TRIANGLES IN SQUARES

Since leaving Drama School Jane has pursued two careers, one as a director of theatre and opera, and the other as a writer. For her own company, the English Chamber Theatre (President, Dame Judi Dench) she wrote and directed over 30 productions. These productions took her all over the world and she has met and worked with many fascinating people including Dame Margot Fonteyn and Robert Helpmann, Jackie Kennedy Onassis, Anthony Quinn, Sir Derek Jacobi, Jessye Norman and many others.

For 10 years she was the Artistic Director of Opera UK – and apart from directing operas and concerts, she wrote 3 English translations of librettos and an original oratorio, *"The People's Passion"* which was filmed for BBC 1. She also wrote an original children's opera, *"Hello Mr Darwin"*. All Jane's productions are now under one umbrella TJM PRODUCTIONS.

She has four children and ten grandchildren and is now based in London.

TRIANGLES IN SQUARES
EUAN'S STORY

BOOK 2 OF THE THREE LIVES TRILOGY

For Toby's Grandchildren

They lived in Squares, painted in Circles and loved in Triangles.

Dorothy Parker in conversation on the Bloomsbury Group

CHAPTER ONE

A great gust of March wind rattled the study windows and the sudden noise startled Euan Mackay out of his dream-like state. With a well-practised gesture he stretched out an arm to reach for his coffee. It was now stone cold. He looked at his watch and realised he must have been sitting at his desk staring into the Square for the best part of an hour. With some reluctance he dragged his attention back to the pad of paper in front of him. Nothing helpful there, it was covered in a series of ink-drawn doodles. With a gesture of irritation he stabbed his fountain pen down on the pad, scattering dots across the page. He stared at it for a moment, then ripping it out he screwed it up and aimed for the bin. Like many others before, it missed and joined the general litter on the floor.

His mind was a blank and into this blank now intruded all the daily sounds of life in the Square. The milkman was doing his rounds and he listened to the clatter of bottles on the doorsteps. His front door slammed. Mrs Gonzales, the voluble but cheerful cleaning lady, was leaving. That meant it must be about eleven-thirty and it wouldn't be long before Ned and Billy returned from playgroup when he would have to abandon all hope of getting any work done. He glanced at the row of books on the top shelf. No help there either. Not an idea in sight. He, Euan Mackay, the darling of the TV literary moguls, was written out, stumped, devoid of all inspiration.

As a last resort he switched on the screen of his word processor and tapped in 'PROPOSAL'. After staring at it for a full ten minutes he took out a cigarette and then remembered he'd given up and put it back.

Tick, tick, tick. The wall clock was becoming hypnotic. It should definitely be removed to another room. What did he need a clock for anyway? He only had to look out of the window to know the exact time of day, so absolutely did the residents of Garrick Square keep to their daily routine. He walked across the room and opened a cupboard revealing a jumble of scripts. What a ludicrous amount of writing he had done in seven years. All those words, the hours spent on re-writes, new versions and added scenes. Maybe he had to face it. He'd written himself out.

This was such a sobering thought he sat down at his desk. Written out at thirty-five? People didn't retire at thirty-five. But could he? Financially it was possible. He'd made money from his screenplay and that, combined with the sale of this house, which had doubled in value since he bought it, would be enough to live on. He could return to Scotland, write a proper book and spend time in restoring himself.

A wave of panic swept over him. That would be a very drastic step and need serious consideration. Did he really want to leave the Square? It had taken him a good deal of soul-searching to arrive here in the first place, dubious as he'd been about becoming a man of property. Thankfully, his initial fears were overcome and he'd now lived in the house for six years. Euan took out a cigarette and this time he didn't return it to the packet. Sitting back in his chair he inhaled slowly and considered the many advantages of living in this particular square.

To an outsider it probably looked like any other London square, but it wasn't. To begin with it wasn't situated in the smartest of areas, being tucked away between Kennington and Stockwell and therefore rather more 'Pooter' than 'Forsyte'. It also boasted an untidy charm not generally found in the squares of Kensington or Belgravia. Indeed the central garden had such a density of foliage it was almost rural. The Annual Residents Meeting frequently put down a motion to attend to the tidying up of paths and the cutting back of roses, but nothing was ever done.

The houses were large, Edwardian and white stucco, with steps up to the front door and down to the garden basements below. They were in various states of dilapidation, most were peeling, but one or two had been repainted. Until the early-sixties many of the houses had families of the original residents living in them, but as they grew old and their children scattered the large houses became too much for them, so they'd departed, leaving a plague of 'For Sale' signs.

Lady Fay Stanhope, who lived at Number 8 and had resided in the Square most of her adult life, busied herself with finding new occupants for the vacated houses, making sure they were populated with her friends and those acquaintances of whose life style she approved. Once, when she had been away on her second honeymoon, an 'undesirable' had slipped through the net and she arrived back to find the ominous sight of scaffolding on the front of the house. Like a galleon in full sail she had swept into the hallway of the astonished new owner and explained exactly how the occupants of the Square were expected to behave. No-one, but no-one, was allowed to alter the exterior look of the houses. What was done inside, she had remarked with a slight shudder as she viewed the G-plan furniture and patterned carpet, was their business, but the outside was to conform to the rest of the Square. We shall never know if the new owners had intended to paint the exterior a different colour, because after Lady Fay's visit the house remained white, if a little shinier than the rest.

As a result of Lady Fay's energies, Garrick Square became a small, elite and tight-knit community and this gave the place its unique quality. She would make a royal progress each morning with her two Pekinese dogs through the mayhem of trees, shrubs and rose bushes that made up the central garden. One year, a braver resident had timidly suggested that perhaps dogs should not be allowed to use the central garden. Lady Fay had turned her full fury on him and the subject was never raised again. Mr Alton, the aged gardener, did his best to keep the undergrowth down, but his efforts were about as effective as Mrs Partington trying to sweep back the Atlantic ocean with a broom.

Another attraction of the Square was its seclusion. Situated off the Kennington Road, it could only be reached by a complicated maze of small roads leading to a dead end. This resulted in it being virtually free of all traffic and unwanted visitors.

Such a quiet haven, conveniently set within easy reach of the West End, had a special appeal for writers and what Lady Fay loosely termed as 'Media People'. She included herself in this category, having had some success with a series of romantic novels and the occasional television script. It was Fay who had introduced Euan to the Square and persuaded him to buy the house after they had worked together on his first television series. Since that time he had made an almost meteoric rise to fame and gained the reputation of being a writer to watch, with several television serials under his belt and last year a prize-winning screenplay.

Fay looked on Euan as her own particular protégée and regarded his arrival in the Square as one of her major triumphs. The Square also suited Euan, at least it had, up until now. On this particular March morning in 1987 he sat in a 'black dog' state, actually contemplating the idea of leaving it.

The noise of Lady Fay's yapping Pekineses, out for a walk in the garden, made him start. He stubbed out his cigarette and made a mental effort to pull himself together. It was time to face the facts. His life was in crisis, brought about by the unspeakable mess on the domestic front, and this was entirely his fault, due to one stupid and reckless moment in which he had landed himself with an impossible woman and her two small, but unruly boys.The work situation he could just about deal with, even his writer's block. In fact he could cope with everything else, but he could no longer cope with Jules. Her presence in the house had become a constant source of irritation and was now driving him mildly insane.And as if to prove the point he lit up another cigarette.

Jules, the Hon. Juliana Stanhope, was the younger daughter of Lady Fay. Soon after Euan arrived in the Square she had introduced him to both her daughters, Marcia and Julianna. Marcia, the eldest, was living in an unsatisfactory marriage and consequently looked on all single men as fair game. She had thrown herself at Euan with such velocity it had momentarily winded him.

"Ma has told me all about you," she breathlessly announced, taking his hand in hers and speaking with dramatic intensity, "how you fell in love with a beautiful woman who was tragically killed in a car crash, so you plunged yourself into writing and became an overnight success. Added to which," she paused, allowing her eyes to devour his body, "you're sort of ruggedly handsome. It's just too much."

With difficulty Euan extricated his hand, which was slowly being massacred by Marcia's chunky jewellery and made a vow never to tell anyone details of his life again, especially a person of Fay's romantic inclinations. So it was with some relief that he'd seen Marcia despatched from the Square a few days later, back to Buckinghamshire, the dull husband and the bridge parties.

Julianna, or Jules as she was known, was entirely different from her sister in every way. Although both brought up in the seventies, Jules was a definite throwback to the sixties. In appearance she rather resembled a Beardsley drawing, with a mass of black curls, round face and large dark eyes. Her ample figure was always swathed in long ethnic robes. She was totally amoral and had a habit of falling into bed with anyone she happened to meet, of either sex, especially after an evening of mild debauchery. By her mid-twenties she'd produced Ned and Billy and wasn't even certain who their fathers were. Euan met her several times at Fay's famous suppers and been fascinated by her sheer eccentricity. It was after one of these encounters that his disastrous error of judgement was made. While rather drunk he had suggested, from the side of the bed he unexpectedly found himself, that as he had a lot of room in his house and she was temporarily homeless, it might be sensible for her and the two boys to move in with him. The next day she had installed herself, much to Fay's delight, relieved to have Jules off her hands at last.

In some ways early on, it had been quite pleasant to have the company. Since Celia's death he'd remained uninvolved. The occasional affair had left him dissatisfied. Something so undemanding and merely of a practical nature seemed quite a good notion at the time. Now, two years on, he was deeply regretting his decision. Jules's lifestyle was becoming increasingly bizarre and he had a thorough dislike of her friends, who appeared to him layabouts and spongers that spent most of their time dabbling in noxious substances. Apart from one or two nights at the beginning he did not feel any further urge to sleep with Jules and although he had a fondness for the boys, they were starting to get decidedly wild and out of control. This situation was disrupting his life to such a degree he realised something had to be done about it. But the question was what?

Euan stubbed out his cigarette and was mulling over possible solutions, when the telephone rang. After a quick search and then unearthing it from under a pile of papers he heard a prim voice say, "Mr Mackay? I have Walter Simmons for you. Can you hold please?"

Wal was Celia's cousin and had been a close friend, although their friendship had rather lapsed of late. After a long pause and a series of clicks Wal's voice boomed down the line. "Euan, I'm glad to have found you in. We seem to have lost touch. How are you keeping?"

Euan replied cautiously, "I'm fine thanks Wal and keeping busy."

The voice boomed again and Euan held the receiver a little further from his ear.

"Glad to hear it. Did you get our invitation?"

Euan looked at the chaos on his desk. He had a vague memory of seeing an invitation but didn't hold out much hope of finding it. "Fill me in on the details Wal. I can't quite recall it."

Wal sounded irritated, "A party, next Thursday at our house, about eight. Do try and make it. We'd really like you to be there." He paused, "especially as Natasha is coming."

At the mention of Natasha, Euan's heart missed a beat. He said nothing. Wal asked if he was still there, and he managed to say that he was, so Wal continued. "I was telling you that Natasha Roxby Smith will be coming, Celia's daughter. You must remember her? She remembers you."

Euan heard his voice, remote and unemotional. "Yes, of course I remember her."

Wal chuckled. "She's quite something now. Wait until you see her. Not beautiful like Celia but damned attractive. So you'll come?" Before he had time to make a decision Wal said, "Oh, by the way, I thought your film was excellent. Miriam and I both enjoyed it. You must have done pretty well out of that. I trust your agent did a good deal."

Euan smiled to himself. He could tell it still rankled that he hadn't taken his contract to Simmons and Woolcock. "My agent got me a great deal thank you Wal."

The voice the other end of the line sounded slightly miffed, "Well I'm glad to hear it. This firm spends its time trying to unravel the damage ostensibly good agents have done."

Euan said drily, "If I have a problem I shall certainly come straight to you Wal." Then he tactfully changed the subject. "How is Dolly? Didn't I hear she'd been ill?"

Wal sounded surprised. "No, Mother is fine as far as I know. It's her husband who's not well, but he's such a hypochondriac we are not taking it too seriously. See you Thursday."

The telephone clicked and the line went dead.

Euan smiled. Even when he'd first met Wal at Cambridge his telephone conversations had a habit of ending like that. One minute he'd be in full flight and the next he'd have rung off. Of all Celia's relations Wal was the only one he really liked.

He stood up and poured himself a Scotch. It wasn't usual for him to have a tipple in the middle of the day but he suddenly felt in need of it. It was the mention of Natasha. He hadn't seen her for seven years, not since Celia had died. How old would that make her, twenty-one, twenty-two? He sipped his whisky slowly. He hadn't even written to her after the car-crash. It wasn't that he hadn't tried, but what could he say? 'Dear Natasha. I'm sorry your mother has been killed, leaving you to be brought up by your appallingly awful father. It's all the more unfortunate because I happened to be in love with her...'

He drained the glass. Maybe he should give Wal's party a miss.

A sudden noise interrupted his thoughts. It was a screaming child. He left the study, and walked down the corridor and into the kitchen.

Jules, draped in a large silk shawl, was sprawled in the rocking chair and dragging on an odd shaped cigarette. Her eyes were closed. He took the cigarette from her mouth and flung it into the sink. The eyes half opened and Euan rounded on her.

"Jules, what the hell is the matter with Ned? He's bawling the place down."

"Not Ned darling. Billy." Her drawling tones infuriated him even more.

"Well Billy then. What's the matter with him?"

"Temper tantrum darling. I used to have them. He'll be over it soon."

The eyes closed again.

Euan strode from the kitchen and up to the first floor room that had become the boys' nursery. On one side of the room Ned was quietly playing Lego, with a virtuous expression on his face. On the other side was Billy, his mouth wide open, emitting loud screams. Euan stooped down, picked up the screaming child and carried him back to his study. Billy was so surprised by this move his crying stopped, except for a series of hiccups. He sat Billy down in his desk chair. Billy stared up at him, wary. Euan wiped his face with a handkerchief and said, "How old are you Billy?"

The boy's face took on a concentrated expression. "Four years," he said and then paused before adding, "I'm five soon."

Euan smiled. "Well that's far too old to be making that racket." He pointed to the screen, "Do you know what that is Billy?"

There was another pause and then, still hiccupping, he said, "Work."

Euan nodded. "Yes and I can't work if you are making that awful noise. So if you want to make *five* I suggest you make no further sound. Yes?"

The boy nodded and looked back at the screen. His hands crept towards the keyboard. "No not that," Euan said firmly. "You can do some drawing." He put Billy on the floor with some paper and pencils.

The pencils were instantly handed back. "I want to do cut-outs."

Euan sighed. "Very well," he said and handed Billy some scissors.

He sat back in his swivel chair and turned it from side to side, thinking. It was definitely time for positive action. The initial fascination with Jules had worn off and her total lack of responsibility, especially towards her children, was making too many demands on his time. He disliked the way she loaded affection and neglect on the two boys just as the whim took her, especially as in the neglectful moments he felt obliged to step in. It was not as if they were his offspring, he had merely offered them a roof over their heads.

He looked across at Billy cutting at the paper with gusto. Poor kid, he would certainly have to be a survivor with a mother like Jules. It was no good remonstrating with her, she wasn't going to change. If anything, she was getting worse. Her late night dope sessions were becoming far more frequent. At first he had turned a blind eye, but he couldn't any longer. He looked again at Billy who was hacking with the scissors at a piece of rug. "Just the paper Billy," he said wearily, "just the paper."

Maybe there was somewhere else Jules could live? He sighed. It seemed unlikely. Although he was only charging her a peppercorn rent she was always behind with the payments, being permanently short of what she called 'scratch'. There would have to be a good reason for her to leave such bargain accommodation. It wasn't as if he could accuse her of taking advantage of him, because it was entirely his own fault. He'd made the offer in the first place. He swivelled the chair slowly round in a circle. Maybe he should offer to set her up somewhere else and help with the rent? After all, he could afford it and the price of freedom was worth almost anything. It might be the only solution otherwise he'd be stuck with Jules for ever.

As if on cue she swept into the room and flopped into a chair.

"Darling Euan, you are a miracle worker. How did you get Billy to stop crying?"

"It's called occupational therapy," he told her drily. "However I'm not getting much work done, so if you could now remove him I'd be grateful. Perhaps it's time for him to be fed?"

Jules ignored this. "I meant to tell you Euan, I have invited some friends over on Thursday, after Jasper's Art Show."

Euan shuddered. Jasper was his least favourite of her crowd. He was affected and spoiled, with enough private income to indulge in whatever latest whim took his fancy.These days he was usually to be found in drag and half insensible from dope. When Euan had first met Jasper he'd been quite a successful interior designer. Now he'd given that up and was painting weird pictures which unsurprisingly nobody wanted to buy. Around him clung a collection of similar types and Euan was well aware that they despised him as much as he despised them.

He stopped staring at the ceiling and regarded Jules thoughtfully.

She was looking at him a little anxiously. It wasn't like Euan to be difficult.

"I just thought I ought to warn you darling. I mean, I know you don't desperately like Jasper..." She broke off, rather at a loss. "It's all right," Euan suddenly said. "I've been invited to a party myself on Thursday night so I won't be around."

Jules sighed with relief. "That's wonderful darling. I just didn't want you to feel I was imposing on you."

And with that she swept out of the room, leaving Billy behind.

CHAPTER TWO

Wal's house, at the smart end of Walbrook Grove, had been purchased in the early-seventies for a modest sum and was now worth a great deal more. The interior, which originally had been minimalist with black leather sofas and palm trees, Wal's choice, had now been changed by his wife for a more 'Conran' look, with large cream sofas, cool blinds and some good antiques. Wal had rescued the two black leather Chesterfields and removed them to his office reception area. Miriam hadn't objected, remarking that they were far more suited to a lawyer's office.

The house was now rather too big for them. The two boys were away at school and their eldest child, Belinda, was doing a course that was loosely called 'Business Studies' and had just moved out to share a flat with two other girls. A year back Wal had suggested moving to a house in the country while keeping a small flat in London for him.

"Ridiculous!" had been Miriam's swift reply. "Let's face it Wal. You're a workaholic. I'd never see you. I'd be stranded in the country which I hate, and be cramped if I ever came up to London which I love." So that idea was never mentioned again.

Wal, a highly successful divorce lawyer, knew that the first rule of a tranquil and surviving marriage was to keep your wife as happy as possible. This was especially necessary during all those tricky stages like children's teenage years, moving house and the menopause. So putting this rule into practice he generally gave way to whatever Miriam wanted on the domestic front. Apart from anything else he occasionally had a twinge of guilt over the fact that Miriam had given up a promising legal career when she married him. She was older than him and already in her thirties, so they had decided to have children straight away, which rather put an end to her working. It had been her choice and she had seemed happy enough about it, investing her enormous energies into running the house, their social life, and her endless committees. Even so, he sometimes wondered if she had regrets.

As he readied himself for the party and struggled with his bow tie, he thought with some complacency that their marriage had been a good one, on the whole. There had been the few inevitable hiccups and two minor crises, once when he had behaved badly and once when she had. These had quickly blown over, mainly because they were both far too busy to make too much of it.

Miriam came into the room and stood in front of him. "I'm not at all sure about this dress. Hermione chose it. Some designer she's promoting. I feel a bit like a guinea-pig."

Wal observed her. "No, not a guinea-pig, more like a zebra. It's rather giddy-making, all those black and white stripes. Like that artist woman. What's her name?"

"Bridget Riley?"

"That's the one." He looked at her again and chuckled. "It's a pity we don't have the black sofas with the white cushions still. You'd have merged perfectly."

She ignored this. He sat down on the bed. "Can you help me do this tie?"

With dextrous efficiency the task was completed in seconds. Wal started to put in his cuff links. "Did I tell you Euan was coming tonight?"

"No you didn't. He never replied to the invitation." There was implied criticism in her voice. Miriam was a stickler for good manners.

"That's why I rang him yesterday," Wal told her. "He was very apologetic. He'd mislaid it."

She gave herself a puff of perfume behind each ear. "Is he still living with Jules Stanhope? I've always found that a very bizarre relationship."

Wal was struggling with the cuff links so with a touch of irritation Miriam took over.

He shrugged. "I have no idea if the Stanhope girl is still around. I haven't seen him for some time. He's been away working on that film. Anyway he's coming alone."

His wife gave him a long look. "Have you warned him about Natasha?"

"Warned him?"

"Yes warned him. I mean, Natasha being Celia's daughter and all that. It might look a bit contrived."

This annoyed him. "Contrived? Why should it be contrived? Celia was my cousin. It's perfectly natural I should ask her daughter."

Miriam shot him another look. "He might not see it like that, and," she added with a sigh, "of all your Cambridge friends Euan is the one I most want to mother."

Wal was startled by this. "What on earth for? I thought you rather disapproved of him. Anyway, of all my Cambridge friends, Euan is certainly the most successful. He's made a small fortune from his writing."

Not for the first time Miriam wished her husband wouldn't judge everyone by the amount of money they made, but all she said was, "He's just looked rather lost since Celia died."

Wal's eyebrows went up. "Euan lost? Are we talking about the same man?"

Miriam sounded impatient. "You wouldn't understand. What Euan needs is a proper woman. I can't imagine Jules Stanhope being very satisfactory, particularly in the sex department. She's always doped to the eyeballs."

Wal said reprovingly, "I don't think he took her in for sex. From what I could gather I think he felt sorry for her homeless state, with two small boys."

This was received with a snort from his wife. "It really is monstrous. She's totally irresponsible. That whole family is a disaster. Both girls were left a considerable amount of money and they just squandered it away, and now she's sponging off poor Euan when he's at his most lost and vulnerable."

Wal decided to ignore that. "How do you know so much about Jules Stanhope?"

"She was expelled from the school during Belinda's last term," Miriam said casually.

Wal looked surprised. "Good God! I didn't know she went to the same school as Belinda. But then why should I? I don't remember anything about that school or Belinda's friends. It was appallingly mediocre. I can't think why we sent her there."

"It came highly recommended," Miriam said impatiently. "I don't think Belinda learned much but then she's not remotely academic. She was very happy there." She looked at him before saying severely, "I suppose you realise your daughter has a huge crush on Euan? She'll probably throw herself at him tonight."

Wal shrugged. "Well, he is her Godfather."

Miriam flashed him a look of annoyance. "Oh really Wal, that has nothing to do with it. She adores the man, has done for years. She was terribly upset when she heard about Jules Stanhope."

Wal was hunting through the wardrobe. "Where the hell is my smoking jacket?"

Miriam retrieved it and handed it to him. He said, "Belinda will grow out of it. Euan gives her no encouragement." And then he quickly changed the subject. "By the way it was clever of you to track Natasha down. I'd completely lost touch with her and I thought Mother had as well."

Miriam brushed his shoulders with a clothes brush. "Dolly had, but somehow managed to find her, in Italy I think. It would have looked decidedly odd if his only grand-daughter hadn't turned up for Bernard's funeral."

Wal made a face. "Miserable old bugger. I don't think he would have minded. He hated everyone towards the end, particularly his family."

"Wal, that's a terrible thing to say."

He gave a shrug. "It's no good you looking shocked. There seems to be no end to the skeletons in our family cupboard. What about that secret woman in Bernard's life that nobody knew about? What about his Will leaving everything to her? What about..."

Further revelations were cut short by the sound of the doorbell, and Miriam, magnificently swathed in black and white silk, glided down the stairs to meet her guests.

*

The party had been going for nearly two hours when Euan finally arrived. He had dithered about going, worried about the potential danger of an encounter with Natasha. However the noisy arrival of Jasper plus his entourage had sent him diving for his car keys.

As he looked around he noted with some relief that Natasha wasn't there. He also noted everyone else was formerly dressed, while he was in corduroys and a linen shirt.

Belinda rushed across the room and kissed him on both cheeks. "Hello Godfather. You're looking very artistic." Euan winced. He was a lapsed Godfather and this habit of kissing even the most distant acquaintance was somewhat alien to him. He looked at Belinda. She was a pleasant, jolly girl who had inherited her mother's capable character and her father's looks. The latter was a little unfortunate. On Wal the ginger hair, large features and florid colouring just looked a bit eccentric. On Belinda it looked rather odd, although tonight there had been a major effort made. The hair and make-up had obviously been professionally done and her Rubenesque figure was crammed into a turquoise silk cocktail dress. The result was not altogether unattractive.

They chatted for a while until Wal came over. "Euan, glad you could make it."

Belinda made a face. "He's being very dour and Scots tonight."

Wal smiled indulgently at his daughter. "It's probably the effect your chatter has had on him. Anyway, I'm taking him away. There are people I want him to meet."

Euan was led to the other side of the room.

Another hour passed and one or two of the guests were beginning to leave. Then the door opened and a slip of a girl came into the room. She was in a skimpy black dress, fashionably tanned and her face was framed with a mass of light brown curls. Euan looked across the room in amazement. It wasn't Celia. The colouring and height were completely different. Celia had been tall, fair and elegant. This was a waif-like creature. Yet there was something that so uncannily reminded him of Celia it took his breath away.

Wal crossed the room. "Natasha, we thought you were lost" and he kissed her on both cheeks.

The voice that replied was low and husky. "Wal, I'm so sorry. Father insisted I took his car and then it broke down ten miles out of London. I had to wait ages for the RAC. I nearly gave up. I hope I'm not too late."

Wal put an arm round her. "Of course not darling girl. Come and get a drink."

Euan stood rooted to the spot as he watched her being introduced to various guests. His mouth had gone dry. Maybe he should leave? No. It was too late. She had seen him. Her large eyes were regarding him with something nearing hostility.

To give himself a bit of time he went to the drinks table, poured a large whisky and noticed that his hand was shaking. When he finally turned round she was right there in front of him. For a second they eyed each other. Then she spoke. "Why didn't you write?"

Euan looked down at his glass.

"Euan answer me. Why didn't you write to me after Mama died?"

There was a long pause and then he mumbled, "I'm sorry."

"Sorry!" She almost shouted. "Is that the best you can do? You're sorry! You were the only person I wanted to hear from. You were the only person I wanted to see. It's been seven years since she died."

For the first time Euan looked at her. "I know. I did try to write. I just didn't know what to say."

Natasha was scornful. "Don't give me that! You're a writer for fuck's sake!"

The swearing gave him a shock. His voice became clipped and he chose his words carefully. "Yes, I'm a writer. I write a lot of words that are totally impersonal. A letter to you would have been different." He hesitated. "After a few weeks had gone by I thought it would be best if I just disappeared out of your life." He took a large gulp of whisky.

Natasha's eyes were blazing. "Oh that's just wonderful. My mother is about to leave my father so she could be with you. Then she gets killed and you think it best to disappear?"

Her voice was raised and angry. Several heads in the room turned towards them.

Euan put down his glass and walked into the garden. He'd always hated emotional scenes. To calm himself he lit a cigarette.

A minute later she joined him. She took the cigarette out of his hand and started smoking it herself. He made no comment but stood in silence. Natasha was the first to break it and her voice was calmer. "Sorry. It was the shock of seeing you. You have to realise I have seven years of resentment and anger to get off my chest."

He looked at her. "Not much of a chest to get it off."

This made her laugh. "You haven't changed."

He smiled. "You have. I suppose it's not surprising, fifteen to twenty-two. You were a lumpy teenager last time I saw you."

Again the low gurgling laugh. "I was never lumpy."

"Well you were certainly plumper than you are now. A puff of smoke would take you away. And talking of smoke, when did you start on the filthy habit?"

She dropped the remains of the cigarette and put it out with her foot. "I don't really. I only smoke when I'm nervous."

He picked up the cigarette butt and threw it into a nearby bush. "And are you nervous now?"

Natasha shook her head. "Not now. But I was. I was nervous about seeing you again and pretty sure I was going to be angry. Then when the car broke down I panicked in case I missed you." She looked at him shyly. "It's odd, as I came into the room I just knew you were there."

They stood in silence. Euan spoke first. "I was nervous too."

She looked surprised. "You were? Why?"

He shrugged. "Well for one thing I felt badly about not having made contact. And for another..." He turned away. "I thought seeing you would remind me."

In spite of herself she was curious. "And does it? Do I remind you of her?"

He turned back to study her. "Yes, surprisingly you do. It's not that you look like her, but there are definite things..." He broke off then added, "Your voice is different from what I remember, more husky."

Natasha smiled. "Yours is the same. You haven't lost that hint of Scottish." She looked wistful. "Do you remember our holiday on Iona?"

He nodded. "Of course."

In the semi-darkness he could see that her eyes were suddenly shining. "That was the best holiday I ever had. I'm going back to Iona one day. Have you been back?"

His jaw tightened and he said abruptly. "No, I haven't." It still hurt him, the memories of Celia. She looked at him and seemed to understand. "Shall we sit down?"

They walked to the garden seat and as they reached it he said, "You have a remarkable suntan for this time of year."

"It's an accumulated tan," she explained. "I've only just got back from Florence, where I've been for the last three years."

"Doing?"

She laughed. "*Doing* Art School."

"Art School eh? I remember you drawing a lot in Iona. And wasn't your grandmother a painter?"

Natasha nodded. "She was quite famous. Audrey Maddington. She illustrated children's books. Her work is very sought after these days."

Euan thought about this. "It's interesting. The talent seems to have skipped a generation. I don't recall Celia being able to draw."

Natasha shook her head. "No, she never did. But she was brilliant at the piano." Her voice was suddenly sad. "I think I missed her playing more than anything else when she died."

They fell silent again.

"How's your father?" Euan asked.

She shrugged. "He's all right. He's not a headmaster now. He left Civolds at the end of that term, after the funeral. I'm rather vague about what he does. I think it's a sort of educational consultant. Anyway I know he's made a lot of money." She paused and her expression changed. "And he's re-married. A woman called Inga."

Euan looked at her. "What's she like?"

Natasha turned away and said abruptly, "Very German." From the tone of her voice Euan decided not to pursue the subject and she went on briskly, "I hardly see them. I'm now in London looking for a flat, although I'm not sure what I'm going to do yet. I've only been back from Italy a couple of weeks and it's been a bit frantic catching up with things. And then there was Grandfather's funeral. You knew about that?"

Euan nodded. "I read the obituaries. They were quite complimentary. I always thought the man a right bastard and from what Celia told me he was a terrible father."

Natasha sighed. "He was pretty difficult with everyone, but Dolly said he was very upset by Mama's death and I suppose she should know, after all she was his sister and knew him better than anyone." There was a pause before she remarked, "Isn't life a mess?"

Euan was startled by her bitterness of tone but said lightly, "So young and yet so cynical."

"No I'm not," she said with a flash of defiance. "It's from careful observation. Life is a mess. Everything gets in such a muddle."

In the distance there was the sound of the party fading. They could hear the goodbyes drifting down the garden. Natasha shivered. "Perhaps we should go in." As they reached the door she said, "Wal tells me you've become famous."

Euan gave a short laugh. "Wal exaggerates. I've written one or two things that have attracted attention that's all. And I've made some money. I think that's what really impresses Wal." He turned to her. "Would you like a last drink?"

"Why not? I arrived so late I have some catching up to do."

He poured her a glass of white wine and they sat together on one of the vast cream sofas. She suddenly seemed small and childlike, but he wondered if that was misleading. Underneath that waif-like exterior he had the impression she was quite tough and certainly had the air of someone who could look after herself.

A thought struck him. "If you are looking for somewhere to live, I happen to have a flat that is empty."

Natasha sat bolt upright. "You do?"

He nodded. "Yes. Some years ago I bought this large house in Garrick Square, off the Kennington Road." He paused and frowned.

He really didn't want to go into the complication of Jules. "It has a garden flat. There's quite a lot of space, and it's not being used at the moment."

She looked at him. "Do you mean that? It could be perfect."

"Why don't you come over tomorrow? We could have lunch and then you can see the flat and make a decision." He paused. "Where are you staying in London?"

She laughed. "Here. I'm staying here for a few days with Wal and Miriam."

At that moment they were interrupted by Belinda. "Natasha, how mean of you to monopolise my Godfather all evening. I've hardly seen him."

Her face had developed a rather unattractive red flush. Euan reflected that with her strange colouring Belinda was going to have to watch the amount of wine she drank.

Natasha stood up and smiled. "He's all yours Belinda," and she moved away.

Euan also stood up and tried to keep the irritation out of his voice. "I really should be going Belinda. I didn't mean to stay this late. Where are your parents?"

A fat freckled arm waved him towards the front door. He made his goodbyes and left.

*

As he climbed into the car he wondered if he would regret having made yet another impulsive decision. Natasha's presence in the house might disturb him. Rake over old embers. Had he landed himself with yet more problems?

He drove home slowly, aware that he was well over the limit. Even so, he only narrowly avoided a tramp who launched himself off the pavement and into the road.

"Tomorrow I give up smoking and drinking," he muttered, but without much conviction.

CHAPTER THREE

Euan was well aware that the plan for Natasha to take over the flat would bring things to a head with Jules, but as she never emerged before eleven o'clock he had to wait until late morning to break the news to her. As anticipated, it did not go well. She sat huddled in an Indian bedspread and her usual drawl became a wail.

"Euan darling, how could you? I'd practically promised the flat to Jasper."

This came as a total shock to Euan who leapt out of his chair knocking over his cup of coffee. "You did what?" he shouted. "Do you mean to say you actually offered the use of my flat to that awful man?"

Jules felt a touch intimidated. It was rare for Euan to raise his voice. "Well, yes, I did. I mean it was just an empty space darling and he needs space like that for his painting. It would have been ideal."

Euan's head was pounding. For the first time in years he had the trace of a hangover and this latest piece of news severely aggravated his condition. He mopped up the spilled coffee and poured himself some more. Then he sat down and looked across at Jules and his tone became curt and cold.

"I think it's time you and I got a few things sorted out Jules. Firstly, this house is mine. It belongs to me. When I invited you, Ned and Billy to move in, it was a very loose arrangement and not in any way meant to be a permanent fixture. Secondly, I am the only person who can invite people to stay or use the flat. That is my business and my business alone."

Jules was alarmed. Euan had never behaved like this before. She had obviously chosen the wrong moment and soothing tactics were required.

"Darling Euan, of course I know that. We are eternally grateful to you for letting us stay and of course the boys simply adore you."

"Fine." Euan cut her short not wanting to prolong the discussion. "As long as we all know where we stand. You presumably realise I'm not over-keen on most of your friends, particularly Jasper. In fact, he would be the last person on earth I would let anywhere near my flat!"

With this Parthian shot he left the room, leaving Jules staring after him in amazement. Until now Euan had been extremely laid back about their arrangement and it had suited her wonderfully. Jerked out of her usual inertia she realised she was going to have to be very careful indeed. But it was definitely awkward. Jasper was expecting to move in at the weekend and she didn't want to upset him either. He was an important source for her dope.

She poured the remainder of the coffee into a mug and considered her position. There was always the possibility that Natasha wouldn't like the flat. After all it was completely undecorated and fairly primitive. Surely she would want something smarter and more comfortable? Somewhere at the back of her mind she vaguely remembered hearing Natasha was some sort of heiress. Hadn't Belinda said she'd inherited money from her mother? She wished her mind wasn't such a fog. Maybe her mother would know about Natasha, she knew everything about everybody. If she had money, it was almost certain she wouldn't want the flat. Then the subject of Jasper could be broached again, when Euan was back to his old self. Last night had obviously upset him, meeting Celia's daughter. He would be back to normal once Natasha had decided to move elsewhere.

Feeling more cheerful Jules rolled herself another cigarette.

*

Back in his study Euan tried to calm down. He felt exasperated and almost inclined to ask Jules to leave at once. The situation was an awkward one. Apart from anything else, what was Natasha going to make of her, let alone the two boys? He looked from the whisky bottle to his cigarettes, wondering which one would soothe him best, but before he could decide the telephone rang. It was Murdo Struthers from Number 29.

Murdo was a charming and cultivated man, much given to quoting Lord Chesterfield. He had once been a distinguished publisher but was now retired. Of all the Square inhabitants Murdo was the person he had most time for. The same could not exactly be said of Murdo's other half. Desmond, a well-built man in his early forties and a good deal younger than Murdo, worked in railway catering. Unfortunately his brain rather matched the thickness of his frame. It was therefore a strange pairing and difficult for outsiders to fathom, although according to Fay they had been together for at least twenty years. Even so, it did seem odd that Murdo, so articulate and well-informed, should choose as his partner a man who rarely uttered a word, except to pass on occasional information about the latest railway sandwiches. Again, according to Fay, there had been times when Desmond had strayed, disappearing from the Square for weeks on end. But he'd always come back, and on the whole his silent devotion to Murdo was touching to observe. In his turn Murdo was always gentle and patient with Desmond, reminding Euan of a parent with an erring son.

Murdo's telephone voice was rather thin and quavery.

"Euan, I'm glad I've caught you. Your presence is required. We're giving our annual supper party for acquaintances in the Square, that is, the ones I can remember. So you're expected."

Euan smiled. There was a pause and then he said, "You haven't mentioned when this party is Murdo."

"Drat, nor I have. I did tell Desmond he'd be better at this sort of thing than I. Now let me see. Oh yes, of course, it's May 1st, just over a month from now."

Euan unearthed his diary. "Is there any significance in that date? Should I arrive on a tank or a missile?"

There was a chuckle. "No, no. I'm no 'reddo' as Fay's dear husband would say. Not even faintly pink. We chose it as a day that would be easy to remember."

Euan checked the date and could only see 'morning script conference' written in large letters. "That would be fine. What time?"

The voice sounded flustered again. "Oh goodness me, yes a time. When do these things usually begin?"

"Seven-thirty, eight?"

"Seven-thirty would be fine."

Euan was about to ring off when a thought struck him. "Murdo, I might have let my flat by then. Would it be all right if I brought someone with me?"

Murdo sounded intrigued. "By all means, do I know him?"

Euan smiled. "It's a *her* and I don't think you do."

The voice the other end became more animated. "Does this female have a name?"

Euan hesitated then said, "Natasha. Natasha Roxby Smith."

There was a pause. "Any relation to George Roxby Smith?"

Euan replied cautiously, "Daughter."

There was another pause. "Wasn't he the headmaster of Civolds prep school?"

Euan was relieved he hadn't made the connection with Celia. "That's the one."

"Fascinating," was Murdo's response, "because I seem to remember there was a scandal about him that I can't quite recall at the moment. Tell you next time I see you."

The telephone clicked. Euan stared at it, startled as always by the abrupt end to the conversation. Murdo and Wal should go into competition. He replaced the receiver and almost immediately it rang again.

"Darling Euan, what a popular man you are. Your line is always busy..."

The unmistakeable lush tones of Lady Fay came down the line. Euan sighed. This call would be a longer one. "Good morning Fay. Yes, I'm sorry it does seem to have been one of those mornings." He decided it was better not to mention Murdo's call in case Murdo either forgot or intentionally didn't invite Fay and Boffy to his May 1st supper. Boffy, Fay's second husband, was a rather senile military man who, although harmless enough, tended to sound off in loud tones about his obsessions which included 'Commies' and 'Nancy Boys'. The latter had been known to upset Murdo.

Fay was burbling on. "...I just want to book you up for dinner, a week today."

Euan suddenly felt in need of a social secretary. Once again he looked at the scribbled entries in his diary. "That seems fine," and then again on impulse he added, "I might bring someone with me. Would that upset your numbers?"

Fay sounded brisk. "I've already asked Jules you silly boy."

Euan frowned. "It wasn't Jules I was meaning."

An excited gasp, "Oh duckie, the plot thickens. Of course you can bring someone else, but only if you tell who me who it is. I hate mysteries."

Euan hesitated, knowing the effect the name would have. "Natasha Roxby Smith."

There was the predictable spluttering on the end of the line. "You can't mean... you do mean... the daughter?"

In spite of himself Euan smiled. This information would keep Fay's telephone busy for the next twenty four hours. "Yes Fay, Celia's daughter. She may be moving into my basement flat." He could hear the excitement in Fay's voice.

"Oh my dear, what a dark horse you are. Where on earth did she spring from?"

Euan's head began to throb again. He said wearily, "Florence. She's been at Art School." There was a pause while all this information was digested.

"Dare I ask how *my* daughter has taken this news?"

He sighed, "Not well. She wanted the flat for Jasper."

Fay sounded shocked. "You are well out of that one duckie, I know Jasper's family. All three boys had to be dried out. Endless problems..."

By the time Euan had extricated himself from Fay he felt quite exhausted. He rang Natasha suggesting they met at the restaurant and gave her instructions how to get there. Then he sat back suddenly feeling decidedly nervous about her impending visit.

She arrived late completely unaware of his agitated state. As she joined him at the table he said, "I thought you might have changed your mind."

She looked surprised. "Why should I? Did you think I was still angry with you? Well I'm not." She immediately dived into a bowl of olives. "No, the reason I'm late is that I think I took your directions down wrong. It's difficult to concentrate in that house, there's so much noise and distraction. Miriam is very kind but incredibly bossy. She shouts instructions at people all the time. Poor Belinda, no wonder she's such a mess. Do you know, she's not even allowed to wear a dressing-gown to breakfast as it's considered sloppy." She mimicked Miriam: "'Sloppy habits, sloppy minds!' I felt almost guilty for wearing my old kimono." She took another olive. "These olives are really good."

Euan made a study of her. She was a strange mixture. On the one hand she had an innocent, child-like quality and on the other this bubbly personality. She also had a remarkable self-assurance, almost sophistication. It left him feeling uncertain how to proceed.

Natasha was studying the menu. "Great! Italian food. I can't tell you how much I've missed it." She summoned a waiter and gave directions in what to Euan sounded like very fluent Italian. The waiter gave a broad smile and hurried off to the kitchen. Natasha looked anxiously at Euan. "Sorry, that must have looked like showing off. It's just that I like my pasta done a special way."

"Very impressive," he remarked drily. "You're actually lucky to have hit a real Italian waiter. Usually they come from Surbiton."

Moments later the chef himself arrived with two plates of pasta. "I hope you don't mind, I ordered for you as well," she explained. "I'm sure you'll like it." She thanked the chef and more Italian was exchanged. He then left and she tucked into her food with gusto. "Isn't that amazing? That chef comes from a town I know well, near Florence. He understood exactly the way I wanted the pasta because it's a local recipe."

The next moment a carafe of wine arrive, 'with the compliments of the chef'.

Euan suddenly felt like a small boy who had been given his first Knickerbocker Glory. It reminded him of how raw and socially ill at ease he had felt when he'd first arrived up at Cambridge, unable to compete with the likes of Wal and his public school cronies. These feelings now came flooding back and all produced by the urchin-like creature opposite him. She looked up from her food. "Euan, you're not eating. Don't you like it? Oh God how terribly bossy of me. It's Miriam. Her constant organising must be having an effect on me."

Euan felt tempted to tell her not to eat with her mouth full, but merely said, "No it's fine. It's just taking me a little time to adjust to seeing you again, as a grown-up."

She made a face. "I so hate that expression. I suppose you're considered grown up once you've reached your eighteenth birthday, but Belinda's over eighteen and she doesn't seem grown up to me. Do you know she has a really pathetic crush on you?"

Euan gave a wry smile. "It's difficult not to notice it, although I've hardly seen her lately."

Natasha gave a laugh. "Oh well, they say that absence makes the heart grow fonder."

Euan dropped his fork with a clatter. He looked in shock and she stared at him anxiously. "Oh God. Have I said something wrong?"

He shook his head. "No, no. It's only that what you just said is exactly what your mother also said to me, the very last time I saw her – 'absence makes the heart grow fonder'. They were almost her last words."

There was a moment of silence and then Natasha asked, "Have you changed your mind, about letting me have the flat?"

He shook his head. "Not at all, you can see it as just soon as we've finished lunch." He hesitated. "However, I think I ought to tell you about my set-up."

Natasha looked startled, "Set-up? You make it sound as if you keep a harem!"

He thought grimly of Jules wrapped up in her Indian bedspread. "Nothing so exciting I can assure you." He hesitated again. "I think you ought to know that I do have someone staying in the house. Not on a permanent basis mind. And it's not what you think. We lead totally independent lives. It's just that she has two small boys and they needed somewhere to live..."

Natasha burst out laughing. "Oh really Euan, you are funny. I know all about Jules already. Belinda moaned on and on about it last night. Anyway, I am not at all shocked. I would have been rather surprised if you hadn't been with someone. After all you're still quite sexy." She pushed the finished plate of pasta away and tucked into the salad.

Euan felt as if he'd been in a rugger scrum and had just had all the breath knocked out of him. This lunch certainly wasn't going quite the way he expected.

He decided on a change of subject. "You'll find Garrick Square quite social. If you do take the flat there are already two supper invitations for you."

She felt surprised by this. After all she hadn't even made any decision, yet here was Euan including her in his social life. However all she said was, "I do? Who are they with?"

"Well the first is with Jules' mother, Fay. I think you'll like her. She's a bit eccentric but fun."

"What about Jules' father? Where does he fit into the picture?"

Euan smiled. "I think he's no longer with us. Fay lives with her second husband, Boffy. He's not so much fun. In fact he's been pretty gaga ever since I've known him. Luckily after the second bottle of wine he generally falls asleep."

Natasha laughed. "I can't wait. What's the second invitation?"

"Murdo Struthers, a publisher..." He hesitated then. This was ridiculous. He'd never felt inhibited before but she looked such a child, even if she was twenty-two. He chose his words carefully. "Murdo lives with a friend called Desmond..."

Natasha said briskly, "Oh you mean he's gay." Euan's eyebrows went up as she went on, "You don't have to be so po-faced about it. I went to Art School remember? Lots of my friends are gay."

At something of a loss Euan summoned a waiter and ordered coffee. When it arrived he said firmly, "I think it's about time you told me what has happened to you over the last seven years."

So she did. At first she spoke sadly and wistfully of her mother's death. The following years had been difficult. She had spent most of the holidays with her cousins in Norfolk and seldom saw her father. After

Celia died he had stopped being a Headmaster and left Civolds School. He lived in the States for a while and when he returned it was with Inga. Here Natasha screwed up her face with disgust. This Inga was a dragon. Although she'd lived in America she was from a German family and still had definite traces of the accent which sounded aggressive even if she said something as innocent as 'pass the Cornflakes'. When her father and Inga returned to England she had lived with them for a while. In flat tones she told Euan that she'd never had a particularly good relationship with her father and Inga soon took on proportions of the wicked step mother.

"She tried to change me, to make me a clone of her. Everything I did was wrong. I looked all wrong. I behaved all wrong. We were different in every way and she was so anal. As for my wanting to go to Art School..." Natasha sighed. "If it hadn't been for Edward I might have ended up at cookery school, or worse."

Euan looked at her and said sharply, "Edward? Do you mean Celia's Edward?"

Natasha looked surprised. "I don't know much about him being my mother's Edward, although she was going out to see him just before she died. No, he was more my Grandmother's Edward. They were lovers and he was the first to encourage her to paint. Anyway, wonderful Edward sent me a letter, out of the blue, inviting me to have another holiday with them in Florence. His wife is called Francesca. She's wonderful too, typical Italian, very voluble but really kind. Once I was in Florence, Edward arranged everything, the Art School and somewhere to live while I was studying. Apart from Mama, Edward has been the most important person in my life. Oh I'm fond of my cousins, especially Libby who is about my age, but Edward is someone I love to be with. He never crowds me, or bosses me or tells what I should or shouldn't do. But he's always there if I want advice and he always listens and gives me time when I prattle on, unlike my father."

She broke off and there were tears in her eyes which she angrily brushed away.

Euan said gently, "So what made you come back to England?"

Natasha shrugged. "Well, I had finished my course at Art School and had decided to work in Stage Design. Edward agreed that it was really much more sensible to do this in England. However, there's always a place for me in Florence, a haven where I can go if things get bad and that's so important." She spoke fiercely and then took a gulp of coffee. Her voice changed. "In some ways I have been lucky, with money and things like that." This last statement was said in a rather dismissive way. "My mother inherited my Grandmother's entire estate and when she died it all came to me. I'm not an heiress or anything, but it's plenty to live on if I'm careful. I think my father resented this. He paid for the Art School but stopped my allowance the moment it finished. Probably bloody Inga saw to that. She likes to live in what she would term 'style' and I would call ghastliness. It costs a great deal I should imagine."

Euan couldn't help smiling at the scorn in her voice. "So you need a place in London."

She nodded. "Yes, I was only staying with my father on a temporary basis, just until Grandfather's funeral was over."

"Had you seen your grandfather much?"

She shook head. "No, I hadn't. The Funeral was quite an ordeal I can tell you. So many relations and most of them I hadn't seen since my mother's Funeral. God! Families are weird and our family seems weirder than most. Did my mother tell you about them?"

Euan hesitated. Celia had indeed talked a great deal about her family, especially about her awful husband George, Natasha's father. He said cautiously, "She did tell me about some of them and of course I knew Wal from Cambridge and I think I met Wal's mother Dolly there once."

Natasha smiled. "Did you ever meet Dolly's second husband, Tinker?"

Euan shook his head. "No, Celia talked a good deal about both Dolly and Tinker, but I never met him." Her face lit up in a way it always seemed to when she liked something. "Tinker is one of the great people, although he looks quite odd. He has this round face and eyes like an owl that blink a lot. Dolly, Tinker and Wal are the only sane ones in the family. Wal's brother Luke is completely off the wall. I think he's some sort of monk. He's shaved his head and wanders around in the weirdest clothes. Apart from Libby, the cousins are a boring bunch. There was one called David who I know my mother used to like, but I thought him fat, bloated and affected. He got terribly drunk afterwards." She paused dramatically, "That is when the dreadful revelations happened."

She broke off, so Euan asked, "What dreadful revelations?"

Natasha took a deep breath. "It was the moment when the Will was read. Apparently Bernard, my grandfather, had this woman. Well, I suppose she was his mistress, although in the Will she was called 'my friend and companion'. Anyway, Bernard had left everything to her; the house, the contents, everything, the lot. No bequests to anyone else."

Euan stared at her in amazement. "That's shocking. I'd always heard he was a dreadful man, but that beats everything. What a terrible thing to do to you."

She said briskly, "Don't you start. Everyone was upset and shocked on my behalf. In fact there was uproar, Wal shouting that he was going to contest the Will, Dolly crying, David swaying around drunk and swearing at the Solicitor and the poor Solicitor trying to calm everyone down. It was like a scene out of a film, only not an English film because people were being so un-English, you know, loud and emotional." She paused. "Funnily enough, I was the calmest of all of them. In a strange way I sort of understood. Although I'd made an effort to see my grandfather after Mama died, it was a pretty thankless task because he was so grumpy, bitter and sorry for himself. In the end I just stopped visiting. I hadn't seen him for about four years. I also knew he resented my grandmother leaving all her money to Mama and indirectly to me. It was probably his way of getting back at us, so I didn't mind as much as everyone else. The only things I would have liked were some of my grandmother's paintings."

She stopped as if considering what to say next. Euan looked at her. For the first time during the lunch Natasha seemed to have lost some of her self-assurance.

After a moment she continued, "You're probably going to be really shocked by this, but I decided to go and see this woman, Gemma

Woods."

Euan leant forward. "What was she like?"

"Very ordinary really, nothing much to look at and I suppose in her late forties. Apparently she owns a dress boutique in Oxford. I don't know how she and my grandfather met but she seemed fond enough of him and kept saying how lonely he'd been and how glad she was to have offered him companionship in the last years of his life. I think this was directed at me for not having visited him more often. Or maybe it was her justification for having been left everything. I was tempted to tell her that he hadn't even written to me after my mother died, nor did he speak to me after her funeral. But I didn't." Her voice became brisk. "Anyway Gemma Woods gave me tea and told me of her plans to sell Grandfather's Oxford house and move to London. It was when she talked so calmly about selling the house that I plucked up courage and asked her if I might have one or two of my grandmother's drawings" She paused. "Gemma Woods just stared at me as if I had committed a criminal act. I felt dreadful and wished I hadn't asked for anything. Then she left the room and came back with two framed photographs, one of my grandmother and one of Mama. She told me quite calmly that she would be keeping the rest of the contents herself because after all, that was what Bernard had wanted. She knew I'd understand."

Natasha stopped talking and looked away. Euan couldn't tell if she was crying and he felt an impotent fury at the way life had treated her. After a moment he said, "And that was that?"

She turned back to him. "Yes, that was that. Wal was furious. He's convinced Gemma Woods knows just how much the paintings and illustrations are worth. I was hurt at first. After all, I hadn't asked for much. But then I got to thinking that she had put up with that grumpy old man for at least seven years. She probably deserved his possessions. Anyway, life's too short to go on moping about it."

She gave Euan a smile. "Should we get the bill? We're the last ones here."

*

As they walked into the kitchen they were confronted by Jules, sprawled in a chair smoking and there was a recognisably pungent smell of weed in the air. Euan frowned, but Natasha appeared not to notice. He made the introductions. There was no sign of Billy, but Ned was painting. He was completely naked except for a pair of red boots.

Euan said sharply, "Don't you think Ned should have some clothes on Jules? After all, it's not warm in here."

Jules shrugged, "His choice darling." She stood up and said a little ungraciously, "Would you like some tea?"

Euan said coldly, "No thanks. We're going straight down to the flat."

They made their way downstairs and Natasha walked into the middle of a large room. She stood silent for a moment. Then she turned to him and said, "I really like it."

Euan was apologetic. "It's in a pretty dilapidated state, although structurally sound. I never bothered to decorate as it hardly seemed worth it. I used it mainly for storage."

Natasha paced round the room. "That doesn't matter at all. I have this penchant for white paint. I'll slap it on everywhere." She walked to the window. "And it's very light for a basement."

Euan smiled. "It's only a half basement. There are a few steps down to your front door and then up to a small patio at the back. I haven't done much to that area either. You can have a free hand."

He led her into the small kitchen and then the bathroom. This had all the original Edwardian fittings and Natasha seemed delighted. Euan said with some amusement, "In that case I suggest you leave it as it is. It looks a bit primitive but it does work. The hot water and the heating run off the top of the house. I'm afraid the radiators tend to gurgle a bit."

She laughed. "It adds to its charm."

"What about furniture?" Euan asked. "Do you have any?"

She shook her head. "Not really, except for a few possessions. But I will enjoy finding my own stuff. Father and Inga said they would give me furniture if I found a place, but I wouldn't touch their offerings with a barge pole! It's all heavy teak and Scandinavian. I will start scouring the junk shops at once." She turned to him. "When can I move in?"

41

He tried to conceal his pleasure, "As soon as you like."

"And rent?"

Euan felt awkward about this but her face had a shut, stubborn expression and he knew she'd be offended if he didn't ask for something. "I'm rather vague about this sort of thing, how about fifty pounds a month?"

Natasha considered this. "It seems awfully little."

"Not at all." To reassure her he added, "you'd be doing me a favour by re-decorating it." He looked round. "I'll get a telephone line put in for you as well."

Her eyes were shining with excitement. "That's great. Are there any house rules?"

He smiled. "None. I'll hunt out the front door key for you."

"Thanks Euan. I'll move in tomorrow. I'd better dash now. I promised Miriam and Wal I'd be back for drinks. They've some people coming. Awfully social aren't they?"

And with that she was gone.

*

Later, sitting in his study Euan thought over the day's events.

Although pleased Natasha had taken the flat, he found it a little unsettling as well. He tried to convince himself that he was doing this for Celia, but after today's lunch he wasn't quite so sure, about anything.

CHAPTER FOUR

A week later Euan was invited downstairs to inspect her progress.

Natasha sat cross-legged in the middle of the floor. "Well, what do you think?"

Euan walked slowly round the main room. The walls and woodwork had been painted white and various rugs lay scattered over the floor. At the far end of the room behind a Victorian screen was a brass bedstead, covered with a patchwork quilt and a scattering of cushions. Near the bed stood a pine chest of drawers, a rocking chair and a hat stand covered with clothes and shawls. The opposite end of the room was taken up with a heavy pine kitchen table covered in books, magazines, and various interesting pieces of what he took to be Italian pottery. There were two solid farmhouse chairs at the table and halfway down the room on one side was a desk already covered in papers, and on the other, taking pride of place, an impressive chaise longue covered in faded green velvet. The whole room now had a sort of decadent elegance, almost the feeling of a film set.

Natasha pointed to the chaise, "Isn't that an amazing piece? I've always wanted a chaise longue and then yesterday I saw it in the antique market round the corner. It was a bit of an extravagance even if I did beat the man down. But what the hell, it will be with me for the rest of my life."

Euan smiled. "I'm impressed. You've achieved a transformation and all in such short a time. I was worried at not having offered you help, but you obviously didn't need it."

Natasha laughed. "I am forced to admit that for the first time I really appreciated Miriam's organising skills. One of her charities had a spare van driven by a wonderful man called Bill. With Belinda's help the three of us did all the furniture in one afternoon, including collecting my stuff from store." She indicated the antique desk. "That was the one piece of piece of furniture I inherited from my mother. She told me it was her most treasured possession." Euan looked more closely and then noticed the photograph. It was of Celia. Not elegant, unhappy Celia, but a beautiful woman relaxed and glowing in the sunlight, throwing her head back and laughing. He stared at it and then realised where it was taken.

"That was on Iona."

Natasha nodded and there were tears in her eyes. "She was so happy there Euan. You made her so happy."

They both fell silent.

After a moment she said, "Would you like a drink, to celebrate the end of phase one?" Without waiting for a reply she went into the kitchen and emerged with two large goblets and a bottle of white wine. "I don't have a fridge yet so I've been standing the wine in cold water. It should be all right. Get us in the mood for tonight."

Euan took the glass, "Tonight?" Natasha flung herself onto the chaise.

"Yes. Aren't we going to one of those suppers you mentioned? I think you said it was tonight."

Euan sat down opposite her. "Oh God. Yes, at Fay's. I'd forgotten all about it." He looked at her. "You don't have to come. The company might be rather ancient for you."

She looked back at him and said with a touch of irony, "Surely Jules will be there? Anyway, don't be silly. I'm looking forward to it."

Euan continued to study the room, ignoring the Jules taunt. A pile of canvasses, propped up on the wall beside him, caught his eye. "Are those your grandmother's paintings?"

Natasha nodded. "Yes. The few I inherited from my mother."

For the first time a trace of bitterness had crept into her voice so Euan quickly went on, "What other pictures will you be putting up? You have a lot of wall space. Do you have a favourite painter?"

Natasha put her head on one side considering. "It's difficult to say really. I mean, I like so many painters and they're all so varied. It's easier to pick out one particularly painting."

Euan remembered a similar conversation he'd had with Celia, except that it had been about music. She'd said she loved many composers but had been unable to choose a favourite, so she had chosen one single piece. With her it had been the Schubert Quintet. He couldn't play it anymore. Not the slow movement. It was still too painful.

"Well what is your favourite painting then?"

Again she gave it thought. "There's actually a painting in the Tate that I love, partly I think because it has a flavour of me, or at least a flavour of what I would like to be me. It's called 'Minnie Cunningham at the Old Bedford' by Sickert and it's the sort of painting that makes you want to know more. There's a young woman, completely dressed in red, a beautiful red dress and a red hat. Then just at the edge of the canvas there's a red rose bush. The rest of the canvas is mysterious and dark, although someone told me Minnie Cunningham was a music hall singer and at the top corner there is a building which I think must be the Old Bedford Music Hall. It's very effective. I wouldn't mind that on my wall." She stood up and re-filled their glasses. "Now Euan, tell me about all the people in your famous Square."

He laughed. "It's not *my* famous Square. In fact, it's much more Fay's. She knows everybody. If a house goes up for sale she's on to it like a hawk and then rings round all her acquaintances in order to find suitable occupants. It's how I arrived here. I happened to mention to Fay how unsatisfactory it was, living with friends and that I was looking for a place of my own." He broke off.

"I was actually staying with Wal and Miriam at the time."

Natasha said scornfully, "No wonder you wanted a place of your own!"

He smiled. "Oh Miriam's all right once you get used to her abrasive character. I was far more irritated by Belinda's dogged devotion, even then. Anyway, Fay told me about this place and I liked it at once. Of course it was far too big for me but that didn't seem to matter..."

He paused and Natasha said helpfully, "Because you managed to fill it up with Jules, Ned and Billy?"

This produced a frown. Jules was not someone he wanted to think about at this moment. Since Natasha's arrival she had been moody and even more neglectful of the boys than usual. How wonderful it would be if the whole problem of Jules were to disappear. Natasha was looking at him expectantly.

He shrugged. "Jules was not a deliberate move on my part. One of those instant decisions I've rather ended up regretting."

She smiled. "I hope you won't end up feeling the same way about me."

He said rather too briskly, "Of course not. You're different. You don't have all of Jules' baggage. Unless there are various offspring you haven't told me about."

Natasha laughed. "Continue with the inhabitants of the Square. So far we've only got to Fay. She's the mother of Jules, right?"

Euan nodded and added, "And Marcia, who doesn't live in the Square, thank God."

She looked at him. "Why the 'thank God'?"

Euan said testily, "Because she's an absolute pain that's why, but I'll leave you to make up your own mind about her."

Natasha suddenly sat bolt upright. "That's it! I know how you've changed. I couldn't put my finger on it until now. You don't swear anymore. In the old days you would have described Marcia as 'fucking awful'."

Euan laughed. "Oh believe me, I can still swear, but now I reserve it for when I'm really stressed." He gave her a quizzical look. "Shall I get back to the Square?" She nodded. "Well, Fay's second husband is called Boffy."

Natasha frowned as if concentrating. "He's the gaga military man who managed to upset the man with our second supper invitation?"

Euan nodded. "Yes, that's Murdo, who lives with Desmond. I told you about them when we had lunch."

Natasha poured the last of the wine into their glasses. "I think it might be easier if you went round the Square by numbers."

Euan deliberately didn't pick up his glass, mindful that there was the evening ahead at Fay's, where the wine always flowed.

"Right, the numbers go from 1 to 40. Fay is number 8. In number

11 we have our mystery man, Mr Pendlebury. He lives with his ancient mother. According to Fay they have always lived in the Square, one of the few original residents left. They have never been social. The curtains are always drawn and the old mother never leaves the house. Pendlebury looks like an undertaker. He must be in his fifties. I imagine he's a civil servant or something of that sort. He keeps to an absolute routine, leaving the house at the same time every morning, and returning at the same time each night. He's always in a brown suit and carries a brief case. Fay actually called on them once and reported that it was dark and Dickensian. Most of the doors were locked and she was taken into a back room that resembled Miss Haversham's, covered in dust and looking as if it hadn't been touched for years."

"How fascinating," Natasha commented, "perhaps he's a Dr Crippen and storing bodies under the floorboards. Go on. Who's next?"

Euan thought for a moment. "The next people I actually know live in number 15. Well, it's both 15 and 16. They've knocked it through, although you wouldn't know it from the front." He gave a laugh. "They are what Fay calls 'the undesirables', which is very unfair because they are perfectly pleasant. But they are 'new money', which is a sin in Fay's eyes." He looked at Natasha and smiled. "By some strange coincidence they are actually called Rich. Arthur and Doris Rich, and rich they are. Arthur makes huge amounts of money from a firm which has something to do with bathrooms, plumbing, that sort of thing."

"Makers of loos?" Natasha suggested helpfully.

"Yes, except they'd refer to it as 'toilet'. Fay mutters on about them being an example of Maggie Thatcher's Britain, but then Fay blames Maggie Thatcher for almost everything, so be warned, never get her on that subject." He chuckled. "There's a story that when the Rich's first moved in, Fay went to see them in order to give them instructions as to what they were allowed to do, and what they were not allowed to do in the Square. Doris Rich was so impressed by the fact that she was a 'lady' she obeyed her every command. According to Fay she kept on saying 'Yes your Ladyship, no your Ladyship.'

Natasha sounded mildly disapproving. "That's ridiculous. The poor Rich's, I shall reserve judgement on them until we meet. "

Euan said in mocking tones, "Oh they'll love you, with your double-barrelled name."

She chose to ignore this. "Are there any Rich children?"

"Yes. Three. Martin the eldest has gone into his father's firm. He's all right, doesn't have much to say for himself. The second son, Peter, is quite different. He's alarmingly artistic, alarming for his parents that is. They don't seem to be on his wave length at all and he barely keeps his contempt for them concealed. Of course, they've only themselves to blame. They've overloaded their children with expensive education, which was totally wasted on Martin who can't string three words together, but Peter is up at Cambridge and never lets you forget it."

Natasha looked at him reprovingly. "Perhaps we shouldn't forget you also went up to Cambridge, nor the fact that you taught in a smart English Prep School?"

A shudder went through him at the memory of Civolds, but all he said was, "That was different. I was a poor boy getting by on scholarships and then trying to earn enough money to support myself as a writer."

Natasha smiled. "What a paragon of virtue."

He picked up his glass and took a gulp of wine. "Where was I? Oh yes, Peter, a pretentious and conceited eighteen year old. He's tall, willowy and blond, rather like that boy in *Death in Venice*, although not so beautiful. In fact there's something rather nasty about him." He laughed. "Marcia jumped on him the last time she was here. He was very alarmed. Mind you, Marcia jumps on every man, especially if they're remotely good looking and single."

Natasha sighed, "Which I suppose means she jumped on you."

He smiled, "Of course, although I managed to extricate myself pretty quickly."

"There's a third Rich child?" Natasha asked.

"Yes, a daughter, still at school. I've seen her crossing the Square clutching a cello case." He picked up his glass. "What I should have explained is that all the houses on that side, numbers 11 to 20, have large gardens at the back. The Rich's have knocked their two large gardens together and put in a swimming pool and a tennis court. Play your cards right and you'll be asked round for summer sports."

Natasha made a face and said briskly, "That's quite enough of the Rich's. Who else?"

Euan did a mental calculation. "The other person on that side of the Square is Dr Fenby at number 19. I don't know him well as we've only met at Murdo's. He has slightly matinee idol looks, rather like David Niven."

"Is he married?" she asked.

Euan shook his head. "I don't think so. I vaguely remember someone telling me that his wife died a few years back. Fay would know." He paused. "That's everyone I know on that side, so we get to our side of the Square." He smiled and added, "the houses with the smaller gardens, or in most cases, patios."

Natasha turned her head and looked out of the window. "I think that's good. It means they aren't such a problem to take care of. In any case, you have the central garden as well."

Euan smiled. "Very true. Well, we're at 23 and Murdo and Desmond are at 29. Then on the corner at 31 we have none other than," he paused for effect, "Maria Linowski."

Natasha's eyes widened. "You mean the soprano?"

Euan nodded, "The great Diva herself."

She looked impressed. "Wow! I was hoping for a celebrity or two."

He laughed. "Well it's not for lack of trying on Fay's part I can assure you. She's away a good deal but when she's around at Christmas she gives a party which is a very lavish affair. Otherwise she doesn't socialise much, except to see the doctor. He visits her a good deal. I'd always presumed it was professional, but it could be more than that. I wouldn't blame him, she's rather dazzling."

Natasha looked at him questioningly and he laughed. "No, no, she's not for me. Apart from anything else she must be very high maintenance, and of course a good deal older than I am."

She said mildly, "You have been known to go for the older woman."

Euan frowned. He felt tempted to remind Natasha that Celia had only been five years older but decided to make no comment and merely said, "So finally we get to number 36 and the Coopers. Gavin is a sort of celebrity, albeit a minor one. He's the Editor of one of the tabloids but I can never remember which. They have one of those impossibly complicated set-ups, both been married several times and it's impossible to sort out which children belong to which. They have one issue from this latest marriage, a fat and highly unpleasing child called Henry. The present wife is one of those formidable Australian women. I think her name's Lorraine and she tends to hit the bottle."

Natasha looked at him, "You don't seem to like the Coopers much."

"Not much, although I don't know them well." He didn't want to expand on what after all had only been a gut feeling. He stood up and stretched. "As I said, numbers 2 and 39 are up for sale. Garrick Square houses are now so sought after they are never vacant for long. It'll be interesting to see who moves in."

Natasha also stood up. "So that's it? You've given me the full run-down?"

"Of all the people I actually know, yes. There are others I know by sight. Fay will be able to tell you more tonight."

She threw the empty wine bottle into a large wicker bin. "I find it fascinating. It's like a little microcosm of the whole of England."

Euan looked amused, "And where does that social observation come from? "

"Don't mock me. You'll probably find my theories very naïve and simplistic, but it strikes me that this Square is sort of representative of the whole country. There's such a huge gap between the Pendlebury's and the Rich's, and then another huge gap between Fay and Murdo, who represent the old world." She paused. "I'm not going to explain this very well, but having been away for three years I've noticed changes since getting back in a way that you, living here, might not have done."

Euan looked at her curiously. "What sort of changes?"

"Well, to the casual eye everything appears flourishing and thriving in 'Thatcher's Britain'. Yet when you look deeper you can see that below the surface all is far from well. It's more a dog eat dog society. Everyone is worrying about how much money they can make. And the people who don't make it just go to the wall. I know there's a great deal of new wealth and we thrashed the Argies and we're over the Recession so all would appear to be rosy. But it isn't. The attitude seems to be that as long as you're doing all right, you don't have to worry about those who aren't." She paused. "I mean, take my contemporaries. I've only seen a few of them since my return, but what I have seen I haven't liked at all. In fact I've found them pretty awful. They only seem interested in the outward trappings of wealth. My male cousins and their friends flash their filo-faxes, drink champagne and talk about their fast cars. If you try and talk about anything more serious or even mention those who are less well-off, they look at you with total bewilderment. I even tried talking to Wal and Miriam about it." She shrugged, "Miriam just patted my hand and told me to stop being such a serious little thing."

She stood staring out of the window.

"Where do your father and Inga come into all this?" Euan asked.

Natasha couldn't keep the contempt out of her voice. "They're just typical, and exactly what I mean. They don't think about anyone but themselves. Their life is taken up with the golf club and putting a new extension on their horrible neo-Georgian house."

Euan smiled. "I hardly dare ask, but where do I fit into your theory?"

Natasha turned to look at him and also smiled. "Oh, you've just about hung on to your integrity and of course you are doing your bit for those less fortunate. Look at the way you have offered somewhere to live to Jules and the boys." The smile faded. "I suppose you'll agree with Miriam and think that I should lighten up."

He shook his head. He wasn't thinking that at all, but before he could say anything she went on, "My mother always used to say how sad she was that she had missed the Sixties. Well, I think I agree with her. There was definitely more equality, more idealism, more social union in the swinging Sixties than there is in the avaricious Eighties."

And she suddenly sang, almost fiercely, "A working class hero is something to be. If you want to be a hero, then just follow me."

She turned back to the window and there was silence between them.

The sun was setting and it threw a light across the room leaving a warm glow on the floor and furniture. It also threw a light onto the top of Natasha's head giving her hair a tint of gold.

Euan was shaken. Shaken by *her*. She was so different from what he'd expected. He'd thought he would feel fatherly towards her and would want to protect her, because of Celia. But that wasn't how he was feeling at all. She disturbed him, and disturbed him deep down. He remembered Celia saying how startled she had been by Natasha's shrewd and observant views, especially about marriage. She had only been fifteen then. Now seven years on...

He forced himself to make a move. "It's getting late. I must go. Shall I come and collect you?"

She shook her head. "No, I think it best if I make my own way to Fay's, don't you?"

Euan was silent, not knowing how to take what seemed to him like a definite snub.

She saw this and said tactfully, "I mean, I presume you'll be taking Jules with you? So I don't want to cause any upset." She gave a gurgling laugh and added, "After all, we don't want to give people the impression we're a threesome, do we?"

CHAPTER FIVE

Euan was not in the best of moods as he set out for Fay's supper party. To begin with, he was still uneasy about Natasha's rather abrupt dismissal. In fact the whole afternoon had left him feeling unsettled and confused. Then to make matters worse, he had arrived upstairs to find a cryptic note from Jules, "Gone to Ma's. Have taken Ned and Billy with me. She needs help with the extra numbers for tonight." This was obviously a dig at him for having invited Natasha along. Jules behaviour was fast becoming intolerable.

He had taken a cup of black coffee to his study to be met by a machine with a red light blinking at him furiously and a message from his Editor at the BBC saying they needed a fresh proposal by the morning. Where on earth was he to conjure that up from?

As he stood in the shower he reflected on the changes his life had wrought in a week. He wasn't at all sure he hadn't added to his problems.

His mood wasn't improved when the door of number 8 was opened by Marcia.

"Darling Euan, how absolutely divine to see you." She pulled him through the door and kissed him on both cheeks. "Now what is all this I hear about you keeping a string of women? I always knew you were one to watch."

He was momentarily thrown off balance by the power of her embrace. Clutching the hall table he told her he hardly thought her sister and the daughter of an old friend constituted a string of women.

She kissed him again. "It's enough to make me violently jealous darling."

He was saved from further ordeal by Fay emerging from the kitchen looking a little flushed. She relieved Euan of the two bottles of wine that he had almost lost under Marcia's onslaught. "Oh bless you ducky for bringing the plonk. Everyone drinks so much these days I always worry about running out. Desmond has brought over the food and it looks extremely exotic." She waved an arm. "Come through, come through," and with an air of a chatelaine showing off a stately home she sailed into the living room.

As always Fay was resplendent in flowing robes which masked most of her bulges and long rows of beads adorned her neck. There was also that usual aroma so particular to her, of damp Pekinese and eau de cologne. She was obviously relishing her role as hostess and beamed with excitement at the thought of the evening before her.

Euan looked down the room. At the far end sat Boffy, cigar in one hand, whisky glass in the other. He was in conversation with Murdo, who sat opposite him. There was no sign of Marcia, who had obviously rushed upstairs to put the final touches to her face before making an entrance. There was no sign of Jules either, but in the distance Euan could hear the faint cries of children and presumed she was putting the boys to bed.

The fascinating thing about Fay's house was that it was crammed from floor to ceiling with 'objets d'art'. Every time one of the family houses had been sold up, Fay had taken a selection of pieces and thrown them into Garrick Square. The result was a shabby but glorious mess. Most of the antiques were mortally wounded. The Chippendale had a wobbly leg, the Meissen plates were cracked and chipped, the Georgian silver tea service was missing a sugar bowl, the Venini cocktail glasses were down to two and the Aubusson carpet was covered in coffee stains and dog pee. In fact, the two pekineses had wrought their own very special brand of havoc to the family heirlooms. The only object that seemed to have survived in the living room was a large and handsome Louis XV gilt mirror, but that could still go the way of the family portrait which boasted an ancestor who had lost an eye. According to Fay, a billiard cue had been pushed through it.

Murdo turned and waved. Fay thrust a glass of wine into Euan's hand and hissed, "Well, where is she then? Don't tell me you've forgotten to bring her."

Euan sipped his wine and winced slightly. This *was* plonk, unlike the two, rather fine bottles he had brought. "Natasha? No, she's coming. She's making her own way over."

Fay's plump frame was quivering with excitement. "Oh ducky, I can't wait to see her. Jules has been frustratingly silent on the subject which means Natasha must be wildly attractive. Has she fallen for you already?" Her fat fingers dug him in the ribs.

Euan didn't know whether to be amused or irritated. "Really Fay. Natasha looks on me as a father figure, or at the very least a friendly uncle."

Fay shot him a quizzical look. "And how do you look on her?"

He didn't dignify this with a reply because in all honesty, after this afternoon, he didn't really know. Instead he decided to change the subject. "So, tell me who is coming tonight? Have you any surprises for us?"

Fay beamed in triumph. "I have the most wonderful surprise for you. Our new neighbour is coming. I've only just met him myself. He's bought Number 39."

"Who?' Euan and Murdo said at the same time.

Fay chuckled. "I'm not telling you. You'll have to wait and see."

Then everything began to happen at once. Marcia and Jules arrived together, Marcia seductive, Jules scowling. A glance round the room told Jules that Natasha hadn't arrived and she looked at Euan with a questioning expression. Desmond came into the room with a huge silver tray of canapés and everyone crowded round to admire his labours.

The doorbell rang. Euan's mouth went dry. How would Natasha cope in these strange surroundings with all these new people? It wasn't Natasha that Fay ushered in, however, but a youngish man with a pale complexion, dark hair and a trim beard, and, more surprisingly, wearing a dog-collar under his well-cut suit.

The company stood dumbfounded.

"Straight out of Trollope," whispered Murdo to Euan.

In ringing tones Fay announced, "Now everybody, this is Gerry

Masterson, our newest neighbour. He has just bought Number 39."

There was a general murmur of welcome as Fay started to make the introductions.

Marcia immediately began to glow, sensing a new victim. She held out a bejewelled hand and said languidly, "Welcome Gerry." She then looked at him more closely. "Haven't I seen you somewhere before? Your face looks very familiar."

Fay's triumph was complete. "Of course you have ducky. You've seen him on television. Gerald, or Gerry as he likes to be known, is the clergyman in residence at the BBC."

"The acceptable face of the Church of England," Murdo murmured in Euan's ear.

Marcia spoke in a rich deep voice that she only kept for special occasions. "So you're the famous Reverend Gerald Masterson. Of course I remember you now. It's too exciting to actually meet you in the flesh."

Euan watched as the rest of the introductions were made. He observed that Murdo didn't smile but that Desmond did. Fascinating he thought to himself. Murdo doesn't like him, Desmond does.

"And this is Euan Mackay. He'll hate me for saying it but he's a brilliant writer."

Euan winced at this description. Gerry took Euan's hand and held on to it.

"What a privilege to meet you Euan. I've heard so much about you at the BBC."

This surprised Euan. Up until now he'd always worked for the independent companies and had only been at the BBC for a short while, hardly long enough time to gain a reputation. Gerry's tones were smooth and full of unction. Euan felt as if he had just received a Papal blessing and was just wondering if he'd ever get his hand back when the doorbell rang again.

This time it had to be her.

Fay, now in triumphant vein, declared, "Aha, our other surprise guest has arrived. Help yourselves to drinks everybody," and she sailed out of the room to open the front door.

"Is your protégé going to cause as a big a sensation as Fay's?" asked Murdo in sardonic tones.

His question was answered as Natasha entered the room.

There was a definite moment of frisson, an almost audible gasp of admiration. She was dressed in an under-stated way. Her low-cut, olive green dress clung seductively to her skinny figure. She wore no jewellery but a black velvet choker at her neck. No make-up either, except for some pale pink lipstick. She was carrying a large bunch of white lilies. The effect was stunning.

Natasha glanced across at Euan and gave him a shy smile and in that moment he knew that he was lost.

She turned back to Fay and handed her the bunch of lilies. "These are for you," she said in her low husky voice.

Fay beamed with pleasure. "Oh ducky, how perfectly marvellous of you. We haven't had anything in the 'Famille Rose' vase for far too long."

There was general bustle while the vase was found and then further drama as the 'Famille Rose' vase was found to have a leak. By the time the lilies had been transferred to a large chipped jug, and the water mopped off the console table, Natasha had been introduced to everyone.

"Well, well, well," Murdo murmured in Euan's ear. "I'd say you've scored a triumph there, quite a 'coup de theatre'."

Fay clapped her hands. "Now come along everybody. Food time! Follow me to the dining room."

Everybody obediently followed her. Fay beamed at the assembled company. "Oh dear, I do so hate 'placements'. Now, let me see. Gerry you shall sit by me and Natasha on the other side of Gerry. Euan, you must come on the other side of me and Marcia will kill me if I don't put her next to you. Murdo, you go on the other side of Natasha with Jules next to you and then Desmond between Marcia and Jules. There. I think that's everybody!"

Jules drawled out wearily, "You've forgotten Boffy, Ma."

Fay let out a shriek. "Darling Boffy, so I have. He can go next to you Jules. Desmond is doing the food so he will be in and out a good deal."

Euan noticed a flash of annoyance cross Murdo's face. He obviously disliked the way Fay treated Desmond as if he were the family butler. However it was certainly a relief that Desmond was in charge of the food. There had been several occasions when he had left Fay's with the distinct feeling that he had been poisoned.

The meal passed pleasantly enough with Fay in full swing as the perfect hostess. She seemed determined to keep the conversation general, and took the lead by firing questions at her new guests. She first turned her attention to Natasha.

"Euan tells me you have been at Art School in Florence. What are you going to do, now that you have returned to dismal old England?"

Natasha smiled and said almost apologetically, "I'm afraid my plans are rather vague. I'd like to work in stage design, but I think I may have to apply for further training as it's such a specialised field."

Jules drawled from the end of the table. "Jasper says all art training is a waste of time. You've either got it or you haven't."

"Well in Jasper's case he hasn't," Euan said crisply. Jules shot him a poisonous look.

Fay gave a little laugh and said by way of explanation, "Jasper is a painter friend of Jules."

Murdo spoke in precise tones: "It doesn't really matter how much talent you have, if the work is specialised you need specialised training."

Natasha gave him a relieved smile.

"You certainly do with catering," said Desmond suddenly. Murdo looked alarmed. Desmond didn't usually join in the conversation.

Gerry looked across at Desmond with a kindly expression. "I felt sure you had to be a professional caterer, Desmond. This food is quite superb."

Desmond looked as if he were about to faint with pleasure as everyone chimed in with their appreciation.

Fay turned back to Natasha. "And where were you staying, before you took Euan's flat?"

Natasha put down her knife and fork, giving up the task of eating while the questionnaire was in progress. "I stayed for a short time with a cousin of my mother's, Wal Simmons. He's a lawyer. He and his wife were extremely kind, but I was relieved to move into a place of my own. Miriam, his wife, is rather bossy." She gave a little laugh. "It was a bit like living with Margaret Thatcher." The moment she said this she regretted it, remembering Euan's warning about Fay's views on the lady.

Sure enough it set Fay off. "Oh you poor child, I can't think of anything worse than living with a clone of that dreadful, bullying, Philistine woman! Isn't it bad enough we've had to suffer her as PM twice? I'm sure the greedy woman will want a third term."

There followed a five minute diatribe in which she aired most of her views on Mrs Thatcher's shortcomings. These were mainly to do with her attitude to the Arts.

Euan watched Gerry's expression throughout this outpouring. It never changed from a beatific and benevolent smile. As Fay paused for breath he said in his most calming tones, "My dear Lady Fay, aren't you being a little harsh? I think it is only fair to point out that Mrs Thatcher does have her good points as well as her bad ones, as do we all."

He talked on pouring oil on the troubled waters of Fay's 'Mrs Thatcher obsession' and Euan had the uneasy feeling that she wasn't going to take very kindly to the Reverend Gerald. He was too nice, too all things to all people.

Marcia leaned across the table, exposing a good deal of her frontage.

"Are you going to be living in that big house all alone Gerry? Or do you have a wife?"

Gerry smiled a special sort of smile he reserved for women. "Alas Marcia, I do not yet have a wife. But I do have a mother..." (That's significant thought Euan. I had a feeling there'd be a mother around.) "... and I shall be converting the bottom half of the house especially for her."

At this moment Jules mentioned that Boffy had gone to sleep and Fay suggested everyone repair to the drawing room for coffee.

"Euan!" she commanded, "come and help me with the coffee. Desmond! Please see that everyone has the drinks they want. You'll find an assortment of liqueurs in the corner cabinet. Be careful of the

59

door, it tends to come off at the hinges."

Euan obediently followed Fay into the kitchen and she firmly shut the door.

"Well," she said, as she plugged in an ancient looking coffee percolator, "Your Natasha is certainly a sensation. Quite frankly ducky, I knew, from the moment she entered, that here we had someone with star quality."

Euan laughed. "She's not one of your thespians Fay."

"Well I know that." She started putting an odd assortment of coffee cups on the tray. "But you don't have to be in show business to have star quality, and I'm telling you that child has that certain something, an ethereal quality. It will be fascinating to see how things develop." She didn't give Euan time to comment on this enigmatic statement, but sat him down and spoke in conspiratorial tones. "Now, while the coffee is doing its thing, tell me, what do you make of our new neighbour?"

Euan decided to move cautiously. "Perhaps it is a little early to make a judgement."

Fay shook her head and sighed. "I think for once in my life, I might have made a teeny mistake. He seemed rather different when I met him at the BBC. I mean the horror of it, to turn up to dinner in a dog collar. I'm terribly afraid he comes from low Anglican stock. No sense of humour either. He probably has a fondness for twanging guitars and those awful born-again hymns."

Euan thought that Fay's second thoughts about the man were more to do with Gerry's defence of Margaret Thatcher, but he refrained from saying anything as Fay continued, "And then, there's the mother." She said this in deep, ominous tones.

"The mother? You've met her?"

Fay's voice was laden with doom. "I'm afraid I have. She's completely ghastly. Not one of us at all. She talks about 'My Gerald' all the time." Fay shuddered.

Euan had to laugh. "Perhaps she'll keep a low profile, like the mysterious Mrs Pendelbury."

Fay leant across the kitchen table to pick up the sugar bowl and Euan rescued a row of beads that had fallen in the jug of cream. Wiping the beads on her kaftan she said mournfully, "Not a chance of a low profile. Joy Masterson will be out there pushing 'her Gerald' socially, trying to find him a suitable wife. You'd better keep an eye on Natasha."

Euan burst out laughing. "Oh really Fay, you are absurd. And you'd better do something about your coffee machine. It's gone into overdrive."

Once everyone had been given coffee Fay declared it was so early they had time for a game, in spite of the fact that Boffy was already fossilised in his armchair, snoring loudly. But Fay was not to be deterred. "Now, I'll give everyone pencil and paper and then all I want you to do is to write down three of your favourite things – as it says in the song."

At the mention of the word 'favourite' Natasha looked across the room at Euan and smiled. He held her gaze for as long as he could but eventually turned away, only to find Murdo regarding him over the top of his glasses with a quizzical expression.

Having distributed the pencils and paper Fay shook Boffy, scattering his cigar ash down his waistcoat. "Now," she said, "we all write down three favourite things," adding, "of course, to play the game properly we should actually write down our three un-favourite things as well, but that would take too long. We can leave that until the next time we are all together. It's best if you write in capital letters. Some writing is so illegible."

Euan felt relieved that the game was so simple. It meant that Murdo would be spared the humiliation of explaining the rules to Desmond. He was also relieved that they were leaving out their dislikes. That could have turned nasty. Boffy would probably have written 'Commies' and 'Nancy Boys', causing yet another upset.

Fay was clapping her hands. "Hurry up everyone, just three favourite things. Oh Boffy, do wake up darling. Natasha, give the Colonel another shove."

Natasha obeyed and explained to Boffy what he had to do.

"Now," said Fay, "Everyone must fold up their pieces of paper. Jules! Fetch the Japanese bowl from the dining room." Jules left the room and returned with a very large chipped bowl. "Now everyone," commanded Fay, "put your folded pieces of paper into the bowl." They all obediently did as they were told, except for Boffy who had fallen asleep again. Natasha retrieved his piece of paper from the floor, folded it and added it to the rest.

Fay vigorously mixed them up. "Now we come to the exciting part. We all draw out one piece of paper and then try and guess which bit of paper belongs to which person."

Natasha drew out two pieces, one for herself and one she put on the arm of Boffy's chair.

"This won't be very difficult I imagine." Murdo remarked drily.

"Visitors first," said Fay. "Natasha ducky, read out yours."

Natasha obediently read out, "ANTIQUE PEN, TOMATIN MALT WHISKY, LEATHER DESK CHAIR."

There was a moment of silence then Jules drawled, "It has to be Murdo." Murdo shook his head. Natasha smiled at Euan. "I think it's you. The malt whisky gives it away."

Euan smiled back. "She's right," he admitted.

Fay beamed. "Well done Natasha, although of course you do have the advantage of knowing Euan better than the rest of us."

"An obscure brand of malt?" remarked Murdo.

"It is. I'll tell you about it some time," said Euan.

"Gerry next," called out Fay.

He obediently opened up his piece of paper and a slow blush suffused his face. He cleared his throat: "PURE SILK UNDERWEAR, A LARGE BOTTLE OF HERMES CALECHE, A HOT TUB."

Marcia jumped up. "Go on. Read it all out. And…"

Gerry said quickly, "A HOT TUB FULL OF RAMPANT MEN."

Fay looked annoyed. "You shouldn't have interrupted Marcia. The whole point of this game is that we have to guess. Euan, your turn next."

Obediently he read, "CRUFTS, A GOOD CORSET, A DAY AT THE RACES. " He looked at Fay. "That wasn't very difficult."

She smiled. "Not very. I shall make it harder when we come to do my dislikes. Marcia, you go next."

Marcia said sulkily. "I think this is a ludicrous game." Then catching her mother's glare she read out, "SEX AND DRUGS AND ROCK AND ROLL." She looked at her sister. "Brilliant Jules."

Fay said, "Oh dear, how disappointing of you girls. I'll read out mine." She put on her most theatrical voice and spoke clearly, giving resonance to each word, "SLIPPERS, WISDEN, PANAMA HAT." There was another silence. At last Fay said, "Well I really think that has to be Murdo."

Murdo shook his head and Boffy burst out, "Damn it woman! Don't you know your own husband's tastes?"

Fay stared at him and said in bewildered tones, "But Boffy darling you didn't mention Navy Rum."

He said testily, "No. I wanted my Panama Hat."

Murdo said tactfully, "Perhaps I should read out mine?" He looked at his piece of paper and said, "Interesting, very sensuous. CHOPIN PRELUDES, OIL PAINTS, PAISLEY SHAWLS."

Euan glanced at Natasha but said nothing. It was Gerry that spoke. He smiled sweetly across the room. "I think that must be our little art student."

Natasha felt rather embarrassed at this and said, "Guilty."

"Boffy! Read out yours." Fay commanded.

"I haven't got my glasses."

"Borrow mine," said Murdo, handing them over.

Boffy fumbled with the piece of paper and then read out, "DR JOHNSON'S DICTIONARY, A BOTTLE OF CHATEAU MARGAUX, A SET OF OLD LEATHER TRAVELLING CASES."

Euan said, "I think we have finally pinned down Murdo." And Murdo nodded.

"Only two left." Fay looked round the room. "Jules, your go."

Jules drawled out in bored tones, "A SET OF GOLF CLUBS, A ROLEX WATCH, A TRIP ON A CRUISE SHIP."

Marcia clapped her hands together. "Oh Gerry how romantic, that has to be you."

Gerry shook his head and Murdo suggested she try Desmond. Desmond went red and nodded. Marcia looked cross.

Euan came to the rescue. "So, by logical process of elimination,

Desmond must be in possession of Gerry's choice. Let's hear it Desmond."

Desmond obediently read, "A BOTTLE OF ARMANI COLOGNE, A CASHMERE PULLOVER, A CAROL SUNG BY KING'S COLLEGE CHOIR." He smiled admiringly at Gerry.

"How nice," murmured Murdo, with just a touch of irony.

There was silence for a moment and then everyone made a move at once. Jules went upstairs to check on the boys and Marcia followed her. Natasha collected up the pieces of paper and looked for a bin to put them in. "Try the kitchen," said Euan.

Boffy poured himself a large brandy and then passed the bottle to Murdo.

Euan poured out coffee for himself and Gerry.

"A fascinating exercise," Murdo told Fay.

She beamed with pleasure. "I'm so glad you enjoyed it. I think you'll find, when you go back over everyone's choices, that they will actually prove to be rather revealing."

The evening came to a close soon after that. Jules decided to leave the boys where they were for the night and she joined Euan and Natasha to walk back across the Square.

Fay stood at the window watching the three of them. Murdo came and stood beside her. "Well ducky," she said, "I think we are in for a very interesting summer."

"With a few thunderstorms no doubt," agreed Murdo.

CHAPTER SIX

The following day did not start well. Euan had set his alarm clock for six a.m. in order to give himself time to put together a quick proposal for the BBC. For some reason it didn't go off and he awoke nearer seven and from then on everything became a scramble. He cut himself shaving, couldn't find a clean shirt and when he went to the pile of ironing he found Jules had dumped all her damp washing on top of it. He only had time to grab a quick cup of coffee before dashing from the house in order to avoid the worst of the rush hour traffic. As he drove out of the Square he thought of all the post mortems that would be taking place that morning, dissecting the events of the night before. He allowed himself a brief smile of satisfaction. At least he would be missing those.

In their small Belgravia flat, Joy Masterson looked across the breakfast table at her son, elegant in the dark blue silk dressing gown she had given him last Christmas.

"Well?" she said with a touch of impatience, "I'm waiting Gerald."

He looked over the top of his newspaper. "Waiting?"

"I'm waiting to hear about last night. Did you have a pleasant time?"

"It was very pleasant thank you Mother."

Joy put her cup down onto the saucer with rather more force than was necessary. "I need to know about the guests Gerald. After all, they are soon going to be our neighbours."

Gerry put down his newspaper and said somewhat wearily, "I told you who was there, when I returned last night. You were waiting for me. Remember?"

"But you didn't tell me what they were like. For instance, how did you like Lady Fay's husband?"

"Colonel Boffington? Well, he's a typical ex-Army man. He didn't have much to say, in fact he spent most of the evening falling asleep."

From his mother's expression he knew he wasn't going to get off that lightly so he continued down the list. He told her first about the Honourable Marcia and the Honourable Juliana, taking care to include their full titles because he knew she would like that. He refrained from telling her that he disliked them both intensely, because his mother found it difficult to think any ill of anyone with a title. He did, however, feel it worth pointing out that Marcia was married and Juliana had a relationship with Euan Mackay, a scriptwriter of some promise who also lived in the Square. He didn't want his mother to get any ideas of match-making where the Stanhope girls were concerned. He briefly mentioned Murdo Struthers and was rather vague about a man called Desmond who was responsible for the catering.

Joy Masterson looked at him. "So they had caterers, just for a dinner party? I am impressed. Such a good idea, it takes all the strain from the shoulders of the hostess."

Gerry explained as patiently as he could that Desmond did not belong to a catering firm but had merely overseen the food.

His mother seemed disappointed. "Was there no-one else? Were there no young people invited?"

Gerry hesitated. It would have gone against his principles to lie, but his heart sank as he said, "There was a young girl called Natasha."

His mother's eyes lit up. "Does this Natasha have a surname?"

"Natasha Roxby Smith

"Natasha Roxby Smith," repeated Mrs Masterson, mentally flipping through the pages of Debrett's. "And what was she like?"

"She was an art student."

Here Mrs Masterson's face fell. She wasn't sure that sounded very promising.

Gerald folded his paper neatly and stood up. "I have to go Mother, I've things to do."

"Anything exciting dear?" she inquired. She liked Gerald to know she took an interest in his work.

"It could be. I'm listening to a young singing group. There's a possibility I might use them for a series of Sunday programmes to sing religious songs. I will provide the spoken word. It will be a sort of musical sermon."

"That sounds lovely dear," murmured Joy.

Gerry continued, "Their recording studios are over in Wembley so I may be late back."

He kissed her on the cheek and left.

Joy sat back and thought how well things were going for Gerald. If only she could find him a suitable wife. What was that name again? Roxby something. Roxby Smith? She would look it up.

*

Jules had already had an early post mortem with her sister the night before, and very unsatisfactory it had proved to be. They had sat on the edge of Jules' bed while Marcia did her best to repair a broken nail. Jules rolled herself a cigarette and wailed.

"I just don't understand Euan. I mean what on earth does he see in her? She's so frightfully young." She drawled out the last word as if it were an insult and added, "He's probably feeling guilty about having had an affair with her mother and is trying to make up for it by behaving like a father towards her. It's pathetic. "

Marcia looked at her sister and sighed. "You've played this one all wrong darling. I should give up now if I were you. He's obviously totally smitten already and believe me it's not fatherly feelings he has for her. I wish he'd look at me the way he looked at her." She gave up wrestling with her nail and broke it off, then ignoring her sister's mulish expression she said, "Mind you, she definitely has something. I mean, just look at that entrance, clutching all those lilies. It was like a character out of an Andrew Lloyd Webber musical, or do I mean 'Les Mis'? Anyway, whichever it was, you have to admit it was a bit of a show-stopper. Hard to compete with that."

Jules dragged on her cigarette and said nothing. Marcia stood up and spoke in brisk tones: "If I were you Jules, I'd give Euan a break. After all it must get on his nerves having you and those noisy boys under his feet all day. Personally I think he's been a saint." Jules still said nothing and Marcia added more kindly, "You're welcome to come and stay with me for a week or two. I could do with some company. The long evenings alone with Tim are so dreadfully boring I could scream. Stay with me and then, when you get back things will be resolved, one way or another."

Jules wasn't happy with the doomish way Marcia had summed up her situation, but she could see the truth in what she said. It might be good to get away. Things had become a little tricky in London, especially since she'd had to inform Jasper that the flat would not be his. It could be a good time for her to disappear for a while.

"I'll think about it," she said.

Natasha sat cross-legged on the bed sipping her coffee and running through the events of the previous night in her mind. Rather to her surprise she'd enjoyed it more than expected. It had been amusing seeing all Euan's descriptions come to life. How accurate he'd been. She smiled at the thought that it was sometimes more for what he hadn't said than for what he had. Euan's reticence on the subject of Marcia had spoken volumes. She really was pretty ghastly. Jules wasn't much better and definitely in sulky mode last night. On the positive side she had liked Murdo, as Euan knew she would. As for Desmond, with his kind but rather vacant expression, she had no feelings at all. They were a strange pair.

Finally there was the Reverend Gerry, with his tortured poet look, or was that John the Baptist? He'd been rather patronising in his manner but maybe, like her, he'd been nervous at meeting everyone for the first time. In spite of this, there was something rather fascinating about him. He'd obviously worked hard to cultivate those beautiful tones. It was almost as if he was acting out his role, more like a stage vicar than a real one.

She was so lost in her thoughts that the sound of the telephone made her jump. It was Belinda, wanting to know how the evening had gone. Natasha smiled, well aware that Belinda wasn't actually interested in the Square's social life, she just wanted news of Euan.

"It was interesting," she said. "I quite enjoyed it."

The voice at the other end sounded impatient. "Well go on. Tell me everything." Natasha gave her a brief account and when she finished Belinda gave a groan. "You're so lucky. I'm green with envy." There was a pause and then she asked, "How are you getting on with Euan?"

Natasha became evasive. "Fine, and the flat is great. You must come over now I've done some more to it."

"I'm so jealous. Is Euan madly in love with you?"

"Of course not," Natasha said crossly. "He's just trying to be helpful, that's all."

They chatted on for a while, ending with a lunch date the following week.

Natasha replaced the receiver thoughtfully. Irritating though she was, Belinda had finally forced her into thinking about Euan. She refilled her coffee cup and then sat down to confront the situation. She would never have admitted it to Belinda, but she had been besotted by Euan after their Scottish holiday and had kept a photograph of him in her bedside table. To her he had been the great romantic hero. She also remembered how happy he and her mother had been together. Sometimes she'd felt guilty about her crush on him, but felt sure her mother hadn't noticed. For seven years she had longed to see him again and now here she was, living in his house and seeing him all the time.

She moved over to the window and stared out.

Maybe it had been a mistake, taking the flat. He hadn't really changed, and slightly to her alarm she realised that her feelings for him hadn't really changed either, except they could no longer be put down to a schoolgirl crush. She'd known it the moment she saw him again. He had this strange effect on her. God knows what it was.

She turned back from the window and sighed. There wasn't much point in speculating. She was quite sure Euan was only being kind to her because of her mother, and it was good to see him again as an adult, as an equal. It would be sensible just to settle for that.

*

After a difficult morning at the BBC, Euan had a late lunch in the canteen and then decided he'd get more done if he took his work home. As he parked his car he noticed Murdo putting out the rubbish. Murdo looked up, gave a wave and called out, "Have you time for a cup of tea?" Euan hadn't, but he nodded, locked the car and walked over. It was hard to resist the invitation. Murdo's teas were always a most civilised affair and today there were slices of homemade ginger cake.

They sipped their tea in silence for a while. Murdo patted the tea-pot appreciatively. "Good blend," he said.

"Delicious," agreed Euan, although he wasn't really a tea connoisseur. Then, placing his cup back on the tray, Murdo said, "Well that was an interesting evening."

"Rather a strain I thought." Euan helped himself to another slice of cake. "I wasn't altogether taken with the Reverend Gerald."

"No," was the reply. "Rather a curious choice of Fay's."

With his mouth full Euan could only nod, but he then added, "I think she's already regretting it. Apparently the mother is dreadful. According to Fay she has only one ambition in life and that is to get 'her Gerald' a suitable wife."

Murdo put his hands together as if he were praying. "That is unfortunate," he finally said.

Euan was curious. "Unfortunate? Why?"

There was a short pause. "Well, you must realise that Gerald is gay." Murdo added irritably, "I do so hate that word, but to say homosexual these days is to appear very old fashioned."

Euan smiled at this, "Are you quite sure?"

Murdo nodded. "Oh yes, I recognised it at once, I know the type well. And of course Desmond is a marvellous barometer in these matters. You only have to watch the way he reacts."

Euan privately thought that it must take one to know one, but out loud he said, "Well I must say I'm a little surprised. That wasn't my reading of the situation at all. I rather presumed Gerry was nothing very much sexually. In fact he seemed to pay nearly all his attention to the women, particularly Natasha."

Murdo smiled. "I think we all paid a good deal of attention to your Natasha."

Euan felt tempted to say that she was not 'his Natasha' but didn't want to interrupt Murdo.

"Gerry's attention to women is very significant. To use another expression I loathe, he hasn't yet 'come out'."

Euan thought about this. "What you're telling me is that the Reverend Gerald is in denial and won't admit he is gay?"

Murdo nodded. "Precisely. He may not even admit it to himself. He has everything against him, poor man; the Church, his very public television career, and now you tell me has an ambitious mother. It's very difficult for him, especially with the added stigma of Aids. Dangerous too."

Euan was intrigued. "Why dangerous?"

Murdo's expression changed and he sighed. "Well the poor man will go on denying it to himself, until he is bullied, or shamed into marriage, which of course will be a disaster, with both parties ending up unhappy. Eventually his true sexuality will come out. It always does. And then, after all those years of suppression, it could have terrible consequences." He paused. "That's what I mean by dangerous."

Euan was about to say he thought Murdo had all this a little out of proportion when Murdo added in almost apologetic tones, "You see that is exactly what happened to me."

Euan looked astonished. "Are you telling me you were married?"

Murdo nodded. "Indeed I was. For almost twenty years. It was only after I met Desmond that finally I had the courage to leave."

Euan sat dumbfounded. Then he said, "But why did you get married in the first place? Wouldn't it have been better for you to stay single?"

Murdo said sadly, "Far better, but that's not the way things worked then. You see I was the elder son of a highly respectable Edinburgh family. By the time I reached my early-thirties it was made very obvious that marriage was expected of me. The pressures became too great and I opted for the quiet life."

Euan stared at him in amazement. "But I'm thirty-five and I feel under no obligation to get married."

Murdo looked at Euan over the top of his glasses. "I think your case is a little different from mine and happily you are not suffering from family pressures, or, as in the case of Gerry Masterson, professional and career pressures." He paused, "And you are very obviously something of a 'ladies man'." He sighed. "Yet another expression I dislike."

After a moment Euan asked, "Is your wife still alive?"

Murdo shook his head. "Elizabeth? No. The poor lady died a few years back."

They were silent again. Euan didn't like to appear to pry but his curiosity got the better of him. "Were there any children?"

Murdo again shook his head. "Sadly no, I should have liked that but it wasn't to be. It was poor Elizabeth who wasn't able to have any. Ironic really but this was my excuse to be relieved of any physical obligation towards her. It was all most unsatisfactory and unhappy." He seemed momentarily lost in thought. "I finally made the break and she returned to Scotland. Of course, I should have done so earlier. It was sheer cowardice on my part. However, I'm glad to say Elizabeth re-married and I hope she found some contentment in the last years of her life."

Euan sat in silence digesting all this new information. Murdo watched him and then asked, "So what about you and Natasha?"

Euan looked at him. "You don't miss much do you? I wouldn't admit this to anyone else but I am finding the situation rather unsettling to say the least. When I first suggested the flat to her I was trying to be helpful, you know, to make up in some way for having lost touch with her after her mother's death..." He hesitated.

Murdo said helpfully, "And this father-figure relationship isn't quite working out?"

Euan gave a rueful smile. "Well, I thought it was until yesterday?"

"So, what happened yesterday?"

Euan shrugged. "Nothing very dramatic. I just saw her in a different light that's all. She ceased to be Celia's daughter and became someone in her own right."

Murdo chuckled. "And very formidable she is too."

There was another silence which Murdo broke. "My poor boy, you're quite right. I had forgotten about you and Celia. You are in for a difficult time."

Euan sighed. "It's not just Natasha. Jules is becoming impossible and I don't know what to do about it."

A note of irritation crept into Murdo's voice. "You should have sent that young woman packing a long time ago."

Euan shook his head. "If it had just been her I would. But there are the two boys. They have a pretty raw deal already..."

"They're not your responsibility," Murdo snapped, adding, "if only Fay could help."

Euan sighed. "I have no illusions where Fay is concerned. She could never take them back. It nearly killed her last time they stayed with her." He stood up, "I really ought to go. I've a lot of work on at the moment."

Murdo made a gesture, as if remembering something. "Before you do, tell me about the mysterious malt you mentioned last night. I'd never heard of it."

"You mean the Tomatin." Euan smiled. "I wrote it down to put people off the scent. But I think I must have told Natasha the story behind it. It's a bit technical, and I don't want to bore you."

"You won't and I should like to hear it if you have time."

Euan sat down again. "Well, it started about ten years back, when I became friendly with the managing director of the Tomatin Distillery. He gave me a few of their very special twelve year old bottles. These were unique because they came from the only hogshead of one million gallons ever produced by a malt whisky distillery in one calendar year." He paused. "Are you with me so far?" Murdo nodded and Euan went on. "Well this particular hogshead, laid down in 1964, initially contained sixty proof gallons, which, twelve years later had only forty-four gallons remaining, sixteen gallons having been lost through evaporation during the ageing process. Thus there were only thirty-eight cases, or 456 bottles of this very unique whisky."

"And do you have any of these bottles left?"

"A treasured few, but I only keep them for friends who will really appreciate its unique quality." Euan smiled. "I actually offer it in 'balloon glasses' so that they are tricked into thinking they are drinking cognac."

Murdo looked sceptical. "Surely you could tell the difference at once?"

Euan shook his head. "On the contrary, I fool them every time. You see, aged malt whisky is much smoother than brandy because the French top up any evaporation in the brandy casks with new spirit each year. Scotch whisky casks are not topped up, and although it results in a financial loss due to the evaporation, it means that the aged whisky is of finer quality."

Murdo chuckled. "Well I'm blessed. How interesting. You must allow me to taste this famous Tomatin some time."

Euan stood up again. "You most certainly will, next time you come to dinner." As he reached the front door he added, "I'm looking forward to May 1st."

A shudder went through Murdo. "I can't say I am. It will be an ordeal of the worst kind. Desmond is already panicking and the kitchen is totally out of bounds. I will be greatly relieved when it's all over!"

*

As Euan reached Number 23, Natasha came out of the basement. "Have you got a moment?" she asked.

He hadn't, but of course said yes. They went inside and she waved him towards a chair.

"Are you all right?" he asked. "You look rather pale. Are you suffering from a hangover?"

"Of course not," she said impatiently. "I've had a shock that's all."

"What sort of shock?"

She sat down opposite him. "Do you remember me telling you about Gemma Woods?"

Euan mulled over the name. "Gemma Woods. Oh, you mean your Grandfather's mistress, the one who's been left all the money?"

"That's the one." She paused and then burst out, "She's turned up here."

Euan looked surprised. "To visit you? How did she know the address?"

Natasha made an impatient gesture. "Not at this house, in the Square. She was looking at number 2, the house for sale. I think she is going to buy number 2." The husky voice was almost tearful. "I don't think I could bear it. I mean, to spend my Grandfather's money on a house in this Square. It would be a constant reminder, just as I thought I had put all that behind me?"

Shades of *Casablanca*, Euan thought, 'of all the Squares in all the world...', but it did seem a horrible quirk of fate. He had the urge to take her in his arms and comfort her, but instead he said, "Don't let's panic yet. This Woods woman may not actually buy the house. She's probably looking at several London houses and she won't be the only person going round number 2. I expect there are quite a few potential buyers. This Square has become very popular recently. Stop worrying Tash. I'll ring the Estate Agents and find out what's going on."

Natasha smiled, "Thanks." She hesitated, "Why did you call me Tash? No-one has done that since Mama..."

Euan was immediately contrite. "I'm so sorry. It just came out on the spur of the moment." She looked up at him. "I don't mind. In fact I rather like it. As longs as it's only you."

His heart missed a beat. She'd done it again, thrown him completely.

He stood up and said abruptly, "I really have to go. I'm up against a bloody deadline."

"What are you working on?" she asked.

"Nothing very interesting I assure you," he said and left.

He reached the kitchen to find another cryptic note from Jules. "We are going to stay with Marcia for a few weeks. Will let you know when we are coming back. Jules."

Euan felt a sudden lightness of heart. Life was getting better already.

*

On the other side of the Square, things were not so happy. In fact it had been an awful day. Fay's hostess performance the night before had left her in a state of exhaustion, and this was only increased by the sight of the chaos in the kitchen and dining room. The boys had woken her far too early and when she had gone to Marcia's bedroom to ask her to take the dogs out for a walk, a crumpled heap had informed her that she was suffering from a migraine. On top of all this, Boffy suddenly had one of his funny turns and she'd had to send for Dr Fenby. The Doctor hadn't stayed long. His quick diagnosis was that Boffy was suffering from nothing worse than over-indulgence bringing on acute indigestion. He didn't even prescribe anything, just told Boffy to moderate his lifestyle for a day or two.

The only welcome news was that Marcia was taking Jules and the boys back to stay with her. By the time Marcia had recovered enough to drive, however, and Jules and the boys had squeezed all their stuff into the car it was mid-afternoon and Fay was near to collapse.

Boffy regarded his wife anxiously. "Feeling worn out, old thing?"

"Well of course I am," she said crossly as she sank into a chair.

"Maybe we shouldn't go in for these evening 'do's' if it takes so much out of you."

Fay looked at him with some annoyance. "It wasn't the evening 'do' as you put it. If you want the truth Boffy, I'm worn out by my daughters, my grandchildren and you."

"Me?" Boffy sounded shocked.

"Yes you. Giving me the impression you were having a heart attack."

Boffy's face wore a hurt expression. "Well, how was I to know that I wasn't? In fact, I may have been. Doctors have been known to get it wrong you know."

Fay gave him a wan smile. Patting his hand she said, "Well there's no harm done. You seem fine now."

Boffy said more cheerfully, "Yes I feel quite recovered. In fact old girl, I thought I might have a tiny glass of Port..."

"No you may not!" snapped Fay. "You heard what the doctor said. No booze for at least two days." She ignored his sulky look and poured him a glass of water. "Actually, I rather enjoyed last night. I'm convinced Euan has fallen for Natasha, although of course he hotly denies it. But 'methinks he doth protest too much'. It's really quite romantic. Didn't you find her quite charming Boffy?"

Boffy grunted, "Bit too skinny for my taste."

"Well what did you make of the Reverend Gerald then?"

He lit a cigar and puffed thoughtfully. "He seemed a decent sort of chap. Damned good of him to turn up in the old uniform. I like a uniform. It reminds me of dinners in the Mess."

Fay exploded, "Oh really Boffy, how could you say such a thing? I thought it was too dreadfully vulgar of him and I have to admit I'm not at all sure about the Reverend Gerald. Just wait until you meet the mother."

"I did meet her," he said huffily. "We bumped into her outside the house. I've forgotten her name."

"Joy," answered Fay. "And there's a misnomer for a start." She put an ashtray on Boffy's lap. "By the way, we must remember the party at Murdo and Desmond's on May 1st."

Her husband looked gloomy. "I can't say I'm looking forward to it myself. I always feel I have to stand with my back to the fireplace in that house."

"Oh don't be so ridiculous Boffy," snapped Fay. "Sometimes I lose all patience with you."

*

In the kitchen of Number 29 Desmond was also thinking about the previous night. As he started in on the *vols-au-vent* cases he made a mental note to remind Murdo to invite Gerald Masterson to their party. It would be nice to see him again and they should also invite the mother. Gerry would like that.

CHAPTER SEVEN

In the weeks that followed, Euan's mind was filled with many distractions and this inevitably affected his work. He spent most of his time, when he wasn't at the BBC, staring at a blank sheet of paper, or an empty screen. Murdo's revelations had left him shaken, even though it clarified a great deal that had puzzled him before, not least Murdo's air of world-weariness and suffering. The problem of Jules also occupied his attention. Since the arrival of Natasha it was more urgent than ever to sort it out and he was running out of time. Marcia would tire of her soon, then she and the boys would be back.

However, it was mainly Natasha who occupied his thoughts. She filled his waking hours and a good deal of his sleeping ones as well. He found it impossible to concentrate and could only think of the next time he was going to see her. Just lately that had been frustratingly difficult to organize. So on the morning of May 1st he set out for the BBC with a sense of excitement, knowing they would be going to Murdo's party together.

*

In the late afternoon London was hit by a huge thunderstorm, and the flash floods that followed sent whole areas into a state of chaos. Natasha found the flat flooding from overflowing drainpipes. She placed buckets in strategic positions round the room to catch the water leaking through. This caused rather a maddening drip, but she decided the situation was not worrying enough to bother Euan at work and went back to the task of painting the antique bath.

Fay also had problems with the storm. She'd been in the process of taking the Pekes out and although only in the Square garden, the violence of the rain penetrated her clothes and she arrived home completely drenched. Worse was to follow. As she ripped off her outer layer she inadvertently caught her raincoat on the heavy iron umbrella-stand knocking it over. This landed on the paw of Ming-Ming, who immediately gave out great yelps of pain. Boffy hurried out of the kitchen to find Fay in hysterics, Ming-Ming pouring blood and Tang leaping about yelping in sympathy. When order had finally been restored and after a large swig of brandy, it was decided that Fay should take the wounded Ming-Ming to the vet and she departed with the yapping dog under her arm.

There was hysteria of quite another kind in the Belgrave flat. Joy Masterson had laid out her entire wardrobe on the bed, trying to decide which would be the best outfit for the evening party. It was to be her first foray into Square society and she didn't want to make the wrong impression. Gerald had been no help at all, merely remarking that she always looked nice. She had tried consulting her friend Muriel, who had suggested she couldn't go far wrong with black, but Joy had thought this might be a little dull. She wanted to make an impression. For a moment she toyed with the idea of ringing Lady Fay but decided that would be a little forward after such a short acquaintance.

Her gaze went to the window and she watched the driving rain. What a relief she'd made her hair appointment in the morning. Looking back into the mirror she patted her golden locks. Tracy was such a good little hairdresser and always knew exactly what she wanted, which was to resemble the ladies who attended the Conservative Party Conference. Indeed she felt that her hair was not unlike that of her great heroine, Margaret Thatcher.

In his office, high up in Television Centre, Euan also regarded the blackened skies and driving rain, but nothing could dampen his spirits. On top of the knowledge he would soon be seeing Natasha, he had just won a minor victory by persuading his colleagues that yet another police series would be boring and it would be far more interesting to make a series based on the experiences of a war correspondent. To his surprise they had agreed and it was now up to him to choose the war.

Someone rushed in and announced that Shepherd's Bush was completely flooded and the traffic at a standstill. The Police didn't think it would improve for several hours. Euan picked up the telephone and called Natasha to explain he would be late back and that if she wanted she could go on ahead to the party without him. She looked at the dripping buckets but decided he had enough problems and didn't mention it. Instead she told him not to worry and that she would wait until he returned.

*

Over at Number 15 Doris Rich was not feeling her usual cheerful self, in fact she was decidedly ragged. Just lately Arthur's snoring had become a terrible problem and for the last few nights she'd hardly been able to sleep at all. Although she'd moved into the spare room she could still hear him through the wall. The whole house seemed to shake. Arthur put it down to the new air-conditioning system aggravating an old boxing injury. He tried to be sympathetic to his wife's complaints but secretly was delighted to have the bed to himself. For the first time in his marriage he could fart, cough and spread himself at will. There was also another reason. Just recently Doris had taken to covering her face with a thick layer of cream and it had a pungent and unpleasant odour which left Arthur feeling nauseous. When he'd mentioned this to her she'd looked very offended and told him it was something Lady Fay had recommended for suppleness of the skin. Apparently it was Japanese and based on products from the ocean. Arthur thought this might account for the smell of rotting fish but didn't pursue the subject. He now had a more pressing problem in finding something to wear for this party. He came out of his dressing room carrying a jacket which had a red Lurex thread running through it.

"Hey Doris, I haven't worn this in a long time."

Doris regarded her husband's stocky figure and the ever-expanding paunch and reflected that if he hadn't worn that jacket for some time he might have difficulty getting himself into it, but she nodded encouragingly. Personally she didn't mind what she wore as long as she felt comfortable. The room was bound to get hot with all those people from the Square jammed into it.

Arthur wrestled with the jacket and grumbled as he did so. "When I think how worried you were about coming to this Square, thinking we'd never get any invites. Well how wrong could you be? We never stop getting invites. It's bloody exhausting. All I want, after a hard day's work, is to get home and put my feet up in front of the telly."

He gave a little jump and with one last effort the jacket went on.

Doris was well aware her husband's hard day's work usually ended with a visit to the dog-track followed by a session in one of his drinking clubs, but all she said was, "I don't enjoy these evenings much myself Arthur, but we do have to think of what's good for Peter. It's nice for him to meet all these clever people."

Arthur had other ideas about what would be good for his younger son Peter and it wasn't polite conversation with a lot of posh people either, but it was more than his life was worth to air his views. Since Martin had gone to live above the firm he had become aware of how much his wife doted on Peter.

"Where is he anyway?" he asked.

Doris sounded vague. "I think he said he was going to some afternoon theatre in a pub."

Arthur gave a snort. "That's the best excuse for afternoon drinking I've ever heard."

Doris sniffed, "You always try and see the worst in him," and she went into the bathroom, slamming the door. Arthur shuddered as he remembered the one theatrical experience he had shared with his son. Doris had insisted on dragging him up to Cambridge because Peter had directed the thing. Three men had sat on dustbins and talked a lot of bloody rubbish for two hours. Then one man had got up and shot the other two and then turned the gun on himself. It was the biggest load of bull he'd ever witnessed.

His wife came back into the room looking anxious. "I hope Peter calls us from the station. He'll get drenched if he walks back in the rain. It's a proper downpour."

Do him good thought Arthur to himself. I'm not turning out in this.

*

Gavin Cooper also struggled getting home. His mood, like the weather, was distinctly gloomy. As he sat in the traffic jam he considered his present situation and decided that on the domestic front things could hardly be worse. Ever since his wife had found out about his affair with the actress Lucy Peppard, due to *Private Eye* exposing it, their lives had become one continual wrangle. Lorraine was in a permanently neurotic state, aggravated by large doses of gin and sedatives. For the last four weeks she had been in something called a 'Stress Therapy Programme' with her own 'Personal Healer', but in spite of the vast expense, there had been little sign of improvement. Even her raunchy Australian looks, which had first attracted him to her, were fast disappearing.

What the hell was wrong with women today? All his male friends were having problems with their wives and girlfriends. He was darned if he could fathom it out. Lorraine would moan at him because she didn't have enough freedom, and then moan at him when he left her to get on with it. Well, these women just had to realise they couldn't have it both ways.

He yanked at the gears and moved forward a few feet. It was bumper to bumper right across the bridge.

He thought again of Lorraine. She was his fourth wife and although none of the previous three had been up to much, she was fast becoming the worst of the lot. For a couple of years he had been given a reprieve when her attentions were taken up with a toy boy. Then the toy boy dumped her. You couldn't blame him, but that's when the trouble really started. She turned all her neurosis back on to him and her endless moaning sounded so much worse in an Australian accent.

He moved forward another couple of feet. At this rate he wouldn't get back for at least an hour. Lorraine would never believe he'd actually made the effort to leave the office early.

Gavin stared at the rain bouncing off the windscreen. He had to face it, he was in trouble. He couldn't afford to divorce her, not with the other three still making demands and then there was the added problem of Henry. Here Gavin gave a sigh. He was forced to admit he had fathered a truly ghastly specimen. Yet Lorraine doted on this obese, unpleasant child. It was quite extraordinary.

He eased the XJS forward as the traffic at last began to move.

A wonderful idea came to him. He would send the boy and his mother somewhere far away for the summer holidays. It would have to be expensive to keep Lorraine happy and far enough away to make it impossible for her to return early. This would at least give him a breather. Meanwhile he somehow had to get through tonight.

*

Fay arrived back from the vet's exhausted. Ming-Ming had yelped the entire time and only finally stopped when the vet plugged the dog with a large dose of sedative. She had been reassured that the wound was not serious but was filled with horror at the thought of what might have been. Supposing darling Ming-Ming had been directly under the umbrella stand. Her noble head, not to mention her body, would have been quite crushed. It was a disaster too awful to contemplate. The tears poured down Fay's face as she struggled back through the rush hour traffic.

Boffy took one look at her wan, tear-marked face and poured her a large brandy. She took it gratefully and said, "We'll have to take Ming-Ming with us tonight."

This was greeted with alarm. "I don't think that's a good idea old girl. The dog won't like it with all those strange people milling around and I don't suppose Murdo and Desmond will like it much either."

Fay was adamant. "Ming-Ming won't notice the people, she's been sedated, but I must be there when she wakes up properly. The poor little thing will be traumatised. She's had a terrible shock."

Boffy said brightly, "I know, you go to the party and I'll stay with the dog."

His wife wouldn't hear of it and said briskly, "Nonsense Boffy. You're no good with her at all. It's me she needs."

Thus it was that Fay arrived on the doorstep of Number 29 with Ming-Ming in her arms. At first Murdo thought she was wearing a large fur muff and reflected that it was rather odd of Fay to go to such lengths when the weather, although wet, was really very mild. Then the fur muff gave a little shudder. Murdo recoiled in shock and Fay explained what had happened. Murdo ushered them in and immediately turned the whole thing over to Desmond, who took the dog from Fay's arms and arranged for Ming-Ming to be placed on a velvet cushion in a seat in the alcove.

"Damn good of you," said Boffy, and for the first time that day was able to relax.

Joy Masterson was anything but relaxed. After three changes of clothes she had finally decided on a dress of red and gold brocade with big bows on the shoulders. Gerry had made no comment but secretly thought his mother resembled a rather large Easter egg.

The result of all this changing was a delay in their departure for Garrick Square, and they were now stuck on Chelsea Bridge with the rain pouring down and their windscreen wipers going at full speed.

"It's too dreadful," complained Joy. "They should sort out the traffic problems on these bridges."

Gerry adopted his most soothing tones. "I think you'll find that the problem today is the excessive rain, rather than the excessive traffic. Don't worry. We'll be there soon."

"But we are the only guests coming from across London," wailed his mother. "Everyone else only has to cross the Square."

"Will you stop panicking Mother" Gerry's voice became a little sharp. "People in the Square still have to get back from work. In any case, it only said 'seven onwards' on the invitation. It's a buffet supper, not a sit down affair. Look we're moving now."

*

By the time Euan and Natasha made it to the party, most of the guests had arrived.

"Are we the last?" inquired Euan.

"No, no. A few more to come," Murdo reassured him. "The Mastersons aren't here yet and I'm still hoping the Diva might turn up. Go through and help yourselves to a drink." He hesitated. "I think I should warn you, Lorraine Cooper's pretty tanked up already."

Indeed she was. Gavin had arrived home to be met by horrible fat Henry who declared 'Mummy's pissed' and one glance in her direction had told him that Mummy most definitely was. She was clad in a very tight black leather dress which covered only the bare minimum of her body and in Gavin's opinion left far too much of her exposed. Her mane of yellow hair was scraped back into a pony tail and her make-up had all the appearance of being applied with an unsteady hand.

Euan noticed she had poor Arthur Rich pinned against the fireplace and decided to stay as far away as possible. Arthur was looking extremely uncomfortable, although this could have been due to the tightness of his jacket rather than to Lorraine Cooper breathing gin fumes over him.

Euan handed Natasha a glass of wine and asked her if there was anybody she would particularly like to meet. She shook her head. "I think I'll just watch to begin with."

At that moment Joy and Gerry were ushered in. Joy, resplendent in her red and gold, was effusive in her apologies for being so late.

"Poor darling Gerald was delayed at the BBC. Some new programme he is working on. They work him so hard." Gerry looked embarrassed and steered her towards the drinks table.

Fay came up behind them. "What did I tell you," she hissed at Euan. "Just look at that hair. It looks like yellow wire wool." They laughed and then she told them about the day's dramas and Natasha was taken away to see Ming-Ming. Boffy joined them and Natasha noticed with some amusement that the waistcoat he wore under his relatively clean blazer was quite filthy and covered in egg yolk, wine stains and cigar ash.

"Who's the good looking blonde woman with the bows on her shoulders?" he enquired of his wife. Fay explained patiently that it was Joy Masterson and that Boffy had already met her. "Dammit. I wouldn't have known it was the same woman," he said and set off across the room to meet her.

"Joy m'dear," he called out. "Good to see you again."

Joy turned and catching sight of Fay flashed her most dazzling smile and gave a little wave. She then turned back and held out her hand to the Colonel who gallantly bent down and kissed it.

"I don't think I can bear to watch anymore," murmured Fay and left the room.

Desmond was in the process of changing the cassette and Natasha went over. It turned out he had a passion for seventies music and Natasha, relieved to have found a topic on which they could so easily converse started to tell him of her favourite singers. She mentioned Janis Ian, James Taylor and Neil Young. Desmond added Carole King and Natasha enthusiastically agreed. "All those wonderful lyrics," and she quoted, "My soul in the lost and found, you came along to claim it."

"That's one of her best," Desmond agreed, but they didn't have time to get any further because Joy Masterson suddenly thrust herself between them.

"You must be Desmond," she said, bestowing on him one of her most winning smiles, "My Gerald has told me all about you."

"He has?" Desmond looked a little bewildered, but Joy was unstoppable.

"Oh yes. He says your catering skills are quite superb. Now do tell me, are you very booked up? I'd love you to do our little house-warming when we move in next month."

Natasha decided to leave Desmond to it.

Arthur was loading his plate with food. "Bloody good tucker," he said to his wife.

Doris nodded. "You can always be sure of good eats here. Desmond puts on a really lovely spread." She looked at Arthur. "I don't know where you're going to put all that food Arthur Rich, I really don't. You're bursting at the seams as it is and your face has gone all red."

Arthur put his plate down. "I think I might take this jacket off. It's bloody hot in here."

As he did so he made a decision to dispose of the jacket in the morning. It had already done terrible things to his breathing and he dreaded to think what it was doing to his digestion.

Doris looked fondly across the room at Peter.

"Look Arthur. Doesn't Peter mix well with all these people? He's been talking to that TV clergyman for ever such a long time."

Arthur stared at his son and his companion. "How do you know he's a clergyman? He doesn't look like one. He hasn't got that white collar thing round his neck."

Gerry had sensed Fay's disapproval of his dog collar the other evening, so tonight was wearing a black cashmere polo-neck.

Doris said, "I've seen him on the telly. Of course you wouldn't have, because you always go out of the room when the God slot comes on."

Arthur ignored this. "I'm going to have to sit down," he said, and they moved away to the far corner of the room.

Natasha replenished her drink and took stock. Euan was talking to someone she presumed was the tabloid editor. He had a rather oily, almost Greek look and from Euan's expression she could tell he was not enjoying the conversation much. The swaying Australian wife joined them. Natasha couldn't hear what was being said but gathered it was a pretty spicy exchange between the two Coopers. Fay came up behind her again. She had a habit of doing that. "Well ducky," she whispered, "I just hope the Coopers don't start throwing things. They usually do." Then in her normal voice she said, "How are you getting on? Have you met Arthur and Doris Rich yet?"

Natasha shook her head and Fay dragged her over to the corner where Arthur and Doris had taken up residence. After the introductions were made Natasha realised she was actually rather hungry and as Arthur had tried out nearly everything he walked her over to the food to supervise her choice. Then they re-joined Doris and Fay who were discussing the merits of various face creams.

Arthur said to Natasha, "You'll enjoy living in this Square. We see all sorts here I can tell you." And he gave her a big nudge in the ribs.

They chatted happily for a while. She liked his friendly squashed face and he made her laugh with his Square anecdotes. She told him she was re-doing her bathroom and Arthur immediately offered help. "I've got a lovely little suite in the showroom that would just suit you. I could let you have it cost price"

Natasha thanked him and smiled inwardly when she thought how horrified he would have been to see her old antique bath covered in dark blue paint. She was just about to take his advice on the desserts, when she received a tap on the shoulder and a loud voice said,

"You must be little Natasha Roxby Smith?"

Natasha winced slightly at 'little' and turned round to find herself face to face with Joy Masterson, who continued, "Gerald has told me so much about you. Now do tell me, is your family the Roxby Smiths who have an estate in Norfolk?" Natasha nodded in surprise as Joy went on, "Then your grandfather must be Sir Malcolm Roxby Smith?"

Natasha nodded again, feeling embarrassed and wishing this woman would keep her voice down. She ventured nervously, "Do you know my grandfather?"

Joy gave her a knowing smile, "I know of him dear. I know of him. Now you must tell me all about yourself. Gerald has made me so curious."

Meekly Natasha allowed herself to be cross-examined and in spite of desperate looks in Euan's direction it was a good ten minutes before she was able to escape. She wandered down the corridor and on opening the first door found it was the kitchen. The Coopers were the only occupants and were screaming at each other from either side of the kitchen table. Natasha heard Lorraine shout, "If you think I am the least bit interested in what you do with your inadequate little..." She quickly shut the door. Moving further down the corridor she found a cloakroom on one side and a door opposite leading into another room she took to be a library. There was a wonderful smell as she entered, a mixture of old leather and tobacco, and every bit of wall space was covered from floor to ceiling with books.

A voice behind her said, "So, you needed to escape as well."

She turned to find Murdo sitting in a leather armchair, a cigarette in one hand and a glass of scotch in the other.

Natasha smiled. "I think I just interrupted an argument in the kitchen."

Murdo said in his driest tones, "I presume you mean the Coopers. Desmond asked if he should pull them apart but I told him there was no point. It happens every year. She'll either throw something or have hysterics and then, thank God, they will leave."

Natasha said "I don't understand why they choose to have their rows in public."

"Because my dear," explained Murdo, "it is the only relationship they have now. They are quite appalling people, but they are part of the motley group that make up this Square, so we always invite them." He sighed. "I'm sorry the Diva hasn't arrived. You'd like her." He took another sip of whisky and asked, "Have you met Arthur and Doris Rich yet?"

Natasha nodded and then gave a laugh. "I probably shouldn't say this, but they remind me of the Flintstones. You know the cartoon couple? I think they were called Fred and Wilma."

Murdo chuckled. "I shall look at them with fresh eyes in the future. Doris Rich is a kindly soul but..." He got no further because Peter Rich walked into the room. Murdo introduced them and Peter gave Natasha only the briefest of glances before returning his attention back to Murdo.

"I'm looking for a book," he said importantly, "Gerry and I are having a slight argument about it. It's Burke's *Philosophical Enquiry*. Do you know if you have it?"

Murdo's eyebrows went up slightly, but all he said was, "It's quite possible. By all means have a look. I'm afraid I don't keep my books in alphabetical order."

Peter started to look and Natasha noted the excitable voice, the peculiar flush to the face and rather fevered eyes. She knew those symptoms. She'd seen it in her cousins. Peter was high on something and she rather presumed it was cocaine. She looked away, only to find Murdo watching her with his penetrating gaze. She was sure he knew what she was thinking.

There was the sound of broken glass coming from the kitchen area. Murdo sighed and put out his cigarette. "That will be the signal for the Cooper's to leave. I'll go and see them out."

He left the room and Natasha asked Peter if he'd like some help. He looked at her blankly as if he didn't know who she was. Then he said, almost rudely, "I'm looking for Burke's..."

"*Philosophical Enquiry*, yes I know." Natasha said. "I'll start at the other end of the book case."

After a minute or two Peter said, "Don't bother any more. It's obviously not here. It really doesn't matter." And he quickly left the room.

Natasha idly went on looking and then suddenly came upon it. She took it off the shelf and was flipping through the pages when Euan came in.

"I'm sorry to have left you so long. I got caught up. Have you been very bored?"

Natasha looked at his worried expression and laughed. "Not at all, in fact I was having a conversation with Murdo when he had to leave to show the Coopers out."

Euan made a face. "Poor Murdo. It happens every year. Usually she throws a plate..."

"It was a glass this time." Natasha told him.

Euan flung himself into a chair. "God they're exhausting. I knew they were having a row. It might have been something I said that started them off. Mind you, it doesn't take much."

There was some sort of commotion in the other room and then a loud peal of laughter. Euan smiled. "I do believe the Diva has arrived. Come along and meet her, with a bit of luck she might be persuaded to sing."

Natasha put the book back and followed Euan out. The great Diva was in the centre of the room with the rest of the guests crowded round her.

Natasha hung back and after a moment Gerry joined her and said, "Oh good, I'm glad you haven't left, I was afraid I'd missed you." He paused. "Are you still keen to do something in stage design?" Natasha nodded and Gerry continued. "I have a friend, someone I met at Oxford, who runs a theatre in North London. He has a resident designer but I was telling him about you and he said he could do with some extra help on his present production."

Natasha was touched. "Thanks Gerry. It would be great to get the experience."

He looked apologetic. "I don't think the money will be very good."

She was quick to reassure him. "That doesn't matter. It sounds just what I need."

Gerry handed her a piece of paper. "I wrote down the details. My friend is expecting you to call."

"That's really kind of you." Natasha put the piece of paper in her jacket pocket.

She looked up to see Euan watching them. His face had a curious expression that she couldn't quite read. He beckoned her to join him but before she could, there was the most terrible shriek from the alcove. Joy Masterson had sat on Ming-Ming, who had promptly reacted by biting her. Luckily her thick girdle and the brocade of her dress acted as protection and there was little damage done, but a noisy scene ensued. Fay flew across the room gathering Ming-Ming in her arms and giving Joy Masterson a look of fury. Gerry went to his mother's side and did his best to calm her down.

"I'm not at all sure I can take much more excitement tonight," murmured Murdo in Euan's ear and Euan felt it his duty to start the general exodus.

As he and Natasha walked back to the house he said, "Would you like to come up for coffee?"

She hesitated and then decided against it. "I don't think I will tonight Euan. I'm actually pretty tired."

He wondered whether he should kiss her, but before he could make up his mind she had disappeared down the basement steps.

CHAPTER EIGHT

No post mortems bombarded Euan the next morning because an event occurred, which quite took everybody's mind off the party of the night before.

Around six o'clock, a silent convoy of police cars made its way into Garrick Square and stopped outside Number 11. Although the dawn raid was conducted in a discreet and quiet manner, the sudden increase in traffic brought several residents to their windows.

Fay immediately instructed Boffy to get dressed and find out what was happening. After much grumbling he put his coat on over his pyjamas and in his slippers hobbled across the Square to Number 11. A few minutes later he returned and reported he had found out nothing except that it was 'Police business'. As he climbed back into bed he pointed out, a trifle crossly, that it hadn't really been necessary for him to stagger across the Square at such an uncivilised hour, only to find out what he already knew. That wasn't going to satisfy Fay and ignoring his grumblings she decided to ring Euan. This was after she had abandoned the idea of ringing Gavin Cooper. The Cooper's behaviour of the night before had been so dreadful nothing would have induced her to ring him, even if he was the editor of a tabloid.

Euan had also risen early, not because of the police raid, but in order to get some work done. As he walked into his study the telephone started ringing.

The voice sounded odd and shaky. "Euan, it's Fay."

He was immediately worried. "Is something wrong?"

"Well, there must be." There was an added note of excitement. "What do you make of it?"

Euan was puzzled. "What do I make of what?"

"The police raid on Number 11. Hadn't you noticed it?"

He stared out of the window again. "Good Lord. What a lot of cars. What's happened?"

Fay tried not to sound impatient. "That's exactly what I am trying to find out. I sent Boffy over but all they would say was that it was 'Police business'. It's so frustrating not knowing. I mean, the Pendleburys. What could they have possibly done? If it had been Arthur Rich with some crooked deal I could have understood it, or even Gavin Cooper with some sort of sex scandal. But the Pendleburys! And why the raid?"

"It is puzzling" Euan agreed. "Mr Pendlebury doesn't look like your average terrorist."

Fay sounded alarmed. "Terrorist? You mean the I.R.A.? He's not Irish is he?"

Euan laughed. "I don't think so Fay. I shouldn't worry. We'll find out soon enough."

"Well I'm not going to wait that long." Fay was back to her brisk self. "Boffy has a friend who's a friend of the Assistant Commissioner. I'll find out from him and ring you back."

One pot of coffee later she was back on the line.

"Well!" she said, in the voice she kept for her most sensational news. "It's a major story but I'll put your mind at rest at once and tell you it has nothing to do with terrorists."

This didn't come as a great surprise to Euan and he waited for Fay to continue.

"I have to warn you ducky, it's almost as nasty. The raid wasn't the bomb squad but the vice squad. It seems our Mr Pendlebury was at the centre of a child pornography ring."

This came as a shock and Fay heard Euan's quick intake of breath.

This news took him back to his childhood in Scotland and the abuse he and his brother had endured at the hands of their father. Until now he'd put those memories firmly behind him but now they quickly re-surfaced.

Oblivious of this Fay went on, "It's all just too ghastly. Apparently Mr Pendlebury was responsible for storing and distributing the stuff. You know the sort of thing, videos, photographs and so on. Can you believe it? That horrid little man has been doing this right on our doorstep. The police have been taking away boxes all morning. I can't bear to think about the dreadful contents."

Euan made an effort to sound normal. "I presume they've taken him away as well?"

"Oh yes. They removed him first and then went back for all the evidence."

"And what have they done with the old mother?"

Fay was rather vague about this. "I suppose they'll have taken her into care." There was a moments silence and then she burst out, "Child pornography! That's what's so terrible. I mean it's the lowest of the low. Boffy says he should be taken out and shot."

Euan reflected that by the time Mr Pendlebury had served his prison sentence, being shot might have been a happier alternative. His father had avoided all that. He had walked up into the mountains the afternoon his mother had discovered his secret. His body was brought back the next day. A terrible accident was the inquest verdict.

Fay's voice cut into his thoughts. "It makes me shudder to think of that house with all its locked doors. Those rooms must have been where the ghastly material was stored. Do you think his mother knew about her son's activities?"

Euan thought of his own mother and all those years of being silent. Had she known about her husband before that final day of reckoning? He'd always given her the benefit of the doubt. All he said to Fay was, "I wouldn't have thought the mother had any idea."

He suddenly gave a laugh.

Fay sounded shocked. "I don't know what you can possibly find funny about this situation."

He explained that when he had first described Number 11 to Natasha she'd said it sounded like the sort of household where they kept bodies hidden under the floorboards.

Fay said sharply, "She may not be so far wrong," Fay said sharply. "Who knows what further evil lies behind those locked doors."

Another thought struck him. "I suppose this means their house will go on the market."

At this Fay sounded more cheerful. "I suppose it will. Did you know that an offer has been accepted on Number 2?"

"No I didn't. Do you know who it is?"

Fay sounded irritated. "No, but I'm not best pleased with whoever it is. They gazumped my candidate on two occasions. I had such a suitable buyer as well."

He smiled. "Cheer up Fay. Your person might buy Number 11 now."

"So they might. I'll go and see my friend in the Estate Agents." And she rang off.

Euan sat back and considered this latest news.

If Gemma Woods had bought Number 2 he would have to break the news to Natasha before she actually bumped into the woman. With Gemma Woods in residence it might mean Natasha would leave the Square and that was something he really didn't want to happen.

Damn! It was yet another problem to sort out and just when the BBC expected him to be at his creative best.

Picking up his pen he made a great effort to go back to his work, but after a couple of fruitless hours he gave up and took the opportunity to ring Murdo to thank him for the night before.

Murdo sounded surprisingly chirpy. "It's a pity you left when you did. Once Gerry had removed the hysterical mother the Diva started to sing. We had a marvellous session, with Cole Porter, Gershwin and even a little *South Pacific*. Dr Fenby accompanied her, except for *South Pacific* when Desmond played."

Euan was surprised. "I didn't know Desmond played?"

Murdo chuckled. "His piano playing was the reason we met. I'll tell you the whole story some time. Desmond's a useful player and good at sight reading, but in a different league from John Fenby. The doctor is a fine pianist and I gather accompanies Maria a good deal."

Euan suddenly saw Desmond in a new light. He'd never got beyond railway catering before.

"By the way," Murdo asked, "do you know what has been going on outside Number 11? The milkman told Desmond there had been a police raid of some kind."

Euan repeated everything Fay had told him and when he finished

Murdo said, "Oh dear what a terrible business."

"Feelings are running pretty high," Euan said, "Boffy's solution is to have Mr Pendlebury shot."

Murdo sounded sharp. "Well, that's typical of Boffy. However, my feelings for Mr Pendlebury are tinged with pity. He will endure the most dreadful time inside, as I'm afraid I know only too well." He paused. "Some years ago an acquaintance of mine was sent to prison, convicted of gross indecency against two teenage boys. He endured three months of his sentence then hanged himself."

Euan was silent, again remembering his father. At least he had managed to escape the indignity of prison. He decided to change the subject.

"Do you know who has made an offer for number 2?"

Murdo said, "No I don't. Ask Fay, she's bound to know."

Euan sat back. This Pendlebury business disturbed him. The Press coverage was going to be massive with every lurid detail reported. He smiled grimly. Gavin Cooper would be having a field day.

He was wrong. Gavin Cooper was quite oblivious of the whole thing. He had been in such a fury with Lorraine the night before, he had taken himself off to his club and consequently missed the one major news story that was to break on his doorstep The first Gavin Cooper knew about the Pendlebury scandal was along with everyone else on the lunch time news.

Euan stared out of the window still trying to find some inspiration. He watched Fay take the Pekes into the central garden. She started talking to old Mr Alton the gardener, then catching sight of Doris Rich, crossed the Square to meet her. They immediately plunged deep into conversation and after a short while Doris turned and ran back into her house. Euan could imagine what that conversation had been about. The Pendlebury scandal was going to keep tongues wagging and telephones buzzing for days.

Arthur Rich sat in his kitchen sipping his second cup of black coffee. He had felt so ill first thing he'd made the unusual decision not to go into the office. His guts were definitely in a bad way and there was a nasty throbbing in his head, so he was just about to take some more aspirins when his wife burst into the kitchen in a very agitated state. It was when her voice had reached an unusually high note that Arthur held up his hand to stop her. "Doris for pity's sake will you keep the volume down? You're killing my head. And why are you back? I thought you were on your way to collect the scarf you left at Murdo's."

"Well I was," she said, "but then I met Lady Fay and she told me about the Pendlebury's."

Arthur was baffled. "What Pendlebury's? I don't know anyone called Pendlebury."

He looked at his wife, "Sit down Doris and talk slow. Your words are coming out all jumbled. Start with bumping into Lady Fay."

So she told him the whole story and when she'd finished Arthur whistled through his teeth. "Blimey! A nice little place we've landed ourselves in and no mistake. It's full of bleeding perverts. I tell you Doris, men like that should be stood up against a wall and shot, the whole ruddy lot of them."

Doris was pleased to have her husband's undivided attention for once. "That's just what the Colonel said," she said, adding with a reproving look, "but he put it more nicely."

Arthur ignored this. "I've got a lot of time for the Colonel. He's a good bloke and the only one around here with any common sense."

Doris looked worried. "I do hope this won't upset Peter."

Her husband looked at her in amazement. "Why in hell's name should it upset Peter?"

"Well you know how sensitive he is." Doris said.

Arthur was on the point of saying something rude, but thought the better of it and went back to his coffee and aspirins.

*

Euan was also in need of coffee. He had been studying the long list of late twentieth century wars and was nowhere nearer making a decision. It was ridiculous. He had finally persuaded the BBC into having the series about a war correspondent and now he couldn't decide on a war. Having already thrown out the Falklands, he now also ruled

97

out Vietnam and Cambodia because they'd already been extensively covered and in any case were a sensitive area for the Americans. He didn't really want to open up the Israeli can of worms either. Maybe the answer was to close his eyes and stab his pen onto the world map and see where it landed.

He stood up. This was no good, he was getting nowhere. Feeling the need to clear his head he decided on a walk round the gardens.

As he opened the front door he saw Natasha running up the basement steps carrying a large portfolio.

Euan called out, "Are you going anywhere exciting?"

She turned and smiled. "I'm going to see a man about a job. Gerry gave me an introduction last night."

The Gerry factor was not welcome news but he said, "What about supper tonight?"

"Great. I'll be back about three. Ring me after that."

Euan watched her drive away and then walked over to the gardens.

So that explained what Gerry and Natasha had been talking about the night before. Damn the man. He didn't trust him. Murdo's words of warning came back to him. Surely Gerry couldn't have marriage designs on Natasha? If that was his plan, once he was in the Square, he'd have plenty of opportunity to pursue her. He stopped walking and sat down on a bench. For God's sake! What was the matter with him? He had to stop thinking like this.

With a major effort he forced his attention back to the world's war zones.

Suddenly it came to him. Afghanistan could be the answer. There was plenty in its favour, with its brave war-lords and tribesman, struggling against the mighty Russian Army. A David and Goliath contest. His war correspondent could be a sort of T E Lawrence character. It was a definite possibility. He would look at some film footage.

*

Natasha arrived back in the early afternoon. She changed out of her interview clothes and had just opened the pot of paint ready for a fresh attack on the bath, when the telephone rang. It was the rich tones of Gerry Masterson.

"I just thought I'd ring to find out how you got on at the theatre."

"It couldn't have gone better," Natasha told him. "I'm starting next week."

Gerry sounded pleased. "That's wonderful news, how about dinner tonight to celebrate?"

She hesitated. "I can't tonight I'm afraid."

"What about Friday then?"

"Friday would be fine. Thanks again for the introduction."

Gerry replaced the receiver. After a moment he dialled another number.

Doris Rich came on the line. "Hello? Who is this please?"

"Mrs Rich, it is Gerry. Gerry Masterson."

There was just a hint of suspicion in her voice. "Oh yes?"

Gerry persevered. "Could I speak to Peter please?"

"Hold on." The receiver was put down with a clatter.

After a minute Peter arrived. "Hello, Gerry?"

"Peter, I was wondering if you would like to join me for dinner this evening? We could carry on that very interesting discussion we were having last night."

Peter seemed pleasantly surprised. "Thank you. I should like that."

"Good. I'll pick you up about seven-thirty."

Gerry sat back in his chair feeling pleased with himself. Garrick Square was full of wonderful possibilities and he was going to take advantage of every single one of them.

*

Natasha, as instructed, arrived in Euan's study at eight o'clock. He was sitting behind his desk scribbling away and it was a few moments before he looked up. When he saw her he smiled. She smiled back. "If you want to carry on working I won't mind. You don't have to take me out you know."

He stood up and put on his jacket. "I don't have to take you out, but

I want to. In any case I have done quite enough work today."

They walked to the door. "Where are we going?" she asked. "I wasn't sure how smart to be."

He looked at her and said with a smile, "You'll do." This was a deliberate understatement and he added, "You have a very good line in jackets. I liked the one you were wearing last night as well."

Natasha shrugged as if clothes were the last thing she wanted to talk about. "You can't really go wrong with Italian clothes. Are we walking, or going by car?"

"Car. I'm taking you to a French restaurant tonight." He looked at her. "Do you speak fluent French as well as Italian? I want to be prepared this time."

She gave her gurgling laugh. "No, I don't. My French is terrible."

They climbed into the battered Saab and as they drove out of the Square she remarked, "I like this car. It has this incredibly beaten up body but the engine is still really good."

Euan said, "You sound as if you are describing Fay." Over the meal Natasha told him about the interview and how pleased she was to be doing a job, rather than starting on another course.

"I couldn't face going back to being a student again so I'm grateful to Gerry for giving me this introduction. His friend is the theatre director. Wasn't it kind of him?"

Euan frowned and didn't answer that. "Tell me," he said, "What was this friend of Gerry's like?"

Natasha chuckled, "Very theatrical. When I first went into his office he was with a theatre critic and the two of them were being very camp together." She mentioned a name and Euan made a face. "He's a loathsome man. Apart from his reviews being vile there is something sinister about him."

Natasha laughed. "He would make an ideal Richard III." She looked at Euan. "You don't seem to have a very high opinion of critics."

He shrugged. "Probably not, but it must be a lousy job. Think how many enemies you must make. Most critics are failed writers, actors or musicians who take out their frustration by destroying the careers of others. There are very few nowadays who really write from a love

100

of actual criticism. Most are just trying to catch the attention of their editors by destroying a piece of work."

He refilled her glass and she asked, "Have you suffered from many bad reviews?"

"Oh yes." He emptied the bottle into his own glass and called for another. "My first television series had some extremely bad reviews but the public loved it and we shot up in the ratings. In contrast, my second series had great reviews but wasn't nearly so successful. It about sums up what I feel about critics."

"Which did you think the better series?" she asked.

Euan considered this. "In their way they were both good television, although quite different. The first was lighter in content with a fair amount of rather explicit sex, which may have helped with the higher ratings. Some critics went for the jugular in the most ridiculous way. It was like taking an atom bomb to crush a deck chair but the result of their reviews was that the series gained a cult following." He shrugged. "I don't take much notice of them, but sometimes personal vendettas can be responsible for destroying careers. You only have to look back at past reviews to find how often the critics got it totally wrong. Look at Shelley, Keats and Byron. They all came in for a thrashing, not to mention what they said about Beethoven."

The evening drifted happily on, but both were aware that beneath the chatter and gossip, something was happening that neither of them could quite admit to. Occasionally there was a touch of hands, or a long held look, but these moments were quickly and deliberately broken.

They finished the meal with large brandies and as she got out of the car Natasha realised she was rather tipsy. She therefore didn't resist when Euan took her in his arms and kissed her. It definitely wasn't a fatherly kiss and feeling rather shaken she stammered out her thanks and ran down the steps to her flat.

Euan stared after her and asked himself yet again what on earth he thought he was doing? It was at this moment his attention was drawn to a car pulling up outside Number 15.

In the lamp light he could see Gerry Masterson at the wheel. After a minute or two the passenger door opened and Peter Rich got out.

That's an interesting development, Euan thought, Gerry and Peter. Could this be a potential relationship in the making? They'd certainly spent a good deal of time together at Murdo's party. Well good luck to them. At least it would take Gerry's attention away from Natasha.

CHAPTER NINE

The immediate days that followed were without any major incident. The shock of the Pendlebury scandal died down, Murdo took to his bed with a bad cold and Fay went to stay with Marcia, so all was relatively quiet on the Square front.

Euan immersed himself in his work and saw little of anyone, including Natasha. This was probably just as well. He realised from the moment he'd kissed her that there was no turning back. He had crossed the Rubicon. The situation between them would have to be resolved one way or another, but for the moment he was content to let things take their course.

Natasha started her job and found it pleasant enough. Painting scenery was not exactly mentally demanding but it was physically exhausting and that, combined with the time it took her to travel to North London and back, meant her hours were long. She arrived home each evening ready to grab some food, fall into a hot bath and crash out.

At least this routine gave her a chance to recover from the evening with Euan, which had left her both uncertain and confused. Half of her knew she ought to resist any serious relationship with him and the other half wanted him desperately. The only solution was to keep her distance until she could think more clearly.

As Friday loomed ever nearer she regretted having agreed to go out with Gerry but had left it too late to cancel. He took her to a smarter Italian restaurant than the one she'd been to with Euan, and this time she carefully resisted the temptation to show off her fluent Italian and meekly let him order for her. At Fay's she'd found him patronising and his unctuous tones had annoyed her, but on his own he dropped these affectations. At some point she asked him about his childhood. Hesitant at first, he gradually opened up and although he didn't elaborate, she had the impression his early years hadn't been particularly happy. His father, an insurance salesman, worked in the Croydon area, where they had also lived. Gerry described it as an ordinary middle-class home, but his account drew a picture of a lonely child saddled with parents trapped in a loveless marriage. Then, when he was nine years old, his father had suddenly walked out giving no reason. Gerry never saw him again.

Natasha was shocked. "That's terrible. Was it another woman?"

Gerry shrugged. "It could have been. We never found out. He just sent a note saying that by the time we received it he would be far away and wouldn't be coming back."

"You mean he left the country?" Natasha asked.

"It's possible. For a few months my mother tried to trace him but finally gave up. Of course the most immediate consequence of his disappearance was the loss of income, but my mother scrimped and saved and through sheer determination made it possible for me to have a good education and go up to Oxford." He smiled at Natasha. "Everything happened rather quickly after that. I went to theological college and then became a curate. During that time I applied to work at the BBC and to my great surprise I was offered the job. I've been with the Religious Broadcasting department for six years now."

Natasha looked at him and thought he must be about thirty although he had one of those faces that didn't really age. She could understand why he was such a success on television. Added to his beautiful speaking voice, he was good looking in a sombre sort of way, with a vulnerable quality thrown in. It gave him a special sort of appeal, especially, she thought, for older women.

"Where do you live now?" she asked.

"We have a flat here in London," he told her, "but it's a little cramped. I wanted my mother to have her own space, which is why I've bought the house in Garrick Square."

Thinking of the over-possessive and rather ghastly Joy Masterson, Natasha had the feeling that Gerry probably needed his space as well.

Almost as if he could read her thoughts he smiled and said, "I know people find my mother a little hard to take, but after everything she's gone through I can forgive her. She never, for one moment, let her standards drop and in all those years of struggle she never asked for any sympathy and hardly ever complained. I admire her for that." He paused. "And of course I owe where I am today entirely to her, to her sheer determination to see me succeed."

He spoke so sincerely Natasha felt a little guilty and made a mental note to be more sympathetic towards Joy Masterson in future.

"Was your mother fond of your father?" she asked.

Gerry shrugged. "There may have been some affection at the beginning, but quite honestly there was no outward show and they communicated little." He hesitated. "They certainly had no physical life together. In fact I dimly remember they had separate rooms."

He gave a thin smile, "Let's put it this way, my mother didn't suffer from a broken heart when he disappeared. It was just the manner in which he went away that was the shock and of course, the fact he left her with no income."

There was a moment's silence and then Natasha burst out, "Marriage is such an odd institution. You almost never find one that works and yet everyone goes on getting married. I'm more and more convinced a marriage can only last if two people live completely independent lives and only meet up when they really want to." She added, "I'm even beginning to think separate houses could be the answer, or houses divided into two parts. Then you wouldn't get on top of each other. People need their own space."

Gerald was quite startled. "That's certainly a novel idea," and he looked at her with fresh interest.

As they arrived in the Square he suggested they should have another evening out soon. She thanked him and he agreed to call her the following week.

Running quickly down the steps she noticed with some relief that Euan's lights weren't on and presumed he was either out for the evening or had gone to bed early. It was totally irrational but something told her it might complicate things if he knew she'd been out with Gerry.

Her instincts were right. It did.

Euan's day had already started badly when he received a letter from Jules informing him that she'd be returning the following week. This was not welcome news. A confrontation was now inevitable and he didn't look forward to it.

He then spent the morning looking at news footage about the Afghan war and the images were so horrific they left him further depressed. He returned home, but couldn't settle to anything. Then the telephone rang. It was Fay.

"I have news," she said.

"No more police raids I hope."

She laughed. "Nothing quite so dramatic ducky, I just thought you'd like to know I've found out who is moving into Number 2."

Euan's worst fears were confirmed as Fay told him it was a Mrs Woods. "Damn!" he said and told her about the Natasha connection. Fay was immediately sympathetic.

"Oh that's too dreadful. I had a feeling in my bones this woman wasn't going to be suitable. Apparently she's going to open a boutique of some kind in Chelsea."

Euan gave a mirthless laugh. "She sounds right up Joy Masterson's street."

Fay cleared her throat. "I'm sorry to be the bearer of more bad news but Jules tells me they are returning at the end of next week."

Euan smiled, "I actually knew that Fay. Jules wrote and told me."

"Jules wrote a letter? Miracles do still happen then. Actually ducky, I think she knows you want her to find somewhere else so you may not have to endure her much longer."

There was a pause and then she said in ominous tones, "I suppose you heard that the dreadful Mrs T has called an election. The greedy woman wants a third term which will mean we have to endure her for another five years. It's almost more than I can bear..."

After a few more pithy comments about the Prime Minister she rang off.

Euan sat back in his desk chair and wondered how on earth he was going to break the news about Gemma Woods to Natasha. On top of everything else it now seemed the wretched woman was spending Natasha's inheritance on a boutique in Chelsea. Looking at his watch he made a quick calculation. She usually arrived back around six thirty. He'd give her an hour and then go down to the flat and tell her.

Duly at seven thirty he got up from his desk and was about to go down to the flat when he caught sight of Gerry Masterson's car drawing up outside. In a second Natasha had run up the stairs, climbed into his car and they had driven away. Euan stared after it in shock. Why was Gerry taking her out? More to the point, what on earth was Natasha doing going out with Gerry Masterson? He paced round the room his heart beating fast and his mind in turmoil. He couldn't survive the evening alone in this state, so he rang Murdo.

An hour later Euan was making his way to Number 29.

As he walked into the study a civilized sight met his eyes, a decanter full of claret and a superb cold collation laid out on a tray.

"No Desmond?" he asked, trying not to sound relieved.

Murdo poured him a glass of wine and said, "He's out at some catering do and left me this meal, which I have extended to two. Desmond always leaves far too much and I'm delighted to have the company." He handed Euan his wine and said in similar tones, "No Natasha?"

Euan scowled. "She's gone out," he said, adding, "with Gerry Masterson."

Murdo gave a wry smile. "Oh dear, that's bad news all round. Desmond will be devastated if he gets to hear about it. He's formed one of his attachments, which is rather tiresome, involving a lot of sighing and banging of doors."

Euan gave a mirthless laugh. "Gerald Masterson seems to be ruffling quite a few feathers one way and another. Did you know he was out with Peter Rich the other night?"

Murdo considered this piece of news. "Well, well, well. It would appear he is making quite a few inroads into the social life of Garrick Square."

There was more than a hint of irritation in Euan's voice. "The blasted man seems to be everywhere and he hasn't even moved in yet."

Murdo gave a wicked smile. "Just wait until the formidable Joy Masterson starts throwing round invitations."

Euan gave a short laugh. "I don't think I'll be on her number one guest list."

"But Natasha will." Murdo said and Euan scowled again.

Murdo made a study of the man opposite. "Well Euan, I have noted the furrowed brow and the various growls emitting forth. Would I be right in saying that all was not well with you, my friend?"

Euan smiled, stretched out his legs and sank back in the soft leather armchair. "Yes you probably would."

"Is it Natasha?" Murdo asked.

Euan crossed his legs and then uncrossed them again. Did he want to talk about it? Could he give a rational explanation as to what he was going through? If anyone could understand it would be Murdo, but then he didn't really understand it himself. Why should he mind Natasha going out with Gerry Masterson? Yet he did, he really did. He wanted her to himself, but that was a terrible thing to want of anyone.

Murdo was watching him and Euan was forced to smile. "Of course you're right. Natasha is the main cause of my problems. The trouble is I just don't know what to think anymore. With any other woman, if I felt like this, I would have made a move by now, but with Natasha I feel I am treading on eggshells. I know it's partly because of Celia, but it's more complicated than that."

He hesitated and Murdo said gently, "It's only natural that her mother should be a complication."

Euan burst out, "But that's just it. She's not really. It's as if Natasha has completely taken me over. What I feel for her is something totally different from the way I felt about Celia." He paused. "It's difficult to explain."

"Why don't you try?" Murdo said. "It might help to talk it through."

Euan sipped his wine thoughtfully and then said, "When I fell in love with Celia it was a gentle and protective feeling. We certainly had a passionate affair, but I was always careful, knowing how broken she had been by her past. But with Natasha, who actually *is* the child, I have no such gentle feelings at all. She has quickly become an obsession.

In fact, I'm not sure I like what I'm feeling at all. Pure lust would be nearer the mark."

Murdo smiled. "My dear boy, lust is never pure."

Euan smiled back. "I suppose not. Anyway, I was trying to take a step back from Natasha, give us both a bit of breathing space, but then she has to go out with Gerry." He looked at Murdo. "I know it's irrational to feel jealous, but I do. I also don't trust the man, or his motives."

Murdo handed him a plate of food. "Maybe you should try a little patience. One supper with Natasha isn't much of a threat. Let's give the man the benefit of the doubt for the moment. It could be he's just trying to make friends in the Square before he moves in."

Later, when they had finished the meal, Euan said, "Tell me about your first meeting with Desmond. I think you said he was playing the piano."

Murdo smiled. "Yes he was." He paused. "You already know that for years I had been trapped in a somewhat disastrous marriage. Well, I finally realized that if I was to keep my sanity I had to get away for a while. The opportunity arose when Elizabeth had a major operation and went into a convalescent home. Rather out of character, and quite on impulse, I booked a cruise. On the very first evening I made my way to one of the bars..." He paused as if remembering, "...and there was this golden haired youth with a glorious tan, playing the piano." He gave a rueful smile. "That was more or less that."

Euan had a vision of Murdo, elegant in blazer and flannels, gazing at this beautiful youth, no doubt a rather slimmer version than now, sitting at the piano and playing romantic music. It was like something out of Somerset Maugham. He looked at Murdo. "So you decided to leave your wife?"

Murdo nodded. "Yes, I arrived back in England and moved in with Desmond. I don't think Elizabeth was that surprised, in fact the poor lady seemed almost relieved. I left her well provided for and a few months later she returned to Scotland. The divorce followed and I bought this house. In those days you had to be very discreet about our sort of relationship and for a while it was all rather trying and difficult.

Desmond was both patient and supportive during the time the divorce was going through. I owe him a great deal. It's why I tend to overlook the occasional indiscretion. In any case, our days of passion are over." He sighed. "But it was true passion. I had never known anything like it."

They both fell silent. Murdo cleared the tray away and offered Euan a whisky.

"Tell me," he said as he fetched the decanter, "what is it you're working on at the moment?"

Euan explained about the war series and the affect the film footage was having on him. Murdo listened attentively and commented drily, "It's no surprise you are disturbed by all those grotesque images. You are not the first to be affected by visions of war. You've only to consider Picasso and Guernica." He chuckled. "Do you know the story of Picasso and the SS Officer?" Euan shook his head. "It was during the war, in Paris. Picasso was visited by this SS Officer. After walking round Picasso's studio he stood for a long time in front of the paintings of the destruction of Guernica. Finally the Officer turned to Picasso and asked, 'Did you do all this?' Picasso stared at him and replied, 'No. You did.'"

There was silence. Then Euan gave a nod. "I like that."

Murdo looked at him and remarked, "You know, you remind me of Picasso in some ways."

Euan was taken aback. "I do? Whatever way is that?"

Murdo smiled. "You both possess those inner demons. The 'Duende' Picasso called it. It's a special sort of anger and although only given to the artistically gifted, it can be both dangerous and self-destructive."

He didn't elaborate further and after that the conversation became more general.

As he was leaving, Murdo said, "Go gently with Natasha my boy."

*

Gerry had a late breakfast the next morning and was thankful to find that his mother had already left, which meant he would be spared the endless questioning about his dinner the night before. Enjoying the solitude he sat back and considered his present situation. He was not usually given to self-analysis, but this did seem a good moment for some form of assessment of his life. Looking back, he was well aware that luck had played a large part from the beginning. Even his father's abrupt departure had turned out an advantage. There had been a certain amount of kudos in being an only child with a struggling single parent left in such sad circumstances. This fact, combined with his sensitive looks and excellent exam results had brought him to the attention of the masters, the most influential of which had been the Deputy Head, who taught Religious Studies. He had taken Gerry into his special care. He coached him in the art of beautiful speaking, making sure he lost every trace of an accent, and it was he that advised him to read Theology at Oxford, knowing it was a subject where Gerry would excel. In this he was right. He was awarded a scholarship and as a scholar, with his El Greco looks and cultivated voice, Gerry was immediately noticed. However, his greatest stroke of good fortune was in meeting Sir Cyril Ford.

Gerry sipped his fresh orange juice and thought about him. Sir Cyril had been a very wealthy industrialist and a patron of the Arts, who lived on an estate near Oxford. He involved himself with the University and was greatly sought after by the Colleges for his generous endowments. Apart from his art collection he was also a collector of good looking young men. Each year he would select a few of the cleverest and most attractive undergraduates for his very special attention and they became part of his social scene.

Gerry had met Sir Cyril at a dinner party in his first term and quickly moved into the favoured inner circle. There followed many social occasions where he encountered the rich and famous and to his amazement soon found himself on equal terms with the most elite in the land. He learned fast and was quickly promoted to being Sir Cyril's favourite. It was never a physical relationship and although unmarried, no sexual demands were ever made. However constant companionship was expected and Gerry spent more time on the Ford estate than he did in Oxford. The vacations were taken up with travel, often abroad and especially to Venice where Sir Cyril had an apartment in one of the Palaces.

It was therefore hardly surprising that Gerry did not get the expected first but had to settle for an upper-second. In the circumstances this mattered little. On hearing the Church was to be Gerry's chosen profession, Sir Cyril used his influence to ensure his swift promotion up the Church of England ladder. He was introduced to the right people and by the greatest stroke of fortune met the Head of Religious Broadcasting just two weeks before the television job became vacant.

Gerry smiled as he thought of his early television days. Everyone, even Sir Cyril, had been surprised by his impact on audiences. His appeal seemed to be universal and although the fan mail poured in from young and old alike, it was mainly letters from middle-aged ladies that filled his postbag. They couldn't get enough of his bland message of hope, his beautiful voice introducing beautiful hymns, or his gentle reasoning with their personal and spiritual problems. He was asked to open Church fetes, to appear at charity functions and to help with appeals. In short, he became a television personality, even appearing on talk shows and games panels. He also acquired an agent, a publicist and a financial advisor. Six months after Gerry's appointment at the BBC, Sir Cyril died of a sudden heart attack. His final gift to Gerry was a Renoir, and Gerry, not being a connoisseur of Art, had immediately sold it at Auction for a very large sum. Although he missed his mentor, he had little time for mourning. It was almost as if, Sir Cyril's usefulness being over, he'd tactfully departed. Gerry sold the house in Croydon and purchased the small flat in Belgravia. He had bought it at the bottom of the market and sold at the top. By the time he'd negotiated a bargain price for Garrick Square he found himself with a large surplus of money, most of which he handed over to his financial advisor for investment.

His one worry, when he had decided to take Holy Orders, had been the financial aspect. He liked to think this wasn't for selfish reasons but a determination not to see his mother go through any further hardship. Luck had again played its part. Thanks to the sale of the painting, the lucrative side of his television work and a few sharp moves on the property front, he had become a wealthy man. It was a fact which still surprised him.

Gerry poured himself a cup of coffee, spread a thin layer of butter on his toast and thought about Natasha. It was a surprise to find out how much he had enjoyed her company. She was the first woman in a very long time to whom he had felt remotely attracted. Could he embark on a physical relationship with her?

Here he frowned. Sexual matters were something he didn't like to dwell on. Occasionally he visited a smart and exclusive private house in Chelsea. It was a club that prided itself on its discretion and had been started by an Oxford friend as a place where men could indulge in almost anything they wanted. There were elegant drawing rooms and private bedrooms. Young girls or young men, or both, could be hired for the night. Every indulgence was catered for. There was a gym, massage parlour, sauna, swimming pool and drugs on demand. Gerry had once or twice dabbled with cocaine, but had given it up before the craving took over. He had also had the odd sexual encounter with various young men, but again been careful never to become involved.

Just occasionally he questioned how he managed to square this double life with his work as a member of the clergy. It was not a subject he cared to dwell on, but quite honestly he wasn't even sure why he had chosen the Church as a profession, other than he'd enjoyed reading Theology and it had seemed the next logical step. The two years preparing for the priesthood hadn't deepened him spiritually but it had given him a strong belief in the status of the Established Church. He also liked the hymns, the language and the structure. The pageantry of the rituals and feeling of theatre also suited his personality. As for his conscience, he kept that well under control.

Gerry reached for another piece of toast.

It was now time to think of the future. He'd always been aware that being in the glare of the media required a little more from him by way of a private life and had taken the trouble to be seen out with the odd secretary and even formed a brief relationship with one of them. The girl had been devastated when he broke it off and confided the fact to all her friends. The news went quickly round the BBC and to his astonishment Gerry acquired the reputation of being a minor Don Juan. If this reputation wasn't to fade he had to make a move towards another woman and this time it should be of a more serious nature. So what about Natasha? He had liked her independence and her ideas on marriage had certainly appealed to him. Maybe she could be the answer.

He finished his toast, sat back and warmed to the subject. His next move should be to introduce her to his colleagues and indicate that they were an 'item'. Wasn't that the current word? Of course it would all be a great deal easier when they were settled in the Square. He was at a slight disadvantage at the moment. He'd observed the way Euan Mackay had watched Natasha when he was talking to her the night of Murdo's party. Hadn't he heard that Euan was involved with Natasha's mother before she'd been killed in a car crash? Surely he wouldn't embark on an involvement with the daughter having had an affair with the mother? That would be rather shocking. However he ought to try and find out.

Here he gave a frown. Euan was one of those moody, powerful men of whom he had a deep suspicion. The rough, rugged looks didn't appeal to him at all. There was something almost primitive about the man and the sort of person whose passions could easily get out of hand. Gerry gave a shudder. Emotional scenes were an anathema to him and he was thankful he'd always managed to keep his own feelings well under control.

He wiped his hands on a napkin and touched the sides of his mouth.

Natasha had certainly seemed to enjoy herself last night. He would now monitor the situation carefully, keeping up the pressure and making sure it wasn't too long before he took her out again. Meanwhile, he would still have time for Peter. It would be a shame to give him up just yet. He was a charming boy. It might be good to go up to Cambridge and stay over a couple of nights, away from the prying eyes of the Square.

Feeling pleased with his deliberations he picked up the *Daily Mail* and turned to the television reviews.

*

A week went by. Euan was aware he still hadn't warned Natasha about the imminent arrival of Gemma Woods but had found it difficult to find a suitable time to tell her. She'd been leaving the house early and arriving back late. He'd also been extremely busy with long hours at the BBC. On top of this a sudden heat wave, with temperatures soaring into the eighties, had left everyone feeling frazzled.

It wasn't until the following Saturday that he saw an opportunity, after she arrived back unusually early in the afternoon. He left it a couple of hours and then made his way downstairs to the flat.

He was totally unprepared for what he saw next. Natasha was lying on her bed, asleep. She was wearing her kimono but it had now slipped open, leaving her virtually naked. The evening sunlight streamed across the room turning her skin to a gentle gold.

It was a vision so beautiful it took his breath away.

Hardly thinking what he was doing he undressed and carefully eased himself into the bed beside her. Very gently he stroked the contours of her body and then he took her in his arms. She opened her eyes wide and for a moment stared at him. He stared back, not moving, until finally she broke the tension by smiling.

"Hello Euan," she said in a sleepy husky voice. Sometime later he sat on the edge of the bed. She was still lying beside him and although her eyes were closed he knew she wasn't asleep.

"Are you all right?" he asked.

She smiled without opening her eyes. "Yes very. And you?"

"Very."

They were silent again.

After a minute he said, "No regrets?"

She shook her head. "None."

He started to get dressed. "Tash, I've something to tell you. It's actually the reason I came down to see you..."

She opened her eyes and held up her hand to stop him. "Euan could it wait? I came back early because I was exhausted. I need to get some sleep."

He kissed her on the forehead.

"Of course, I'll tell you tomorrow." And he quietly left the room.

As he reached the top of the basement stairs he noticed a figure standing by the kitchen door. It was Jules. On seeing him she drawled out, "Well darling, so that's where you were. I didn't know where to find you although I knew you must be in, windows open, car outside, everything unlocked. It was like the *Marie Celeste*."

Euan frowned, walked into the kitchen and took a beer from the fridge.

"Have you been back long?" he asked and looked around. "Where are the boys?"

She leant against the door watching him. "We actually arrived back in the Square about two hours ago. I've been over at Ma's catching up on all the gossip. My, my, hasn't a lot been going on? And I've only been away a few weeks."

Euan ignored this and said, "Are the boys still with Fay?"

Jules nodded. "Yes. I thought if we all arrived at once you might find it a trifle overwhelming."

Euan finished his beer, crushed the can and threw it into the bin.

"Jules, I have a heavy load of work on at the moment, so I'd be grateful if you and the boys could start looking for somewhere else to live. I'm sorry, but it was only meant to be a temporary arrangement."

Jules gave him a shrewd look. "Ma warned me you'd probably want the house back to yourself, although she didn't say anything about it being due to your work-load."

Euan let that one pass and Jules added in an offhand manner, "I'll see what I can do."

"Thank you," said Euan and returned to his study.

CHAPTER TEN

The following day Jules made an extra effort to be up at a reasonable hour. It was Sunday, so there was no play-school for Ned and Billy and she was anxious to keep them out of Euan's way. Yesterday's conversation had made her well aware they had outstayed their welcome. Extreme care was going to have to be taken if she and the boys weren't to be thrown onto the streets. As she made herself a pot of tea and tried to unscramble her brain from a rather heavy session the night before, she reflected that life had become rather tiresome of late. She had almost no money left from her inheritance and the family allowance was hardly enough to cover her for booze and fags. On top of all this she now had to find somewhere else to live. Although she was fairly confident Euan wouldn't actually throw them out, it wasn't very pleasant living in a place where you obviously weren't wanted.

She looked out of the window and wondered where the hell he was.

Ned and Billy fell into the kitchen yelling and fighting, almost knocking her over. She prized them apart and told them to keep quiet or they would disturb Euan.

"He's gorn out," said Billy. "He's gorn out in his car. He gave us our breakfast and then went out."

Jules thought crossly that she needn't have made the effort to get up so early and was just considering returning to her bed when there was a knock at the door. Surprised at this she called out, "Come in," and Natasha entered the room. For a moment she and Jules eyed each other warily. Then Jules, realising Natasha hadn't met the boys, introduced them and they solemnly shook hands.

"I'm sorry to bother you," she said, "I was looking for Euan."

"He's gone out," Jules told her, picking up a chair that the boys had knocked over. "Billy," she said, grabbing hold of him, "when did Euan say he'd be back?"

"He didn't," said Billy. "He just told us he was going out and he'd see us later. He said he would come back and play cricket with us."

"Could we go and play cricket now?" asked Ned.

"We could go and practice. Can we? Can we?"

"No you can't," Jules said crossly. "I'm not even dressed yet."

The boys jumped up and down. "Please Mum, we don't need you?"

Natasha looked at them. "Well I'm dressed and I'd quite like a game of cricket." She turned to Jules. "Would that be all right?"

Jules said grudgingly, "Fine, if you really want to. I'll get dressed and come and relieve you."

The boys, delighted to have found a new friend, busied themselves with getting a bat and ball together. It took some time and they finally emerged with a football and a rather small bat and the three of them set off for the garden.

Natasha was so engrossed with organizing the boys she didn't notice a small, neat looking woman walking across the lawn towards her. On catching sight of Natasha the woman stopped and stared.

"Run, Billy, run," Natasha cried out. "No, not across the flower beds, go round it. Yes Ned, I know, it will be your turn next."

The woman tapped her on the shoulder. "Natasha?" She hesitated, "It is Natasha Roxby Smith isn't it?"

Natasha spun round and her face went a little pale. "Mrs Woods," she stammered out.

The woman said, "I couldn't believe it when I saw you. Isn't this a coincidence? What are you doing in this Square?"

"I live here." Natasha said in clipped tones.

"But that's extraordinary," Mrs Woods said brightly, aware of the hostile look on Natasha's face. "I've just bought a house in this Square myself." She waved her arm in its direction. "Which house are you?"

Ned and Billy were not impressed with this interruption to their game and before Natasha could answer Mrs Woods, Billy called out, "Come on Natasha. It's your turn to bowl."

"What sweet little boys," she said. "I presume they don't belong to you?"

Sweet was hardly the word Natasha would have applied to the boys and looking past them she saw, with some relief, the sight of Jules crossing the lawn towards them.

"No, they're not. That's their mother coming over now."

Jules, looking rather magnificent in an Indian multi-coloured robe, arrived at their side and Natasha couldn't resist the full title. "Mrs Woods, this is the Honourable Juliana Stanhope."

Mrs Woods looked slightly awestruck. Jules held out her hand. "I'm known as Jules," she said.

Natasha started to explain, choosing her words carefully, "Mrs Woods was a friend of my grandfather's and has just bought a house in the Square."

By this time the boys were thoroughly bored and Ned deliberately kicked the ball into the middle of the road and then tugged at his mother's sleeve.

"The ball's in the road. The ball's in the road." He chanted.

"I'll get it," Natasha said, pleased to have the excuse to get away.

As she walked out of the garden she noticed the battered Saab drawing up outside the house. She threw the ball back to the boys and then went over to meet Euan. Jules and Mrs Woods were deep in conversation. Euan looked at them and then at Natasha's face and took the situation in at a glance. "Mrs Woods?" he asked and she nodded.

He grabbed hold of her arm and led her into the house.

As soon as the door was closed she cried out, "Why didn't you tell me she had bought the house? You promised to find out."

"I only found out myself yesterday. I was going to tell you..." he broke off.

She looked at him and blushed, realising what had happened. "Of course," she said, "I remember. You were going to tell me and I put you off. I actually came upstairs this morning to find out what it was that was so urgent, but you had gone out. Then I took Ned and Billy into the garden and there she was." She gave a wan smile and then looked out of the window. "My God," she burst out. "What on earth can she and Jules be talking about?"

"Lord knows." Euan joined her at the window adding grimly. "Look at those boys. They are ruining the rose bushes. Fay will be furious. Jules has no control over those children whatsoever."

Natasha flopped into a chair. "Damn, damn, damn! Well at least I now know the worst." She shrugged. "Maybe I won't see too much of her and when the initial shock wears off I'll get over it. I just wish she hadn't chosen this Square, that's all."

Euan continued to stare out of the window. "She's rather a drab wee person. Not my idea of a femme fatale at all."

Natasha laughed. "A drab wee person? What's brought on this Scottishness all of a sudden? Actually it's not the drabness I mind, it's her voice. It's like a child and she has this odd way of giving a giggly laugh at the end of every sentence. It's so annoying. My grandfather must have been very lonely to put up with her."

There was silence between them and then she stood up. "I should be going."

Euan said, "You don't have to go on my account. I'm taking a day off work. What about a coffee?"

She shook her head. "No thanks, I've been drinking coffee all morning."

As she moved towards the door he said, "What about supper tonight?"

She hesitated. After the events of yesterday she knew perfectly well where supper would lead and wasn't sure she could cope with that. "I don't think so Euan. I'm back at work tomorrow and I really must sort out the flat. It's a bit of a mess and I haven't even finished painting the bath yet."

At this he smiled. "All right, but I want to see you soon."

Once she reached the safety of her flat Natasha thought about her decision not to stay. It would have been all too easy to have given in and spent the evening, and no doubt the night with Euan. Did she really want to launch into a full blown affair so soon? It had all moved very fast. She hated to admit it, but when she was with Euan she lost all ability to make rational decisions.

Crossing the room she went to the fridge and poured herself an iced tea and then sat on the bed. There was another thing worrying her. It was no good pretending the problem of her mother didn't exist because it patently did. When Euan had turned to her afterwards and asked her if she had any regrets, she knew perfectly well what he meant. It had been unspoken, but they were both thinking the same thing. Could a relationship work with this shadow from the past hanging over them? She sighed and stood up. The subject would have to be broached before they took things much further.

*

Euan watched Natasha leave and thought with some annoyance that the reason she had declined his invitation to supper was because she was inhibited by the presence of Jules in the house. After all, it was a bit difficult to try and have a relationship with one woman with another hanging around. It was all the more annoying because after yesterday's unexpected break-through, he longed to follow it up and spend the night with her. In fact he'd thought of little else all day. Damn Jules.

As if on cue, and showing unexpected energy, Jules burst into the room and deposited herself like a beached whale onto the nearest chair. She almost lost the languid drawl as she spoke excitedly. "Well darling, I think I've found us the answer and it's quite, quite extraordinary."

Euan said with as much patience as he could muster, "Found the answer to what Jules and what is so extraordinary?"

"That woman is darling, Gemma Woods, the friend of Natasha's."

Euan said coldly, "I'd hardly call her that."

Jules waved her hand dismissively. "Well, whatever she is, she has provided the answer to all our problems. I'm going to move in with her. I'm going to move into her house in the Square. Isn't that great news?" Euan for once was completely lost for words as Jules went on, "We were chatting away after Natasha disappeared, and she asked me where I lived. So I explained that we only had a temporary residence with you and I was simply desperate to find somewhere else before you threw us out."

With a hint of irritation Euan said, "Oh really Jules. I was never going to throw you out."

"I know darling, but it sounded much better and more of an emergency. Anyway, it turns out Gemma needs someone to be in the house with her. It's far too big for her alone. Also she is opening a boutique and needs to store her stock. So for security reasons alone, she has to have someone in the place she can trust."

Euan thought there had to be a snag in this somewhere and asked, "What about rent?"

Jules waved her hand airily. "Oh I explained I had absolutely no money. Amazingly that didn't seem to worry her either. She said I could be a great help to her one way and another. She probably thinks that because I am a Hon, I'll be able to find her clientele and in some ways that's true. I can send Marcia along to her, and from Ma's description, Gerry Masterson's mother is just the sort to use her boutique. I'm sure I can drum up plenty of others. I could even get Jasper to do the décor." Euan shuddered at this thought.

Jules rolled herself a cigarette. After a few drags she said, "So there you have it darling. Miracles do still happen. By the end of next week I'll be out from under your feet and the great thing is the boys will have continuity. Children do need continuity you know. It was why I was so worried about leaving here. Now they will still have the Square and will still be able to see you."

At this moment the boys came into the room chanting, "Dog shit, dog shit, shit, shit shit!"

Jules yelled at them to keep quiet and Euan asked, "What's brought that on?"

She hauled herself up from the chair, "It's their new word. Billy trod in some dog shit in the garden. It's all over the place. I really must tell Ma to do something about the bloody Pekes."

The boys started shouting again, "Bloody Pekes! Dog shit!"

Euan fled to the comparative calm of his study and poured himself a drink. As he sipped his whisky he smiled to himself. The awful Mrs Woods had just landed herself with one hell of a problem while simultaneously he had been relieved of one.

*

The next day Natasha was halfway up a ladder, absorbed in painting a rather tricky area of the scenery, when someone called out she had a visitor waiting for her in the theatre bar. Somewhat surprised she made her way to the foyer and found Gerry chatting to Alan, the theatre's director. Gerry moved towards her and kissed her on both cheeks in a rather theatrical way. "I'm sorry to drag you away from your work Natasha, but I have exciting news that just couldn't wait. I've managed to get two seats for *Don Giovanni* at the Royal Opera House tomorrow. I know it's very short notice, but I wondered if you could possibly make it."

Natasha looked at Alan. "It's really up to you Alan, because it means I would have to leave work early."

He gave her an indulgent smile. "I think we can manage that as it's for something so divinely special. I'm terribly jealous. I hear it's a heavenly production."

Natasha turned back to Gerry. "In that case, I'd love to."

"Good," he said, looking pleased. "I'll pick you up at six."

Natasha went back to the scenery. The Opera House! That would mean dressing up. What on earth was she going to wear? There was no time to buy anything.

That evening she thumbed through her wardrobe trying not to panic. Then she saw it. It was a dress she'd forgotten about, crushed velvet, ankle-length and in a deep wine-coloured red. She'd only worn it once and that was in Italy, when Edward had taken her out on her twenty-first birthday. She remembered feeling guilty at the time for buying something that had taken up most of her yearly allowance. Now she had the opportunity to wear it again.

The next day, Jules, watching from the window, saw Natasha climb into Gerry's car and muttered to herself, "Bloody hell, that girl's done it again. Where on earth is she going dressed up like that?" She wondered if Euan knew and had the feeling he wasn't going to like it very much.

She was right. He arrived back late and tired from the BBC and Jules spared him no detail.

"I can only say darling," she drawled, "Natasha looked a million dollars. She'll be a sensation wherever she's gone. Lucky old Gerry with her on his arm! He was all togged up too."

As Jules had predicted, Natasha did cause a sensation and Gerry revelled in it. He prided himself on being a bit of an opera buff and had a circle of male friends who all shared his enthusiasm. They were rather taken aback to see Gerry with a female companion, especially one so stylish and they fussed around her and bought her champagne at the interval. Natasha found herself enjoying the whole scene. Alan had been right, it was a wonderful production and Gerry had thought of everything, even down to her own opera glasses. They finished the evening with a delicious meal and more champagne.

As she said good night and thanked him she added, "This really has been the most wonderful experience for me Gerry."

He kissed her on the cheek and as he drove home couldn't help indulging in a quiver of satisfaction. All this was going remarkably well to plan.

No such lovely thoughts filled Euan's mind as he saw Natasha return. His jealous rage kept him awake for most of the night. This whole affair with Gerry was getting out of hand. The very word 'affair' sent him into a panic. Was it moving towards that? Surely it couldn't be. Not after what Murdo had said. But he didn't trust the man. Natasha on the other hand would trust him. She was a naturally trusting person and Gerry was making enormous efforts to ensure that she did. It was imperative he tried to warn her, but how? How could he do that without upsetting her?

After many sleepless hours he climbed out of bed and took two aspirin. The sun was just coming up, the central garden was bathed in a soft misty light and he could hear the dawn chorus starting. There was no point in going back to bed now. He dressed and went down to his study.

*

As Natasha arrived back from work that evening Euan called out, "Do you feel like a drink?"

She hesitated and then said, "Give me half an hour. I need to have a bath as I'm covered in scenic paint."

It was nearly an hour before she arrived upstairs washed and changed. Euan waited for her impatiently. "Let's go into the living room," he said, handing her a drink.

It was the first time Natasha had been in this room and she was pleasantly surprised.

"It's good you have managed to keep your rooms uncluttered. All the Square houses I've been in so far have been terribly over-furnished. I'm convinced that when you have such great proportions the rooms only need the bare minimum."

Euan waved a hand. "Miriam organized most of this. I was working flat out and didn't have the time, so she offered. I told her what I wanted, just the 'bare minimum' as you put it, and this was the result."

"That was very trusting of you," Natasha said, "Suppose you'd hated it."

Euan smiled. "Believe me, I gave very strict instructions that everything should be plain and bleached and absolutely no patterns. I hate patterns and frills."

Natasha laughed. "Just wait and see what Joy Masterson does with that house. I imagine the whole place will be patterned chintzes and ruched curtains."

She sank down onto the sofa and Euan looked at her. "You look tired."

"I am. This job is exhausting, added to which I was out late last night."

"I know," said Euan. "I saw you come in."

She burst out, "Honestly Euan, I do believe you are clocking me in and clocking me out."

He looked suitably contrite. "No, I'm not. It just so happens that my desk is right in front of the window, looking out on the Square. So inevitably I see everything that is going on."

Natasha said a trifle crossly, "You should move your desk if it's so distracting."

He wasn't to be put off. "Where did you go? You were very dressed up."

"I went to the Royal Opera House to see *Don Giovanni* and then we went out to dinner."

"We?"

Natasha put down her glass. "You know perfectly well who took me out Euan, because you saw him drop me back." She looked at him and said, "Is it because Gerry took me out? Is that what all this is about? You don't like him do you?"

He said drily, "How very perceptive of you."

Natasha tried to keep the irritation out of her voice. "Why don't you like him? It's very irrational of you. He's kind and quite harmless."

Euan spoke sharply. "Harmless he is not!"

She looked genuinely surprised. "What on earth do you mean? Of course he's harmless."

Euan remained silent. Natasha leant forward. "Come on Euan, out with it? There must be some reason you feel so antagonistic towards him."

He took his time in replying, knowing he had to tread carefully.

"You're right. It's probably irrational of me. Call it gut instinct if you like, combined with the fact that I have a deep suspicion of all things religious." He picked up the bottle of wine and replenished their glasses. "Look around the world. Ninety per cent of all the trouble that is going on has its roots in religion. It produces bigots and extremists who inflict huge damage on everyone else."

Natasha held up her hand. "Hang on a minute Euan. What's all this got to do with poor Gerry?"

Euan shrugged. "He's part of the religious merry-go-round isn't he? I have a terrible suspicion he's one of those 'born-again' clergymen, indulging in shallow sound-bites, twanging guitars and dreadful hymns. You've seen his television programmes haven't you?"

She shook her head. "No I haven't, but he's obviously good at his job. Blame the BBC, it's what they want from him. In any case, I think you're being very unfair. You've only met him twice."

"Quite enough to form a judgement," Euan said gloomily. "Look at his ghastly unctuous manner."

"That's only when he's in public. He's not like that on his own." She suddenly laughed. "I do believe you're jealous because I went out with him."

Euan said a little too quickly, "Nonsense, why should I be jealous? You've just told me he's harmless." He looked at her and felt frustrated. He needed to tell her of Murdo's warning about Gerry's dubious sexual leanings. However, this obviously wasn't the moment so instead he changed the subject. "Actually I have some news that may interest you. Jules and the boys are moving out."

Natasha looked surprised. "Isn't that rather sudden? I do hope it isn't because of me."

Euan hastened to reassure her. "No, absolutely not, I've wanted her to move out for a long time but this is the real surprise. Guess where's she's going?"

Natasha shook her head. "I've no idea."

Euan paused for maximum effect. "She's going to live with Gemma Woods."

She looked stunned. "When did this happen?"

"Yesterday," said Euan and told her the whole story.

When he'd finished Natasha asked, "Where is Jules tonight? Has she moved out already?"

"No, she's over at Fay's for the evening. She moves next week and I have to admit, I can't wait." He sat down beside her and kissed her. "Do you want feeding?"

She thought about it. "I don't think so," and she got wearily to her feet. "I feel slightly done in. Do you mind?"

"No. Off you go and get some rest."

It was true. He didn't mind, because after next week he would have the whole place to himself and then he and Natasha would have all the freedom they needed.

CHAPTER ELEVEN

As May moved into June the Square was like a beehive, buzzing with activity.

Gemma Woods moved into Number 2, the Mastersons moved into Number 39 and Jules and the boys moved out of Number 23. There seemed to be a permanent fleet of removal trucks and vans parked in the roadway and Fay remarked to Euan that judging from the proliferation of Peter Jones delivery vans in the Square they must have been suffering a sudden shortage for anyone else. "You'd think they were breeding," she added gloomily.

Her voice cut across Euan's thoughts as they sat on a garden bench watching the activity.

He smiled. "The Peter Jones vans are only parked outside the Masterston's at No 39."

Fay shuddered and added, "Well at least we have some idea of what their décor will be like." Euan remembered Natasha's remark about chintzy patterns and ruched curtains and nodded. They sat in silence for a while and then Fay said, "It really is vitally important we find suitable people to take over the Pendelbury house." She waved her arm towards the lorries and vans in an exasperated gesture. "I shall be glad when this week is over. It's like living in a giant car park. I feel my life is at risk every time I cross the road and I'm terrified one of those ghastly vans is going to crush my little dogs."

The upheavals in the Square were having an effect on most of the inhabitants and some took the opportunity to disappear. Gerry decided to go up to Cambridge to see Peter. The day after their move into Number 39 he had felt quite drained and one look at his mother, with a sheaf of plans in one hand and a sample of curtain fabric in the other, was enough to send him diving for his weekend case. Surprisingly Joy had raised no objection to his going as she was far too pre-occupied with organizing the builders and decorators. She was in her element and had never been so happy.

Not so happy, but still getting away from it all, was Lorraine Cooper. She informed her friends that she was going for a short stay in a Health Hydro. Gavin Cooper informed his friends that his wife was going away to be dried out. Horrible fat Henry combined the two and informed his friends that his mother had been taken off to a funny farm. Whichever it was, most of her acquaintances were quite relieved to see her depart. They all felt they deserved a breather.

Natasha didn't go away, but found she was seldom in the Square. There was little time for anything outside her theatre work. The first production opened and she was asked to stay on for the next. This she agreed to do, although she was certain she wasn't going to make a career out of painting scenery.

On the home front Jules had now left and she knew it wouldn't be long before Euan summoned her upstairs, something she looked forward to and dreaded in equal measure.

The Rich household was not particularly put out by the activities of the Square, because they were far too taken up with activities of their own. The time was drawing near for their annual summer party and Doris Rich was working herself up into the frenzied state that always hit her three weeks before the party and stayed on for three weeks afterwards. Arthur Rich knew the symptoms well and asked himself, as he did every year, why they bothered to put themselves through all this aggravation for a lot of poxy people they didn't care tuppence for. Their initial mistake had been to give the first party and now they were lumbered with it. His wife sat slumped at the kitchen table with a large pile of invitations in front of her. She looked at the list of possible guests and for the fourth time that morning she gave a great sigh. Arthur could ignore it no longer.

"What is it Doris?" he asked, making little effort to keep the irritation out of his voice.

"It's this Square," she complained. "You have to make sure you give everyone an invite, otherwise they'll feel they've been left out on purpose. There have been so many new people moving in lately, it's difficult to keep up."

Arthur chucked. "Well you can cross pervert Pendlebury off your list anyway."

"Don't be silly Arthur," she snapped. "We never invited them." She looked at him, "I wonder who will move into their house now they've gone. Lady Fay says it's up for sale."

Her husband said gloomily, "It'll be some sort of villain. A bigamist I shouldn't wonder or a toff who's either into drugs or an arms dealer."

Doris took no notice of this. "Lady Fay tells me a politician is interested."

"There you are," he said," what did I tell you? Politicians are the worst of the lot. A political scandal is all we need in this bloody Square."

His wife went back to her list. "There's a new lady moved into Number 2 and she sounds ever so nice. I'll send her an invite. She's living with that Jules Stanhope."

Arthur did his best to be helpful. "What about the vicar bloke and his God-awful mother? They'll be moved in by now. When are we having this shindig anyway?"

"The first Sunday in July as Peter will be back by then." She paused and said a little nervously, "I thought we could have a marquee this year?"

"A what?" Arthur exploded.

"Well a tent, for the drinks, in case it rains," and she added, "you remember that year we had the bad storm? It got really messy indoors." She thought grimly of the mud and grime left all over her cabbage rose carpet. It had taken her weeks to get the marks out. She didn't want to face that again.

Arthur was considering the idea. A beer tent might not be such a bad thing. At least he and his cronies could disappear and have a good booze-up. "All right," he said, much to his wife's surprise. "Go ahead and order a tent. I leave it up to you. I'll just pick up the tab at the end."

"I do hope it doesn't rain though," murmured Doris. "People enjoy it much more if they can use the facilities."

"Facilities?" echoed Arthur. "You make us sound like a bloody fitness centre."

"You know what I mean dear," Doris tried to be patient. "We are the only ones with a tennis court and a swimming pool." A thought suddenly struck her. "Mind you, talking of fitness centres, did I tell you about that Australian woman, Lorraine I think her name is? She's gone to one of them fitness places. Well, more like a health farm really."

Arthur snorted scornfully. "Health farm my arse! She's gone to be dried out and about time too. I don't want her chucking plates all over my house. I suppose they're invited?"

"The Coopers? Well yes, they've always been invited before."

Arthur groaned. "That means they'll bring that horrible fat kid along. He's one of the few kids I wouldn't mind handing over to Mr Porno Pendlebury."

"Arthur! How could you say such a dreadful thing?" His wife looked shocked and Arthur went back behind his newspaper.

For the next half hour he found it sufficient just to give the occasional grunt.

"Well, I think that's everybody," he heard her finally say and at last felt it was safe to abandon his paper.

"Oh no," Doris said. "I've left out that girl we met at Murdo's. She had a complicated name. I'll have to ask Lady Fay. She would be the right age for our Peter and it would be nice for him to have a girl of his own age at the party."

Arthur looked exasperated. His wife was deluded where Peter was concerned. "I'm off to work. Get on to Martin about the beer tent. He'll organize it for you."

*

The Rich invitations plopped onto the Square doorsteps a week after everyone had moved in. Joy Masterson beamed with pleasure. "Isn't that lovely Gerry?" It means I'll be able to get to know everybody before sending out invitations for our own house-warming."

Gerry frowned. "I don't think there's any need to rush into a house-

131

warming Mother. Surely it would be best to wait until the house is finished?"

Joy looked alarmed. How could Gerry not have noticed? The house *was* finished, with the exception of his study. She was still a bit puzzled that her son had gone away, leaving her to make all the decisions, but thanks to an expensive firm of builders and a truly wonderful interior designer recommended by her friend Muriel, the work had been completed on time and to a very high standard. However, she understood that Gerry was a busy man, and he had been generous in financing all her ideas, so she forgave him his absence.

The kitchen and drawing room were her particular pride and joy. Every gadget known to man, or at least to Peter Jones, had been installed in the shiny white kitchen.

"You don't think it looks a little clinical?" Gerald had asked.

"You can't have too much white in a kitchen dear," she had reassured him.

In contrast she had gone for colour in the drawing room, using an abundance of Chinese silk in a peacock blue, red and gold design. William, her interior designer, had excelled himself she reflected, although the Chinese vases had been rather an extravagance and not totally necessary, but they did add a touch of class. Now her only wish was to have a house-warming so that the residents of the Square could see their beautiful home.

She turned to face her son and said in a voice that had a hint of reproach, "The house is finished dear, all except for your study. I didn't like to interfere with that."

He was immediately contrite and adopted his most soothing tones. "Of course I realise that. You have done a wonderful job Mother, but I know you haven't stopped for the last two months and that must have exhausted you. In all the excitement I think you might have under-estimated how tired you really are." He smiled at her indulgently. "Of course you must have your house-warming, but let's leave it for a while and give you a chance to restore the old batteries, yes?"

She was immediately mollified. "Would you like me to reply to the Rich's invitation?"

He patted her hand. "Yes, you do that."

He'd already promised Peter he would be there and as he left the house he thought again of the delightful weekend he'd spent with him in Cambridge. He found the boy extremely attractive and it was gratifying to know that the feeling was mutual. There was certainly no need to end things just yet.

*

Murdo cut open the envelope with an Asprey's paper-knife, read the invitation and gave a sigh. He and Desmond were having an unusually late breakfast because Desmond wasn't going in to work that morning. He'd put his back out playing squash the day before and had decided to see an osteopath before it became any worse.

"Is that an invitation?" he inquired.

"It is," Murdo said with little enthusiasm. "It is a request for our company at the Rich's summer party. I suppose we really ought to attend, it might look churlish if we didn't."

He paused. "Mind you, it could be more interesting this year, with several new additions to the guest list. Natasha Roxby Smith is one, and of course there will be Joy and Gerry Masterson." At the mention of Gerry, Desmond reacted, as Murdo knew he would.

"I think we really ought to make the effort Murdo," he said, adding in a casual manner, "I will go in any case, so you could back out if you wanted to."

Murdo smiled. Desmond was so transparent, but all he said was, "We'll see nearer the time. I'll reply for both of us and I can always make my excuses later. It is one of the advantages of being a geriatric. You can get out of anything at the last minute on medical grounds."

*

The conversion of Number 2, where Gemma Woods now resided with Jules, had been organised in similar fashion to the Masterson's house, but there the similarity ended. Where Joy Masterson had order,

Gemma Woods had chaos. No silks and chintzes adorned the living room and there was certainly no fitted kitchen. In fact, when the Rich's invitation arrived Gemma and Jules were sitting either side of a tea-chest, wondering which room to tackle next.

As with nearly all houses in the Square, the basement had a self-contained flat and into this Jules had happily installed herself. The boys had been given a small room with enough space for their bunk beds and toys. Jules took over the large room for herself, and this combined with a separate entrance, small kitchen and bathroom, gave her total independence. The rest of the house was solely for Gemma's use, with a design room on the top floor. She had sold most of her furniture along with her small Oxford house, which put together with the sale of Bernard's large Oxford house, gave her a very tidy sum. Even so, it had been a big step coming to London and she knew she was taking a risk with the boutique, but having taken on a business manager, she felt quietly confident. Letting Jules Stanhope take the flat had been an impulsive gesture and very out of character, but the more she reflected on it, the more she was convinced she had made a shrewd move. If she had let out the flat properly it would have needed a good deal of expensive modernising, whereas Jules was happy to live in it just as it was. And she liked the company. There was something about Jules that Gemma found fascinating. She was certainly unlike anyone she'd ever met before. The last year had been a lonely one for her. In spite of Bernard being a miserable old bugger, his death had deprived her of a companionship which she'd strangely missed after he'd gone. It had been an odd coincidence meeting the grand-daughter and awkward too. She was well aware how much resentment there was over her inheritance. But why shouldn't Bernard have left everything to her? Natasha wasn't poor. Bernard had told her his wife had left her entire estate to his daughter Celia, with nothing to him, not even a mention, and of course, on her death in that car crash, it all went to Natasha. By all accounts it had left her quite comfortable. Gemma knew how much his wife's action had hurt Bernard, because she'd had to pick up the pieces and put up with his dreadful moods and excessive drinking. His snooty grand-daughter had only bothered to visit him once or twice, so she really didn't deserve his money. If Gemma experienced any guilt at all it was over the grandmother's art work which for the moment was stacked up in the hallway. A valuer had told her she'd make a good deal of money if she sold it as a collection but she felt a bit worried about putting them all on the market. Maybe if she gave Natasha one or two to salve her conscience, she could sell the rest at a later date.

Jules had told her Natasha was now involved with this man Euan Mackay, who had previously had an affair with Natasha's mother. Really! What a family!

She sipped her tea and looked across at Jules, who had the invitation from the Rich's in her hand. The drawling voice said, "I think we really ought to give this party a go Gem. You never know, you might pick up a few clients."

Gemma took the invitation and looked at it. "In that case Jules, we'll definitely go."

*

On the day the invitation arrived, Fay extended her morning's walk as far as Euan's house. He saw her approach and with a sigh immediately abandoned his work.

Once settled in the kitchen she said, "I presume you'll be taking Natasha to the Rich's party?"

Euan shrugged. "Actually I've hardly seen her, so she doesn't know about it yet. She's working long hours at this theatre job."

"Is that the one Gerald Masterson found for her?"

He nodded and from his expression Fay decided it wouldn't be a good idea to pursue that subject. "How are you finding life without Jules and the boys?"

Euan smiled. "Very peaceful."

Fay laughed. "I can only say ducky that my daughter appears to be in seventh heaven with the Gemma Woods woman. She bored on last night with her 'Gem this' and her 'Gem that' until I thought I'd scream, but I've never known her so content and settled."

After a moment Euan said drily, "It would appear we have another

'Jules et Gem' on our hands."

Fay looked puzzled. "Like the film, *Jules et Jim*?" She collapsed with a shriek, her whole body rippling with laughter, causing the entire kitchen to shake. Tears ran down her face. "Oh, that's priceless. Maybe that is what she should call her ghastly boutique."

Half an hour later she left him and still chuckling about 'Jules et Gem' she tottered back across the Square.

*

That evening, for the first time since the departure of Jules, Euan asked Natasha upstairs. They had supper and he told her about the invitation. "You don't have to go to this, but you might find it amusing."

"Of course I'd like to go," she told him.

They sat listening to Chopin Nocturnes, with the candles flickering in the fading evening light. He handed her a glass of Tomatin Malt. "I know you don't usually drink spirits but this is something special. Sip it very slowly."

She did as she was told until she had drained the last drop. The moon came up over the Square and was shining through the window. Euan blew out the candles and stood looking at her. "I want to take you to bed."

"I know," she said, and found she didn't have the will to resist.

Later that night as she lay beside him, she said, "Euan, I think we should talk about Mama."

Euan shifted restlessly. "Why? What is there to talk about?"

Natasha sat up on one arm and looked at him. "Well your relationship with her for a start, and how that affects us..." she broke off.

Euan said lightly, "That's easy. I once loved her. Now I love you."

She ignored his flippancy. "You must be serious Euan. Please?"

He was silent for a moment and then said, "What is it you want to discuss?"

She hesitated. "Well, do you think it wrong, you and me? Are we betraying her in some way by being together? I feel so confused."

136

Euan lit a cigarette as he pondered how best to answer her. "I don't see how it can be wrong, and as for betrayal, that's ridiculous. Celia died in a tragic accident. We both lost somebody we loved, but that's all in the past? Of course, if she were alive today, it would be a different situation. But she's not."

Natasha persisted. "But aren't we the ones who were partly responsible for her death?"

Euan felt a rising irritation but seeing her look so desperate he tried to curb his impatience. "How could we possibly be responsible Tash? It was an accident for God's sake. It was nobody's fault, except the bloody fog which caused the pile-up in the first place."

She turned away from him. "I know that, but she was on her way to see me when it happened. And the reason she was visiting me, was to tell me she was leaving Father for you. Anyway, that's how Father sees it."

Euan stubbed out his cigarette angrily. Bloody George! What a dreadful thing to do to his daughter, to make her feel in some way responsible for her mother's death.

"Now hang on a minute. Your mother didn't actually leave your father for me. She was leaving him because quite frankly she hated the man and couldn't bear to live with him any longer. She had made no other plans, except to take you away for the summer and she told your father nothing except that she was leaving him. It was in a letter that Wal drafted for her and sent on after she died. I saw a copy of it. My name was never mentioned. Celia and I were going to pick things up when she returned from Italy and the holiday with you. We thought we had all the time in the world so there was no rush. We never got a chance to have that future. That's what made it so damnable."

Natasha noted the anger and bitterness in his voice. After a moment she said, "Even so, I just can't help feeling guilty..."

Euan chose his words carefully. "Please Tash you have to stop this. You have no reason for guilt, any more than I have. When Celia died I was devastated. Not just because I had lost someone I loved, but because she had been robbed of the freedom she had so longed for. The positive thing you have to remember is that she *did* manage to break away. She had been so unhappy with your father. The last time I saw her she was really excited about the future. You have to cling on to that."

Natasha lay back. "Do you think you and Mama would have ended up being together?"

Euan lay down beside her. "I thought so at the time, but it was not to be."

Natasha turned to him. "So where does that leave us?"

"Where we are," he replied, "in the present. It's no good trying to live in the past, trying to think what might have happened. What I do know is that we are absolutely free to make our own decisions." He looked at her and smiled, "And for starters I think we ought to get some sleep. We both have to be at work in the morning."

She nodded and quite soon fell into a deep slumber, but Euan lay awake puzzling over this latest conversation. What was it about women? Why did they always have to over-complicate their lives with all this emotional baggage and useless feelings of guilt? Celia had been the same, always worrying, always feeling guilty. It was completely alien to him. He suddenly wondered if his mother was tortured like this, living with her guilty memories all these years.

It was several hours before he finally managed to drift off to sleep as well.

CHAPTER TWELVE

Three weeks went by and it was the day of the summer party. Doris Rich, in her bed of self-exile in the spare room, awoke early. She opened her eyes and looked out of the window and what she saw filled her with horror. Crossing the room she peered out at a layer of thick grey mist that covered the lawn and obscured the pool and tennis court. In the far corner she could just see the outline of the white beer tent which had been erected the day before. A terrible scenario presented itself, of guests wandering around in the semi-darkness, maybe even walking into the pool. Supposing someone was drowned?

In panic she rushed into Arthur who lay spread-eagled over the entire bed, his mouth open, snoring happily. It took her some minutes to wake him and even longer to impress upon him the urgency of the situation. Finally, he staggered to the window and looked out across the garden.

"It's only morning mist Doris," he said crossly and looked at his watch. "Good God woman it isn't six o'clock yet. What's the panic? I'm going back to bed and advise you to do the same."

Doris pulled on her dressing gown and went down to the kitchen. As she poured herself a cup of tea she reflected, not for the first time, that her family offered her little or no assistance on these occasions, least of all Arthur. If this party was to happen, it would be entirely due to her efforts.

Arthur finally arrived downstairs at around ten o'clock, by which time the proceedings were well under way. He sat in the kitchen and thought gloomily of the day ahead. He was further depressed by the sight of his younger son, mincing his way around the garden in a scanty silk dressing gown. Picking up his mug of coffee he decided to go and join Martin in the beer tent. It would be a good place to hide for a while.

Peter, meanwhile, stopped his wanderings in front of the ornamental pond, where he had a moment of rare inspiration. He instructed the caterers to form a pyramid of white wine bottles underneath the fountain. This would not only look decorative but have the added merit of keeping the wine cool.

Doris clapped her hands with delight. "Oh Peter, you are clever. That looks really artistic."

The waiters were not so overjoyed. "That's brilliant that is. We're now going to get our bloody feet wet every time we open a bottle of white wine."

Peter, having made his contribution to the proceedings, took himself off to his room where he pulled down the blinds and put on a Philip Glass cassette. He lay on the bed thinking of Gerry and the weekend they had spent together. For the first time he actually liked one of his parent's friends and he really did like Gerry. He liked him a lot. Until now he'd spent as little time at home as possible, well aware that his father knew he was gay and although fond of his mother, his family was like another species and he had absolutely nothing in common with them. He wouldn't even have bothered coming back for this party if it hadn't been for Gerry. He was now rather regretting having arranged to go to Greece for the whole summer. Maybe a few evenings with Gerry could be managed in the following week, before he had to leave.

*

By eleven o'clock the mist had totally cleared. By twelve noon, when people began to arrive, it was evident they were in for a scorcher. Doris repeated over and over again as she greeted her guests, "Aren't we lucky with the weather?"

It was a remark she was later to regret when the combination of heat and alcohol had done their worst.

By one o'clock the guests were lying sprawled out in the full midday sun, and it was now that the pool came into its own. Alison Rich, having gone through all her summer clothes, finally emerged in a very scanty bikini, which Doris noted with alarm revealed a good deal of pubic hair. Her daughter, oblivious of this, lay Lolita-like by the shallow end of the pool, delicately dipping her brightly painted toes into the water.

Euan sat in a deck-chair beside Murdo, who was looking distinguished in a battered plantation hat. They watched the various bodies cavorting in the water and after a while Murdo remarked, "I've always thought swimming pools were responsible for bringing out the very worst aspects of human behaviour."

Euan agreed. "The attire seems to be another give-away."

They both sat studying individual pool performances.

Lorraine Cooper, fresh from her spell away, was ploughing up and down the pool, goggles on, head down, in true Olympic fashion. Ruthlessly she destroyed anyone who was in her path and Boffy, floating gently around on his back, was twice sunk by this aquatic bulldozer. Gavin Cooper wore baggy swimming shorts that filled with water giving them a pantaloon effect. He wasn't actually swimming at all but stood in the shallow end talking to Alison, obviously mesmerized by the nymphet-like body.

Peter and Desmond, both in very tight-fitting swimming trunks that left nothing to the imagination, were demonstrating their water skills for the benefit of Gerry, who sat elegant in white trousers and black shirt on the opposite side of the pool to Euan and Murdo. Into this tranquil scene came a human bombshell in the form of horrible fat Henry, who insisted on leaping into the water with his legs tucked under him for maximum splash, and shouting at the top of his voice, "Bomber Command!"

Occasionally, when a particularly large amount of water had been displaced, his father would say, "Stop that Henry," and then there would be a few moments respite before it started all over again.

*

Joy Masterson picked her way over the lawn with some difficulty in her very high sling-back shoes. She had forgotten to bring a summer hat and was now desperately trying to find some shade. There was only one tree and the ground beneath it was already occupied by Jules and Gemma Woods, so Joy decided to join them.

Natasha explored the entire garden and finally ended up in the beer tent. Up at one end Arthur and his cronies were already well into their beers, and at the other, a splendid buffet was being laid out. A large ice sculpture had been placed in the middle of the table. Natasha took this to be a swan, although the heat had rendered the shape a little obscure. As she peered at it Doris joined her and wailed, "They promised me it would last for twenty-four hours. You can't even tell it's a swan now and it's only been out for a short while."

Her wails brought Arthur over and he wasn't sympathetic. "Of course it won't last in here you stupid woman. It's bound to melt in a bleeding tent in a heat wave. It's like a bleeding sauna in here. And I told you to put the food in the house and keep the tent for the drinks but you wouldn't listen. I expect the food will go off as well and we'll all get bleeding food-poisoning." With which cheerful pronouncement he left her and re-joined his friends.

Doris looked panic-stricken and Natasha was just about to reassure her that this really wasn't necessary, when there was a terrible commotion from the garden. They both left the tent to find that Marcia had fainted and was out cold underneath a rose bush. Fay was fanning her with a large straw hat from which there flowed a selection of multi-coloured chiffon scarves. Dr Fenby also went to Marcia's aid and as she came round he and Fay managed to get her inside the house. The Doctor assured them both it was nothing to worry about, just the rather lethal combination of white wine and hot sun, upon which Marcia burst into tears and informed him it was nothing to do with the bloody wine or the bloody sun but that she was bloody pregnant! Dr Fenby tactfully withdrew at this point, leaving her to the ministrations of her mother. Fay regarded her daughter with something nearing dislike and said in brisk tones, "If you really are pregnant Marcia, you'll have to get used to this sort of thing."

Marcia wailed that she thought she was going to be sick and Fay instantly became practical. "We'd better get you to the bathroom. You can lie out on the floor until you feel better. At least it will be cool in there." She looked at her daughter's wan face and relented a little. "Cheer up ducky. The worst is usually over after the first three months."

Marcia muttered, "I'd get rid of the bloody thing if I didn't think Tim would demand a divorce." As she lay down on the bathroom floor she bust out, "It's all Jules's fault. After she and the boys left he gave me an ultimatum. Either I had a kid, or else."

Fay put a wet cloth on her forehead and left, reflecting that you couldn't blame the poor man. Tim wasn't possessed of enormous intellect, but even he realized he needed an heir. She shuddered to think what the offspring would be like. Another horrible fat Henry was more than likely. She sighed and then thought more cheerfully that it was possible having a baby might be quite good for Marcia. She put on her hat and re-joined Boffy, Euan and Murdo.

The swimming pool had now emptied of bodies and everyone was having lunch. One of the waiters offered to fetch Fay some food and she happily accepted. Murdo found her a chair and as she flopped into it Boffy asked her if Marcia was all right.

"Marcia is pregnant" she announced dramatically, and the shock of this news caused him to lose all the contents off his fork. As he embarked on the difficult operation of retrieving the pieces of prawn embedded in the hairs of his chest he asked, "Do we presume this offspring is sired by Tim?"

Fay shrugged. "I didn't ask. And talking of offspring, where's your son Roddy?"

"Ah," said Boffy, re-loading his fork, "a slight hitch there. He isn't coming."

His wife said sternly, "Not coming? He pestered us for an invitation, saying how much he'd enjoyed it last year."

Boffy looked uncomfortable. "I know. I forgot to tell you. Poor Rodders fell off his horse at the Army Horse Trials. He's bust his collar bone."

"I thought you said he was a good horseman."

"Well he is," her husband looked a little indignant, "but accidents can happen to the best riders, even Prince Charles."

"Well what about his awful wife?" Fay said impatiently. "Surely she could have driven him over?"

Boffy looked uncomfortable. "Don't think things are too happy there. I get the feeling she's gone back to her mother's, but after the dreadful publicity I didn't like to inquire too closely."

Before Fay could ask him what dreadful publicity, Murdo tactfully changed the subject.

"Joy Masterson seems to be getting on extremely well with Jules and her new friend."

They all looked across the garden to where Jules, Joy Masterson and Gemma Woods were sitting in a group, engrossed in animated conversation.

"The sexual permutations of this Square are becoming more and more interesting," murmured Murdo.

Without fully realizing it, Murdo was right. At that particular moment, Gemma Woods was happier than she had been in her entire life. In fact, the events of the past few days had left her in a state of euphoria. Some nights previously she had been lying in bed reading, when Jules had come into her room. Although aware that Jules was probably high on dope, Gemma had not resisted when she had climbed into bed beside her. There then followed a highly charged few hours of sex after which they'd both fallen asleep completely exhausted. The same thing had happened the following night and Gemma saw no reason why it shouldn't continue.

Up to that first encounter with Jules, her sexual experiences had been limited. Mr Woods became an invalid just after the outset of their short marriage and apart from the odd encounter in the first weeks there had been no physical contact at all. Then followed the relationship with Bernard and after a few drunken couplings early on, it had quickly drifted into a platonic state where it remained until his death. Since then there had been nobody, until now. That first night with Jules aroused in Gemma Woods a sensuality that took her totally by surprise. She was under no illusion about Jules, having observed her decadent lifestyle, but this didn't seem to matter. Now she sat, with the object of her passion, in a lovely garden full of interesting people. Added to this she was listening to Joy Masterson, who under Jules' skilful guidance, was about to order a new wardrobe from her boutique.

She would have been further heartened if she'd been able to read her lover's mind. Jules had also been surprised by the sexual delights she had enjoyed with Gemma. Now as she worked on Joy Masterson for the sake of the boutique, she felt a surge of contentment completely new to her and for the first time in her life experienced a sense of purpose as well.

Joy too was in her element, feeling she had been accepted by these new friends and was now on her way to ordering a set of designer clothes, just hoping that Gerry wouldn't mind all the expense.

*

The afternoon wore on and the pyramid of wine bottles began to shrink.

Gerry, after more than his usual quota of drink, suggested a game of tennis and Natasha, looking particularly fetching in white Bermuda shorts and skimpy top, readily agreed. Tennis was one of the few outdoor games she enjoyed. Euan and Murdo both declined, Euan because he didn't play, Murdo on the grounds he was too old. Desmond, glad to have the opportunity of sharing an activity with Gerry, accepted the invitation with enthusiasm. Gerry then asked Doris if Peter would make up a four. Doris, delighted, that Peter had been included, felt sure he would and Natasha was despatched to find him. She made her way to his room, knocked on the door and was told to enter. Peter was wrapped in a towelling bath robe, sitting cross-legged in the middle of a darkened room which smelled strongly of incense. On seeing her, he made no attempt to turn off the music.

"Oh" she said, "Philip Glass. I'm not keen on him myself."

He stood up then, as if irritated she should know what the music was. He switched it off and said almost rudely, "Yes?"

Natasha thought again what an obnoxious individual he was, but merely said, "I was sent up to ask if you would like to join us for a game of tennis."

"Who else is playing?"

She ignored his abrupt manner and told him it was herself, Desmond and Gerry.

At the mention of Gerry's name Peter forgot his languid pose. "I'll change and come down."

It took some time to get the equipment together but at last they made it onto the court. Natasha was the only one of them who was actually interested in playing for the enjoyment of the game. Gerry was out to show Natasha that he possessed the necessary social graces, and also to show Peter how well he looked when playing. Desmond and Peter, who had been partnered together, were playing entirely to impress Gerry. Desmond in particular pushed himself rather more than was sensible. His back had only just recovered from his squash injury and as the play became more intense, it started to deteriorate again.

In spite of the heat and alcoholic intake, the game was fast and furious.

Marcia, looking pale and wan, joined the onlookers and placed herself beside Euan. She glanced at Gerry and Natasha and whispered maliciously in his ear, "Don't they make a lovely couple?"

Euan didn't rise to this but replied calmly, "Which couple do you mean Marcia?"

He was spared further conversation with her as he was cornered by Gavin Cooper who sat down on the other side of him. He remained trapped for the next half hour. Finally he was rescued by Murdo who explained to Gavin Cooper that he was needed to deal with some crisis involving his child and a minor accident.

"That man's a dangerous fascist." Euan muttered through clenched teeth.

Murdo regarded Euan's scowling expression with some amusement. "He's much beloved in high places. I hear he's tipped for a knighthood."

Euan growled, "How predictable."

Murdo closed his eyes and murmured, "'If you want enemies excel others. If you want friends let others excel you'."

"Lord Chesterfield I presume?"

Murdo nodded.

Euan closed his eyes and allowed his thoughts to drift back to Natasha, which they did a great deal these days. Their affair had progressed rapidly and they now spent nearly every night together, but he couldn't help wondering if their relationship wasn't rather one-sided. Apart from their love-making, they spent little time together. Since the slightly tortured conversation about Celia, the subject had not been touched again, but he knew she still worried about it. For his part he knew he had to try and curb his jealousy of Gerry Masterson. As soon as he let it surface her irritation became apparent and if he pushed her too far it could prove damaging. He let out a sigh. It was difficult because he still needed to warn her about Gerry's sexual orientation.

The tennis game was in its final throes and the sun at last began to lose some of its heat. A shout went up and the four of them met at the net and shook hands. Peter scowling at having narrowly lost left the court in a less than gracious manner. Gerry called out after him, "We can go over to my house if you like Peter and collect those books you wanted?"

Peter nodded and went indoors with the racquets.

Lorraine Cooper peeled off her top and lay back in a deck chair, wearing only the skimpiest of bras that left nothing to the imagination.

Murdo murmured to Euan, "It's easy to see she's a mammal."

Natasha flung herself onto the grass. "I'm exhausted."

Euan offered to get her a drink and she accepted gratefully.

"Who won?" Murdo asked.

Natasha looked at Desmond sitting dejectedly a little apart from the rest of the company. It was unfair, she thought, he had really played the best of all of them.

"Desmond should have won," she said. "He played the best. I think Peter rather wilted. Maybe he was feeling the heat."

Murdo was also looking at Desmond anticipating a difficult evening ahead. The man was not only suffering the humiliation of defeat, he was obviously suffering from severe back pain as well.

Euan returned with a glass of water and said to Natasha, "I have to go back to the house and make a call to LA Will you be all right?"

"Of course," she said irritated. "Why shouldn't I be?"

Murdo saw this exchange and sighed.

*

Euan left by the side gate and started to cross the Square. He hadn't gone far before he heard a rustling in the bushes rather similar to one of those nature programmes when, after a certain amount of scuffling, an animal would emerge. As he drew level he could make out two people locked in an embrace and on looking more closely saw that it was Gerry Masterson and Peter Rich. He hurried on, mildly surprised at their indiscretion in such a public place. Then it struck him that the central garden at this particular moment was not very public, as most of the occupants of the Square were in the Rich's garden.

As he reached his front door he saw Desmond, who had obviously crossed the garden a few yards behind him. Judging from the expression on his face Euan presumed he had also witnessed the Gerry and Peter embrace. By the time he had made his call to the States and returned to the party there was no longer any sign of Gerry and Peter in the central garden.

In fact, they were in Gerry's house. Gerry by now was thoroughly sexually aroused. So they did not go straight to the study but instead went into his bedroom, where Gerry bent Peter over the bed and despatched him with speed and efficiency.

Neither of them spoke a word.

They then collected the books and returned to the party, arriving back just after Euan.

Peter went upstairs to shower and Gerry went and sat beside Natasha.

Desmond, having returned to his house also to shower, was so upset by what he had seen in the garden, decided not to return to the party, but lay down in a darkened room to await the return of Murdo.

*

One of Arthur's friends, in an extremely inebriated state, fell out of the beer tent and into the swimming pool with all his clothes on. Arthur, Martin and some others, with a great deal of mirth and general palaver, managed to haul him out, and they all repaired back into the beer tent.

Joy Masterson, having observed this little diversion and also the sight of the nearly naked Lorraine, decided that it was time she left the party before it turned into a Bacchanalian orgy. She suddenly longed for the cool civilization of her own beautiful surroundings and went in search of her hostess.

Murdo also concluded it was probably time to leave, especially as Desmond hadn't returned.

Fay looked across at Boffy stretched out on a steamer chair. His torso was now scarlet and his mouth was wide open emitting the odd snore. At least she had taken the precaution of protecting his head with a knotted handkerchief. Such a pity she hadn't been able to find his Panama hat. She had a horrible feeling that Ming-Ming or Tang might have devoured it.

"I really think we ought to be going too," she said. "I don't like leaving the Pekes for too long, especially in this hot weather. I would have brought them with us but last year there was the most terrible fight when the poor darlings were attacked by a visiting dog and Desmond got his hand bitten pulling them apart. So I didn't think we should risk it." She gave Boffy a shove and he grunted himself awake. "I do hope you haven't overdone it Boffy. We always presume it doesn't get hot in England but the forecasters said today would be in the nineties." She looked at him, "Oh dear, you've gone the colour of a lobster. It's going to be bad enough with Marcia throwing up every five minutes, without you having sunstroke as well."

Gavin Cooper wandered over and joined them. "What about us all going on to my Club in Soho? It would finish the day off nicely."

He looked at Natasha who said, "Why not? It could be fun."

At this, Gerry said he would also like to go. Euan frowned and said he wouldn't. Murdo declined as well. Peter joined them and the invitation was extended to him. On hearing that Gerry would be in the party he accepted and this time it was Gerry's turn to frown. After the events of the afternoon he would like to have distanced himself from Peter. He also wanted Natasha to himself.

Gavin Cooper said with as much sincerity as he could muster, "I'm afraid Lorraine won't be able to join us. Unfortunately we don't have a baby sitter for Henry tonight. I suggest we get changed and meet over at my house in half an hour."

The party began to disperse. Doris Rich was relieved to see the main bulk of her guests depart but she still had Arthur and the tent contingent, and by the sound of it they were set to continue well into the night. She decided to dismiss the caterers and put her feet up with a nice cup of tea. It had been a tiring day, especially with the heat, but on the whole it had gone all right, with only a couple of dramas. Things could have been a good deal worse.

*

Euan and Natasha walked back across the Square. "Quite a party," he remarked.

"Very eventful," she replied.

They walked on in silence.

As he reached the door he said, "Do you really want to go to this Club? I'm not sure it's a very good idea."

To be absolutely honest, Natasha wasn't sure it was a good idea either, but she didn't like being told so by Euan and her manner became slightly hostile. "What's wrong with it?"

He didn't know whether to say that any Club of which Gavin Cooper was a member was bound to be suspect; or whether to report the dubious behaviour of Gerry and Peter that he'd witnessed that afternoon. In the end he decided it was safer to say nothing.

Irritated she burst out, "It's because of Gerry Masterson isn't it? Well, if you're so worried why don't you come too and chaperone me?"

He said coldly, "Because it's not my scene."

And he went quickly up the steps and into the house.

CHAPTER THIRTEEN

Euan, having passed a restless night, rose early and went straight to his study. His parting with Natasha at the end of the party had left him annoyed. He knew he was handling the situation badly but was under no illusions about Gerry. The man was both clever and ambitious and certainly wouldn't allow scruples of any kind to stand in his way. He obviously had some plan that involved Natasha, he was convinced of it. But how was he to convince her? The mere mention of Gerry's name made her defensive and now, adding to his worries, it looked as if he had to go to LA for three weeks, which would leave the field clear for Gerry to do his worst. It was a damnable situation.

This trip was going to throw up other problems as well. His work on the 'War Correspondent Series' had reached a critical stage and without him it could well falter. The BBC weren't over-keen on it anyway. It just wasn't the right time for him to go away.

He paced up and down, turning things over in his mind.

Maybe he should refuse to go to LA. Tell them to stuff their offer. But could he really do that? It would be madness to turn down such a great opportunity and probably give his agent a heart attack. There was also the financial aspect to consider. It was a generous deal that could set him up for years, leaving him free to write whatever he wanted. Could he possibly turn his back on that?

He suddenly stopped his pacing, stared out of the window and looked at his watch. That was odd. It was well past eight, yet nothing had stirred in the Square. Usually by this time on a Monday it was bustling with activity. He looked across at the Cooper's house. Gavin's XJS was still parked outside. The golden Rolls hadn't moved from outside the Rich's and Gerry's flashy Japanese car was also still there.

Immediately in front of him Natasha's little Citroen was still parked behind his, she should have left for work by now along with everyone else. What was the matter with them all? Could it be that the entire Square was suffering from a giant hangover?

He left the study, walked down the stairs to the flat and let himself in. He could hear a low moaning coming from a heap in the middle of the bed. Natasha was lying hunched up with a pillow over her head. Euan walked over and gently removed it. She half-opened her eyes and then shut them again.

"Go away!"

Euan smiled. "I take it you are suffering. How bad is it?"

"Bad. I think I'm going to die."

He laughed and she thought this extremely callous but felt too ill to tell him so.

"I take it you won't be going to work?"

There was another groan from the bed. "Oh God I can't even face making the call."

Euan fetched a wet flannel from the bathroom and a glass of iced water from the kitchen.

He put the flannel on her forehead. "Don't worry. I'll make the call and come back and see you later."

She made no reply and he frowned. She did look pale. What on earth had happened at that Club? He returned upstairs. None of the cars had moved. He now noticed Desmond hadn't gone to work either. It was if the entire Square had been struck down by plague.

Feeling unsettled he abandoned his work and walked over to Murdo.

"What's the matter with everybody?" he asked, as Murdo let him in.

"I don't know about everybody," Murdo said drily, "but Desmond is certainly in a parlous state."

Euan was surprised. "I thought he kept rather sober yesterday, compared with the rest of us."

"It wasn't the alcohol. It was the tennis and his back. He's even too bad to see the osteopath." He led the way into the kitchen. "Of course this humidity doesn't help."

Euan flopped into a chair. "That party seems to have had a disastrous effect on everyone. Natasha can't move."

Murdo's eyebrows went up. "She seemed quite all right when we left." He paused. "Didn't she go on to that Club? It could be more to do with that."

Euan looked grim. "I'm quite sure it is. I could cheerfully strangle Gerry Masterson."

At this Murdo said, "I thought it was Gavin Cooper who arranged it." He handed Euan a cup of coffee and gave him a long look.

Euan was scowling and he spoke with scarcely disguised anger. "Gerry insisted on going with her, so the least he could have done was to look after her." He took the coffee and gulped it down. "Seriously Murdo, I'm getting worried about Gerry's designs on Natasha. Everywhere Natasha goes, Gerry goes. Everything Natasha does, Gerry does. He's been inviting her out, taking her to the opera and expensive restaurants. He's involving her in his life and of course she's such a little innocent she's totally bowled over by it."

Murdo said mildly, "Maybe he just likes her company."

"Come off it Murdo," Euan slammed down his mug, "you were the one who first warned me. Of course he likes her company but I'm damned sure it goes further than that."

Murdo poured out more coffee. "Do you think you might have things a little out of proportion?"

Euan gave a bitter laugh. "No I don't. I'm sure he's making future plans for her."

Murdo could see that Euan was genuinely worried. "You mean marriage?"

Euan nodded and said bitterly, "Yes, I do. She'd be a perfect choice for him. She's attractive, classy, everything he'd need to make his image complete."

They were both silent for a moment.

At last Murdo said, "Have you tried to warn her about him?"

Euan shook his head. "That's the worst part. I've messed up there. I stupidly showed her I was jealous early on and ever since then she has reacted badly if I even mention his name. The more I say, the more she defends him. She's now making him out to be some sort of saint. She's grateful to him for finding her a job and he obviously behaves impeccably when they're out together. The man's a bloody good actor, I'll give him that."

Murdo sighed. "I can see the dilemma. However, I think you need to tell her where his sexual preferences lie, before things go too far."

Euan burst out, "She won't believe me. She'll put it down to spite because I am jealous, although if she'd seen what I did yesterday, I don't think she'd have much doubt."

Murdo looked questioningly at him so he explained about seeing Gerry and Peter locked in an embrace. "I think Desmond witnessed it as well."

Murdo put his hands together. "Ah, that explains a lot. I didn't think Desmond's collapse was entirely due to back pain."

Euan said angrily, "It's all Fay's fault. She brought the bloody man to the Square in the first place and the damnable thing is I now have to go away for three weeks. It's not a good time to leave Natasha right now."

Murdo said soothingly, "I'm sure Natasha can take care of herself during that time. Where are you going?"

"Los Angeles. I've been asked to discuss a new television series."

Murdo smiled. "That sounds like a great opportunity."

Euan said gloomily, "That's what my agent keeps saying and of course the money is good. But it has come at the wrong time. It's not just Natasha, it's also my War Series. I should be around. I've told the BBC it'll only be two weeks, but I know it will be longer. I leave on Thursday." He hesitated. "Murdo, could you keep an eye Natasha while I'm away?"

Murdo was startled. "Me? I don't know what an old buffer like me can do."

Euan persisted. "She likes you. Ask her over. It would be a relief to me."

"I can certainly do that." Murdo hesitated, "But my advice to you is to forget all the London problems and concentrate on your work."

Euan smiled, "I thought you never gave advice."

Murdo also smiled. "I don't usually, but on this occasion I am risking it. There's a good Lord Chesterfield quotation, 'Advice is seldom welcome; and those who need it most, always like it least'."

Euan considered this then nodded. He left soon after that.

As he walked out into the heat of the Square he saw Fay talking to Doris Rich and went over to join them. He thanked Doris for the party and she said, "I feel ever so worried. Lady Fay says poor Colonel Boffington isn't at all well."

Euan was concerned. "What's wrong? Is it serious?"

Fay spoke with some irritation. "He overdid the sun that's all, a touch of sunstroke."

Euan laughed. "The Square is full of the walking wounded this morning." Then catching sight of Doris's worried expression he said, "It's the sign of a good party Doris."

She said doubtfully, "I don't know about that, but I do know I haven't seen Arthur yet this morning. Mind you they were in that tent till well gone midnight. I just hope they didn't disturb Dr Fenby."

Fay chuckled. "I don't think you need worry about John Fenby. I happen to know the Diva arrived home last night and he was summoned round to her house and is still there."

Euan's eyebrows went up and she added quickly, "I only know because I tried to get hold of him this morning to visit Boffy and his number had been transferred."

All this was rather lost on Doris Rich who was too taken up with her own problems to worry about anyone else's. "As for my Peter," she went on, "I don't know what time he got back from that Club, but there's no sign of him either."

Euan decided not to mention the state of Natasha and took his leave. As he walked over to the house he noticed Gerry's car still parked outside his house and fervently hoped he was suffering from a major hangover as well.

*

Gerry was suffering more from a bad conscience than the effects of alcohol. It irritated him that the end of Sunday had gone so badly wrong. He didn't like losing control but that is exactly what had happened. After getting to the Club he'd found himself split up from Natasha almost at once and then spent a couple of hours stuck with some very dubious people. It was not the sort of scene he enjoyed at all and on top of this Peter had bumped into a friend from Cambridge and had also disappeared. By the time he'd found Gavin Cooper again, Natasha had gone.

He sipped his green tea and thought about Peter. He had to take great care to guard against any further indiscretions. Yesterday's incident had been a stupid mistake. Luckily Peter was not likely to get possessive or make demands. The boy was obviously promiscuous and hardly likely to accuse Gerry of rape or indecent assault. The very thought filled Gerry with panic. He wiped the sweat from his forehead and poured himself a glass of mineral water. No, the sensible thing was to fade out the relationship with Peter altogether. This would be easier now that the boy was away until September, so his full concentration could be given to Natasha, taking no more risks that might jeopardise his plans for her.

Joy entered the room and told him of her intentions to give a dinner party the following week. Gerry glanced at her guest list and was pleased to note that it included Natasha but had left out Euan Mackay.

*

The day dragged on and the humidity worsened until early evening, when the skies darkened and a tremendous thunderstorm ensued. After this it became cooler and it instantly made life a good deal more bearable.

Around six Euan made his way back to the flat. Natasha was up or at least out of bed. She was lying on the chaise with an ice pack clamped to her head.

"Don't say it!" she said as she saw him coming in.

"Don't say what?"

"Don't say 'I told you so' or 'you have only yourself to blame'."

He smiled. "I wouldn't dream of it." He sat down beside her. "At least you're now speaking which is a step in the right direction. This morning you couldn't string two words together. Do you want to tell me what happened?"

She shrugged. "There isn't much to tell. We all arrived at this Club. It was a house in Soho on about five floors I think and it was absolutely heaving. Our party split up early on. I was introduced to someone and after that I didn't see either Gerry or Peter again. I kept being given these blue drinks and rather stupidly kept drinking them." She looked at Euan. "I was thirsty after all that sun and the tennis. I knew it wasn't a good idea but it wasn't the sort of place you could ask for water or lemonade."

Euan said grimly, "The drinks were probably spiked. How could Gerry Masterson have been so irresponsible? At least I thought he'd look after you."

Natasha frowned. "I should have been able to look after myself. And it wasn't Gerry's fault. He thought I was with Gavin and in any case he was probably looking out for Peter."

Euan thought that more than likely but didn't say anything.

Natasha went on, "After a while Gavin Cooper started coming on a bit strong, nothing serious but enough to be irritating, so I left him and wandered through some other rooms. It was all pretty dark and I'm sure there were illegal activities going on. I kept drinking the blue things and it was while I was talking to some guy I suddenly realised I was feeling very odd and that if I didn't get myself home I was going to pass out. I told Gavin I was leaving and he objected at first, but I think I must have looked odd and I know my speech was slurred. Anyway he found me a taxi which I think he must have paid for." She gave a rueful smile, "the taxi man was brilliant. Poor guy, I had to stop on the way back and throw up. In fact I spent most of the night being sick. It's been awful."

She removed the ice-pack from her head and shook her hair free. "It's not a pretty story. I wish I knew what they put in those drinks. I've never felt so ill."

Euan was silent. In some ways he was relieved to hear it hadn't been worse so decided to make light of it. "Well if it's any comfort at all, you're not the only one who's been ill. It seems the whole Square has been in a state of collapse today."

She closed her eyes and said wearily, "I wonder what became of Peter and Gerry?"

Euan felt it safer not to comment. "Would you like any refreshment?"

She shook her head. "I don't think so, except another glass of iced water. I think that's all I can manage at the moment."

When he returned he told her about going to LA and the possibility of a television series.

"Wow," she said. "That's impressive."

Euan looked worried. "It means I will be away for three weeks. Will you be all right?"

Natasha frowned and spoke almost angrily. "Will you stop this? I'm not a child. Of course I'll be all right. I admit last night wasn't very sensible but there was no real harm done. Please stop trying to look after me. I don't like it."

There was an awkward silence. Euan had wanted to take this moment to warn her about Gerry but that wasn't possible now.

Natasha suddenly looked contrite. "I'm sorry, I over-reacted. It's just I'm still feeling lousy." She gulped down the water. "Why don't you let me drive you to the airport on Thursday? What time is your flight?"

"Twelve o'clock, but I have to be there about nine."

"That's fine," she said. "I'll drop you off and then go on to work."

He started to protest but she stopped him, "I'd really like to so no arguments." She stood up. "Sorry Euan, if you don't mind I think I'll go back to bed, otherwise I won't make it to work in the morning."

*

The thunderstorm had cleared the air and the weather gradually returned to a normal English summer, cool, wet and windy. By Wednesday most people in the Square had fully recovered.

Fay looked at Boffy's torso and after a few last dabs of calamine declared he was on the mend. She also felt encouraged by the news that Marcia would be returning home the following day. Marcia normal was bad enough, Marcia pregnant was beyond endurance.

In the cool of the evening she poured herself a large dry sherry and reflected that after three difficult days she was starting to feel almost normal again. For the last twenty-four hours Boffy had been almost civil and even her agent seemed to be doing some work on her behalf. All in all things were looking up.

*

Doris Rich, having survived the party, hoped all her troubles might be over for a while. Sadly they weren't. Arthur had been grumpy and difficult since Sunday and his mood showed no signs of improving. He didn't even apologise for the state of the garden. She thought crossly of the damage his friends had done. There was no delicate way of putting it. Someone had found a pot of red paint and daubed it on the private parts of the fountain statue.

"How could you let it happen?" she demanded. "It's disgusting that's what it is, painting the statue that way. And don't try and look so innocent, you know just where it was painted. It gave me the fright of my life when I saw it. Shocking, that's what it is."

Arthur did his best not to laugh. "It was just high spirits Doris. No real harm done, so don't get your knickers in a twist. I never liked the statue anyway. It's a bit of posy nonsense."

Doris said indignantly. "It is not. It's very tasteful. Peter chose it. He said it was Greek."

Arthur made no further comment and Doris was left with cleaning the paint off. It was a task she found highly embarrassing and she made sure everyone was out of the house before she set about it. It had taken a lot of rubbing and left her very hot and bothered.

If Arthur had proved unhelpful, the children were even worse. As she poured herself a cup of tea, she reflected that her mother might have been right. Their move to the Square had been a mistake. Maybe she should suggest to Arthur they sold up and moved back to Dagenham.

It wouldn't affect the children. Martin and Peter were more or less off their hands and Alison could be sent to a local school where she might drop all those silly airs and graces, not to mention her expensive tastes. It wasn't that she had any complaints about the people in the Square. They'd been very nice and welcoming but they weren't real friends, not like the ones you could have a moan or a laugh with. Not like the ones she'd left behind in Essex. She poured another cup of tea and decided she would mention this idea to Arthur, when he was in a better mood.

*

The drive to the airport on Thursday morning passed almost in silence, both Euan and Natasha wrapped up in their own thoughts. Euan was regretting Natasha hadn't spent the last night with him. Since the night club incident she'd been subdued and each night had pleaded fatigue. At some point she told him she was going to be working flat out while he was away and this reassured him a little. The more time she spent working, the less time she would have for Gerry Masterson. Nevertheless, as the car turned into Heathrow, he couldn't resist saying, "Tash do me a favour. Don't go out with Gerry Masterson while I'm away."

Her face immediately adopted a mulish expression and she said, "I wish you wouldn't keep on about him Euan. It really isn't any of your business. It's up to me who I see and who I don't."

He was silent for a moment then put his hand on hers. Although he knew it was probably hopeless to pursue the subject he said, "Believe me, I do have my reasons."

She pulled her hand away and yanked at the gears. "It is Terminal Three you want isn't it?"

"Yes," and he said again, "I do have my reasons."

"I heard you the first time," she said shortly. "So what are these reasons?"

"I can't go into them now." They were driving through the underpass and were nearly there. His voice became more urgent. "You must trust me on this because I have valid reasons for not wanting you to go out with him."

She said nothing until they drew up outside the terminal. Then she turned to him and said, "You've no right to ask me that Euan. However, I will promise not to do anything stupid while you're away."

A traffic warden was hovering. They both got out of the car. She handed him his luggage. He kissed her but without passion and her response was also half-hearted.

"I'll ring you," he said. "Thanks for the lift."

She slipped back into the driving seat and said, "Good luck with the series. I'll come and collect you if you let me know when you're due back."

With that she waved and drove away. She had just about kept her temper, but he'd left her pretty angry. Why keep on bringing up the subject of Gerry? It was ridiculous. She wasn't sleeping with Gerry, she was sleeping with him. Did this mean she couldn't even see other men?

She swerved to avoid a lorry and tried to concentrate on her driving.

Why was Euan behaving like this? He was like a Victorian father and jealous husband rolled into one. It was almost worse in public. He would hover near her, watching her every move, asking her if she was all right, if could she manage, was she happy, was she tired? It was so controlling, so possessive. She couldn't remember him treating her mother like this. She wiped away an angry tear. How long could any relationship survive under that sort of pressure?

She arrived in the theatre car park, turned off the ignition and for a moment sat thinking. Diversions were what she needed, to remind her that she had a life apart from Euan. She'd go out, see people, organise some entertaining of her own. An invitation to Dolly and Tinker was long overdue. Then, when Euan returned, they could make a fresh start. This break was what they both needed.

*

Similar thoughts occupied Euan's mind as his plane stood in a long queue waiting for take-off. He stared out of the window onto the bleak grey landscape of Heathrow thankful that his cabin was fairly empty and he had a row of seats to himself. He shifted restlessly. He knew he'd upset Natasha. She'd seemed close to tears as she drove off. But what was he to do? Even Murdo had said he should warn her, but she was now so touchy about Gerry it was almost impossible to say anything at all, let alone warn her about the man.

The plane started to roar down the runway. He settled back and closed his eyes. Maybe this time away would do them both good. He fervently hoped so, because he didn't see how he could possibly live without her now.

CHAPTER FOURTEEN

Gerry Masterson sat having his morning coffee. He had given Peter a farewell supper the night before and thought with some relief that by now he would be half way to Greece. The Sunday incident hadn't been mentioned, but it had decided him on not renewing their friendship when Peter returned, although this was a matter of some regret. There was definitely a mutual attraction and at any other time he would have been happy to continue seeing him, but not now. Now he had to concentrate on Natasha especially as the coast was clear. Euan had apparently gone to the States for three weeks which was good news indeed. It was therefore the moment to take advantage of his absence and see Natasha as often as possible. His producer had already asked if he would like to bring her over for supper and that could be an exceedingly useful move.

He suddenly frowned. There was his mother's dinner party the following week and this gave him a few qualms. He was not altogether happy to see she'd invited Murdo and Desmond, but when he'd raised an objection she ignored him, insisting they repaid their hospitality. Nevertheless he was uneasily aware of Desmond's infatuation and could tell that Murdo had noticed it as well. Added to this he felt uncomfortable in Murdo's company, feeling it was possible the man knew more about him than he would have liked, especially in view of his great friendship with Euan.

He sipped his coffee thoughtfully. What he needed now was to find out the exact nature of Natasha's relationship with Euan Mackay. It was difficult to know how to proceed until he knew what he was up against. That had to be his next task.

*

Sitting at her kitchen table Doris Rich felt happier than she had for some time. In the last few days she had seen Peter off to Greece, Alison off the Channel Islands, and Martin and Arthur had yesterday left for Benidorm. Arthur had rather half-heartedly suggested she go with them, but she had said no. She had a pretty good idea what sort of holiday it would be. The look of relief on Arthur's face when she declined his invitation said it all.

There was another thing that had lifted her spirits. Last week she'd noticed an advertisement in the window of the local post office, advertising flower-arranging classes and on the spur of the moment she had enrolled herself. She'd only attended one class but already had met some lovely people. They'd been given a project to work on and she was already dreaming up designs. She might even be adventurous and try Japanese. It was amazing what you could do with a bulrush, a single flower and a bowl of grit.

*

Fay received Joy Masterson's invitation to dinner with mixed feelings. Could she really face it? There was no good asking Boffy because he always left these decisions to her. It was also for the following week, which meant Euan would be absent and that was a definite drawback. His presence always added something to the proceedings. It was quite likely Joy wouldn't have invited Murdo and Desmond either. On the other hand she was curious to see just what Joy had done to the interior of that house. With a sigh she put the invitation on her desk, deciding to put off any decision until the weekend.

Two days later however, Fay made a terrible discovery which quite put the dilemma of the dinner party out of her mind. It all started with the discovery of a severely chewed leather slipper in the dog basket. She didn't have to be Sherlock Holmes to realise what had caused the slipper's ruin and she angrily waved the remains at the Pekes, hoping to find out which one had been responsible. This didn't work as both dogs dived under the sofa, so she told them that she found them both guilty and vowed to dock their dog chews for a month. After which she went off in search of the other slipper in order to take it to the shop and buy a replacement pair.

In ordinary circumstances Fay didn't go into Boffy's dressing room. On the odd occasion she had peered round the door it seemed such a scene of chaos she had ventured no further, but this time it was different as she felt obliged to find the missing shoe. She gingerly began to remove one or two garments from the chair and then heard a mysterious clanking sound. On shifting more clothes she came across two empty bottles of Navy Rum. Fay smiled indulgently to herself. Dear old Boffy, he'd always loved his drop of Navy Rum. She continued her search, looking under the wardrobe. Here she was perturbed to find several more empty bottles and then a couple more appeared under the chest of drawers and more inside. This now left her feeling decidedly worried. She flung open the wardrobe doors and a cascade of empty bottles fell at her feet. By the time she had gone through his entire dressing room the floor was covered in bottles. There was even one half-full bottle, stuck in the remains of his Panama hat.

Fay, in a state of shock, went back to the bedroom and sat on the bed. Boffy, her Boffy, was a secret drinker and judging by the sea of bottles must have been that way for years. She glanced back into the dressing room and told herself it had to be faced. Boffy was an alcoholic and she'd known nothing about it. Up to now she'd presumed that his slurred speech, loss of memory and falling asleep in his chair, was just the result of old age. Once or twice she had vaguely wondered if he was suffering from dementia, but obviously this was not the case. Her Boffy was a drunk.

What should she do? Should she face him with the evidence? It was a serious problem and must be damaging his health. If only Euan hadn't been away. He would have been able to advise her. It was no use asking Boffy's son for help. Rodney was an overgrown moron and quite useless, and far from helping the situation would have sent his father diving for another bottle. No, there was nothing for it. She'd have to make an appointment with John Fenby. The only sensible way out of this situation was to take medical advice.

She returned to the dressing room and put the empty bottles back.

It wouldn't be good for Boffy to know she had rumbled him until she knew the best way to proceed. Thank goodness he was spending the whole day at his Club.

She went downstairs, made an appointment with the doctor and then wrote an acceptance note to Joy Masterson. From now on it would be best to have Boffy where she could keep an eye on him. Calling the dogs, who were still cowering under the sofa, she relented and gave them both a chew. After all, without their criminal activity she would never have discovered the truth. Then, pouring herself a very large sherry, she collapsed into her favourite chair to await his return.

*

Natasha kept herself fully occupied in the days following Euan's departure, giving no time for further introspection. Every evening had been filled. She spent a night out with Belinda, a meal at the bistro with friends from the theatre, the whole of Sunday at Wal and Miriam's and twice went out with Gerry, once to *Rigoletto* which she had loved, and the second time to a French film which she hadn't, although dinner afterwards at the Ivy had been fun because there was a 'first night' party and she'd been able to goggle at all the celebrities.

There had also been a visit from Dolly and Tinker, who dropped in on their way to supper with Wal and Miriam. Apart from being her mother's aunt, she'd always had a special fondness for Dolly and this extended to Tinker as well. They were an eccentric couple. Dolly was always forthright in her opinions, whereas her husband was reserved and shy, letting his wife talk for them both. They were, however, absolutely devoted and Dolly required Tinker's opinion on everything.

They arrived in their old Riley, which she'd bought in 1947. Wal had tried to persuade her to sell it, explaining that her vintage car would now be worth a small fortune. She had been shocked by this mercenary attitude. Why should she change it? It took them everywhere they wanted to go perfectly adequately.

She walked into the flat and clapped her hands with delight. "Oh darling, it's quite lovely. How did you find it?"

Natasha became a little evasive and explained it had been through a friend of Wal's. She was not quite sure how Dolly felt about Euan since her mother's death, or indeed how she would react if she knew she was now in a relationship with him. It was definitely not worth the risk, so she added, "The flat hadn't been let because it was undecorated, but that suited me fine."

Dolly nodded. "I do so agree, much nicer to do your own thing."

Tinker sat on the chaise while his wife went on a major exploration. She wandered about studying everything in great detail making little appreciative noises. On entering the bathroom she gave a great whoop of delight.

"Oh Tinker, do come and look at this bath. It's too wonderful."

Natasha gave an apologetic smile as Tinker meekly got up and followed his wife's instructions. She heard him say, "Oh yes, wonderful."

"You have your mother's style," Dolly declared coming back into the room. "Don't you think so Tinker? Don't you think Natasha has Celia's style?"

Tinker nodded, "Yes indeed."

As Natasha handed them a glass of wine Dolly said, "Now, I want to hear all about this Square. Have you met anyone? Do you have any interesting neighbours?"

Natasha mentioned Fay. As she said the name Dolly sat bolt upright, her birdlike features alert with interest.

"Fay Stanhope? Fay Stanhope? I know that name. Why do I know that name Tinker?"

Tinker blinked in his owl-like way trying to remember.

Natasha suddenly panicked in case they connected Fay with Euan so she said quickly, "It might be because Belinda was at school with Fay's daughter, Jules."

She was just about to add that Jules also lived in the Square, when she stopped herself, realising it wouldn't be tactful to mention Gemma Woods. After all, it was she who had been responsible for relieving Dolly's brother of all his worldly goods. Family feelings were still running high on that subject. Natasha began to sweat. This conversation was turning into a minefield. She started to talk about her work hoping she'd be on safer ground, but Dolly brushed this aside with some rather scornful comment about all thespians being extremely tiresome and asked, "Have you seen your father lately?"

"No I haven't, not for some time. I don't think he even knows this address."

Dolly snorted. She'd never liked George. "His new wife is appalling. We took an instant dislike to her at Bernard's funeral, didn't we Tinker?"

Tinker nodded, "Instant."

Dolly continued, "Wal tells me they've spent an absolute fortune on their new house."

"They have," Natasha agreed. "I don't think you'd like it at all. It's not very 'us' if you know what I mean."

Dolly smiled ruefully. "I do darling, I do. George never had any taste, but what can you expect from a family who made all their money from a poisonous soft drink? That drink is full of sugar and chemicals. I refused to buy it for the grandchildren."

Natasha laughed. "I think Grandfather sold out very early on. Mama told me that's how they'd enough money to buy the estate in Norfolk."

Dolly sniffed. "I always told Celia the Roxby Smiths were a 'nouveau riche' bunch of Philistines." She gathered herself together, "Now darling we have to leave you, or we'll be late for dinner and that would never do. You know what a stickler for punctuality Miriam is. Are you ready Professor?"

Tinker drained his glass of wine and stood up. Dolly kissed Natasha. "You look a bit tired. It's all those theatricals. Come and stay with us for a few days when your next play finishes."

The Riley lurched uncertainly out of the Square. Natasha watched them go and reflected that lovely as all this was, she had socialised quite enough for one week. In two day's time she had the Joy Masterson dinner, an event she dreaded.

As she drove wearily into the Square the following day she thought with relief of a quiet evening ahead. She locked the car and had just turned to go inside when she heard someone calling her name. It was Murdo.

"Natasha, I'm glad to have caught up with you. Are you busy tonight?"

Her heart sank but she said, "Not really, why?"

"Well Desmond is out for the evening, so I wondered if you'd be kind enough to keep me company. He's left the most delicious cold collation and it seems a pity not to share it."

She hesitated. An evening alone with Murdo was probably a rare event and something of an honour, so she didn't feel she could refuse.

Murdo seemed delighted, "I'm so glad you could come at such short notice."

He was actually responding to a frantic call from Euan, who had repeatedly rung Natasha but received no answer. Murdo had promised to find out if all was well.

*

An hour later Natasha arrived at Number 29 and Murdo, looking elegant in bow tie and velvet smoking jacket, led her into the living room. He handed her a glass of wine.

"Dry white wine is your tipple I believe?" She smiled, surprised he should have remembered and was immediately stuck by his similarity to Edward. Maybe all aged publishers became like that.

"Have you heard from Euan?" he asked.

Natasha shook her head. "Well no I haven't, but he would have found it difficult to find me. I seem to be living an extremely social life at the moment." She made a face. "Tomorrow I am bidden to dinner with Joy Masterson, which I'm afraid I'm not looking forward to."

Murdo put his hands together as if he were praying. It was a little habit of his that Natasha had noticed before. He sighed, "Ah yes, I believe we've been asked to that as well."

Natasha burst out laughing. "This Square is unbelievable! It's like a holiday camp, you know, 'everything we do we must do together'!" She stopped. "Oh dear, that must sound terribly rude."

"Not at all," Murdo smiled, "you are absolutely right. Of course this is mainly down to Fay, because if you are one of her chosen people you are expected to socialise. She thrives on all the intrigue and gossip."

Natasha sighed. "It's fascinating of course, but I sometime wonder if there's a life outside the Square."

Murdo thought for a moment. "I don't actually think this Square is all that unusual. The English love their little 'sets'. However, some of us in the Square do have lives elsewhere. I have my Club and so does Boffy, and most of the residents go out of the Square to work. It's the ones who don't get out, like poor Doris Rich, who must feel the most claustrophobic." He stood up. "Are you hungry? It's cold, so the food is all ready for us."

Natasha followed him into the dining room and gasped. The table had been elegantly set for two but on the sideboard was a minor culinary vision, with a large dressed salmon, cucumber salad and various other delicious looking dishes.

Murdo smiled. "I can assure you this has nothing to do with me. It's all down to Desmond. Grateful as I am, I do know he enjoys doing it. When I first met him he insisted on organising all my publishing lunches. They were quite superb. We became renowned for them."

Natasha found Murdo easy to talk to, just as she had done with Edward.

Halfway through the meal he suddenly asked, "How old was your mother when she was so tragically killed?"

She was a little startled by this question but replied, "She was just thirty-five."

"And Euan, how old was he when she died?

"I think he was twenty-eight or twenty-nine. I know there was a slight age gap."

They were silent for a moment.

Natasha finally said, "My mother was very beautiful. I often wonder how she would have coped with getting older." She added quickly, "It's not that she was vain, but nowadays so much emphasis is put on women keeping their looks. They seem to go to any lengths to try and look younger than they are."

Murdo smiled. "I do so agree. However I know some very beautiful women in their eighties who certainly don't spend time worrying about their appearance."

The meal went happily on until Natasha declared she couldn't eat another thing. They returned to his library for coffee. He asked her about her work and she told him that she was now sure she wasn't going to pursue a career in stage design.

"What does Euan think about that?" Murdo asked.

Natasha looked surprised, "Euan? I don't think he's given it much thought."

Murdo tried to choose his words carefully. "I'm quite sure he has. He worries about you."

She made a face and sighed. "I know he does and I don't want to appear ungrateful but just lately I've found this really irritating. He seems to want to control my life and I find this difficult. You see, I've been so used to coping on my own."

She didn't want to say too much because it was hard to explain to an outsider. Over the last few weeks she had come to the conclusion there were two Euans, the one she wanted to be with and the one she didn't.

Murdo put his cup down. "I suppose it's only natural he should feel a certain responsibility towards you. After all, apart from the shock at your mother's death, he must have been left with certain feelings of guilt over their relationship."

Natasha shook her head. "Euan despises all feelings of guilt. I'm the one who feels guilty about her death because she was on her way to see me when the accident happened. I can't help how I feel, although everyone tells me I was in no way to blame, even Edward."

"Edward?" Murdo asked.

"Edward Cunningham. He's a great family friend."

"Do you mean Edward Cunningham the publisher?"

Natasha said, "Yes. Do you know him?"

"Well yes, our paths did cross in the publishing world, although I haven't seen him for years. I heard he'd gone to live in Italy."

She nodded. "He did," and added, "Edward has probably been the most important person in my life. Well, not just in mine, it all started with my grandmother, Audrey Maddington..."

Murdo interrupted, "Do you mean the book illustrator? I didn't know she was your grandmother?"

Natasha spoke with some pride. "Yes she was. It was actually Edward who first suggested she should take up book illustrating. They became lovers. It was a terrible mistake she didn't leave my grandfather for Edward." She looked at Murdo. "When my mother told Edward she was leaving my father, he was wonderfully supportive, offered her a job and a place to live. Then a few years later he did the same for me. Well, not a job exactly, but he found me a place in an art school in Florence. I was in Italy for three years." She sighed. "I am far closer to Edward than I am to my father. He's kind and generous, and always there if I need him, without ever being possessive or overbearing. I just know that if I'm ever in trouble Edward will somehow sort it out."

While she had been talking so animatedly, Murdo had a nagging worry at the back of his mind. He felt sure he'd seen Edward Cunningham's name recently and fairly certain it had been among the obituaries in one of the publishing journals. Obviously Natasha knew nothing of this and he certainly wasn't going to say anything until he had checked it out.

A little while after that she'd left.

*

Joy Masterson's dinner party the following night was a truly dismal affair. This was in no way due to the lack of hospitality. On the contrary, the evening had been organised on a lavish scale. It was her guests who were the problem. None of them wanted to be there and most of them were wrestling with their own personal problems.

Fay was in a state of uneasiness over Boffy. She'd talked at length to John Fenby, who'd impressed upon her that urgent action had to be taken. He ruled out Boffy's complete withdrawal from alcohol, explaining this could be quite dangerous unless done under medical supervision. Fay listened to all this with alarm, and was relieved when she was told a severe cutting down would be the best option, combined with a large daily dose of vitamin pills. Of course this would mean keeping a constant watch and Fay was dismayed at the sudden upheaval in her life. For years she had regarded Boffy with a mixture of affection and irritation, sometimes worried about his vagueness and loss of memory, but it had never caused her loss of sleep. Now that was all about to change. First there was the task of getting him to acknowledge he had a drinking problem. After that she'd have to clear out his dressing-room and check his daily intake. The doctor warned her alcoholics could be cunning and Boffy would be sure to find another hiding place. Fay thought sadly that all this spying would change their relationship for ever. She regarded him across the table and wondered how much damage he'd already done to his liver.

Boffy caught sight of her watching him and guiltily put down his wine glass. Fay had been most unlike herself the last few days and he was rather perturbed. He tried hard to recall if he'd done something to upset her, but as usual his damned memory let him down. He hadn't wanted to come tonight, but she had insisted. In fact she'd been very sharp and told him she wasn't leaving him behind on his own. It was most unlike her. He had to find out what was bugging the old girl. He knew he wasn't the most sensitive of husbands but he was very fond of Fay and didn't like seeing her in this state, especially if he was the cause.

Natasha was also not at her best. She had longed for an evening to herself and Joy Masterson was not her favourite person. Now as she looked round the gloomy dinner table her worst forebodings were realised. The usual company had been joined by a perfectly dreadful woman called Muriel, who was introduced as Joy's best friend. Nobody seemed at ease and the evening was filled with embarrassing lulls in the conversation, quite unlike any of the previous Square gatherings she'd attended. Even Gerry looked strained and was unusually silent. Boffy appeared totally traumatised by Muriel and only stammered out one or two words during the entire meal. Desmond sat scowling throughout the entire proceedings, no doubt because he had been placed between Muriel and Fay, neither of whom spoke to him at all. It also surprised Natasha that Fay was so quiet. Normally she would have kept the conversation bubbling along, but tonight she was silent and seemed unhappy. Even Murdo hadn't produced his usual dry comments but sat wearing a rather hooded expression. The entire meal was kept going by Murial and Joy who chatted ceaselessly. Each new course, of which there were several, was greeted by Muriel screaming, "Joy my dear, this is sensational. How do you manage it?"

And each time Joy would look arch and reply, "My little secret Moo, my little secret."

Secret or not, Natasha was quite certain Joy hadn't been slaving away in the kitchen herself. The evening must have required a good deal of outside help and planned down to the last detail. It was more in keeping with a Lord Mayor's banquet than supper with friends.

Towards the end of the meal Fay suddenly spoke.

"I have a piece of news. Dr Fenby is getting married."

There were general exclamations of surprise and delight.

Murdo said, "Do we presume it is the Diva he is marrying?"

For a moment Fay was almost back to her old self. "Yes, it is. John Fenby told me yesterday. It's going to be a quiet ceremony next month, in Vienna. She's over there for a series of concerts."

"How thrillingly romantic," gushed Joy.

"Are they going to return to the Square?" Murdo inquired. "If so, which house will they live in?"

Fay put up her hands, "That's all I know. We will find out more when they get back."

That announcement was to be the only excitement of the evening.

During coffee in the exotic drawing room, Natasha went to sit beside Murdo to thank him for the previous evening and commented, "It's all fearfully grand here isn't it."

Murdo's eyes were riveted on the two Chinese vases. He said in tones that made her laugh, "Fearfully."

Gerry opened up a drinks cabinet that resembled the Duty Free at Heathrow. Everyone said no to his offer of a liqueur, except Boffy who seemed about to say yes, when Fay intervened and said no for him.

After that, greatly to everyone's relief the evening came to an end.

Murdo walked Natasha to her front door. "Quite ghastly," he murmured, almost to himself, "quite, quite ghastly."

Natasha laughed and then added, "Poor Joy, she really had made a huge effort."

Murdo snorted. "Poor Joy my foot! At this very moment she and that awful Muriel will be knocking back the liqueurs and congratulating themselves on their huge success. They are probably under the impression that they have brought a touch of class to the Square."

And as usual, Murdo was right.

He watched Natasha run down the steps to her flat and sadly wondered the best way to tell her the news of Edward's death. He had looked up the obituary after she'd left. It said some complimentary things about his career and then stated that he had died quite suddenly in Italy. His age was given as seventy-seven.

I'm not far off that thought Murdo.

He decided he would ring Euan in LA and ask for his advice.

CHAPTER FIFTEEN

A week later Euan sat looking down on London, as his plane circled in a holding pattern for the fourth time. It had been a long and tiring flight and he was still suffering from a farewell party in LA the night before. The flight's chosen film *Good Morning Vietnam* hadn't relaxed him either. Although admiring the antics of Robin Williams, it was a reminder of the problems he was about to face with his War Series and the BBC. He'd turned it off and let his thoughts return to Natasha. Murdo had assured him she was well but now he had to face telling her about the death of Edward. His role seemed to be that of a Greek messenger, always the bearer of bad news. First it had been Gemma Woods, now this death of Edward, which would be a far greater blow.

The noise of the engine changed and there was a clunk and a shudder which indicated that at last the bloody thing was going to land.

He saw her at once. She was standing on her own a little apart from the rest of the waiting crowd. She looked pale and he noticed at once her expression was sad and drawn. Obviously she'd already heard the news about Edward. Damn! He'd told Murdo he would break it to her.

There was no greeting as he walked over to her. She just clung to him for a moment and then they walked to the car in silence. As she put the key in the ignition he put his hand on hers. For a moment she hesitated, then burst into tears, "It's Edward," she said. "He died."

Euan said, "I know."

"How do you know?"

"Murdo told me. Wasn't it Murdo who told you?"

She shook her head. "No. It was Wal. How on earth did Murdo know?"

"It was after having dinner with you. He remembered having seen

Edward's obituary in some literary journal and looked it up. After that he rang me and asked me what he should do. I told him to wait until I returned so that I could break the news to you myself." He looked at her. "How did Wal know about it?"

Natasha started up the engine and they moved out of the airport. "He didn't really, he just sent on the letter with the news. They'd been trying to get in touch with me from Italy but that stupid Inga never passed the message on. Finally they sent a letter to my father's house, and he sent it on to Wal, who sent it on to me. It only reached me yesterday. By which time Edward had been dead for over three weeks. Wal's now handling everything."

Euan was puzzled. "Handling what?"

She yanked at the gears and burst out, "Apparently I'm mentioned in the Will, money or something. What do I want with bloody money? The two people I love most in the world have to die on me and all I get is bloody money by way of compensation. I don't want it. I want them."

Euan was silent. She briefly turned her tear-stained eyes to him, "I feel terrible. I should have gone out to see him, or at least been in touch. He didn't have my address in Garrick Square. Even my father doesn't have this address..." She broke off.

They both knew why she hadn't told her father the address.

They reached the motorway and Natasha put her foot down. The little Citroen shuddered as the needle neared the top of the speedometer. In normal circumstances Euan would have said something but on this occasion he made no comment.

Natasha went on angrily, "If only that stupid Inga had passed on the message, I might have been able to fly out for the funeral. As it is, I missed it and now because of work I can't get to Italy for at least four weeks."

Euan said nothing, but to his great relief she slowed the car down and when she spoke again she seemed calmer. "I had a long conversation with Francesca last night. She was so understanding and calm."

"Did they have children?" Euan asked.

Natasha shook her head. "She and Edward married late, so no

children. I think that was why he was so fond of me. I suppose in a way my mother and I were the children and grandchildren he never had." They were both silent for a moment and then Natasha said, "Francesa told me his death was very sudden. One minute he was talking to her and the next minute, bang, a massive heart attack and he'd gone. I suppose I should be thankful he didn't suffer. Even so..." She wiped a tear away and said sadly, "I always presumed he'd live forever. I expected him always to be around and to be there for me. Stupid really."

Euan wanted to tell her that he would always be around and there for her. He'd even made plans to take her back to California with him, but she was obviously in no fit state to make any major decisions.

Natasha broke the silence, "Euan, I'm sorry. I should have asked. How did it go in LA?"

He smiled. "It was pretty hectic, but the series appears to be on and it's going to be a long assignment."

"That's great. You must be feeling pleased." She made an effort to be happy for him.

He said cautiously, "There's a great deal to sort out here first..." She shot him a questioning look so he said quickly, "with the BBC for a start. It might mean ditching my work with them. However, right now I'm feeling jet-lagged and rather regretting I drank so much on the plane, so all I want is a hot bath and a good night's sleep. Then I'll be able to face the world in the morning."

They turned into the Square.

"Do you want to come in?" he asked as he unloaded the suitcases.

She shook her head. "I don't think so. It's been a long day. Why don't we meet up tomorrow?"

She looked worn out so he kissed her gently. "Thanks for the lift. I'm around if you need me."

*

The news that Euan was back spread quickly round the Square.

Fay was first on the telephone the next morning. Euan thought she sounded a little odd so suggested they met for a lunchtime drink.

Murdo was the next to call. "Welcome back. How did it go?"

Euan was a little diffident. "I think the series appears to be on, although there are a great many hurdles ahead. Just at this moment I feel extremely tired."

There was a pause then Murdo asked, "Did you break the news to Natasha about Edward?"

Euan sighed. "I didn't have to. Unfortunately she'd heard it from another source. They got in touch with her father and it reached her by a rather roundabout route."

"How's she taken it?"

"Not well. We didn't talk much last night but I'm seeing her this evening."

Murdo was tempted to advise him to tread carefully with her, but all he said was, "See you soon dear boy, when you're over the jet-lag."

Fay duly arrived at noon and her appearance confirmed Euan's suspicions that something was wrong. Her plump features were haggard and there were dark rings under her eyes. He led her into the living room and she dropped like a stone into the armchair.

"You look as if you could do with a bucket of sherry," he said.

She smiled wanly. "I think I probably could."

Euan only kept sherry for Fay and there wasn't a great deal left from her last visit, but he emptied the remains into a glass and handed it to her. She took a large gulp and told him the saga of Boffy and her discovery of the empty bottles. Euan listened with growing amazement, occasionally feeling tempted to laugh, but didn't because Fay was so obviously upset.

When she finished he said, "I can understand it's been a shock. I'm shocked as well. Boffy's never behaved like an alcoholic, you know, loud, abusive or angry. Have you broached the subject with him yet?"

Fay took another gulp of sherry. "That's the worst part of it. I did, on the day after the dreadful dinner party at Joy Masterson's." She looked at Euan. "You will have to get Natasha to tell you about that ducky. It was quite the worst party I have ever attended in the Square. Anyway, the next day Boffy suddenly blurted out that he wanted to know what was bugging me. I suppose I had been a trifle short with the poor old thing. So I sat down and told him what I'd found out." She paused, struggling to choke back the tears. "Oh Euan, it was so dreadful. First he blustered, saying the bottles had been there for years. Then I reminded him he'd only had that dressing room for two years. After that he became angry and started saying it was no business of mine. Finally, and this was the worst part, he collapsed completely and began to blub, saying how ashamed he was but he couldn't stop himself."

Fay was unable to go on because the tears were now pouring down her cheeks. Euan found her a handkerchief and wondered how many more people he was going to have to mop up.

"It's so awful," she sobbed, "and I don't know how to put things right."

"Well it seems to me," Euan said in his most calming tones, "that the worst is now over because it's finally out in the open. Dr Fenby is right. You have to make sure he cuts right down and then stuff him full of vitamins. He'll soon be back to normal."

Although in Boffy's case he wasn't quite sure what normal was.

Fay sniffed and handed him back the handkerchief. "I expect you're right, but the awful thing is, I just don't trust him anymore. He may be at it right now," and she added with a wail, "but nothing will ever be the same again."

Euan tried to sound cheerful. "Of course it will. Boffy's had a shock. He's been found out. From now on he'll be on his best behaviour. It isn't as if he's an out and out alcoholic. He just likes his tipple and has been overdoing it. You've got to get him to cut down, that's all."

Euan's words had a soothing effect. Fay started to look more herself and knocked back the remains of the sherry. As she left she told him about the Diva and Dr Fenby.

Euan remarked, "A great deal seems to have gone on in my absence, although I must say I am relieved to have missed the Joy Masterson dinner party," adding with a smile, "not that I was sent an invitation."

*

That evening Natasha sat in Euan's living room and they talked long into the night. As the daylight faded and the candles flickered out, she told him about the Joy Masterson dinner which made him laugh and then about her relationship with Edward, which made him sad. He then told her about LA and more about the series. There was not one mention of Gerry Masterson. Finally they went to bed.

Euan was woken in the small hours by a series of screams. Natasha was sitting upright, staring straight ahead of her. In the moonlight he could see her eyes wide open. She looked like a frightened animal and she was shaking. He pulled her to him.

"What is it?"

She gasped out, "I've had a terrible dream."

"Do you want to tell me about it?"

"I don't know." She hesitated. "In some ways it's still vivid, in others it's all jumbled up."

Euan gently removed the strands of damp hair from her forehead. "Would you like a glass of water?"

She nodded and he fetched her one. As she took it she said, "I'm sorry Euan. You're still so tired and I've woken you up."

"That's all right, I can go back to sleep. You must too."

As they lay back she said, "I've been having a lot of these nightmares lately."

He put his arm round her. "It's hardly surprising. You've been going through a tough emotional time. Try and get some rest now."

She did try, but although he went back to sleep almost at once, she remained fully awake until morning. The dream had been vivid and full of danger. She couldn't rid herself of the images and it left her disturbed.

*

Gerry Masterson sat at the breakfast table, opening his post and sipping coffee from a gleaming white china cup. The toast popped up in the gleaming white toaster and as he looked round the gleaming white kitchen he reflected it was rather like having his meals in an operating theatre. Even the floor had a white marble effect. Why on earth had his mother insisted on everything being so white? He'd bought her some yellow tulips, just to add a splash of colour, but they had quickly been removed to another room.

He sighed. His mother was beginning to get on his nerves. The dinner party had been a disaster and afterwards he vowed to oversee any future social engagements. With slight impatience he reflected it would be almost impossible to fulfil his plans for Natasha with his mother hovering around. Maybe he should re-organise the house and make her a separate kitchen downstairs.

He ate his toast and with some irritation realised he hadn't seen Natasha for a while. A theatre evening had been arranged but she had cancelled it sounding quite upset. Apparently a family relative had died. Now Euan was back. She had however accepted the dinner with his producer the following week, and that was going to be an evening of some importance.

He turned his attention to the post, and with great precision opened the envelope on the top of the pile and removed the contents. He read the letter through once, took a gulp of coffee and then read it through again. His hands trembled with excitement. He couldn't believe it. This was incredible. The timing was perfect. Yet again the fates were playing into his hands. He stood up, abandoned his toast and the rest of his coffee, picked up the letter and left for work.

After dictating a reply he put through a call to Natasha.

Someone called out, "Natasha, it's lover boy on the phone."

She frowned. She really had to tell Gerry not to ring her so often at work.

The voice on the line was both apologetic and excited. "Natasha, I'm sorry to have bothered you, but something rather extraordinary has happened and I wanted you to be the first to hear the news." She waited and he announced, "I've been offered a living."

"A living?" she queried.

"Yes. I've been asked to become the new Rector of St Peter's Church, Stockton-under-Wold."

There was a stunned silence. Natasha wasn't really sure how to react to this. Finally she said cautiously, "That sounds great Gerry. I'm pleased for you."

Gerry continued, "I'd really love you to come and see it with me Natasha."

She hesitated, "That could be a little difficult..."

"How about Saturday? You don't work on Saturdays do you? "

"Well, no I don't." He was making it difficult for her to refuse. "Where is it?" she asked.

"It's on the edge of the Cotswolds, between Woodstock and Chipping Norton. We could take in a lunch..."

On impulse she said, "Oh, that's very near my father. He lives outside Charlbury. We could call in on our way back."

As she put the telephone down she hoped she wouldn't regret that decision, but a visit to her father was long overdue, so perhaps it was no bad thing.

The following evening she bumped into Euan, who apologised for not having seen her but explained he had been tied up at work.

"Don't worry," she said, "we can meet up at the weekend."

He looked apologetic. "Tash I'm sorry, I'm working all day Saturday. What about Sunday?"

"Sunday would be fine." She hesitated, "In fact, I was thinking of going to see my father on Saturday."

Euan smiled. "I won't ask you to remember me to him."

She also smiled. "Maybe not."

So that was it. The die was cast. She would definitely go with Gerry.

As she went down the steps to her flat she felt a twinge of guilt at not mentioning this fact to Euan, but knew it would only complicate everything.

*

They agreed to set out at eleven o'clock because Natasha told Gerry she wanted to catch up on some sleep. She also wanted to be sure Euan was well out of the way before she left the Square with him.

The weather was balmy, and considering it was August the traffic

183

wasn't too heavy and they made good time. Gerry was a fast driver.

"Isn't this rather a flashy car for a man of the cloth?" she asked.

Gerry smiled. "It looks flashier than it is. I bought it because it's Japanese and therefore reliable."

"How very unpatriotic," she said in mocking tones.

"And that from someone who drives a French car?" he mocked her back and she smiled.

Was he flirting with her?

They arrived in time for a late lunch and parked outside a pub and opposite the Church. Over the meal Gerry told her all about the job. "Apart from St Peter's being one of the most beautiful Parish churches in the country," he explained, "it is also one of the few remaining Collegiate Churches. It's like a Cathedral but it has no Diocese attached. There are only a few Collegiate Churches left in the country."

There was something that had been puzzling Natasha since Gerry broke the news about his appointment. She asked, "What about your job at the BBC? Won't you have to give it up? You have been so successful and it could mean a drop in your salary as well."

Gerry was pleased she was taking such an interest and took great pains to explain everything to her. "Well, of course I will earn less, but I don't think anyone goes into the priesthood for financial reasons. As for the BBC, I've been there nearly seven years and I think now is the time to move on. I'm sure I'll continue to do the occasional broadcast but it will be more on a freelance basis. This appointment they have offered me is an ideal step up the Church of England ladder."

Natasha frowned. "I don't know much about the Church of England. I come from a long line of atheists, although I suppose my father took his Chapel duties seriously when he was a headmaster. But the actual way the Church is run is a complete mystery. If you took on this job, what would be your next step up this ladder?"

Gerry smiled. "There are no organised steps. Usually after you are ordained you become a curate, which I did. Then you might move on to a parish, which I will now be doing, although I did the BBC job in-between. After that you might become attached to a cathedral chapter, or you might take on one of the larger city parishes. The two biggest jobs in the Church are those of the Dean and the Bishop. It all rather depends on where your particular gifts lie. A Bishop is more an administrator and his skill is in running the Diocese. The Dean is only involved in the running of the Cathedral and is often more academic. Some clergy like to remain in pastoral parishes all their lives. Other's like to work among the slums. As I say, it depends on your particular gifts and circumstances."

Natasha thought about this. "And you? What would you like to do?"

Gerry took a moment before answering. "If I take the living of St Peter's, I would like to remain there a few years. After that I'd probably want to become involved in Cathedral life in some way. I've always rather fancied living in a Cathedral Close." He looked at his watch. "Enough of this, we must go or we'll be late."

They walked over to the church and went inside. Gerry was right. It was very beautiful, all light and airy and totally unlike the Italian, incense-laden Catholic churches that Natasha had been used to, crammed with statues, paintings, and old relics. This building, apart from the weathered pews, was empty of adornment. The soft honey-coloured stone was warmed by the gentle summer sun, and the huge windows, which were not of stained glass but of pale green, filled the whole building with a liquid light that seemed to dance. She looked up and above her was a wonderful fan-vaulted wooden roof. Below her were the uneven slabs of paving stone that were worn with age.

She wandered into the chancel and examined the impressive effigies on the tombstones while Gerry talked to the present Rector. Natasha thought the old man looked rather saintly, but well beyond retirement age.

After a while Gerry summoned Natasha over and made the introductions.

He looked at her. "Are you any relation to George Roxby Smith?"

"He's my father," she told him.

The old man chuckled, "Bless my soul, I used to know him well. I went over to Civolds many times to preach during the time he was headmaster. He turned it into a very good school."

Natasha smiled. "We're going to call in on my father on the way back to London. He still lives quite near Civolds, although of course he's no longer headmaster."

The Rector led them out of the church. "I won't keep you, but you might like to look at the Rectory before you go?"

As they walked through the gate Natasha gasped. If she had thought the church beautiful, her breath was completely taken away by the rectory. It was a long, low building of the same Cotswold stone and covered in clematis, honeysuckle and roses. At one side there was another low building of the same stone but with a barn-shaped roof. The Rector's wife, as charmingly ancient as the Rector, took them over and explained that it used to be the Parish Hall, but as a new one had been built the other side of the village, this room was almost never used. Natasha walked round it, taking in the space and the tall windows going up to the edge of the roof. Gerry watched her every reaction. This was going even better than he could have hoped.

The present Rector and his wife were obviously as poor as the proverbial church mice, the house had threadbare carpets and minimal furniture, but Natasha was entranced by the whole scene. It was a completely different world to her.

As they drove to her father's house she said, "That long room would make the most perfect artist's studio."

This remark was made quite innocently. Little did Natasha realise that she had just fitted another piece of the jigsaw into the future plans of Gerry Masterson.

They didn't stay long at her father and Inga's, but long enough for Gerry to strike up a distinct rapport with George. It was the first time Natasha had brought any of her male friends to visit them, so George immediately presumed it was serious. He was also gratified that Gerry was something of a celebrity. George collected celebrities, and the fact that one of them might shortly be connected with his daughter gave him great satisfaction so he turned on the full charm offensive.

Gerry couldn't find any physical resemblance between George and Natasha except perhaps their colouring, and he quickly realised they didn't have a close relationship either. He nonetheless felt it was important to make a good impression, and spent a pleasing hour talking mainly about the new job at Stockton-under-Wold.

Natasha sat beside Inga listening to her father and Gerry talking. She wondered, for the hundredth time, why they had chosen to live in such a hideous modern monstrosity, when with all their money they could have chosen a beautiful period house. As an American Inga should have liked something with a bit of history. Maybe it suited the German side of her character, the side that made her behave rather like one of Rommel's tanks.

Occasionally she felt almost sorry for her father, but not quite.

On the way home they stopped briefly at a country pub. Gerry told her he found George charming and she sighed, remarking that many people found him charming but she knew him too well and could see through the act. Gerry let this pass and added that he liked her stepmother as well.

Natasha was surprised at this. "You do? I can't bear her. She seems to have all the worst characteristics of an overbearing female. She couldn't be more different from my mother if she tried."

Gerry was rather shocked that Natasha should speak in such acid tones. It didn't seem in character. Maybe she was getting tired. It had been a long day.

"Tell me about your mother," he said.

Natasha shrugged. "She was very beautiful, tall and willowy, and she dressed with enormous style. I think a lot of people found her distant and aloof, but I think that was mainly because she was so unhappy with my father. I didn't find her any of those things. I still miss her, every day."

Gerry didn't want to intrude too far, but this seemed a good moment to find out more about Euan, so he said innocently, "If she was so unhappy with your father, why didn't she leave?"

Natasha said sadly, "She did, or at least she was on the point of doing so, when she was killed in the car crash."

Gerry looked suitably shocked, although he knew all this already. "How dreadful," he said. "Was there anyone else in her life?"

"Yes, there was." She hesitated. "As a matter of fact it was Euan. Euan Mackay."

Gerry feigned astonishment. "Euan?" and then added, "Ah, now I understand."

She was puzzled. "Understand?"

"Yes. Now I understand your relationship with Euan. Forgive me, but I wasn't quite sure whether you were involved with him yourself."

He watched her very carefully. A slow blush crept over her face. Finally she said, "Euan obviously feels a certain responsibility towards me, and of course I am grateful to him for letting me have the flat."

There was silence. Natasha felt embarrassed. Had she given herself away? She really didn't want to tell Gerry about Euan. Suddenly a horrifying thought struck her. If Gerry took the job he would be living very near her father and it was more than likely they would meet socially. She said rather quickly, "Actually Gerry, if by chance you meet my father again, I would be grateful if you didn't mention the fact that I am living in Euan's flat." She gave a rueful smile. "For obvious reasons my father dislikes him and it would really complicate things if he knew."

Gerry patted her hand reassuringly. "Of course, I quite understand."

They were both quiet for the rest of the way home. Natasha closed her eyes but didn't sleep. She thought over the events of the day. She had actually enjoyed it. The house and the church had been beautiful and Gerry was good company. It was annoying that Euan had taken against him.

Gerry was also thinking. In fact his mind was racing. He had gleaned a great deal of important information in that brief conversation about Euan. Firstly, he was now convinced Natasha was having an affair with the man. Secondly, he was fairly certain she was feeling guilty about this. Thirdly, and most important of all, if her father ever got to hear about the affair, both Euan and Natasha would be in a great deal of trouble. All he had to do now was to find the best way of using all this information to his advantage.

He glanced across at her and was now certain of what he wanted. He found Natasha more attractive than he'd ever found any other woman and he also enjoyed her company. But above everything else, she would be the perfect asset for all his future plans. He now had to find a way to make it work. He also had to move fast, before she became too involved with Euan Mackay.

He looked at the speedometer. In his excitement he had put his foot down and consequently was well beyond the limit. He slowed down and finished the journey at a legal speed.

They arrived back in the Square about nine o'clock. As Natasha went to get out of the car she noticed, with a sinking heart, that Euan had just drawn up outside his house. Damn! Now she would be called upon to explain her devious behaviour. She quickly thanked Gerry, declined his offer of coffee and walked over to where Euan was waiting for her.

"Hello," she said as casually as she could. "You've been working late."

His jaw was clenched and he sounded odd. "I thought you told me you were going to see your father today."

She started to bluster. "I did. I was. I have."

"Then what were you doing getting out of Gerry Masterson's car?"

She hesitated, not wanting a scene. "He came with me. Or rather I went with him."

"What?" Euan exploded. "Are you telling me you took Gerry Masterson to meet your father?"

"Yes. No. I mean it's not what you think. It wasn't anything special. We just called in on our way back."

Euan was looking really angry. "Back from where?"

There was no point in talking to him when he was like this, so she said, "I can't explain now. I'm too tired. I'll explain everything tomorrow, I promise."

He took a step towards her but she quickly ran past him down the steps.

CHAPTER SIXTEEN

Early the next morning Natasha sat at Euan's kitchen table and watched him as he paced up and down. "Euan!" she said, "I can't possibly talk to you if you behave like a caged lion. Please sit down!"

He glowered and then flung himself into a chair.

Knowing he would have worked himself up into this sort of frenzied state had given Natasha a restless night. Yesterday would need explaining, but she really didn't know where to begin. After all, her day out with Gerry had been totally innocent, yet here he was once again making her feel she had committed a crime. She looked across the table at Euan sitting pale, unshaven and fierce. She couldn't imagine Gerry ever confronting her in such a dishevelled and angry state.

"Speak!" Euan growled.

"All right, I'll tell you, but you're to keep quiet and not interrupt."

She then explained how the trip to her father had come about and of Gerry's new job and the visit to the church. "My father lived so near it seemed silly not to take the opportunity to call in. I see him so seldom and in fact it was quite good to have Gerry as a buffer state. They got on rather well."

Euan said sarcastically, "That doesn't come as any surprise. Gerry Masterson is just the sort of wishy-washy celebrity that would appeal to your father."

Natasha said with some impatience, "Oh really Euan, you don't have to be so nasty."

There was a moment of silence. Then Euan burst out, "What I can't understand is why go at all? Why did Gerry have to take you to see his blasted new job?"

Natasha shrugged. "I don't know. He just wanted someone to go

190

with him that's all." Then she laughed and added, "If you had Joy Masterson as a mother, wouldn't you have taken anyone rather than her?"

He didn't smile. There was another silence. At last he said, "Why didn't you mention it to me? Why be so mendacious?"

Her eyebrows went up. "Mendacious?"

"Yes. What was the reason for all the lies and deceit?"

She became indignant. "I didn't lie to you. I just didn't tell you all the details."

Euan gave a hollow laugh. "So you were being- 'economical with the truth' is that it? What was the reason for that? Why didn't you tell me about Gerry's job? Why only tell me about your father? There has to be a reason Natasha."

She said hotly, "Well of course there's a bloody reason. This interrogation is the reason. I knew how you'd react if I said anything about Gerry. In fact I thought you would try and stop me."

Euan was angry now. "You're damned right I would." He got up and started pacing around again. Then he stood in front of her chair. "Let me tell you something my girl. You're going to have to choose between that man and me. Because if you want anything more to do with me I shall insist that you give up seeing Gerry Masterson."

Natasha suddenly lost her temper. "That is totally unreasonable Euan and you have no right..."

"I've every right..." Euan began but Natasha stopped him.

"No you haven't and what is more what you are asking is blackmail and I'm not going to give in to it. I won't stop seeing Gerry just because you don't like him. In fact, I'm going to have dinner with him next Wednesday. It's all arranged."

She stood up and faced him, even though a little frightened. His eyes were blazing with anger and he shouted, "I'm telling you Natasha not to see him. You can forget about us if you continue to do so."

Her eyes filled with tears. "You can go to hell."

She ran past him down the stairs to her flat, slamming the door and then locking it. Trembling with rage and frustration she went into the bathroom and splashed cold water on her face. Then she returned and sat on the bed.

Why was Euan doing this? Did he want to destroy what they had, because he was certainly going the right way about it. Why should it matter if she liked Gerry for God's sake?

She lay back and in her mind started to compare the two men.

What did she really feel for Euan? Did she love him? There was no doubt they were having a pretty passionate affair, but was that love? At times like this she almost hated him. The more she thought about it the more it seemed strange that when she was away from Euan she longed to be with him, but when she was with him, like now, she wanted him to go away. It was a paradox. To add to the confusion there was the complication of the past. Was she betraying her mother in some way? In her darkest moments she'd been convinced that the death of Edward was some kind of sign, a punishment for her having done her mother a wrong. Perhaps she was going slightly mad. And then there was his possessiveness, his wish to control her. He had no right to tell her not to see Gerry, or to choose between them. It was ridiculous.

Her thoughts turned to Gerry and it struck her how different he was from Euan. With Gerry there were no sudden outbursts, he was always calm. When she was with him everything was on an even keel, there was no danger, no worry or panic.

She thought back over the times she'd spent with him. He was good to be with, in fact she couldn't remember being bored once, except at his mother's dinner party, but that was hardly his fault. He'd made it pretty clear what he thought of his mother and it was to his credit he was so tolerant and kind towards her. He also put no pressure on her, of any kind. He was obviously not the sort of man who went leaping into bed with every female he took out. She guessed he was a bit shy and inhibited. In any case it was only a friendship they had, not a love affair, whatever Euan thought.

She sighed. All this was getting her nowhere, except to give her a headache. She decided to get some air and slipping on her jacket walked out into the central garden.

To her surprise Jules was sitting on one of the benches. It seemed rather early for her to be out, but then she heard noises coming from behind the bushes and presumed Jules was doing her motherly bit with Ned and Billy. As she drew level with the bench Jules drawled out, "Hello darling, you're something of a stranger. I haven't seen you since the Rich's party."

Natasha sat down beside her and said in rather subdued tones, "I've been busy at work."

Jules noted the wan look and said, "Is something the matter?"

Natasha shook head. "No, nothing," but Jules continued to look at her and she realised she had to sound a bit more convincing, so she added, "I've had some bad news that's all. A relation I was fond of just died."

Jules was sympathetic. "What a bugger," then she added gloomily, "mind you, apart from Ma, I'd be quite happy if all my relations kicked the bucket. I can't wait to see them go. But will they? No, they just hang on and on. Every christening, wedding and funeral, there they all are, looking like a lot of old drapes on coat-hangers. They're vultures, the whole pack of them." She gave a sudden chuckle. "Actually there is one old aunt who's all right. She has loads of money and all the other relatives, who are completely skint, sit around waiting for the poor old bird to pop her clogs." She started to roll a cigarette. "But she refuses to shuffle off. She will probably still be with us in the year 2000."

Natasha smiled in spite of herself. Jules was amusing in small doses and always fascinating to look at. Today she was draped in an embroidered kaftan, as if she had just emerged from Outer Mongolia.

"I do love your clothes Jules. Where on earth do you find them?"

Jules was vague. "Oh you know, here and there. I seem to live in jumble sales and charity shops. It's amazing what you can find." She took a lighter from somewhere in the folds of her cloth and lit her cigarette. "Talking of clothes, you must come to the opening of Gem's boutique on Thursday."

Natasha was silent. She wasn't sure she wanted to go to any boutique belonging to Gemma Woods.

Jules noticed the slightly hooded expression and said, "Oh God. I'd forgotten about Gem and your grandfather." She put the lighter away. "You really shouldn't let it get you down you know. Put it behind you. Life's too short to bear grudges, take it from me." She dragged on her cigarette. "And quite honestly money is only annoying when you haven't got any, but you have enough don't you? You're not like me darling. I've got through two fortunes already. I haven't a clue where it all went. What's more I've nothing to show for it. A month ago I was beginning to feel quite doomish and then out of the blue it all happened. I'm happier now than I've ever been. Even more extraordinary, I've started living normal hours, you know, up with the lark and to bed at dusk. It's all deeply healthy." She blew the smoke out in rings. "Do come to the boutique. There are some great designs and they'd suit your skinny figure. Ma is putting on a buffet afterwards and I know she'd like you there."

Natasha thanked her and said she'd try to make it. Jules lent back and closed her eyes. Natasha sat quietly, enjoying the peace, broken only by noises from Ned and Billy up to no good the other side of the garden. She let her mind go blank and started to feel calmer. Jules sat up suddenly. "Is Euan back from LA?" she asked.

"Yes he is. He's been back a week now."

"Tell him to come to Ma's buffet supper." Jules smiled. "I don't think he'd be interested in the opening of the boutique, it's not his sort of thing."

Natasha also smiled. "Probably not," she agreed.

There was a sudden loud wail from under the rose bush. Jules got to her feet.

"Christ, those boys! I'll be glad when the summer holidays are over. Ned! Billy!" she shouted, "We're going home." She moved across the lawn. "See you Thursday darling. Mind you come." She dragged two very dirty children out from under the bushes and made her way back to Gemma's house.

The sun came out and Natasha removed her jacket. The garden was now empty and she was left alone with her thoughts. It crossed her mind to cancel Gerry's Wednesday dinner. She was working late at the beginning of the week and now Thursday evening would be taken up with the opening of the boutique and Fay's supper afterwards. That would leave her with no evenings free. On the other hand, if she backed out of the Gerry dinner it would look to Euan as if he'd won, and that simply wasn't true.

Oh to hell with it! She'd bloody well go and what is more she'd make a real effort. In fact she would dazzle.

Out of the corner of her eye she caught sight of Fay leaving the house with her yapping Pekes, so she quickly made her exit back to the sanctuary of the flat.

Having decided to dazzle, she was now confronted with the problem of what to wear. The evening was apparently of some importance to Gerry because he had rung three times to confirm she'd be going, but the only information he had given her was that the invitation came from the head of his department at the BBC. This surely must mean it would be fairly smart. After wrestling with the problem for a while, she decided on a dress that was plain, but at the same time stylish. It was ankle-length, and as with all her Italian clothes it was beautifully cut, in silver grey silk. She knew it suited her and almost hoped that Euan would see her in it and realise what he'd be missing if he carried out his threat.

*

The moment Gerry drew up outside the drab, semi-detached house on the far edges of Acton, Natasha had the sinking feeling that she was completely over-dressed. If the outside had filled her with foreboding, the interior confirmed her worst fears. It was positively forlorn, with tired paint work and pealing wallpapers and over the entire place there was a pervading smell of cat-pee and damp.

Their host led them into a room which Natasha presumed served as the general living quarters. There were two sofas, which had obviously seen better days and she gingerly sat down on one of them, removing a cushion which had the stuffing falling out, no doubt due to the cats. Brian, the producer, said, "I expect you'd like a drink," which Natasha accepted gratefully, already feeling she might need alcohol to get her through the evening. She was about to suggest a white wine when a rather small glass of sweet sherry was thrust into her hand. She didn't even try the limp looking crisps that were put beside her.

Gerry rather ostentatiously asked for a non-alcoholic drink, explaining that he was driving.

"Would orange squash do?" Brian asked and Gerry nodded. This obviously meant they didn't run to mineral water and Natasha made a mental note not to ask for it.

When Brian returned with the watery squash, she made a study of him. It was difficult to calculate his age because he'd lost most of his hair, except for a few untidy grey tufts that stuck out in an odd way, but she reckoned he was in his early fifties. His clothes were as drab as his house and he had a check shirt with short sleeves. She particularly disliked short sleeves on men, but even worse he was in socks and open sandals. There was no getting away from it, he looked awful and the evening ahead was going to be an ordeal of the worst kind. If only Euan hadn't been so stupid about Gerry she wouldn't even be here.

Brian was talking loudly, his manner over-hearty, rather like a schoolmaster permanently trying to drum up enthusiasm in his pupils. Gerry turned to her and explained, "Brian has been with the Religious Department for over twenty years."

"Twenty-four years this September," Brian said cheerfully. "In the early days Natasha, I thought of moving on, but now we've built up such a happy family in the department it would almost feel like leaving home."

He beamed down at them from his position in front of the non-existent fire. Natasha was relieved that it was summer. There seemed to be little sign of any heating in the house.

Brian's wife Daphne entered the room, rubbing her hands on a wet tea-towel. She gave them both a weary smile. "I'm sorry not to be here when you arrived. Things were a little behind in the kitchen."

"Anything I can do to help?" Natasha asked.

Daphne shook her head. "No, no. The vegetables are on now so we can eat quite soon."

Natasha's heart sank still further as she smelled the powerful aroma of boiled cabbage. Daphne kissed Gerry and then sat down opposite them.

"Am I allowed a sherry dear?" she asked Brian.

He jumped to attention and gave a mock salute. "I think we might allow you that dear."

Over dinner, which was indescribably awful, Brian asked Gerry how he and Natasha had met. Gerry told them about the Square and said rather grandly, "It was at a party given by Lady Fay Stanhope. Natasha and I were the two newcomers to the Square so we were thrown together...."

Natasha, not wanting Gerry to elaborate further on the Square and risk any mention of Euan, quickly intervened. Turning to Daphne she asked, "How did you both meet?"

Daphne looked coyly at her husband. "I'm actually Brian's second wife." This was something of a shock. Brian didn't look like a man who moved from wife to wife but Daphne added, "He sadly lost his first wife, in a car crash."

Gerry looked anxiously at Natasha, who deliberately gave no reaction.

Brian said, "Daphne was my secretary at the BBC. She was very kind to me after my wife died." He gave another of his little whinnying laughs. "Everyone began to guess something was up because we were always the last to leave the office!"

Gerry smiled indulgently and said, "I'm also the last to leave the office but I don't think they'd ever talk about Madge and myself in that way." He and Brian exchanged glances.

Brian explained: "Gerry's secretary, Madge, is an extremely formidable lady. Gerry is the only one who seems able to work with her, but she's been at the Beeb so long they wouldn't dare ask her to leave. She's as much an institution as the BBC itself." He turned to Gerry. "I don't know who will take her on when you go."

Daphne asked Natasha. "What do you do Natasha? You look as though you might be a model."

Natasha winced and shook her head. Gerry explained that she worked in stage design.

"How exciting," Daphne said wistfully. "I have no artistic talents whatsoever."

197

As if to prove the fact she fetched in a very solid, unappetising pudding which Natasha took to be an attempt at a trifle. She stared with some irritation round the room. It would have taken little money to improve it, just a bit of imagination and some white paint. As she struggled with the rubbery concoction, she made a vain attempt to keep the conversation going and asked how many children they had.

"Just the two boys," Brian told her. "They're both away at the moment. James is on a school holiday trip and Dominic's at music camp."

Daphne mentioned one of the minor public schools and Natasha thought of her grandfather's scathing remarks about the standard of education in third-rate English public schools, but all she said was, "That must be very expensive for you."

Daphne dolloped another load of pudding onto Brian's plate, it was evident he was used to her cooking. Natasha declined and Gerry did likewise.

Daphne sighed. "Their school fees take every penny we earn. We tried to sell this house last year but there wasn't a buyer." Natasha was not surprised by that.

Mercifully the meal came to an end soon after that and she offered to help Daphne with the washing up. She was handed a ringing wet towel and while struggling to get anything dry, she listened to Gerry and Brian talking in the other room. Daphne droned on about the struggles and hardships of their life and Natasha occasionally made sympathetic noises. Suddenly Daphne turned to her and said, "So when's the happy day then?"

Natasha was so startled she gave a start. "The what?"

"Your wedding, have you settled on the date yet?"

Natasha stammered out, "What wedding?" There was a pause and Daphne looked a little embarrassed. Natasha said firmly, "If you mean Gerry and me, there is no wedding. We're not even engaged."

Daphne flushed red. She said rather stiffly, "I'm sorry. I must have misunderstood. I thought you were his fiancé."

Natasha shook her head, "No, we're just friends."

Daphne said meaningfully, "Oh that's the phrase the press always uses isn't it? It must be so difficult for you both, with Gerry being such a celebrity. I know he has a great many fans, especially female ones. Brian and I think he's wonderful, such a great communicator."

Before Natasha could make certain she had made herself clear, Daphne picked up a tray of weak instant coffee and walked in to join the men.

*

On the way back Gerry thanked her for accompanying him. "They are good souls, salt of the earth really, and the sacrifices they have made for those two boys. Well, you saw the state of the house."

Natasha felt irritated. She wanted to say that all the house needed was a coat of paint and a good clean. Privately she thought it might also help if they put the cats down, but she didn't say this to Gerry, nor did she repeat the bizarre conversation she'd had with Daphne. Instead she said, "So are you going to Stockton-under-Wold then?"

"Yes. Brian's been very good about it. We've already talked about some programmes I'll still be making for the BBC once I've moved."

She made no reaction and he glanced at her concerned. "Are you all right Natasha? Forgive me, but you don't seem quite your normal self tonight." There was a short silence. Gerry went on, "Please don't think I'm prying, but I'm a good listener if you feel like talking."

Natasha hesitated, "It's nothing really. I've had a few problems lately and I'm still upset about Edward's death."

"This Edward, was he a relation?"

"No not a relation, but he was a very great family friend. He was like a father to me and I'm finding it difficult to adjust to the fact that he's no longer around."

Gerry nodded understandingly. "Mourning the loss of someone close to you is always a difficult time."

Natasha shrugged and without thinking said, "It's not just Edward. It's Euan as well. Since his return from LA we just haven't been getting on." She stopped, feeling disloyal for even mentioning it. Gerry tactfully didn't pursue the subject. He didn't need to because he'd heard enough. It was what he had suspected and hoped for.

As they drove into the Square, Natasha asked him if he was going to the opening of the boutique the following day. He smiled and said it was not his sort of thing and he would be leaving it to his mother to make an appearance. After he kissed her on the cheek she ran quickly down the steps into her flat.

Even so, she knew Euan would have been watching and waiting for her return.

Gerry, meanwhile, now came to a momentous decision. He would visit Natasha's father. It was time George knew about his daughter's affair with Euan.

*

The opening of the boutique was the next day. By the time Natasha arrived, a little late from work, the place was buzzing. Almost immediately she bumped into Belinda and Miriam.

"How did you know about this?" she asked.

"I was at school with Jules," Belinda explained. "She seems to have written to almost every one of her contemporaries. I dragged Mum along because I thought she could do with some new clothes."

Miriam kissed Natasha. "I'm not at all sure there is anything here for me. It seems far more suitable for you girls." She gave Natasha a look. "How are you darling? You're looking tired and a bit pale."

"Well I've been working long hours." She gave a light laugh. "I actually think the paleness of my skin might be due to this lighting. It makes everyone look an odd colour." She looked around. "Talking of odd, who is that very strange man over there with the striped velvet trousers?"

"Oh that's Jasper, a friend of Jules" said Belinda. "Isn't he divinely bizarre? He did the decor, not that you can see much of it. Have you ever seen such a crush? It really is a brilliant launch."

Fay joined them looking harassed. "I can't stop long. I've left Boffy and Desmond doing the buffet and I ought to get back and rescue them." She looked at Natasha, "Isn't Euan with you?"

Natasha shook her head. "It's not really his sort of thing. I think he was going to meet up with Murdo and then go on to your buffet."

Fay turned to Belinda and Miriam. "I do hope you can join us afterwards."

Miriam shook her head. "It's very kind of you but I'm afraid we can't. We're going on to the theatre after this. In fact we ought to be making tracks or Wal will be cross. He can't bear anyone being late."

Natasha felt relieved Wal wasn't with them. He would have disliked the fact that the boutique was owned by Gemma Woods and that this launch was probably being financed with her grandfather's money.

Fay came up and hissed in Natasha's ear, "Oh my God ducky, there's Joy Masterson. I do hope Jules won't invite her to the buffet."

Marcia joined them and gave a wan smile. "We have to now leave Ma. I'm beginning to feel faint."

*

Natasha arrived at Fay's house about an hour later. Murdo opened the door and held onto her in the hallway, preventing her from her from going in. "Natasha I think I ought to warn you, Euan's extremely drunk."

Natasha edged towards the door and looked through into the drawing room. Euan was down the far end of the room. He was waving his arms around and she could see he was pale and unshaven. She stepped back to Murdo. "How long has he been like that?"

"Well, he arrived on my doorstep about six but I rather presume he had been drinking all day."

Murdo wanted to tell her that in his opinion there was more to Euan's state than just alcohol, but she looked so pale he decided not to.

She was alarmed. "I've never seen him like this. I mean he often drinks but he hasn't been drunk."

Murdo said grimly, "Well he certainly is now?"

Natasha asked nervously, "Has he upset anyone?"

Murdo shook his head. "Not yet, but I think it's only a matter of time."

They went into the room. Euan saw her and immediately came over. Murdo left them to it and Euan stood in front of her, swaying.

"So, Madam has managed to drag herself away from her many other social engagements, how very gracious of her."

He made a mock bow and almost fell over in doing so. She put out her hand to steady him which he roughly knocked away. "Where have you been?" His tone was aggressive.

In spite of this she tried to keep the conversation light. "I've been to the opening of the boutique. It should be a great success. They have some lovely things."

He mimicked her rudely: "They have some lovely things." He moved closer to her and she could smell the drink on his breath. "And what lovely things were you doing with Gerald Masterson last night? Tell me that."

She didn't dignify this with a reply but walked past him to where Murdo was standing holding out a drink for her. He looked anxious. They both watched as Euan swayed down the room, narrowly missing Fay's few remaining antiques. He stumbled over one of the sofas and landed next to Marcia. Natasha wondered whether to rescue her. Marcia edged up to the far end and said nervously, "Good heavens Euan, you look a bit wild tonight. What have you been doing?"

Euan looked her up and down then said sorrowfully, "Never mind about me. What have they done to you Marcia? You've got fat."

Marcia gave a tinkly laugh. "Of course I have you silly boy. I'm pregnant."

"You're pregnant?" He leaned towards her and said loudly, "I demand to know, who has violated your beautiful body?"

Marcia backed even further away. "Well, my husband of course."

Euan frowned. "There's no 'of course' about it Marcia." He waved his arm. "Could have been anybody. Could have been the Reverend Gerald for all I know."

Marcia looked shocked and was about to say something when Euan continued, his voice slurring more by the second, "I am of the opinion," he said, wagging his finger in her face, "I am of the opinion, that all girl babies should be shot at birth. Then they wouldn't cause trouble later on. Shoot the lot of them I say." He made his hand into the shape of a gun, aimed it at her stomach and went, "Bang, bang!"

Marcia gave a little scream. Natasha was about to go over, but Fay, who'd overheard the last part of the conversation, pulled Euan to his feet and said firmly, "That's enough Euan. Go and sit by Boffy where I can keep an eye on both of you."

With surprising strength she pushed him over to the sofa on the other side of the room, where Boffy was sipping a glass of mineral water. He looked cheered as Euan sat down beside him. "Hello Euan old boy. How are things with you?"

"Dreadful Boffy, dreadful," said Euan, slurring his words. He examined Boffy's glass. "What's that you're drinking Boffy?"

Boffy looked mournful. "It's water, the old girl's instructions. She caught me with the Navy Rum midday."

Euan shook his head, slurring again "That's dreadful Boffy. What are these women doing to us? My woman is no good to me either. We've got to make a stand. I demand a drink!"

He sat swaying. Murdo walked over and put a small glass of wine in his hand. It immediately tipped to a crazy angle. Murdo straightened it once and then gave up.

To Natasha's great relief, Euan became silent as Boffy launched into some long military anecdote. She turned away as Fay joined her.

"Natasha, what on earth's the matter with Euan. Why's he so terribly drunk?"

She wondered irritably why everyone expected her to know the reason for Euan's behaviour. "I really don't know. He's been working very hard lately and I think he's still jet-lagged."

Murdo joined them. "Something's obviously upset him. He's been drinking all day."

Fay looked severe. "I think it might be wise to remove him now, before he does further damage to either my guests or my furniture." She swept off to her other guests.

Murdo looked at Natasha who shook her head. "I honestly don't think he'll take any notice of me Murdo." Her eyes pleaded with him and he nodded.

"All right," he said. "I'll try and bribe him with a scotch."

At this moment Joy Masterson came over, bristling with indignation. "Mr Struthers, I don't like to bother Lady Fay, but one of her guests is disgustingly drunk and is being most abusive. I can't even bring myself to repeat what he said to me. Far be it from me to complain, but I really think he ought to be asked to leave."

Murdo said soothingly, "You're quite right. I am taking him home right now."

With some difficulty Euan was extricated from the party. He left shouting, "I want to talk to my friend Boffy. Why won't you let me talk to my friend Boffy?"

Natasha walked to the window and watched their progress across the garden. She saw Murdo hunt around Euan's pocket for his keys. With some relief she watched the front door open and Euan disappear into the house. She turned back, her legs were shaking and she felt rather sick. Jules came over and gave her a searching look.

"Why is Euan behaving like Heathcliff on a bad day? I've never seen him so pissed."

Natasha shrugged and said she really didn't know, but possibly it was jet-lag.

Jules shook her head. "Jet-lag doesn't leave you legless darling. Euan has been on a major bender."

Natasha gave the party another hour and then left.

Once back in the flat she stood and listened. There was an ominous silence from upstairs. Reluctantly she made her way to the top of the stairs and listened again. To her relief she heard faint noises coming from the study and then something was knocked over, followed by a good deal of swearing.

She turned and went back down the stairs. At least he was alive. It was probably best to leave him to it and let him sleep it off.

CHAPTER SEVENTEEN

At the very moment the events of Fay's party were unfolding, Gerry was heading out of London and on his way to see George. He'd put in a call that morning saying there was something he needed to discuss. The effect had been immediate. George had summoned him down at once, so Gerry waited for the rush hour to die down and then set off.

As he sped along the motorway he smiled to himself. George had obviously assumed he wanted to ask for his permission to marry Natasha. Well not yet he didn't, but if he played his cards right today, that event might not be so far off. He was sure he had understood right, that Natasha and Euan had momentarily fallen out. This was therefore the ideal moment for her father to intervene and break them up altogether, leaving the field clear for him.

He put on a Maria Callas cassette and prepared for battle.

*

George greeted him warmly. "My dear Gerry, how good to see you again. We were only talking about you the other day. That nice rector from Stockton-under-Wold came over and told us you were definitely taking the job. I'm delighted for you."

He led the way into the living room and offered Gerry a drink. "Inga is out at a meeting but will be back in time for supper. I'm hoping you'll join us."

As Gerry sat down in one of the large armchairs, George said, "Now, what is it you want to see me about? I'm rather presuming it involves my daughter?"

Gerry adopted a suitable expression of regret. "It's a matter of some delicacy George, and I debated long and hard whether to come and see you. I do hope you will not feel I am betraying any confidences or interfering in any way, but I did feel it my duty to impart certain information to you."

He paused and George waited for him to continue. Gerry now added an extra note of sincerity into his voice. "You've probably realised that I have a special fondness for your daughter. However that is not what I have come about" He couldn't resist adding, "on this occasion." His expression changed. "I have actually come to see you because I'm rather concerned about her."

George looked worried. "Concerned? Is there something wrong with her?"

Gerry hastened to reassure him. "It's not her health. Physically she is fine." He put his hands together in a praying position. "I presume you heard about the death of Edward?"

George sighed. "Yes, the news was sent to us because they didn't know where to find her. Of course, I knew his death would upset her." He paused. "I didn't actually know the man myself. He was a friend of my late wife and subsequently very good to Natasha. He arranged for the art school in Italy and during that time she lived with Edward and his wife." He paused again. "Maybe Natasha should come and stay with us for a while. Presumably she can take time off from this job. I gather it's only painting scenery." He said this dismissively before adding, "I'll get Inga to invite her."

Gerald used his smoothest tones, "I'm sure she would like that, but Edward's death wasn't the real reason for my coming here…" He broke off, giving the impression that he was struggling to find the right words.

George leant forward. "Are you telling me there is something else?"

Gerry sipped his drink. "This is where I find it a little difficult because I am somewhat in the dark, so please bear with me." He gave George a significant look. "I believe if I say the name Euan Mackay, it will give you some sort of clue?"

There was a sharp intake of breath and George's usually florid face went a shade paler.

Gerry continued. "You presumably knew that Natasha is living in his house?"

"I knew of no such thing," George exploded.

"Well, she's living in his basement flat," Gerry quickly added.

George was looking aghast. This was having just the effect Gerry had hoped it would. "I'm so sorry," he said innocently. "I presumed you knew."

"No," spluttered George, "I had no idea. Had I known, I would have taken immediate action. All she told me was that Wal Simmons, a cousin of her mother's, had organised somewhere temporary for her." He sipped his drink and then exploded again. "How could she be so stupid?"

Gerry looked at him and put on an expression of deep concern. "I'm afraid it could be worse. I think Natasha is now having an affair with this man."

There was stunned silence while George digested this news and now Gerry's concern was genuine. George had gone a funny colour and seemed to be having difficulty with his breathing. His eyes were narrowed and angry and when he spoke again it was with a voice of cold fury. "I do hope you are wrong my friend. I can hardly believe it of my own daughter. That man is evil, pure evil."

He stood up and walked to the drinks trolley to replenish his glass.

"I know very little about him myself," Gerry said, "only what Natasha has told me. I do understand he was in some way connected with your late wife." He cleared his throat. "Believe me, I was reluctant to interfere in such a private family matter and only do so now because Natasha is obviously unhappy. Just lately I have been alarmed by the state she's in. At first I thought it was the news of Edward's death, but then I realised it was something more." He sighed and added in puzzled tones, "It's almost as if she were weighed down by a terrible sense of guilt."

George turned found and faced Gerry. "Well of course she is." He offered Gerry another drink but when he declined George sat down again. "Believe me, Gerry, I am enormously grateful to you, for putting me in the picture. I am aware how difficult this must have been. But your instincts were right. I needed to know." He paused. "I think it is only fair I now put you in the picture."

George drained his glass and Gerry waited for him to go on, as he launched into what seemed like an almost prepared speech.

"Sadly, my poor late wife was something of an innocent and she completely fell for this man Euan Mackay. There was nothing I could do to save her, although you must believe me, I did try." He gave a mirthless laugh. "The man is devious, but unfortunately extremely attractive to women. I now deeply regret giving him the job at Civolds, the prep school where I was headmaster. He somehow wheedled his way into Celia's affections. What makes it even more tragic is that Celia believed him and convinced herself he was in love with her. I'm certain Mackay was flattered by this beautiful woman falling for him, but he had absolutely no intention of embarking on a permanent life with her. Good God no. Euan Mackay is totally ambitious and single-minded. Had she lived he would certainly have left her."

Gerry regarded him thoughtfully. George had obviously been torturing himself for years and seemed obsessed by Euan almost to the point of madness.

George slammed down his glass. "Damnation!" He looked at Gerry. "How far do you think this affair has gone?"

Gerry hesitated. "It's difficult to say. She has been living there for five months now."

George went to pour himself another drink and gave a mirthless laugh. "Five months? That's plenty of time for someone of Euan Mackay's ability. My God, that man's a public menace."

Gerry cleared his throat. "I'd be grateful George, if you didn't tell Natasha about my involvement in this."

George nodded. "I totally understand. I think the best plan is for Inga to call her the moment she gets back."

Gerry said quickly, "Natasha's not home tonight. I happen to know she's at the opening of a friend's boutique." He smiled. "She wanted me to go with her but I made my excuses. It's not really my sort of thing and in any case I wanted to take the opportunity to see you."

George knocked back another whisky. "I'm damned grateful you did. Hopefully we can get this problem sorted out before it's too late."

Inga came into the room and Gerry was rather surprised when she greeted him like an old friend kissing him on both cheeks. But in spite of this warm reception he declined their supper invitation, making the excuse that he had to get back for an early start at the BBC.

He drove home at speed feeling exceedingly pleased with the way things had gone. It was an absolute certainty George would take swift action. All he had to do now was to bide his time and wait for developments.

*

It took Inga most of the evening to calm George down. His immediate threat was to drive up to London and face Natasha and Euan together. She persuaded him against this, feeling he'd probably antagonise his daughter for life.

"Why don't you invite Natasha to come here for a few days?" she said.

George was sceptical. "I can't wait that long. She might put off the visit for weeks. No, a more drastic action is called for. If Gerry is right, Natasha must be seen at once."

Inga rather wished Gerry had kept his thoughts to himself. George was going to be unbearable until he'd seen his daughter. He turned to her. "You must ring Natasha first thing in the morning. Tell her I'm ill and you feel she ought to be here."

Inga said, with her usual German precision, "I do not think that is a good idea George. It would be a lie. She will never forgive you if you tell her a lie."

George looked irritated. "What do you mean it's a lie? It damn well isn't. This piece of news has made me feel very ill indeed. My heart started to fibrillate the moment Gerry mentioned Euan Mackay. You know my blood pressure is high. A shock like this could prove disastrous. Ring Natasha and tell her in all honesty you are worried about my health."

He loosened his collar, running his finger round it.

Inga looked at him with a mixture of pity and contempt. This obsession with Celia and Euan Mackay was pathetic. However, there would be no peace until she'd rung the child, so she reluctantly agreed.

Natasha was woken early the next day by the clipped Germanic tones of her stepmother.

"Inga, is something wrong?" She blinked at the clock. It was only seven thirty.

"I am afraid there is Natasha. It is your father. He is not well."

"Not well? What's wrong with him?"

There was a pause. "I think it is his heart. You should come down and see him as soon as you can."

"Well of course. How bad is he? I mean shouldn't he be in hospital or something?"

There was another pause. "No, it hasn't come to that. Shall I tell him to expect you?"

"Well yes." Natasha said, "I'll come straight away. I should be with you mid-morning."

She put the phone down and stared across the room. Her clothes lay littered the floor and suddenly the horrors of the night before came flooding back. She'd obviously collapsed into bed exhausted. Well, there was no time to see if Euan was all right now. Of the two men her father seemed to be the more urgent.

She dressed quickly, grabbed a cup of coffee, left a message on the machine at work and climbed into her car. As she drove out of the Square she grimly thought that if she took many more days off they would probably fire her. But this was a genuine emergency. Bloody Inga obviously wasn't telling her everything. She wondered if she would find her father wired up to machines. He might have had a stroke. Maybe he couldn't talk.

She put her foot down.

*

Inga took a large packet of smoked salmon out of the deep freeze and cut it open with clinical precision. She was not at all happy with developments. Until now Natasha had caused few problems and this had suited her fine. She had no fondness for children and had disliked the idea of becoming a stepmother. It was therefore a great relief when Natasha took herself off to Italy for three years after leaving school. George seemed to have little in common with his daughter, although he was extremely touchy on the subject, nearly as touchy as he was on the subject of his first wife and Euan Mackay. Inga did not like untidy emotions and George's irrational hatred of this man Mackay was one of these. It was obvious her husband's ego had been severely dented by his wife's affair, but Celia had now been dead for seven years and this tiresome obsession should have been over long ago.

Here Inga sighed. She was a realist and accepted that George, having lost his prize possession would probably never recover from it, so she was careful to avoid the subject. It was just unfortunate that Natasha had caused the whole thing to surface again.

She laid the smoked salmon on the plate and thought about George.

Their marriage had certainly been no love match. In fact there were moments when she truly despised him, but she did like status and security, so the married state suited her well. When her first marriage failed, she quickly sought another husband. The fact she had a great deal of money made this a good deal easier. She recognised from the outset that George liked money. It hadn't been difficult to find him a lucrative job in her father's public relations firm, nor to persuade him to marry her. She knew about his little sexual indiscretions but this didn't worry her in the least. She had too much power over George for him to risk straying too far. On the whole her life was just the way she wanted it. They took plenty of expensive holidays, staying in the best hotels. They belonged to the local Golf Club. She would go to a health club most days, while George had a London Club. When they felt like entertaining, they did so lavishly. Each day was organized and planned. It was not a life that could possibly have accommodated offspring, so she wasn't about to see it ruined by George's daughter.

She spooned some caviar into a bowl and started to slice a lemon. Maybe they could send Natasha back to Italy. She could well afford to buy a small residence for the child, if that's what was needed to remove her from the scene.

The unmistakable sound of the small Citroen sounded on the gravel drive. Inga looked out of the window and watched with some alarm as the car lurched to a halt only inches from her new Audi. Natasha leapt out and ran towards the house. Inga met her in the hall and felt a momentary twinge of guilt as she observed the girl's dishevelled state and worried expression.

"Your father is in the study, Natasha," she said in her clipped tones. "He is waiting for you."

Natasha looked surprised. "Is he better then?"

Inga gave a curt nod and returned to the kitchen.

*

George had not been looking forward to this encounter, well aware that his daughter would be angry at having been tricked into coming home. However, he told himself that desperate circumstances called for desperate measures. It had been his hope never to hear the name of Euan Mackay again, and now here was his daughter having an affair with the man! The next hour was going to be a testing one for them both.

Natasha flung herself down and looked at him crossly. "What is all this about Father? I've driven here in a state of total panic having been told you were ill."

George laid his hands flat on the desk and looked at his daughter. "When Inga rang you, at my behest I may say, I honestly thought I *was* ill. I'd just had some extremely disturbing news which could have aggravated my heart..."

"What news?" Natasha said impatiently, "Couldn't it have waited until the weekend? I understood it was an emergency. If it wasn't, I needn't have cancelled my work."

"I'm sure they can manage without your scene-painting skills for one day Natasha,' George retorted sarcasticallyz. This is rather more important."

There was silence between them. Inwardly George sighed. He'd never really understood her, nor felt comfortable in her company. After Celia's death he'd made a great effort to get to know her better, but although she was outgoing and bubbly with everyone else, with him she remained aloof and detached.

Natasha sat on the sofa and patiently waited. Although her father wasn't dying, she had to admit he didn't look all that healthy. His cheeks were oddly flushed and there was a puffiness round the eyes which indicated lack of sleep. He also looked extremely angry and this alarmed her. It wasn't that she was frightened, but she knew how unpleasant his rages could be. It would have been so much easier if she'd loved him, or even liked him. But she didn't. In a rather Austenesque kind of a way she merely felt a duty to him as a daughter.

Suddenly George spat out the words, "Euan Mackay," with such venom that she jumped.

She blinked at him in surprise. "Euan," she said nervously, "what about him?"

George's voice was as cold as steel. "It has been brought to my attention that you're living in his house. Is this true?"

Natasha shifted in her seat. "Well yes. No. I mean not exactly. I have taken his basement flat, but it's completely separate."

"So you don't deny you are living in a house owned by Euan Mackay."

He sounded so pompous Natasha had to stop herself from laughing. "No, of course not, why should I?"

George clenched his fists so that his knuckles showed white. "You are sitting there and calmly admitting that you are living in a house owned by the man who was responsible for the death of your mother?" His voice rose to a crescendo, so that by the end he was shouting.

Natasha's mouth went dry. She could see this was going to be very unpleasant indeed. Her voice matched his in coldness. "Yes. I am living in a house owned by Euan Mackay. No. I do not agree he was responsible for the death of my mother." She paused and then said pointedly, "There were a great many factors that contributed to her death, and you and I aren't entirely blameless in that respect."

All George's good intentions to remain calm now deserted him.

"My dear girl, you may not be able to face facts, but I certainly can. So let me tell you a few home truths. Your poor mother was under the illusion that she was in love with Euan Mackay and for this reason alone she decided to break up her marriage and walk out on us both."

Natasha broke in. "You think I can't face facts? Well I'm telling you I bloody well can. I'm probably better at facing facts than you are. The truth is my mother couldn't stand living with you anymore. That is the real reason she was leaving. She'd have left earlier if it hadn't been for me. That's why I feel guilty."

George's eyes were blazing. He shouted, "You're wrong. She was leaving me for Euan Mackay."

Natasha shouted back, "No, she wasn't. She was going away to Italy for the whole summer. There were no other definite plans."

There was a pause as they both got their breath back.

George spoke first. "The fact remains. You have chosen to live with a man who had an affair with your mother."

Natasha shrugged. "I don't deny it. I happen to like him."

George gave a mocking laugh. "Is that what you call it? My information is that you are sleeping with him."

Natasha was dumbstruck. Who could possibly have told her father this?

George spoke again. "I am waiting for an answer Natasha. Are you having an affair with Euan Mackay?"

She was silent. She didn't want to lie to her father, but on the other hand saw no reason why she had to tell him anything.

George said, "I presume from this silence you are admitting your guilt."

Natasha suddenly lost her temper. "I am not in a court of law Father, and I will not be interrogated by you about my personal life. I am over twenty-one, independent, and my life is my own. What I do with it is my business. My God! You get me down here under completely false pretences, making me think you are dying and then you put me through third degree. It's monstrous." She grabbed her bag and started to make a move. "Well I'm not staying..."

"Sit down!" her father thundered, thumping his fist on the desk.

"You will listen to me my girl, because it's about time you heard a few things about your precious Euan Mackay."

She sat glaring at him as he continued.

"When Mackay first came to see me I gave him a job and soon after, to my horror he wasted no time in starting an affair with your mother." Here his voice became emotional. "Poor darling Celia was an innocent when it came to men. Of course she fell for him. He was the sort of man who was attractive to women so your mother became infatuated, even obsessed. He took advantage of this to turn her against me, against her home and her marriage. It didn't matter to him that he was breaking up a family..."

Natasha looked at her father in complete bewilderment. What was this garbage he was spouting? He was completely deluded

"...Believe me Natasha," he went on, "Mackay was extremely clever, I'll give him that. He convinced your mother she should leave me without making any commitment to her. He took no responsibility for her at all, made no provision. That man is only interested in one thing and that is himself."

George took out a handkerchief and mopped his brow.

"My God. I sometimes think death was the best thing that could have happened to Celia when I realise how Mackay would have behaved towards her."

Natasha could bear it no longer and leapt to her feet. "How can you say such things? They're lies, wicked lies. Euan and Mama were happy together. I've never seen two people so much in love. I know because I spent a lot of time with them."

George stared at her blankly. "You did? When?"

"The three of us spent a whole summer holiday together. We went to Scotland when you were in America. It was the best holiday I ever had. They were so happy and Euan was more a father to me than you ever were..." She broke off fighting back the tears.

The barriers were down. George stood up and faced her. "You see? You see? He's even managed to fool you. He'll do anything to get his own way. He'll fill your head with lies just as he did your mother."

Natasha stared at him. "You're mad. There were no lies. Euan isn't like that at all. He really loved Mama. He was devastated when she died. I know because the pain is still there and he still misses her. You don't know the first thing about him, or understand him. You're just filled with your own bitterness and failure. I saw the letter from my mother that Wal sent you. She made no mention of leaving you for Euan. They weren't going to make any plans until she returned from Italy at the end of the summer. We'll never know what might have happened because she was killed in that bloody car crash. But the reason she was leaving was because she couldn't bear to stay with you a moment longer. You can't face up to this, so you twist things around and tell yourself a pack of lies!"

George was shaking with fury. "I'm now going to say to you what I said to your mother all those years ago. If you choose to carry on with Euan Mackay, we're through. Don't think I'll be around to pick up the pieces when you come crawling back. If you continue with this obscene affair I wash my hands of you. I don't want to see you again until Euan Mackay is out of your life."

Natasha snatched her bag and ran out of the room shouting, "Don't worry, you won't!"

*

Inga had been hovering in the hall for some time, listening to the raised voices. She was trying to decide when would be the best moment to interrupt and suggest lunch. However, she had no chance. Natasha rushed past her and out of the front door. She heard the screech of gears and wheels on the gravel.

So that was that.

Peering round the study door she caught sight of George. He was standing white-faced and wild-eyed, staring after his departed daughter.

Inga sighed, went back into the kitchen and put cling film over the smoked salmon and caviar. This would be a good moment to spend the entire afternoon at her club.

Natasha drove like a maniac for five miles and then stopped in a lay-by. She took her hands off the wheel and tried to calm down.

What was happening to her life? It was like one long nightmare.

She thought back over what had just happened with her father. He'd said some terrible things. They both had. Her head was throbbing. At the back of her mind was a horrible feeling that there might be a grain of truth in what he said. Maybe Euan was playing some sort of power game and did like to manipulate women to get his own way.

She sat quietly for a while, taking slow, deep breaths. Then she eased the car back into gear and set off at a more reasonable speed.

The big question remained. Why did the men in her life feel they could tell her what to do? It was ridiculous. Edward was the only one who hadn't treated her like this and now he was dead.

Well, from now on she would stand up to them. She wouldn't give up Euan's flat just because her father told her to. Nor would she give up Euan. On the other hand, she wouldn't give up seeing Gerry because Euan had told her she must. Let them threaten all they liked. She would show them she had an independent spirit and a mind of her own.

CHAPTER EIGHTEEN

"What's wrong with everyone?" Fay burst out.

Murdo was startled. Up to that moment he had been lost in his own thoughts. It was the morning after the ill-fated buffet supper and he and Fay were sitting in the garden, while the Pekes pottered about, happily oblivious of the gloomy atmosphere emanating from the bench. The morning mist had cleared and there was the promise of a warm and humid day.

Fay shifted restlessly on the wooden seat as she continued. "It's as if a great black cloud has descended on the Square. I just don't understand it. The beginning of the year started so promisingly but if things go on as they are, we're in for a very dark and oppressive autumn. Do you know I scarcely bother with events happening in the outside world, there's too much human tragedy right here. I mean, just look at Natasha. She has lost all that wonderful 'joie de vivre' she had when she first arrived. And as for Euan! Well his behaviour last night has left me completely baffled. I've never seen him even remotely drunk before."

"Nor I," Murdo murmured.

Fay went on: "I mean, there are people who drink too much and go pleasantly off to sleep, and then there are people who drink too much and become unpleasantly rude and aggressive." She looked at Murdo before adding, "Joy Masterson was very upset."

Murdo chuckled. "I'd love to know what Euan said to her. I don't suppose he'll remember."

"I think that's probably just as well," Fay said severely. She made an impatient gesture. "You know Euan far better than I do, Murdo. Can you explain what all this is about?"

218

He sighed. "I think the man has a great many problems to deal with at the moment."

She said crossly, "For goodness sake, that's the same for us all, but we don't go round getting blind drunk and insulting everyone in sight. There must be more to it..."

Her speculations were stopped in their tracks. Old Mr Alton the gardener, who had been in the process of trying to prune an overgrown rose bush, let out a yelp of pain. Ming-Ming had apparently bitten him in the ankle. Fay was profuse in apologies. She put the disgraced Peke on a lead and dragged her back to the bench. Then she turned her attention back to Murdo. "So there's nothing more you can tell me about Euan?"

Murdo pursed his lips. "It's probably a case of 'cherchez la femme'."

Fay sounded triumphant. "I knew it! I knew it right from the start. It's Natasha. He's in love with her?"

Murdo was silent. Fay tried again. "He isn't in love with her but she's in love with him?"

Murdo still said nothing. Fay made one final effort. "He's in love with her but she doesn't want anything to do with him?"

Murdo looked amused. "My dear lady, it's no good you firing questions at me. I know little more than you do and what I do know is merely guess work and speculation. We shall just have to await developments."

Fay burst out, "The whole thing is a disaster. It's like sitting in the middle of a Greek tragedy. A few months ago the Square was filling up with new people. Euan had found Natasha and everyone seemed happy." She gave a rueful laugh. "I suppose I've been writing 'soaps' for too long."

Murdo regarded her sadly. Fay at this moment resembled a great, overblown rose, whose petals were beginning to droop. Privately he agreed that life in the Square had certainly taken a turn for the worse. There seemed to be some sort of strange sexual dance going on, where nobody could find the right partner. Fay looked so dejected he tried to sound encouraging: "Well, there has been some good news, your daughters for instance. Jules seems settled since moving in with the

Woods woman and Marcia appears much calmer now she's expecting a child."

"I suppose so," Fay agreed and sighed deeply. "It would all be much better if I weren't so worried about Boffy."

"Boffy?" Murdo said sharply. "I didn't know there was anything the matter with him. Is it serious?"

Fay had forgotten that Boffy's problems weren't universal knowledge and said quickly, "It's just his health. It's been giving us a few problems lately. I have to watch his..." she hesitated, "diet rather carefully."

Murdo looked at her flustered face but made no comment. He had a sudden longing to be back in the cool of his study, among his beloved books.

*

On that same day, Euan arrived at the BBC, late. He wore dark glasses and drank three cups of black coffee before going into the conference room for the crunch meeting. Everyone else was seated, paper cups and mineral water in front of them and lined yellow pads and sharpened pencils at the ready. Euan muttered an apology, eased himself into the one vacant seat and sat scowling. A few glances were exchanged and then the speaker, who had been interrupted by Euan's entrance, started again.

"As I was saying, we now have three projects in place and I think we can agree they have produced a clutch of exciting and interesting ideas. I am extremely grateful for the hard work you have put into this." He cleared his throat and went on. "The task before us today is to choose one of these for our new major drama series. I know everyone in this room is rooting for their own particular project, but I hope you will listen patiently as go we go through the 'whys and wherefores', the 'pros and cons' and in the American way find out just what is 'do-able' at this moment in time..."

Christ, thought Euan, he only has to say 'God is Love' and he'll have used up every cliché in the book.

"...Right, if you pick up your folders, we will start with 'Project One'."

Everyone, except Euan, obediently picked up the packs in front of them. The voice droned on. His eyes closed and he thought of Natasha. To his annoyance the events of the night before remained a blur. His head was pounding and he started to doze. The next thing he knew someone was shaking him. He heard a voice say, "I'm sorry to impose on your time, Euan..." There was laughter here, "...but we'd like to have your ideas on Project Three. I gather this is your particular baby." Everyone looked expectantly at Euan, who stared blankly back and then looked down at the unopened folder in front of him.

He was completely void of all thought so he said, "It's all there, or as you would say, 'in place'. I have nothing to add."

There was a shocked silence. Then the voice, now clipped, thanked him for his contribution. "Right, well at this point I think it would be a good moment to break for lunch. I suggest we meet up again at two, when hopefully we can make a final decision."

"Hopefully," murmured Euan.

As they were leaving the room a colleague came up and hissed in Euan's ear, "For fuck's sake Euan, what the hell's got into you? We need you to sell our War Series. The others have been pushing their projects like crazy."

Euan stared at him with a glazed expression. "I'm going for lunch" he said.

"Well I hope you come back revived. We need a bit of the old Mackay zip if we're going to get our series chosen."

Euan went to the canteen, purchased a bottle of BBC plonk and returned to his office. By the time the meeting was due to start again, he had drunk most of the contents. His colleagues watched dubiously as he swayed around the table and slumped into someone else's chair.

The summing-up took an hour and then each person in the room was asked for his opinion. Euan was the last. He removed his glasses revealing two very bloodshot eyes and looked round the table regarding them blearily. "You want my opinion?" He paused. "Well, my opinion is that this entire operation is being run by a bunch of fucking fairies."

There was an audible gasp but nobody stopped him. "It doesn't matter one jot what I say, because you've already decided to take the easy option, you always do. Your choice will simply be the most mediocre series you can find. No risks will be taken, because as long as it pleases the great mass of the British public, then it's all right. You don't give a toss for innovation or for quality, just as long as you go up in the old TV ratings and the DG continues to smile down on you. You'll get in some poxy stars, pay them far too much and make the rest of it on the cheap. Well, I don't give a fuck, because I refuse to compromise any bloody more! The fact is, you lot couldn't organise a piss-up in a brewery."

He smiled benevolently at them, his speech beginning to slur "That's all I have to say." He put his dark glasses back on.

"And that's a great deal too much,' someone angrily said. I think an apology is due..."

Euan didn't wait to listen. He stood up, waved airily at them and swayed towards the door.

Then he turned and said, "Don't worry, I'm leaving. So I don't give a toss what you do with your fucking series!"

With that he walked out. As he went down the corridor towards his office he heard an outraged babble coming from the room. He started to clear his desk when someone rushed in and started shouting at him. "Good God Mackay! What the hell do you think you're doing? Our series might have stood a chance if it hadn't been for you..."

Euan looked wearily at him. "You stupid little man, don't you understand? Our series never stood a chance. They've been mucking us around for months, a compromise here, a compromise there. They never had any intention of doing it. It was always going to be another Police series. My only regret is having wasted so much fucking time on it."

He opened his brief case, slid the contents of his desk inside and snapped it shut. Pausing at the door he looked at his colleague whose mouth had dropped open like a goldfish, and left.

In the future, similar exits came to be known as 'doing a Mackay'.

*

Euan drove home slowly and with extreme care, knowing how drunk he was. At this precise moment if the police had breathalysed him they would probably have pronounced him clinically dead. Once safely back, he let himself into the house, walked into the study, flung his brief case on the desk and slumped into a chair.

Well, he thought, that's that. LA here I come.

He tried to imagine the scenes he left behind and grinned. However, this brief moment of pleasure was interrupted by a ring on the doorbell.

It was Murdo.

Euan led him into the kitchen. "I was going to make some coffee. Can I get you anything?"

Murdo shook his head, observing that Euan's state hadn't greatly improved from the night before. Suddenly the words he had used about Euan's 'duende' came back to haunt him. The man seemed hell bent on self-destruction.

"How are you feeling?" he asked a touch severely.

"Wonderful." Euan replied. "I've just told the BBC to stuff their war series." He gave a grim laugh. "You've never seen anything like it. I delivered this tirade and left them all speechless, their jaws touching their navels."

"Was that wise?" asked Murdo.

Euan took a swig of coffee. "Best thing I ever did. They never liked me. I'm too much of a maverick for that poxy organisation. I didn't fit into their little ways. I didn't toe the line." He gave another laugh. "I only wish I hadn't been so drunk and used more sober language. Nevertheless it seemed to have the desired effect."

"I'm quite sure it did." Murdo said drily. They fell silent.

Euan looked at him. "I believe I should thank you for getting me home last night."

Murdo nodded.

"Did I behave very badly?"

"On the scale from one to ten I'd say about nine," said Murdo.

"Bad as that?" Euan looked apologetic. "I don't remember much. I'd better send Fay some flowers."

Murdo sighed. "You'd better include Marcia and Mrs Masterson with that Interflora order. You managed to upset them both."

Euan groaned. "Oh well, Marcia can share Fay's flowers. As for Mrs Masterson, she doesn't deserve them."

"That's rather harsh isn't it? What has she done to incur your wrath?" Murdo looked reproachful.

Euan growled. "She gave birth to the Reverend Gerald."

Murdo sighed. "Is that what all this is about, Gerry and Natasha?"

Euan paused before answering. "Basically, yes."

"My dear man, don't you think you're dealing with this in the wrong way?" Murdo sounded a little irritable. "If you ignored it for a while, the whole thing might peter out."

Euan shook his head. "No, it wouldn't. He's too clever. Gerry hasn't put a foot wrong where Natasha's concerned."

Murdo looked at him. "Whereas you have?"

Euan sounded bitter. "Oh, I've done everything wrong. I've behaved like a crass oaf, but I just couldn't stop myself. Now I think I've lost her. But I deserved to. The problem is I love her too much. I'm obsessed with her. I can't get her out of my mind."

He saw Murdo's worried expression and said with a grim smile, "I'm sure you have a suitable Chesterfield quote for my condition?"

Murdo shook his head. He actually did, but in the circumstances didn't think it would help. Lord Chesterfield wasn't charitable towards the lovesick and had rather a dismissive attitude towards women. Instead he murmured, "I do know a Burmese proverb which is quite apt." He paused. "They say 'the more violent the love, the more violent the anger'."

Euan thought for a moment then nodded. "That's very true."

He drank the rest of his coffee. "What really worries me is that I may have made things worse. I may have pushed her into Gerry's arms." He looked at Murdo. "I could understand if Natasha doesn't want to see me again, but if she runs into the arms of Gerry Masterson I won't cope at all." He gave a grim smile. "You see, my friend? I'm beyond all help."

Murdo said nothing and then stood up. "When are you off to LA?"

"In a few weeks," Euan stood up as well. "There are some things to be sorted here first." He looked at Murdo. "We should have another

Tomatin evening before I go."

"I look forward to that," Murdo said.

He hesitated and suddenly took Euan in his arms. He held on to him for a moment, then without a word went out of the house.

Later that evening Euan went down the steps to Natasha's flat. He waited a few seconds before knocking, nervous of the reception he would get. She was sitting on the chaise, almost as if she were expecting him.

"Hello" he said.

"Hello" she replied.

He sat down opposite and looked at her. She was very pale.

"I'm sorry" he said at last.

She shook her head. "It's all right, it was partly my fault. I've always had an obstinate streak. I get it from my father."

He smiled at that, but made no comment.

"Have you been all right today?" she asked.

"Apart from a thumping headache, surprisingly I have." Then he added, "I've thrown in the sponge at the BBC."

She looked concerned. "Oh Euan, I am sorry. Does that mean they won't do your war series?"

He gave a short laugh. "It does but it's probably just as well. All those images of war were beginning to get me down. In any case, I don't think they'd have done the series even if I hadn't made the scene today."

She looked at his grim expression and laughed. "I almost feel sorry for them. Did you give them a hard time?"

Euan nodded. "Yes. I behaved pretty badly, but to be honest I'd never fitted in. I'm just not a corporation man."

Natasha thought of the awful Brian. "No, you're probably not. So what happens now?"

He hesitated. Was this the moment to ask her to go to LA with him? Maybe he should try and heal a few wounds first. "Tash, can you forgive me, for Sunday?"

She gave a shrug. "I've told you. It's all right."

He looked at her. "It's only because I love you."

Natasha said sadly, "I don't know what love is."

He stood up, went over and kissed her. "That's love," he said and walked over to the window staring out.

She was a little shaken and said quickly, "I hardly dare ask. Would you like a glass of wine?"

He didn't turn round. "No thanks. I'm on water for the next few days."

She went to the kitchen and poured herself a glass and returned to the chaise. Euan sat down opposite her again. His face had a strange, intense expression.

"Tash, I have to know. What is your relationship with Gerry Masterson?"

Her heart sank. She dropped her head into her hands. "Please Euan, let it be. Believe me, it's just not the time to talk about it."

But he couldn't let it go. He said pleadingly, "Please, I need to understand."

She shrugged. "There's nothing to understand. I like being with him..." she hesitated, "and I feel sorry for him."

Euan looked startled. "You feel sorry for him?"

She nodded. "Yes, from what he's told me I think he had an awful childhood..."

Euan snorted but made no comment. Natasha looked at him, "For that matter I could ask you to make me understand why you dislike him so much. Last time I asked, you just launched into a long diatribe against all things religious."

Euan walked again to the window, staring out as if considering what to say. After a moment he turned to her, "Gerry Masterson is a completely mediocre person. He and his sort bring everything down to a deadly grey respectability. In normal circumstances I'd do my best to avoid him. But I can't, because of you." He shrugged. "Basically the man's a total jerk."

Natasha shook her head sadly. "Euan, that's just childish."

"All right, you asked me, so I'll tell you," he replied angrily. "I don't trust him and I don't trust his motives where you're concerned."

She looked bewildered. "He has no motives."

"Of course he has." Euan paused. "Has he taken you to bed?"

Natasha said sharply, "You've no right to ask me that but no, of course he hasn't"

"Why 'of course'? You went to bed with me."

"That's different."

"Why is it different?" Euan was firing questions at her like bullets from a gun.

She said, "Because I wanted to go to bed with you and because you asked me."

"Well what if Gerry asked you?"

"He hasn't and he wouldn't."

"Why?"

She burst out. "Well for starters he's a priest and priests have a different code of morals. They don't just fall into bed with people."

Euan moved a step towards her. "Why did you say 'people'?"

Natasha looked a little alarmed. "Well women then. Look, what is all this? Can we drop it?"

Euan came across the room and knelt by her, taking her hands in his. "No, we cannot, because you are being a blind fool. Have you ever asked Gerry about his sex life?"

"No I haven't." She pulled her hands away. "I haven't even asked about yours. You might have gone through a harem of women for all I know."

"Well I haven't, he said shortly. "Before you I only had two serious relationships and one of those was with your mother. Anyone else didn't mean a thing." He stood up. "And you?"

She shrugged. "I had a couple of brief affairs and one serious boyfriend in Italy. That broke up a year ago." She drank her wine and said, "So why should all this matter?"

Euan said quietly, "Have you even thought about Gerry? Tell me, who has he had affairs with?"

"I've no idea," she said impatiently.

Euan went over to her. "So I will tell you. He has affairs with men. Gerry is gay. He's a homosexual."

Natasha looked in shock. After a moment she stood up and walked away from him. When she turned, her eyes blazed with anger. "How dare you say that? How dare you say such a thing?" She walked over and started beating him on the chest. "That's vile. Vile, do you hear? I knew you were jealous but I never believed you'd stoop so low as to say such disgusting things about him."

Euan caught her hands. "I say them because they are true Natasha. Ask yourself about his relationship with Peter Rich?"

She stared at him disbelieving. Then she screamed, "You bastard! He was trying to help Peter. He was being kind. I can't believe you are saying such terrible things." She started to beat him again becoming hysterical with rage. "I hate you, I hate you." she sobbed.

He tried to defend himself by grabbing hold of her.

Looking back on it she was never really quite sure what happened. One moment she was pushing him away the next clinging on to him. Every time he threw her from him she charged back. At some point she ripped his shirt. They fell to the floor struggling, their bodies intertwined. He started kissing her roughly but instead of moving away she came back for more. They wrestled on, gasping, moaning, tearing at each other, until he finally entered her with such force it took the breath out of her body.

When it was all over they clung to each other for a moment then lay side by side, panting and exhausted. Natasha felt she was falling down a deep, deep well and there was nothing for her but the blackness at the bottom. She rolled away from him onto her side.

Euan lay without moving.

Sometime later he stood up and staring down at her felt a stab of pain. Abruptly, he left the room and went upstairs. For a long time he sat at his study desk without the lights on. Quite suddenly and for the first time since Celia's death, he started to howl with great loud racking sobs.

Natasha heard him downstairs. She got up, walked into the bathroom and threw water over her face. Then she went back, fell on the bed and lay staring at the ceiling, listening to his cries. She felt completely numb.

*

The next day she put a note through Euan's door. He picked it up and read:

Euan,

I have decided to move out – back to Wal and Miriam's. I will make arrangements to put the furniture in store next week. I'm truly sorry it didn't work out. I really wanted it to.

I don't know if it's love. All I know is we are going to hurt each other terribly if I stay on.

Good luck in LA.
Tash.

CHAPTER NINETEEN

Gerry heard the news of Natasha's departure from his mother. She had heard it from Gemma Woods, who had heard it from Jules, who had heard it from Fay, who had heard it from Euan, thus proving that the Square grapevine was working as well as ever.

Inevitably there was a great deal of speculation as to what had actually happened.

Joy Masterson was forthright in her opinions. "Quite frankly Gerry, I am relieved to hear that the poor girl is no longer in the clutches of that dreadful man. His behaviour at Lady Fay's party was totally out of order."

Gerry wasn't interested in his mother's opinion of Euan, but he was interested in finding out where Natasha had gone. On this point his mother was rather vague. "To some cousin of her mother's I think."

Gerry eventually tracked Natasha down at work, where they told him she had taken the week off, but they gave him her new number. He rang at once.

"Natasha? It's Gerry. Are you all right?"

She sounded weary and her voice was more husky than usual. "Yes, I am."

Gerry hesitated. "Can I come round and see you?"

There was silence and he waited. Finally she asked, "When?"

"I could come round now."

Natasha thought about it. She was actually alone in the house, so probably now was as good a time as any. It was not going to be possible to avoid him forever, so she gave the address and rang off.

It had been a strange few days since leaving Euan, almost as if she were in limbo. She had no will to do anything. She didn't even ask herself questions any more. Her body felt as if it was suffering from severe bruising, both mental and physical, and she moved around like someone in a dream, pale and listless.

Miriam observed her state and became worried. She suggested to Natasha she should see a doctor, although in private she told Wal that a psychiatrist would have been more appropriate. She remarked crossly that none of this would have happened if Wal hadn't invited Euan to their party. "I knew they'd fall for each other, the moment she walked into the room. It was like Heathcliff and Cathy. Now the poor child is suffering from severe depression."

Wal looked exasperated. "Oh really, it's nothing like Heathcliff and Cathy. Of course she's depressed. She's just had a major bust-up with Euan. They're both powerful personalities and perfectly capable of inflicting deep hurt on each other. My God, if you think Natasha looks bad, you should see Euan. I met him for lunch yesterday and he looked terrible, even worse than after Celia died. I'm just thankful he is going to LA. The sooner he gets these Roxby Smith women out of his system the better it will be, for all of us.

Miriam looked at him. "That's rather heartless isn't it?"

Wal shook his head. "I'm merely being practical. Euan's going to be a huge success in LA. I feel it in my bones. He'll be a millionaire in a couple of years. Meanwhile Natasha will find someone else. "

Miriam didn't agree. She felt deep down that if you offered Euan the choice of a million pounds or having Natasha back, he'd choose the latter. Nor did she think Natasha would recover from such a passionate affair for a very long time, if ever. But she kept these views to herself.

*

The doorbell rang. Natasha opened it and showed Gerry into the living room.

He stood looking at her and then he took her hands in his. "Tell me what has happened. Why didn't you call me?"

She took her hands away and sat down. "I had a row with Euan that's all. I just thought it would be sensible for both of us if I moved out."

Gerry noted the pale face, the listless movements and the blank expression. He didn't know what George had said to her but it must have been pretty brutal. She seemed near breaking point. He felt a faint twinge of guilt but it didn't last long. He looked at her, his face kindly but concerned.

"My poor child, as if you hadn't suffered enough already with the death of Edward.

She gave him a wan smile. "It's for the best. Euan is going off to LA soon anyway."

This was good news indeed. He fervently hoped the Euan episode in her life was over for good. He sat down beside her and put on a cheerful voice. "You know the best thing to do when you are down?" She shook her head. "Think positive. Think of what lies ahead of you."

Natasha gave a brittle laugh. "I'm not sure I can think of anything ahead of me right now."

Gerry smiled at her indulgently. "I think you can. Ask yourself, what is it you want out of your life?"

She said with a touch of irritation, "Oh really, Gerry. At this precise moment I have absolutely no idea about anything, except that my life seems to be one great mess."

Gerry was at his most patient and sincere. "That really isn't true and I'm not going to allow you to think this way. You are a wonderful person Natasha, and have a great talent."

She was almost amused by his efforts to cheer her up. "And what might that be?"

He smiled at her. "Your art of course."

"Oh that," she said flatly. "Quite frankly I'm not even interested in that at the moment. The thought of going back to painting scenery makes me want to scream."

Gerry smiled. "Then you certainly shouldn't go back. Take a break from it all."

He hesitated. The big moment had arrived. He'd rehearsed it many times in his mind and he knew in his bones this was the right time, but just wasn't sure how she would react. He took her hands in his again and this time she didn't remove them.

"I think I might have a solution for you Natasha. Will you listen carefully to what I have to say?" She looked surprised but nodded in agreement. He paused and then said,

"I have only known you for a few months, but in this time I have grown so fond of you and now I know I have a deep and lasting attachment. What I feel for you I have never felt for any woman before. I want you to believe that." He hesitated. "I hadn't been meaning to speak out about these feelings so soon but in some ways the circumstances have changed and I must now say what is in my heart."

He looked at her to see how she was taking this but her expression hadn't changed, so he continued. "During one of our first evenings together you told me how you thought a marriage could work. Do you remember? You said, and I think I am quoting you correctly, you said a marriage could only work if two people lived independent lives and were only together when they really wanted to be."

He paused again and still she said nothing. "Well, that had a profound effect on me. You see, it made so much sense. I suddenly saw marriage in a completely new light." He smiled. "It's difficult for someone in my position not to become a little disillusioned with the frequent breakdowns of the married state, but you suddenly gave me hope. You made me see the possibility of a freedom within a marriage that could really work."

He allowed his voice to become a little emotional here. "That's what I want to offer you Natasha. I want you to be my wife. I want to cherish and look after you, but at the same time let you have your freedom to develop in any way you wish. I know you are young and have a whole lifetime ahead of you, but I want you to consider that life with me. I want us to grow and develop together."

Her eyes opened wide but still she said nothing. It was time for his master stroke, his trump card.

"I hadn't been going to ask you so soon but the fates seemed to have taken things out of my hands." He cleared his throat. "As you know I take up the living of St Peter's in November and I so desperately want you to share that life with me. You could have a completely free run in decorating the house. I wouldn't interfere at all because I know you will make it quite beautiful." He looked at her and said slowly and deliberately, "Of course you could also have that great hall for your painting. You said yourself it was perfect for a studio. Think of the hours you could spend in there. It's as if it was made for you Natasha."

At last he let go of her hands. It had been a brilliant performance.

She sat staring at him. His calm, sincere tones had a sort of hypnotic effect on her. His offer was tempting. She would have peace, freedom and independence. No more bullying from Euan or her father. No more being told what to do, who to see, or how to run her life. She could spend a great deal of time painting in her own studio. She could create a beautiful home. There would be children running around...

At the thought of children she looked at Gerry. It was a subject that needed to be tackled. She cleared her throat. "Gerry, there is one worry. I don't quite know how to put this but you and I haven't actually had any physical experience together. We haven't..." she faltered.

Gerry finished the sentence for her. "We haven't been to bed together? I know." He smiled at her anxious face. "My sweet girl, if you want we can go to bed right now."

She looked very startled and he quickly went on, "I don't think that is what you really want is it? I think deep down, like me, you want to keep some of the excitement back until after we are married?"

She looked a little embarrassed. "As long as you think we will be all right..."

He smiled reassuringly. "Of course we will. 'With my body, I'll thee worship'. You need have no worries on that score." He kissed her gently on the forehead.

She sat back and closed her eyes. All those dreadful comments of Euan's, she'd known they couldn't be true.

Then another thought struck her. She opened her eyes.

"I don't mean to be rude Gerry. But what about your mother, would she be living with us?"

Gerry was quick to reassure her. "No, no. My mother is going to remain in the house in Garrick Square. It's all been arranged already. Her friend Muriel is going to live with her. We would have the rectory to ourselves."

There was silence. She had no fight left in her. There seemed no valid reason to say no. She turned to him and said in rather polite tones, "Thank you Gerry. I will marry you."

He took her in his arms. "Oh my sweet girl, you won't regret it. I will do everything in my power to make you happy." Letting her go he said, "I don't want to rush you Natasha, but because of my appointment, we only have a few weeks to get things organised. Do you mind if we announce the engagement right away?"

Natasha shrugged and said unemotionally, "That's fine by me."

He stood up and kissed her again on the forehead. "I'm going to leave you now. That's quite enough excitement for one day. Tomorrow we'll go out and buy you a ring."

She said quickly, "That isn't necessary, really."

Gerry smiled. "Of course it is. We're going to do things properly."

After he'd gone she sat curled up on the sofa thinking. It was as if she had just come through a long and nasty operation and was now wrapped up in a warm blanket, recovering. A great cloud had been lifted from her. She was going to be looked after, cared for and cherished. Nobody would ever hurt her again. Now all she wanted to do was to sleep for a very long time.

*

Gerry returned to his office in a state of febrile excitement. It had all gone far better than he had expected, even in his wildest dreams. Needless to say he was aware that he had caught Natasha completely on the rebound and her decision might only be a temporary one. It was therefore essential she shouldn't be given a chance to change her mind.

He picked up the telephone and rang George Roxby Smith.

*

George replaced the receiver and said, "Well, well, well, that's interesting."

He looked across at Inga who was deep in a computer magazine. If the news was as he expected, Inga would be delighted. He was well aware that she had been thoroughly irritated by the last furore over Natasha. Inga wasn't an easy person. He could tell Natasha disliked her. He didn't like her much himself but it had been a clever move to marry her. She had brought him money and a good job just when he needed it. Of course he wasn't able to run as many risks as he had done with Celia, but he still managed a certain amount of discreet fun on the side.

"So?" she said, without looking up. "What is so interesting?"

He told her Gerry Masterson was visiting again and that this time it could be good news.

"Do we have anything to give him for dinner?" he asked.

Inga nodded, mentally taking the cling film off the smoked salmon and caviar.

George sat back in a glow of anticipation. His harsh words to Natasha seemed to have worked. He had been right to take a firm line. As a consequence of their row, Natasha had left Euan and Gerry had cleverly taken advantage of the situation and asked her to marry him. It would not only mean that his difficult daughter was being taken off his hands but she was also marrying a very suitable man, who was obviously quite wealthy and a celebrity to boot.

A couple of hours later George pressed a glass of champagne into Gerry's hand.

"My dear chap, I couldn't be more delighted. Natasha's a very lucky girl."

Gerry sipped his champagne, then looked at George and said apologetically, "I don't want you to think it indecent haste, but I would like to announce the engagement as soon as possible."

George nodded. "I think that very sensible. Women are strange creatures. We don't want to give Natasha a chance to change her mind." Then his expression changed. "To be serious Gerry, I do understand the urgency. I am thankful my talk with Natasha seems to have done the trick and relieved she has finished with Mackay, but the danger remains as long as she's under the same roof..."

Gerry interrupted, "She isn't. She moved out of the flat the day after you saw her. She's staying with that cousin, Wal Simmons."

George looked dumbstruck. "That does surprise me. She left me in a very defiant mood." To Gerry's surprise he suddenly became quite emotional. "I don't mind admitting I was very upset after she left. She's my only daughter and I hated getting so angry with her, but she's strong willed, as you are about to find out."

He smiled and poured more champagne into Gerry's glass. "At least I hope that is the last we will hear of Euan Mackay."

Gerry nodded. "I think it will be. He's going to live in the States." He looked at George. "To get back to Natasha and myself. As you know, I take up the living of St Peter's in November. It means I need to be married as soon as possible in order to fit in a short honeymoon."

George beamed. "That's very sensible. Long engagements are never advisable. And please don't worry about the arrangements. Inga and I will make sure you have a splendid wedding with no expense spared."

Gerry thanked him profusely and invited George and Inga to Garrick Square the following week to discuss all the details.

After he left George turned to Inga and said, "What a very satisfactory outcome. I couldn't have chosen a better man for Natasha if I had chosen him myself. She'll soon be happily settled and we won't have to worry about her again."

With this Inga agreed wholeheartedly.

*

At about the same time Gerry and George were discussing wedding plans, Natasha made the announcement of her engagement to Belinda, Wal and Miriam.

There was a shocked silence.

Then Belinda burst out, "Who on earth is Gerry Masterson?" She had wanted to say 'but what about Euan?' but didn't dare.

Miriam said, "Isn't Gerry Masterson that TV personality who does all those religious programmes?"

Natasha nodded.

Wall looked at her. "He's quite a celebrity. I didn't know you knew him, Natasha?"

She gave a wan smile. "I met him in Garrick Square. He has a house there, so we've seen quite a lot of each other." She hesitated. "Actually he's giving up most of his television work. He's going to be the rector of St Peter's Church in Stockton-under-Wold."

Belinda giggled. "I can't see you as a rector's wife."

Miriam frowned and said tactfully, "Stockton-under-Wold is a beautiful part of the country, almost in the Cotswolds."

There was another silence until Belinda, having recovered from the initial shock, became excited and started firing questions at Natasha about the wedding. Natasha answered in monosyllables and after a while pleaded tiredness and said she was going to have an early night. As she reached the door she turned to Wal and asked if she could have a word with him in private. They went into his study.

He looked at her wan face and thought it wasn't exactly the radiant expression of a woman in love. "Are you quite sure this engagement is what you want, Natasha?"

"Yes" she said in flat, unemotional tones and then hesitated. "Wal, could you ring Euan for me? I know Gerry was going to see my father and I'm sure they'll put the announcement in the papers very soon. I don't want Euan to find out by reading it."

Wal stared at her. "Don't you think you ought to tell Euan yourself?"

Her eyes filled with tears. "Please Wal," she pleaded. "I couldn't do it. You must tell him. Give him my love and say I'm sorry."

Wal said gently, "Natasha I don't want to pry, but if you love Euan and have had some sort of row, it won't solve anything by marrying a man you don't love." Natasha said nothing so Wal persevered. "Are you trying to get your own back at Euan in some way? You really can't marry someone just out of revenge. It wouldn't be fair on Gerry."

Her eyes opened wide and she looked genuinely surprised at such a suggestion.

"I'm not. I want to marry Gerry. I think it will be a good marriage. He understands me and will give me plenty of space. I can live a totally independent life and he's going to let me have a large studio for my painting."

Wall felt a little at a loss. "Well that's good," he murmured. She continued almost defiantly, "Gerry won't bully me, or tell me what to do, or say who I can and cannot see."

"Is that what Euan did?" Wal asked?

She nodded. "And my father. I had the most fearful row with him." Suddenly she found she was telling Wal the whole story of how Inga had summoned her home and the scene that followed. As she finished she turned to Wal and said, "I thought it might have been you who told my father about my affair with Euan."

Wal seemed shocked at this suggestion and assured her it wasn't.

Natasha shrugged. "It doesn't matter now. I can see it was wrong of me."

"Wrong, why wrong?" Wal said sharply.

A sad look came over her face. "Well, however much I told myself it didn't matter about my mother's involvement with Euan, I think it did. It's irrational I know but I felt I was betraying her somehow."

Wal thought about this. "And what did Euan think?"

She shrugged. "It didn't seem to affect him in the same way. In any case, he didn't want to talk about it. He just said the past is the past and we are in the present and that was that." Her eyes filled with tears. "I hate myself for having hurt him. I love him terribly and know I always will, but I also know we are bad for one another. We're just so destructive when we are together. It could never have worked. Please Wal, try and make him understand this."

She turned and ran from the room.

*

Miriam looked at her husband. He had been sitting on the edge of the bed, fully clothed, staring into the middle distance for nearly fifteen minutes.

"Well," she finally said, "are you going to tell me what happened with Natasha?"

Wal looked at her. "She wanted me to ring Euan and tell him about her engagement. So I did." He started to undress.

Miriam sounded exasperated. "For goodness sake Wal, what did Euan say?"

Wal shrugged. "Nothing much, in fact he was silent for so long I thought we'd been cut off. Then all he said was 'give her my love'. He then told me he was going to visit his mother in Scotland and that he'd put the Garrick Square house on the market. It should sell pretty quickly. Those properties are very sought after at the moment. Then he's leaving for LA."

He went into the bathroom and slammed the door.

When he returned Miriam said, "Wal we have to do something. Can't you see what has happened? Euan and Natasha have had an almighty bust-up and she's marrying Gerry on the rebound, or even worse for revenge. We have to stop it."

Wal was silent for a moment and then said sadly, "If you want my professional opinion, this marriage may not be such a bad idea. Gerry and Natasha have a lot more chance of working out than Euan and Natasha would have done. They are too alike, too passionate ever to settle down. There are also too many other complications hanging around from the past. I mean, there's Celia for a start. Euan and Natasha could well have burnt out in a couple of years. You can't live with that obsessive intensity and survive. Marriage is a rather boring, but practical institution. The ones that work are those that chug along on an even keel. It may sound cynical but what Natasha needs now is a bit of stability in her life, a good home, financial security and a devoted husband. It could well work out. "

Miriam decided not to take his depressing views on marriage personally. She saw his unhappy expression and said, "All right, that's your professional opinion. What about your unprofessional one?"

Wal sighed and climbed into bed. "I don't like seeing two people I love, suffer so deeply. I think there's little doubt they had a very passionate affair which has left them both damaged. I'll be relieved when this wedding is over and Euan safely installed in LA."

He lay back in bed.

What he hadn't told her was that he had agreed to see Euan and he was dreading it.

For the first time in a long while he took his wife in his arms.

*

The announcement of Natasha and Gerry's engagement sent shock waves through the Square.

Fay tried to ring Euan, only to learn from the message on the machine that he'd gone away.

Murdo read the news with a sinking heart. He looked across the table at Desmond and decided it would be better to keep him in ignorance for the moment. There was no point in sending him into a fit of sulks.

Gemma Woods passed the paper over to Jules. "Well, what do you make of that?"

Jules read it and drawled, "Well darling, it does explain their peculiar behaviour of late. My God, I almost feel sorry for Euan. To have missed out on two women in the same family begins to look like carelessness." She put the paper down. "Joy Masterson must be over the moon with delight."

At that precise moment Joy Masterson was busy cutting out the engagement announcement from the twenty-four newspaper copies she had ordered and then putting them in envelopes to send to all her friends.

*

The news also had its effect outside the Square.

Wal's mother put down the paper and said severely to her husband, "Professor Linklater this is a disaster. We must go and see Wal and once. He will have to put a stop to this engagement."

She handed him the paper. Tinker read it and said, "Dolly, I know your son is a brilliant divorce lawyer but he can hardly be expected to stop a marriage before it has even taken place. Anyway, how do we know it is the disaster you say it is? This Gerry Masterson may be just the right man for Natasha."

Dolly snatched the paper back. "No he isn't, I know he isn't, instinctively in my bones. She's going to make the same mess of her life that her mother made. Well I'm going to stop it. I'll ring Miriam and invite ourselves for supper. We need a council of war."The next day, Tinker and Dolly drove up from Oxford to Walbrook Grove to see Wal and Miriam. Belinda and Natasha were out, having gone to the theatre.

Wal regarded his mother with a mixture of irritation and affection and did his best to conceal his impatience. "It's no good you sounding off at me Mother. You don't even know the man. I met him yesterday and he seems perfectly nice and is obviously devoted to Natasha. I'm sure he will make her a good husband."

His mother snorted. "'Perfectly nice', what sort of recommendation is that? And don't tell me I don't know him because I checked him out on the television. The man is perfectly ghastly, all insipid and soulful. I know his sort, he's a wimp. Aren't I right Tinker?"

Her husband jumped. His mind had been drifting as it so often did when Dolly was holding the floor. "Well," he said cautiously, "Religious Broadcasting has never been my favourite medium..."

"Oh for goodness sake Tinker," Dolly said impatiently. "We don't want a discussion on the media we want your opinion of Gerald Masterson."

Tinker was saved from saying anything more, because she burst out, "Can't you see? It's happening all over again, the same situation as with Celia and George..."

Wal interrupted. "It's not really Mother. Celia wasn't on the rebound from anyone when she married George."

"Rebound, what rebound?" his mother said sharply.

Miriam looked anxiously at Wal. It wouldn't be a good idea to bring Euan into the conversation. Dolly had adored Celia and although she had loathed George, she had also known about Celia's affair with Euan and might not like the idea of him now having an affair with Natasha.

Wal said cautiously, "We're not sure of all the details, but Natasha has obviously just broken up with someone she really cared about."

Dolly sounded triumphant. "There you are, I knew it! She's running away just like her poor mother, although in Celia's case she was running away from her ghastly home life, but it's basically the same. Can we contact this man she's had an affair with? He might change her mind for us."

Miriam said quickly, "I don't think that would be a very good idea Dolly. Natasha's only just getting over it."

Dolly turned to Wal. "Very well, you must use your professional expertise Wal, and dissuade her from this disastrous marriage."

Wal sounded almost cross. "Oh really Mother, I can't give Natasha divorce counselling before she's even got married."

Dolly regarded her son calmly. "I don't care what you do darling, just get to Natasha before her dreadful father does, because George will love this match and do everything in his power to make it happen. We owe it to Celia to stop him."

*

Later than night Natasha sat on the edge of her bed and opened a letter from her father that read:

My dear Natasha,

I cannot tell you what joy the news of your engagement to Gerry has given me, and I give my consent wholeheartedly.

I have been through a good deal of heartache since we last met and feel perhaps I was over-harsh with you. We both said a great many things we didn't mean in the heat of the moment. For my part I hope you can forgive me. Believe me, I only acted out of my deep affection for you. Let us now put the whole incident out of our minds and try to forget the unhappiness of the past. The future is all that matters.

Inga and I will do everything we can to make your wedding

day a happy and joyous occasion. Your happiness means everything to me.

Your affectionate,

Father

Natasha stared at it for a moment. Then she folded the letter carefully, placed it back in the envelope and dropped it into the waste paper basket.

CHAPTER TWENTY

The next day Euan was shown into Wal's office.

As he sat down Wal looked at him in some concern. "Good God Euan, you look terrible."

Euan shrugged. "I haven't been back to the Square since Natasha left, couldn't face it."

"Well where have you been? Sleeping on park benches?"

Euan smiled. "No, staying with a friend. Tomorrow I go to my mother's in Scotland."

Wal handed him a cup of black coffee.

Euan's voice sounded hoarse. "How is she?"

Wal looked at him and said drily, "About the same as you."

Euan took a gulp of coffee then put the cup down. "Why has she done this Wal? She can't hate me that much."

Wal said crossly, "She doesn't hate you, exactly the opposite. But you didn't exactly help things did you?"

Euan shook his head. "No I didn't. I made a complete mess of it."

"Well if it's any consolation," Wal told him, "it wasn't only you. Her father delivered a pretty decisive blow as well," and he repeated the account of her visit to George, just as Natasha had told it to him.

Euan groaned. "I had no idea. She never said anything to me."

This drew a look of reproof from Wal. "She probably didn't think she could. My impression is she felt inhibited about talking to you about Celia anyway. So she bottled up all her guilt and then had to endure the dreadful verbal lashing from her father."

"That man ought to be shot," Euan growled. "What else did she say? I want to know, word for word."

Wal repeated parrot fashion: "She said she loved you terribly and always would, but you were bad for each other and destructive when you were together, and it could never have worked."

There was silence. Then to Wal's alarm Euan's eyes filled with tears.

"She's right. We can't be together and yet we can't be without each other. Jesus Wal what a mess! I never meant to fall in love with her but now I don't know how I can live without her." He paused and said slowly, "I can understand her leaving me, but to marry Gerry Masterson? That I can't accept. I'm telling you Wal, you have to stop it."

Wal sighed again. "You and everyone else. I have daily deputations begging me to break them up." He looked at Euan. "You're not going to like this, but as your friend I am going to say it anyway, so please don't interrupt." He took a deep breath and said, "I'm not actually sure that it's in Natasha's best interest to try and stop this marriage..." Euan started to protest but Wal held up his hand. "No Euan you have to hear me out. There are several reasons for my saying this, but the main one is Natasha's mental state. She is very near the edge and I am seriously worried. I know you'll say I'm no psychiatrist, but I see enough in this room to know when a human being has had enough. Just look at what Natasha has been through in the last six months. She had the shock of being cut out of her grandfather's will and then she had a traumatic affair with you, traumatic because it brought back all the memories and guilt about her mother. She's had to cope with the death of Edward, who was far more of a father to her than George. And then on top of everything else her own father gives her a terrible verbal lashing. The girl's at the end of her tether, she has no reserves left. What she needs now is peace and stability, both of which Gerry will give her. If she were forced into breaking off this engagement I truly fear she might have a breakdown. So if you really love her Euan, you will go to LA and try to forget about her."

He lent back in the chair exhausted. The room went very quiet. Euan's face had a strange expression and his jaw was clenched. He said stiffly, "If that is what you really feel Wal then so be it. But does she have to marry Gerry Masterson? Apart from what I personally feel about the man, I'm pretty sure he's basically gay."

Wal said wearily, "Yes, I also had the feeling he had homosexual tendencies when I met him." He gave a short laugh. "However, I don't have to tell you that half the married men in England are bi-sexual, a fact which doesn't necessarily preclude them from making good husbands."

Euan said impatiently, "I'm fed up with calling them bi-sexuals. It's just an excuse to hide the fact they are gay."

"Whatever category you put Gerry into Euan," Wal said a little impatiently, "I genuinely think he's fond of Natasha and will make her a good husband."

Euan closed his eyes and thought of how he and Natasha had been together when making love. He knew Gerry would never fulfil her sexual needs, but how could he explain that to Wal?

Wal was watching him and said, "We're not exactly sending her to the gallows Euan. If she isn't happy in this marriage she can always end it. I don't want to anticipate failure but a great many marriages do end in divorce." He gave a little laugh. "If they didn't I'd be out of a job!"

Euan didn't smile at this but said gloomily, "Don't forget she is marrying into the Church. It will make things far more difficult."

"Difficult maybe, but not impossible," Wal looked at Euan. "I'm only trying to reassure you that by marrying Gerry, Natasha isn't signing her death warrant."

"It feels like it," Euan said darkly, then he stood up and burst out, "I really loved her Wal. It wasn't just a casual affair. I loved her. After Celia died I didn't think I'd ever feel that way again..." He broke off unable to say more.

Wall also stood up. He felt concerned but could only say, "Go to LA, Euan, and forget about her." As Euan reached the door he added, "Please keep in touch. We will want to know how you are."

Euan nodded. He suddenly turned and spoke almost fiercely. "Wal, I want you to promise me one thing. If Natasha is ever in any sort of trouble, I want to be told. Do you understand?"

Wal looked startled.

"I mean it Wal, any sort of trouble. You must promise me that."

Wal nodded a trifle wearily. "All right Euan, I promise."

With that he left the room.

*

A week later George, Inga, Joy, Gerry and Natasha, gathered in the drawing room of the Masterson house in Garrick Square. Once introductions had been made and everyone was provided with a drink, Joy opened the bowling.

"Now my dears, have we decided on a date for the happy day?"

Natasha looked at Gerry who said smoothly, "I think October 16th is going to be our best date and that, I'm afraid, only gives us seven weeks." He smiled at his mother and Inga. "But as we are in such capable hands I'm sure that it shouldn't be a problem."

Joy said to the room in general: "I've told all my friends this is going to be the wedding of the year." She looked fondly at Natasha, giving her a sickly smile. "If we can just help our little bride-to-be to get over her wedding nerves, everything will be fine."

Gerry shot Natasha a worried look but she gave no reaction, so he said quickly, "I suggest you leave all the Service arrangements to me." Here he gave a smile. "I'm lucky enough to have a certain experience in this area."

George and Inga both laughed at this.

Natasha looked across the room at her father. She was doing her best not to show her feelings of contempt for him but knew she could never forgive him for the things he'd said. For her own sanity, however, she'd decided that for the duration of the engagement she would call a truce, even if it was temporary.

Her glance then went to Inga who was sitting beside Joy and thought grimly that they made a formidable duo. There had been an instant bonding between them and they were now behaving as if they were old friends.

Gerry was still talking. "As I think I've mentioned, we are to be married in St Michael's Chester Square. Luckily I have the right connections so we won't have a problem in obtaining the Special

License."

"Such a beautiful church," murmured Joy. She turned to Inga. "It just lends itself to flower arrangements. I thought a white, gold and orange theme would be good for an autumn wedding."

"Good, yes," agreed Inga, sounding even more German than usual.

Gerry looked anxiously at Natasha. "You will say if you aren't happy with the arrangements sweetheart?"

Sweetheart! How had that crept up? "Of course Gerry," she said. "It sounds fine to me."

"We ought to look at the guest list," said George. He turned to Gerry. "I don't want you to feel you have to stint with the invitations. I imagine a great many of your friends from the BBC will want to come?"

Gerry smiled. "Quite a few, I expect."

George looked nervously at his daughter. Since their row over Euan she had been very distant and cold. He'd been worried about this evening, but although she was showing no emotion, to his relief so far she was behaving impeccably.

"We'll have to invite my side of the family Natasha, so I'll need you to bring me up to date with the whereabouts of your cousins. I've rather lost touch with my brother's family."

Natasha nodded and George turned to Gerry. "Sadly I don't think my father will make it. He's rather frail these days."

Joy lent forward. "Is that Sir Malcolm, George?"

George looked a little startled. "Yes, do you know him?"

"I know of him George, I know of him."

Natasha smiled to herself. She had a mental vision of Joy thumbing her way through Debrett's. She wondered if Joy also knew that her grandfather's fourth wife had been a check-out girl from the local shop. It had caused quite a scandal at the time.

"We can get the invitations printed at once," Gerry continued. "If you send me your lists with the addresses my secretary will send them out."

Joy said, "We need somewhere for the reception."

Inga gave a nod in Joy's direction. "I think I have a solution for that, Joy. There is an exclusive hotel near the church called Ebury Hall. I have arranged to take over the entire hotel for the weekend, so that my friends and relations coming from abroad can also stay."

Joy looked at her admiringly. "That's lovely, Inga. It sounds perfect."

Natasha thought that between them they'd have made a pretty good job at running the Third Reich.

Inga turned to Natasha. "You will need attendants Natasha, flower girls and page-boys."

"No flower girls or bridesmaids," she said firmly, having a sudden vision of lumpy Belinda in pink taffeta.

Inga looked annoyed. "You should at least have a maid of honour, Natasha."

"No." said Natasha firmly.

There was a moment of tension. Gerry broke it by speaking in his most calming tones: "I think we must all respect Natasha's wishes in this." He turned to her. "Do you want attendants of any sort, sweetheart?"

That word again, although she was grateful for his support. She thought for a moment and then had a brainwave. "I'll have two pages, Ned and Billy."

Her father looked puzzled. "Who?"

"Ned and Billy Stanhope," she said. "They'll be charming pages, if we can get them to behave."

Joy turned to George. "I believe they are the two grandsons of Lady Fay Stanhope."

George looked relieved. "I knew her husband, old Freddie Stanhope. Their estate was near ours in Norfolk." He turned to Natasha. "I thought the Stanhope's only had daughters. Who's the father of these two boys?"

Natasha smiled. "Jules isn't married," she said glad to be introducing a little controversy into the bland proceedings. "Jules went to school with Wal's daughter Belinda. She lives here in the Square."

Joy was already thinking of the list of wedding guests in *The Times*, 'Sir Malcolm Roxby Smith, Lady Fay Stanhope, the Hon. Juliana Stanhope and the pages Edward and William Stanhope'. She gave Natasha one of her dazzling smiles.

"I think it's very sensible not to have too many attendants. I always thought Princess Anne's wedding was the most stylish of all the Royal Weddings, and if I remember rightly, she only had two attendants."

Gerry refreshed their drinks and Inga turned to her step-daughter. "What about your wedding dress Natasha?"

Natasha said coolly, "I'm flying out to Italy next week. There's an Italian designer I'd like to use."

Joy looked at her with reluctant admiration. She had to admit Gerald had chosen a girl with style. An Italian designer! Her friend Murial would be very impressed by that.

On the other side of the room Gerry sounded rather annoyed. "Is this a sudden decision Natasha? You said nothing to me about going to Italy."

There was another moment of tension.

Natasha tried to sound contrite. "I'm sorry Gerry, I've only just made the arrangements myself. I was going to tell you tonight. I need to go and see Edward's widow and visit his grave. It just seemed a good idea to organise my dress at the same time."

Gerry's expression immediately softened. "Then of course you must go, sweetheart. I'm sure you can feel confident leaving the rest of the wedding arrangements in the hands of these two ladies." He smiled at Inga and his mother.

Natasha turned to them. "I'm afraid it will mean you'll have to deal with clothes for the boys."

Joy said, "That won't be a problem. After all, they live so near." She hesitated. "There is one last thing. It would be helpful if you and Gerry could decide on your wedding list, where you want it to be and what items you'll be wanting."

Gerry looked at Natasha. She shrugged and said flatly, "As I'm going to be away in Italy it might be easiest if you and your mother could organise the list."

Joy was about to protest, but Gerry recognizing certain danger signals said, "Whatever is best for you sweetheart."

After they all left, Joy reflected that on the whole things were going rather well. So far there had only been one major hiccup and that was over her missing husband. In the end Gerry had decided it would be easiest to assume he was dead and that Gerry was the son of the late Harold Masterson. Considering what a worm the man had been, his name looked quite distinguished in print.

*

A week later the wedding invitations plopped onto the doormats of Garrick Square.

"Well I never!" Doris Rich said, as she read it and passed it across to her husband. "I must say I didn't see those two getting it together. I'd always thought she was more attached to that writer man."

"Well not any more she ain't," said Arthur studying the invitation. "Blimey, this is going to be a posh do. It'll mean hiring the wedding kit."

Doris looked at Peter, who had just returned from his holiday in Greece, "It's for you as well Peter. You're invited too."

Peter snatched the invitation from his father and went rather pale.

"Well that's one marriage that won't last. I give it six months!" he said and left the room slamming the door behind him.

"Well I never," Doris said again, "what's got into him?"

Arthur reflected he'd rather not know.

*

Fay whistled through her teeth and said to Boffy, "So! They're going through with it. I really didn't think they would."

Boffy said gloomily, "You got this one wrong old thing. You told me Natasha was involved with Euan."

"But that's what we all thought, Boffy. It's just too extraordinary." She stared down at the invitation. "St Michael's Chester Square and Ebury Hall. I'll have to sort out your wedding togs." She gave a sigh. "Did I tell you she's asked Ned and Billy to be pages?"

"My God, she must be mad to let those two hooligans loose in a church," was Boffy's only comment and he went back to his paper.

Fay picked up a slip of paper that had fallen from inside the invitation. She clucked disapprovingly. "The wedding list is at Harrods. I thought Natasha would go for something more original." She looked at Boffy, who wasn't paying attention, so she threw it away,

"I don't think we'll bother with the list. I'll give her one of my antiques."

*

Desmond looked at the large envelope and seeing it was addressed to both of them, opened it. On reading the contents he let out an astonished gasp, which caused Murdo to look up from his paper. Desmond handed over the invitation and said in his most malicious tones, "Well dear, I think our little Miss Natasha needs to be told a few home truths about Master Gerald before this wedding takes place."

Murdo spoke sharply. "Desmond I forbid you to say anything. It's none of our business and you are not to interfere."

Desmond put his hands on his hips. "Oh, I'm not to interfere am I? You're just peaked because your beloved Euan has had his nose rubbed in the dirt. Well let me tell you dear..."

But he got no further, because at that moment Murdo made a strange choking sound and fell sideways onto the floor.

CHAPTER TWENTY-ONE

Euan sat on the train, thinking over the time spent with his mother. It had been cathartic for many reasons, but mostly for the evening he'd felt brave enough to broach the subject of his father's abuse. It was the first time they'd ever discussed it, but he needed to know the truth, before he left for America.

She had told him that since his death she'd kept her husband's terrible secret to herself. It was not that she condoned his behaviour, indeed the memory of it still tortured her, but she explained in her quiet way, that living in a small community it was best she remained the widow of their revered Minister, who had come to such a tragic end.

Annie Mackay was a woman of few words so they didn't talk long, but she promised him she had known nothing about his father's abuse until the day she witnessed it for herself. He believed her. It was also a relief that she'd made her peace with his brother Cal, for not trusting him and acting sooner. He thought grimly there was a certain irony in Natasha feeling sorry for Gerry's sad childhood which didn't begin to compare with what he and Cal had endured.

He stared out of the train window as the countryside rushed past and his thoughts drifted to the brae above his mother's house. At its highest point it looked out to Oban and the open sea. There he would sit for hours on an outcrop of rock, by a fast rushing burn. Natasha would have loved it. He'd wanted to bring her with him, to see his mother again and then go on to Iona. Was the terrible pain of losing her ever going to leave him?

On their last evening his mother sat at the piano singing her favourite Burns' song, 'Ae Fond Kiss.' As she sang the lines: 'Had we never loved sae kindly, Had we never loved sae blindly, Never met, or never parted, We had ne'er been broken hearted...' he couldn't stop the tears from falling down his face. His mother finished the song, looked at him and then tactfully made an excuse and left him alone.

Her last words to him were, "Broken hearts do heal in time you know Euan."

He arrived back at the Square in the early evening. There was a note pinned to his door from Fay and it read:

Dear Euan,

I thought I should let you know that Murdo has had a stroke and is in the Westminster Hospital.

I hope you're all right ducky.
Get in touch,

Fay.

Half an hour later Euan arrived at the hospital and made his way to Murdo's ward. The Sister informed him that Mr Struthers had only suffered a mild stroke, but he was not out of the woods just yet, as a first stroke was often followed by another.

Murdo lay with his eyes closed, looking frail and old. His white hair was ruffled and untidy and there were two rather unhealthy flush marks on his cheekbones.

The eyelids fluttered open as he gave a slightly crooked smile. "Ah Euan, I was just thinking about you."

Euan drew up a chair and sat down beside him. He was relieved Murdo could still speak. The stroke must have affected the left side of his body. He only used the right side of his mouth. His left arm lay lifeless on the covers, whereas the fingers of his right hand drummed nervously on the bedspread.

Euan said, "You gave us all a fright. How are you feeling?"

"Not too bad. They tell me I've only had a mild stroke so things could be worse." He added ruefully, "They've confiscated my cigarettes and I would give my left arm for a whisky." He sighed. "All life's little pleasures disappearing one by one."

"How did it happen?" Euan asked.

Murdo shrugged. "It was a trifle unfortunate. Desmond and I were having a minor tiff and I keeled over right in the middle of it. Now the poor man is beside himself with remorse, thinking it was his fault." He looked at Euan. "I'd be grateful if you'd try and convince him it wasn't. They might let me out of here in a day or two and it won't aid my recovery to have Desmond wittering on about his guilt." Euan smiled and Murdo went on, "He just won't believe me when I tell him this stroke was long overdue. I've had high blood pressure for years, not to mention the fact that I drink and smoke too much. I have nobody to blame but myself." He patted Euan's hand with his good one. "So tell me, how was Scotland? You look a great deal healthier than the last time I saw you."

Euan laughed. "That wouldn't be difficult. Actually Scotland was therapeutic and I was glad to have seen my mother."

"So, when do you leave for Los Angeles?" he asked.

"On October 16th." Euan hesitated. "I presume you've heard that Gerry and Natasha are getting married?"

Murdo nodded. "Indeed. The wedding invitation has already arrived."

Euan was shocked. "My God, that was quick."

"Almost indecent haste," agreed Murdo.

Euan burst out, "I've made such an unholy mess of it. While I was in Scotland I kept thinking of all the things I should have done differently."

Murdo said quietly, "'Ah my Beloved, fill the Cup that clears Today of past Regrets and future Fears'."

Euan raised his eyebrows. "That doesn't sound like Lord Chesterfield."

Murdo smiled. "No, *The Rubáiyát of Omar Khayyám* I believe." He looked at Euan. "So what happens now?"

Euan shrugged. "Nothing, it's over, finished. I will go to LA. Natasha will go to married life with Gerald Masterson."

"Like a lamb to the slaughter," murmured Murdo.

"Well you and I think so, but of course her father is absolutely delighted by her choice," Euan said bitterly. "He practically bullied Natasha into making a decision. Someone had told him about our affair. I'm now pretty certain that must have been Gerry. It's the sort of devious move he would make. Anyway, George went berserk."

Murdo looked shocked and said, "That poor child."

Euan said angrily, "At least I know I was right about Gerry's plans for her. There were times when I thought I was just being driven mad by jealousy." He looked at Murdo. "What have I done?"

Murdo said gently, "You really mustn't blame yourself. A great many factors were involved in her decision. The death of Edward must have played some part, and her father. Have you considered she might have needed to settle for a secure and stable life?"

Euan sighed. "It's what everyone keeps telling me, but I can't accept it. She's rushed into this marriage because of me and I am certain it will be a disaster. Apart from what you and I suspect about Gerry, he's so mediocre. Natasha will never settle for that." He groaned, "Why couldn't she have just given us more time to work things out?"

Murdo closed his eyes for a moment, his strength ebbing. When he opened them again he said, "Listen to me, my friend. You and Natasha were too passionate together and caused too much turbulence. No-one can survive that sort of relationship for long. The zenith is reached too fast and there's nowhere to go but downwards after that. Believe me, I know."

Euan was silent and Murdo continued. "I know we've had our worries about Gerry, but lying here I've had plenty of time to think and I've come to the conclusion he could make Natasha quite a good husband..."

Euan was about to say something but Murdo stopped him.

"Think about it Euan. Gerry won't be possessive with her. He'll give her the freedom she needs. It will also give her a chance to develop her own personality. It could just work out."

Euan was silent. He didn't think Murdo sounded very convinced.

He was taking the same line as Wal. The famous British compromise. He was sure that wouldn't work for Natasha, but what could he do? He had promised to back off.

Murdo said wearily, "When I first met Gerry, I understandably compared his situation to my own. Consequently I may have over-reacted."

Euan wanted to tell him that his real worry was that Natasha didn't know the true nature of Gerry's sexuality and he'd made a mess of telling her, but he could see that Murdo was getting tired, so he said nothing.

"The important thing is that you concentrate on your writing, Euan," Murdo said with unexpected vehemence.

Euan looked at him with affection. "What a wise old man you are."

Murdo replied with something of his old spirit. "So I should be at my age."

He closed his eyes.

Euan felt contrite. "Murdo I've worn you out. I'm so sorry."

He got up to leave. "I'll see you again before I go."

He took the limp body of the old man in his arms and held him close. Then he laid him gently back on the pillow and left the ward.

He remembered thinking afterwards it was like holding on to a frail and fluttering moth.

*

Natasha, oblivious of all the dramas, had spent a happy fortnight in Italy and been sorely tempted to send a message saying she was never going to return. Indeed Francesca, worried by her languid appearance, suggested she postpone the wedding and stay on in Florence for a while. Natasha thought about it, but couldn't quite bring herself to embark on such a drastic a step.

After two days back in England, she began to regret this decision.

The first horror to confront her was the wedding list.

"Harrods?" she almost shouted, "I would never have chosen a wedding list from Harrods." She started looking down the list picking out items at random, while Belinda gave out great shrieks of laughter.

"A Plastic Apron, green and blue pattern, An Ice-cream Scoop... a what? Six Crystal Sherry Glasses... I hate sherry, Floral Sheets and Duvet Covers..."

Belinda said, "Ghastly isn't it?" She snatched the list from Natasha and continued to read: "Wooden Party Susan, with glass inserts... what on earth is that?" She looked at Natasha. "It gets worse, listen: White plastic garden furniture with floral design on the fabric – they do love floral – a sun-lounger, a gas barbecue..."

"Stop, I can't bear to hear any more." Natasha paced up and down. "How could they be so tasteless?" She looked at Belinda. "Well with a bit of luck nobody will buy any of the stuff."

Belinda laughed. "You're wrong there. Pa's study is full of parcels. They've been arriving daily by the van load. Have a look."

They went to the study and peered in. Natasha shut the door. "The whole lot can go to Oxfam," she said firmly.

Belinda looked shocked. "Natasha, you can't do that. People have taken time and trouble and spent money. At least you have to write to them." She looked at her cousin's mutinous face. "I tell you what. We'll unpack them, make a list and then you can go back to Harrods and change the worst items. They're really good about that sort of thing."

Natasha accepted Belinda's help gratefully, and after a couple of days the present situation was more or less under control.

Then Jules rang. "Natasha could we meet? I can't really believe you want Ned and Billy to wear these page boy costumes."

Natasha sighed. "Come over here Jules, and bring them with you."

Jules duly arrived and Natasha stared with disbelief at two hideous harlequin costumes, orange with white spots. Jules said apologetically, "Joy Masterson sent them, but I honestly don't think the boys will wear them."

"I should think not," Natasha said. "Send them back. You and I will decide what they're going to wear. I should have known better than to leave it to Joy."

Jules looked greatly relieved and suggested the boys wore naval uniforms. Natasha nodded approvingly. "I think they should have yachting caps as well."

Jules departed happy, and Natasha went into the garden to await the next disaster.

She sat in the gentle autumn sun, thinking back over the days since her return from Italy. They'd not been easy and she'd hardly spoken to Gerry. He'd rung once to welcome her home and then yesterday he'd made a quick call to tell her he'd fixed the honeymoon, at Inga's recommendation, on the shores of Lake Geneva. She didn't want to think about the honeymoon and quickly put it from her mind.

From the moment she'd agreed to marry Gerry, the whole event had been taken out of her hands. Like a coward she had taken the line of least resistance. The day was not for her, nor even Gerry. It was a day for Inga and for Joy and to a certain extent her father. She thought grimly that at least she'd managed to please him at last.

Leaning back in the deck chair she closed her eyes and had just started drifting off to sleep when the doorbell rang. There was no-one else in the house so rather reluctantly she went to answer it, fully expecting another package from Harrods. But it wasn't from Harrods.

It was Euan, looking cool and smart in jeans, linen shirt and blazer, something of a contrast to the last time she'd seen him. Her mouth went dry and her heart began to pound. She stared at him and he smiled at her obvious consternation.

"I won't stay long," he said, "I've just come to say good bye."

They went into the garden and sat down on the wooden seat.

"This is where we came in," he commented, and Natasha thought back to that evening in March when they had re-met. She had told him then that life was a mess. Well, she'd been right.

"When do you leave for LA?"

"On the 16th of October."

"That's the day of..." she broke off.

"Your wedding, I know."

He looked at her in that penetrating way he had, and not being able to bear it she turned away and sat clasping and unclasping her hands.

Finally she said, "I'm so sorry Euan, about us."

Turning back she could tell he hadn't taken his eyes off her. It was almost as if he were willing her to change her mind. She said almost defiantly, "It wouldn't have worked you know. We would only have made each other unhappy."

He said almost angrily, "Are you telling me you're happy now?"

Natasha was silent, unable to give him an honest answer. When she did reply her voice was defiant. "Most people would say I am lucky. I am going to have a lovely house, a devoted husband, a large studio to paint in..." her voice petered out.

Euan remembered a similar conversation he'd had with Celia all those years ago, when he'd accused her of being unhappy. He gently gave Natasha the same answer he'd given her.

"Darling Tash, you're only telling me what you *have,* not what you *are.*"

Her eyes filled with tears. "Don't Euan, please. I can't bear it."

He took her in his arms and said savagely, "Well who are you and I to expect happiness when ninety-nine per cent of the world is suffering appalling agonies? We're obviously not put on this planet to be happy."

She broke away from him and walked down the garden, too shaken to speak.

After a moment he joined her and she said, "I don't care about the happiness bit Euan, but I do know you're a great writer. I would only have got in your way."

Euan gave a hollow laugh and said bitterly, "Well, if the creative artist is helped by suffering I should do pretty well. Let's hope your sacrifice was worth it."

She winced at that. Then decided to change tack and asked, "How long will you be in America?"

He shrugged. "I don't know, probably at least a year. If I like it I may stay on out there. After all there's nothing left for me in England now."

They were silent again. Then she said shyly, "I have a present for you. I was going to send it, but now you're here..." She ran into the house returning with a small box which she handed to him.

He opened it. Inside was a fountain pen made of tortoiseshell and gold. With it was a small card which said: 'Euan this pen was left to me by Edward, but I want you to have it. Tash.'

He appeared stunned, and for once was lost for words.

She said softly, "Write something beautiful with it Euan."

He put the box in his pocket and said, "Wait there."

He walked away from her out of the front door and to the car. A moment later he returned with a brown paper parcel. "I also brought something for you. I'm afraid it's not very elegantly wrapped."

She smiled. "If you knew how relieved I am that it's not in Harrods' paper."

He laughed. "I bumped into Belinda yesterday and she told me you'd been having problems."

They stood staring at each other. Then he took her in his arms and she clung to him in desperation.

Just before he left he whispered in her ear, "If you ever need me Tash, I'll be there. Will you remember that?"

Abruptly he let her go, walked from the garden and out of the house. She heard the car draw away and sat down on the garden seat. Her shoulders began to shake as she cried silently. The tears fell on to the brown paper parcel on her lap, making a pattering sound.

After a while she opened it.

Inside was a beautiful antique silk kimono and a postcard of her favourite painting, Sickert's Red Lady, inscribed on the back in Euan's neat writing, 'My love always, Euan.'

CHAPTER TWENTY-TWO

In the week before the wedding there were two national disasters. The first was a crash on the Stock Market of such dire proportions it gave the City a collective nervous breakdown. It also sent her father and Inga into a panic from which they had still not recovered.

Two days later the South of England was hit by a hurricane and the Great Storm destroyed thousands of trees and caused major disruption to all forms of transport. Many of Inga's relations had struggled to get flights and although Natasha made sympathetic noises this hadn't troubled her in the least.

Now, as she lay in bed on the morning of her wedding, it occurred to her that disasters were meant to come in threes and although her marriage wasn't of national importance, it could well be the third in the line of catastrophes. Maybe that was a little strong, but it set her wondering how people were meant to feel on their wedding day? Whatever it was, she felt nothing. She looked across the room at her wedding dress hanging up on the cupboard door. It was certainly very beautiful but what had all the effort been for? She could have worn a sack and felt the same.

Had she made the wrong decision? So many people had tried to change her mind. Even Murdo, when she visited him in hospital had asked her if she was sure she was doing the right thing? Well, there was only one person who could have changed her mind and he was now out of her life and on his way to Los Angeles. She brushed away a tear. That last encounter with Euan had left her shaken. Why had he spoiled everything? If only he hadn't told her Gerry was gay, they might have been able to work things out. But his absurd jealousy made him act like a madman. She couldn't endure being with him when he was like that.

He'd made it impossible.

Walking across the room she stared out at the garden still covered in broken branches.

Why was jealousy so destructive and dangerous? She'd never really experienced it, but after that last meeting with Euan she'd suddenly thought of him with another woman and immediately had the most violent reaction. There had been a terrible sick feeling in her stomach and her heart started to thud in the most peculiar way. She idly wondered if Gerry would ever give her cause for jealousy and then found it rather alarming to realise that she didn't actually care if he did.

She put on the silk kimono Euan had given her. Maybe she shouldn't have been so hasty. God knows she had tried to make the right decision. Anyway it was too late for regrets now. In a few hours she'd be married to Gerry. The only way to get through the day was to accept that Euan was now in the past.

She sat down on the edge of the bed and tried to think of the positives but the only thing that came to mind was her studio. That was it. Every time she felt panicked or depressed she would think of that great long room, with nothing in it but her canvasses, her easel and her treasured box of paints. That studio would be her salvation.

Feeling a little restored she started to prepare herself for the day ahead.

*

By one-thirty the Church was already half full.

The Garrick Square contingent sat in a little enclave on the bride's side. Fay was looking particularly magnificent in flowing chiffon and an extremely large hat, which had seen her through years of weddings, garden parties and Royal Ascot. She looked around her and whispered to Boffy in loud tones, "There's a very funereal atmosphere in here. Nobody would think it was a wedding." Boffy didn't reply. Not because he didn't agree, but because his wedding clothes had evidently shrunk at the cleaners and he was having great difficulty in breathing. He certainly wasn't going to be able to kneel and if he stood up he wasn't at all sure he was going to be able to sit down again. The whole thing was hellishly uncomfortable.

The Rich's and the Cooper's were stationed in the pew directly behind Fay and Boffy. Poor Doris Rich had her view totally obscured by Fay's hat. She was still upset by Peter's refusal to come with them, especially as she had spotted so many celebrities in the pews opposite. She presumed they were friends of Gerry's from the television, and thought that he might have introduced them if Peter had been there. She glanced along their row. Michael and Lorraine Cooper were having an argument of some kind but at least they hadn't brought that nasty child with them. She looked beyond them to the floral displays.

"Lovely flowers," Doris whispered to her husband.

"Too blooming many if you ask me," said Arthur, "they're going to bring on my hay fever." And as if to prove the point he had a violent attack of sneezing.

There was a little stir as Gerry and his best man walked up the aisle to their places. They both wore dog collars under their morning suits. Gerry's wedding clothes were particularly elegant, having been especially made for the occasion in light grey silk.

Murdo, looking tired and frail, followed them up the aisle and slipped into the seat next to Fay. "What a lot of clergy," he remarked. "It is rather like taking one's seat at the Lambeth Conference."

"Where's Desmond?" Boffy asked.

"He didn't feel quite up to it." Murdo said evasively. "In any case, he's making a cold buffet for when we get back, to which you are cordially invited."

The organ ploughed on through a particularly dreary repertoire.

"I wish they'd play summat a bit more cheerful," hissed Arthur. "How long is this do going to be? Let me have a look at that programme Doris."

"It's the Order of Service," Doris said reproachfully.

There was an audible gasp as Joy and Inga made their entrance together. Joy resembled a rather overblown daffodil. She was clad from head to foot in canary yellow and her hat, which rivalled Fay's in size, was in bright orange and yellow stripes.

Inga, in contrast, wore a severe double-breasted khaki suit, with military buttons right up to the high neck.

"She looks like a five star general," said Fay and turning to Murdo she asked, "What do you make of those two?"

"Excessive," said Murdo.

Precisely on the dot of two o'clock, the wedding car drew up outside the Church. Natasha was momentarily thrown by the crowd of cameramen and photographers that were waiting for them, but in a minute regained her composure and air of icy calm. They were greeted at the steps by the Canon who was taking the Service and then joined by Ned and Billy, very smart in their naval uniforms.

George looked at his daughter in some concern. Her pale, expressionless face had him worried, although he had to admit she looked breathtakingly beautiful. Her dress clung to her like a Roman statue and from her shoulders poured a cloud of thin white silk gauze. Small white flowers like stars adorned her chestnut curls, and she carried a spray of white camellias. It was simple but wonderfully effective.

George felt out of his depth, conscious of her great unhappiness and knowing this marriage was partly due to the pressure he'd put on her. He was now at a loss at what to say but hoped in time she would understand he'd done it for her own good. It would have been different if he could have broken through that barrier of reserve, but he hadn't managed it with Celia, so why should he with her?

Suddenly he blurted out, "You don't have to go through with this Natasha. You can back out now. I shan't mind."

She turned her cool gaze on him. Was it a look of contempt? "No Father, I'm fine."

The boys began to fight behind her and she turned round and said severely, "Boys behave, or you won't get your football kits." There was instant silence and she smiled. "Put your yachting caps under your arms, just like I showed you." They did so and she added, "Good. Now don't you dare tread on my train or you're dead. Understand?" They solemnly nodded.

She turned back to her father and said calmly, "I'm ready."

The organ struck up 'Love Divine, all Loves excelling' and to gasps of admiration Natasha and her father walked up the aisle towards Gerry.

"Like a lamb to the slaughter," murmured Murdo and Fay pulled out her handkerchief as her eyes began to well up.

*

The Service went like clockwork, without one vestige of emotion from either bride or groom. As the wedding party withdrew to the vestry for the signing of the register and the choir embarked on yet another anthem, Jules turned to Gem and said, "Well, as wedding services go that was pretty good. Natasha was so right to insist on no sermon, such a bloody relief. The Diva sang divinely and the bride looked ravishing. So how come I don't feel uplifted and exhilarated?"

Gemma replied, "Probably because you know it's not a love-match and everybody is feeling depressed and miserable about it. I've never seen so many gloomy faces." She paused. "Actually Jules, I don't think I'll go to the Reception, do you mind? I've already had some nasty looks from Bernard's sister Dolly and I won't be able to avoid Wal Simmons much longer."

Jules assured her she understood but explained she'd have to go if only to make sure Ned and Billy didn't sabotage proceedings. Up to now they'd behaved like angels but she didn't want to tempt fate. She wondered what Natasha had done to get them through the Service.

The choir started on yet another anthem and the congregation began to get restless. Murdo took a piece of paper out of his pocket. It had arrived from Euan that morning and he looked down at it now:

Oh Wedding-Guest! This soul has been
Alone on a wide, wide sea.
So lonely t'was that God himself
Scarce seem-ed there to be.

Murdo sighed, folded the paper and returned it to his pocket. Suddenly he was overwhelmed by a great grief and took out a handkerchief and dabbed his eyes.

The Wedding March belted out and with relief everyone stood up. Gerry and Natasha emerged, followed by the rest of the wedding party.

They progressed down the aisle, Gerry smiling and waving, Natasha staring straight ahead. They reached the porch where a watery sun was doing its best to filter through. A barrage of pressmen and photographers circled round them. Natasha stood patiently while the cameras flashed and clicked. Someone shouted, "Give the bride a kiss Gerry!" and others joined in, "Let's have a kiss you two!"

Gerry obediently complied and planted his cold lips on hers. The photographers went wild and clicked away happily, but Natasha knew, in that one moment, without any shadow of doubt, that she had made the most terrible and catastrophic mistake.

She didn't love this man. She could never love him. She had no feelings for him whatsoever, except perhaps a sort of physical repugnance.

They reached the Reception and she made her excuses and went to the Powder Room. She heard Gerry call after her, "Don't be long, my sweet." He was evidently revelling in his role of Bridegroom.

She went in, locked the door, put the seat down and sat on it. Then she dropped her head in her hands. Thoughts of Euan filled her mind. She went through every moment she had spent with him and then went back over it again. Then she thought of Gerry and was filled with a terrible panic. What was she going to do? She felt faint. She loved Euan, yet she'd married Gerry. She must be mad.

Suddenly a great wave of anger swept over her. Damn Euan! It was his fault, all of it. He had driven her into the arms of Gerry and then to add insult to injury had behaved like a martyr and meekly walked away from the whole thing.

She heard other people come into the room. She stood up. It was absolutely no good thinking like this. A cold determination came over her. It didn't matter if she didn't love Gerry. She would somehow make a success of this marriage. She would show everybody who'd thought she'd made a mistake that they were wrong. She'd prove them wrong. She would make a beautiful home, her husband would become even more successful and their children would be wonderful. Yes, everything would be fine. Euan could sneer as much as he liked about Gerry being a mediocre person. There would always be people who felt superior and sneered at others. Those were the people she disliked, the sneerers. Well she would show them all.

She went out and down the stairs to join Gerry.

He seemed annoyed. "What's taken you so long? Everyone is waiting for us in the line-up."

Natasha was alarmed. "But Gerry, I remember saying I didn't want a line-up."

Gerry looked at her with irritation. Gone were the unctuous tones and calming voice.

"Well it's too late now," he said. "Inga and my mother have arranged it and we're keeping them waiting."

She obediently followed him and took her place, listening as the endless names were called out, playing her role as the charming bride to perfection.

"Lady Fay Stanhope and Colonel Boffington!"

"The Honourable Juliana Stanhope!"

"Mr Murdo Struthers!"

"Professor and Mrs Linklater!"

Natasha looked at Dolly's tear-stained face and smiled. "Dolly, this is a wedding, not a funeral."

At which point Dolly burst into tears again and Tinker dragged her off to mop her up.

The shaking of hands and the kissing of cheeks seemed to go on for ever and no sooner was it over than the speeches began. First George made an embarrassingly emotional tribute to his late and beautiful wife Celia, Natasha's mother, who had been so tragically killed, and how sad it was that she couldn't be with them today to see their daughter, the loveliest of all brides...

This set Dolly off again, who sobbed so loudly it rather put George off his stride and brought his speech to an early conclusion.

Then Gerry started on his. He paid flowery tributes to George, Inga and his mother. He then turned to Natasha. "The Good Book says, 'Who can find a virtuous woman?'" He paused dramatically, "Well, I am happy to tell the assembled company that I have done just that..." His voice cracked with emotion and sincerity. Natasha felt the colour rising in her cheeks. How could he say such things? Had the man no idea of what she and Euan had done together? It certainly wasn't what you would call virtuous.

Gerry was now in full flow: "... My Natasha also has a great talent as a painter, handed down in trust to her by her Grandmother, Audrey Maddington, and I am going to see to it that this talent is not wasted..."

Natasha looked down at the floor. Please God make him stop before I vomit over the wedding cake.

At last there was clapping and Gerry introduced the Best Man. Natasha didn't listen any more. The whole day became one great blur. She vaguely remembered Lorraine Cooper getting predictably drunk and Ned and Billy having a water-pistol fight. She moved through it all as if in a dream. At some point, someone ushered her upstairs to a room to change. She slowly climbed out of her wedding dress and laid it on the bed. She removed the flowers from her hair and folded up the long silk train. It was as if it had never been worn. Then she put on the red dress and hat that she'd had copied from the Sickert painting. But why, oh why had Euan remembered it? Now the dress would always remind her of him. She took the postcard from her handbag turned it over and read, 'My love always, Euan'.

With a sigh she put the postcard back and clicked the bag shut.

Then she picked up the bouquet of flowers and walked from the room.

She remembered rose petals being dropped from the top of the stairs, drifting round her like flakes of snow. She remembered seeing Gerry's stern face as he waited for her at the bottom of the stairs. No welcoming smile there. Was he dreading the honeymoon as much as she was? She remembered her father and Inga kissing her goodbye and she remembered being relieved she didn't have to attempt to get under Joy Masterson's hat to kiss her goodbye because in a ghastly affected way, Joy blew her a kiss and said, "Have a wonderful honeymoon little daughter-in-law!"

The drive to the airport was conducted in almost total silence. There was one moment when Gerry patted her hand and made some remark about her looking tired. Otherwise they didn't speak. As they turned into Heathrow she suddenly thought of Euan. He'd be halfway to Los Angeles by now. Oh God! Why wasn't she with him instead of Gerry?

They arrived at the terminal and Gerry checked their luggage through with great efficiency. In no time at all they were boarding the plane for Geneva. He handed her back her passport and she looked down at the alien object. Mrs Natasha Masterson it said. She quickly put it in her bag. That wasn't her. It had nothing to do with her. She thought miserably of other honeymooners, excited and happy to be going away. Her heart felt heavy and full of lead.

She turned to Gerry, making an effort. "How long is the flight?" she asked.

"Not long. About two hours I think, dear."

Dear? My God, that was worse than sweetheart. She'd have to talk to Gerry about his use of endearments. She could just about cope with sweetheart, although she'd have preferred him to call her Natasha. They'd end up like Brian and Daphne if he started calling her dear.

"Do your seat belt up, dear."

There he went again. She was about to say something when Gerry summoned over a good looking young steward and asked for a glass of water. The steward looked down at him and smiled. "I'm afraid I can't get you anything until we've taken off, sir. I'll bring you a drink after that." He smiled again and then the most extraordinary thing happened. He gave Gerry a wink. Natasha thought it most odd and familiar, but Gerry just smiled and was obviously not put out by it at all.

Her eyelids closed and she started to doze.

When she awoke they were airborne and Gerry was no longer beside her. She looked up the plane and caught sight of him in animated conversation with the young steward.

She listlessly flipped through the magazine in front of her, listening to the soft drone of the engines.

After a while Gerry returned. "Sorry to leave you dear. I thought you were sleeping."

She looked at him. His face wore a rather flushed febrile expression. I wonder if he's been drinking she thought. She let her eyelids close but didn't go back to sleep. Instead visons of Euan kept floating before her and her eyes filled with tears. Angrily she wiped them away. This was no good. She had to pull herself together. It was the start of a new life. There could be no more thoughts of Euan, ever. After all, he probably hadn't thought of her. It was a new life for him as well. He would be far away by now.

*

In that, Natasha was wrong. Euan hadn't even left the Airport but was still waiting for his flight to be called. There had been some sort of engine trouble and take-off had been delayed by several hours. Thanks to the generosity of the film company he was travelling first class which meant that at least he could wait in comfort with the advantage of free beverages. As he poured himself another drink, he closed his eyes and thought of Natasha.

Suddenly he sat up and looked at his watch. My God! She'd be Mrs Masterson by now.

He knocked back the drink in one savage gulp. He wouldn't think of it. His English life was no more and in a gesture of defiance he moved his watch to Los Angeles time.

He glanced at the large television screen. The News was on. He was only half paying attention when he heard the name of Gerald Masterson. He stared at the picture on the screen as the announcer said, "For the Reverend Gerald Masterson, today's church visit wasn't in his usual line of duty. For today, the well-known television personality was in church getting married himself. There were many familiar faces among the congregation at St Michael's Chester Square to see Gerry and his beautiful bride, the former Natasha Roxby Smith tie the knot..."

Euan stared in disbelief. There she was. There was Natasha, looking so beautiful he wanted to cry. The cameras went into close-up and he studied her impassive expression. Someone was shouting at them to kiss. Gerry lent over. Euan saw, as if in slow motion Natasha's expression change. It was something about her eyes as Gerry kissed her.

In that single moment he knew she realised, too late, that she'd made the most terrible mistake.

The sweat gathered on his forehead. He lent back in his seat.

"It was my fault," he murmured, "my fault."

A voice came over the Tannoy. His flight was being called. He got up as in a dream.

As he boarded the plane and stumbled into the first class section he was handed a glass of champagne. Hardly knowing what he was doing he took it and sank back into the black leather seat.

"It was my fault," he murmured again, "*my* fault."

He let out a long moan.

The stewardess came over. "Is something wrong, sir?"

He shook his head.

"Would you like some more champagne?"

He looked down at his glass. He'd hardly touched it.

"No thanks." He forced a smile. "I'm fine, maybe later."

She smiled too. "All right sir. Just call out if there's anything you want."

He stared after her as she walked down the cabin. How could she know that the only thing he wanted was now quite beyond his reach?

He closed his eyes.

Moments later the great silver bird roared down the runway and the wheels left the ground.

As they soared into the sky a dark despair closed around him. There was no more England and no more Natasha. It was over, finished and there was no going back.

Printed in Great Britain
by Amazon.co.uk, Ltd.,
Marston Gate.